BEAST WITHIN

LOUP-GAROU SERIES BOOK 3

SHERITTA BITIKOFER

MOONSTRUCK WRITING

Dedicated to those who believe there's a place for everyone and a purpose for every creature, even if we don't readily see it.
Also, big thanks to my husband for supporting me through the production of this novel, and for helping me out with certain aspects. I'd never know what a hollow-point bullet was without your guidance. And thank you to Amy Levinson who came in at the last minute and helped me put the final touches on this manuscript. You are a saint, dear lady.

CHAPTER 1

"We're proud of you, Katherine," the voice whispered, echoing within her mind and shattering the darkness of sleep.

Katey fought through the grogginess to open her eyes. Her bedroom glowed with the amber sunlight that streamed through the window above her writing desk. The scent of prairie grasses and herbs permeated her room like incense. There, blocking some of the light, stood the tall man she had seen so many times in her dreams. He always came in the hour just before dawn, almost as if he were heralding the sun over the horizon and bringing with him the wild aroma.

Gazing at him for what seemed the thousandth time, she marveled at how his presence could seem so real and yet so ethereal. Light seemed to bend around him as if he were the master of nature itself. His skin, as if tanned by years spent in the sun, offset a pair of brilliant green eyes. They were the same color of green that stared back at her every time she looked in the mirror. They shared that much in common, among so many other things. Dark brown hair fell over the back of his neck, thick and glossy. His face had a boldness about it with a square jaw and high cheekbones.

Not only did his presence command respect but there was an air about him she couldn't help but envy. He exuded confidence and peace—something she thought she would have by now, but it eluded her just the same. There was also a wildness about him. Not dangerous, but free. Free from turmoil and strife, soaring above it all like it didn't exist. Katey wanted that badly.

"You're going to do great things," he said. His voice was deep and husky, full of comfort and wisdom from centuries of roaming the earth. If only he were truly there now.

Katey would not move, afraid that he would run away like the woman in white that appeared in her other dreams. Her chest squeezed with desperation, and she reached out to the vision.

"Dad, don't go," she begged. Her own voice sounded like a mere rumbling in her ears.

As soon as she spoke, the man began to fade away, along with her bedroom and everything in it, blurring like a mirage.

Katey's eyes popped open again, and she was met by gauzy blue sheets draped over her canopy bed frame. Just as in her dream, the dawn was there to greet her with another day. She swallowed hard and tried to will away the tightness in her chest that lingered from the dream.

It was a dream that had come so many times now. She should have been used to it. Her father, her real father, would appear and give some sage advice that she couldn't quite grasp, and then vanish.

It had been a couple of weeks since Katey saw them together - her mother and father - but even then, it was a bittersweet reunion. Logan and the others told her that she had been dead for nearly a minute that day at the castle in Alaska. A moment in the world of the living, seemed only seconds in the world of spirits. That was where she met her mother and father for the first time and was able to talk to them, but it wasn't enough. These dreams, these visions, weren't enough either.

Katey found that when she slept in Logan's bed, the dreams didn't come, but those chances were few and far between. Nothing sexual ever took place on the nights she snuck into Logan's room and cuddled with him under the sheets, but they both knew the others were well aware of what they were doing.

They were all mindful of her movements every second of the day and night. None of them reprimanded her or Logan since they were to be mated anyway. When that would be exactly, no one knew for sure. So many factors played into setting the date.

Not only did they have to get John—a high-ranking alpha who happened to live across the country—to officiate the ceremony, but both her and Logan had to be ready for what the mating ritual required. Both would need to shift into their loup-garou forms in front of dozens of other people and have the clarity of mind to clasp hands – paws.

However, neither of them was any closer to learning how to shift voluntarily. Logan had been trying for over a century with no luck. Considering that the loup-garou gene was so diluted in his blood, this was no surprise, but it was nonetheless frustrating to Logan, who continually berated himself for his inability to shift at will like any other born loup-garou.

Katey draped her arm across her eyes and sighed deeply as she tried to calm her racing heart.

She had been a loup-garou for almost two months now, a miracle to the world as the first female to be bitten and changed. Even now, she could feel the wolf within her—a constant presence while she slept, ate, and tried to live her life as any normal high school senior, but she could sense something deeper, something that had been there ever since that fateful morning after Christmas.

In front of a dozen or more witnesses, Katey revealed herself to be the fulfillment of an ancient prophecy. She had shifted for the first time into a white loup-garou, towering above the vampires trying to kill her pack and her friends. It was that day that she ended the feud between the two races and, even though she was not conscious through the transformation, she came to realize later that it was only the beginning of a revolution in their culture. This revolution would not be driven by blood and violence. This was to be a peaceful reform.

The white wolf that appeared to everyone had commissioned Michael - her vampire grandfather - to seek out those whom he trusted and recreate the council that had been torn apart long ago. Soon, vampires and werewolves would come together to discuss grievances and settle laws about cohabitation with their kind and the humans who dominated the world as they knew it.

That was all she knew. As she lay there in her bed, Katey still wondered what exactly she was supposed to do now. She had received no word, no guidance from anyone - werewolf or vampire. As far as she knew it, the world might have been carrying on as it always did and didn't care whether she was alive or not, but there was no way she could forget what happened.

Ever since that day, she could feel something else coursing through her veins and humming in her core. It wasn't just the new knowledge that she had a home and a purpose for living, but also that she was a full loup-garou and the beast that dwelled within her gave her this life that she could be proud of.

Not only that, but a shift in perspective had taken place somehow. Katey had noticed it shortly after Logan had changed her, and more so since they all arrived back from Alaska. After doing a little internet research, Katey attributed her experiences to a newly developed empathic personality trait. She was more in tune with the feelings of those around her. She could not only smell their fear and sadness – as most loups-garous could do – but she felt it in her soul. Their pain was her own, and sometimes it became too overwhelming to ignore.

At the same time, she noticed a change in the others. One morning while Ben and Dustin were arguing, Katey entered the room, and she could sense the ebbing of hostilities immediately. Perhaps it was because they didn't want her to see them fighting, but Katey suspected something different. Her presence had an effect – if only a mild one – on nearly everyone she met. Not only would their sadness become her own, but somehow, she would heal it and lessen the grief for others.

Since she was the first female loup-garou in millennia, there was no one to ask if this was normal or if this had something to do with being the fulfiller of the ancient prophecy. She remembered that Michael said something about a Spirit of Peace that manifested itself within her. Perhaps that was what caused the strange changes in her body.

As her acute senses began to drink in her surroundings, she could hear her pack downstairs cooking breakfast. The scent of succulent meats like bacon and sausage drifted to the second floor and infiltrated her room. Her stomach rumbled in response.

Katey sat up and stretched out her lean, yet muscular arms over her head and yawned. The dreams, as tormenting and exciting as they were, stole away some of her much-needed sleep. Somehow, she managed to make it through the day without falling asleep on her desk as she used to when she was human.

Many perks came with being a supernatural creature that Hollywood distorted to scare audiences. Heightened senses and unnatural stamina were just the start, but many responsibilities came along with it too.

Katey learned these things the hard way when she spent her first few days as a loup-garou in an internal war against the wolf inside that hungered for control and raw meat. It was only recently that she became accustomed to the idea and gave in to the primal needs that kept her from becoming a raging monster. She had seen what hunger could do to a loup-garou and it wasn't pretty. It was downright dangerous.

Living in a world of humans wasn't as difficult as she thought it would be, though. There were moments when she had to keep a tight rein on her temper, but other than that, spending time with her friends was a breeze.

Katey pushed back the covers and slipped from her bed to quickly dress for the day ahead. School was back in to full swing after winter break, and it was still months before graduation. Darren had offered for both her and Logan to continue their studies from their home outside of town, but Katey refused, knowing that she would be separated from her friends and any hope for social interaction with the outside world. Darren always meant well, but she knew that if he were given a chance, he would confine her to the house until her training as a loup-garou was complete. From what she understood that would take a long time; maybe decades.

After brushing out her hair in the bathroom she and her pack shared, Katey followed the voices downstairs. There, she was greeted by a sight that she had become all too familiar with. Darren, Dustin, Ben, and Logan were congregated in the kitchen, each holding their own plate of breakfast meats and leaning against the expansive counters.

Katey walked in just as Dustin was finishing an amusing story about a troublesome student in one of his classes. They all gave a hearty laugh before turning to her with wide grins.

She couldn't help but smile back. In all the years she had been an orphan, all the years she had spent with foster families, never once did she think that she would find a place where she was so openly welcomed. After Mary, her foster mother, died and before she was loup-garou, Darren welcomed her into their home as if she were one of them. They were all just as warm and caring as they had been then and Katey hated to think that one day that may change.

However, she also noticed that they seemed to take special care when it came to her. Except for sleeping and showering, Katey was never alone. Logan was always with her, every waking hour of the day, and one of the other pack members was always close by. Since Darren, Dustin, and Ben were also her teachers, it was convenient for them to keep an eye on her. Yet, they were always professional within the classroom and didn't let on to anyone that there was more between them and Katey.

They were protective - maybe a little overly so - and Logan, especially. Katey had a mind to be offended by their constant hovering and badgering questions about her well-being. Upon further thought, she realized that they were right. Not only was she the youngest and least experienced in the loup-garou ways, but she was far too valuable for her security to be neglected.

Whether they were aware or not, she heard their whispered conversations about possible assassinations and unwanted harassment from both vampires and werewolves. It wasn't surprising that some of their kind didn't want peace. There were plenty of Yaveriks out in the world, lusting after an all-out war between the two races. Her existence defied these plans, and there might have been plenty of people who would pay top dollar for her head on a platter.

There was no evidence of an assassination attempt, yet. Maybe it was too soon to tell, or the guys were doing such a good job that she never knew there was trouble brewing outside her perfect world.

"Good morning, Katey Kat!" Dustin greeted before stuffing a slice of sausage in his mouth.

Logan was by her side in an instant, and Katey felt a pleasant shiver run up her spine when his breath tickled the tiny stray hairs on the top of her head. His presence—powerful and yet gentle—had such an effect on her. She was about to greet her future mate, but the words fell from her tongue when she looked up into his piercing blue eyes. Instead, her smile broadened, and all she could do was slightly blush under his loving gaze.

Each time she met his stare, she was reminded of the lake in Alaska where they rolled around in the snow and where he proposed. She remembered that kiss and how he had touched her so softly in places she never thought any man would touch. The memory kindled a fire in her belly that only he could control. Even her wolf could feel his desire for her and whimpered for attention.

As if he could hear Katey's wolf begging for his touch, Logan slipped his arm around her waist, and their lips met for the first time since last night before they parted for bed. Each kiss felt like the first, sensual, and fully expressive of his love and devotion for her. Katey knew there would be decades, centuries, maybe millennia of kisses to come, but she vowed to value each one as if it were the last she would ever get. What they went through in Alaska showed them how fragile their lives could be.

He pulled away and brushed his nose against hers. "Good morning," he murmured. His voice was the only one that could thrill her soul with just a whisper. Just one word, if it was the right one, could make her melt.

Katey did melt into his arms, her hand resting on his chest that was - to her dismay - covered by a gray shirt. He appeared to be ready for school, just as she was.

"Good morning, Logan," she replied a little breathlessly.

"If you think you can pry yourselves apart for a moment," Darren interrupted, his words marked by a sophisticated British accent, "Katey needs to eat breakfast."

"Of course," Logan said before ushering his lady into the kitchen.

The others were dressed in their typical school attire; the kind of outfits she had seen them wear so often before. If someone had told her months ago that she would have seen them in anything else, like pajamas, for example, she would have thought they had been sniffing the bleach a little too much.

With her breakfast of cooked sausage rolls, she took her place beside Logan as they continued their meals and conversations. As always, she stayed quiet while the others exchanged stories and opinions about things that she knew nothing about. Most of it related to the school board administration, their classes, or even other loup-garou affairs in the city or across the state that they had heard of. In time, Katey was sure that she would meet these alphas and betas that they spoke of and then she would feel more at ease to ask questions and join in the talk. Until then, she leaned into Logan's side and savored the feel of his body against hers.

"You look tired, Katey," Ben asked in his lilting southern drawl after swallowing a mouthful of crispy bacon. "Did you not sleep well?"

Katey looked up and saw that all eyes were trained upon her, waiting for an explanation. Ben was right, she was tired, but a split second of stage fright kept her from answering right away. She cleared her throat and said, "I'm fine."

"Are you still having those dreams?" Logan asked, concern laced in every syllable. He reached around and firmly rubbed her upper arm in a gesture of comfort.

Katey bit her lips together and nodded, letting her eyes fall to the bowl of red soup in her hands.

"If you're tired, you should stay home. I can arrange for Logan to collect your homework before the end of the day." Darren was always quick to give Katey any excuse to stay home. It was better than letting her out of the house where anything could happen to her. "Ben can stay here with you," he added.

She looked up and shook her head. "Really, I'm fine. It's just..." Katey hesitated again, keeping her eyes focused on a crack in the backsplash behind where all the others stood.

Before the change, and even shortly after, she wouldn't have been so eager to confess her deepest thoughts and fears. Darren had made it perfectly clear that they should all be honest with each other. There was no point in keeping secrets from her pack, especially from Logan or her alpha. There was to be no dissension between them. What one loup-garou knew, they all would know. Secrets and lies only created rifts between them as a pack and Katey understood that all too well after the stunts she had played after being turned.

"I dream about my parents so much, but I miss them. How can you miss someone you barely know or have never met?"

"But you did meet them," Dustin offered. "You told us about that yourself."

They didn't talk much about the time when Katey died. They rarely ever spoke of what happened up in Alaska at all. They especially never talked about how they could have been hunted down like animals on a snowy mountainside, shot down by silver bullets from the vampires who had trapped them there.

Katey had told them all about those sixty seconds when she was dead, how she met her parents and talked to them for the first time, but she would have sounded ungrateful to say that it wasn't enough to satisfy her curiosity about who they were. She knew that her father was a loup-garou, and her mother a vampire. Michael had told her all about their tumultuous relationship and short-lived family life.

She didn't know their characters, their pasts, their personalities. She had nothing to understand who they were or what parts of them were living in her that she didn't even know about.

Darren and Dustin did not know their fathers, the ones who had given them the gene to become loup-garou. She was far more privileged than they were and had no room to complain.

"I know, but I guess I wish I just had more time with them."

Logan pulled her closer and sweetly kissed the crown of her head. There were no words that could be exchanged at a time like this. There was no consoling a living being, who had a long time to wait to be reunited with her dead loved ones. Any death for Katey would be far too soon, as long as the council was still to be formed and devoid of proper leadership. She needed to stay alive for the sake of the future of both loups-garous and vampires – whatever that future would be.

Instead of continuing the grave subject of death and the afterlife, Katey asked, "Can I practice shifting again after school?"

From the thoughtful, unsure faces on those of her pack members, Katey knew what the answer might have been. She had been deep in training almost every day for the last two weeks, working at getting closer and closer to shifting into her wolf form at will. It was a small step toward learning how to shift into her loup-garou form for the ceremony, but she could tell her dogged determination was starting to annoy the others. Every day Katey, Logan, and one of the pack members were outside in the cold, pushing the edges of her willpower and coaxing the wolf out into the open. Still, they had no luck.

Katey could feel it coming, though, and just one more try could mean a breakthrough. She thought perhaps the assurance that she could transform at will would give her some insight into her parents or validation in her mission to restore peace. Maybe she would receive a message somehow, anything to give her some guidance.

"Don't you think you need a break?" Ben asked. She knew that he, above all others, was growing impatient with her efforts. As the omega, he was the one assigned to look after her most of the time. If it was one thing Ben hated, it was to have his personal time stolen away by pack responsibilities.

Yet, he was far from weak. Sometimes, he could be perfectly intimidating, and somehow, she could sense he was just as strong and deadly as Dustin – the beta. It was something she hadn't quite noticed before they left for Alaska, but she could sure sense it now.

"I felt a real difference yesterday. I think if I just push a little harder next time, I can do it."

Logan shifted uncomfortably, and Katey instantly felt ashamed for her blatant disregard for his feelings on the matter. He accompanied her during the training sessions to serve as moral support, but he had trained just as much in the past and never had any luck at shifting at will.

He was still only able to shift at his time of the month and never more unless violently provoked. It was pure speculation, but Katey thought perhaps he considered himself beyond help, like he would never shift and shouldn't even bother trying. He had never tried with her, and she thought that could be the difference that helped him finally shatter the glass ceiling that stopped him each time.

"We can try one more time," Darren finally said. "But if you don't make it this time, you're giving it a rest for another week before trying again."

Katey wanted to contest such a plan. If she didn't shift, then that meant another week of rest that would only postpone the mating ceremony. Then again, if Logan didn't take action, there might never be a ceremony. Such a thought did not settle well with Katey and a knot formed in her stomach.

As if sensing her unease, Logan squeezed her shoulder. "You'll get it soon, Katey. You've been making great progress."

She smiled up at him and nuzzled her cheek against his shoulder. Even when he felt defeated, Logan cheered her on and supported her in her training like no one else could. Darren and Dustin could spend all day telling her she was doing a good job, but Logan's word was the only one that mattered.

The others finished off their plates, rinsed them in the sink, and left to finish getting ready, leaving Katey and Logan alone. Before she could open her mouth to speak, Logan had whisked the plate out of her hands and sat her up on the countertop.

She giggled as he rested his massive hands on her knees and leaned in to give her another breathtaking kiss. Lacing her fingers in his hair, she held him close until they were both satisfied enough to release their hold on one another.

"Do the dreams bother you that much?" he asked, keeping his voice low so the others upstairs might not be able to discern all his words. They all had impeccable hearing, so it may not have mattered anyway, but it gave their conversation a level of intimacy Katey enjoyed.

"They don't bother me so much as make me miss my parents more somehow."

"I remember you told me that when you're with me at night, you don't have the dreams." Logan took a strand of her hair between his fingers and lovingly twirled it as if it were the most fascinating thing on the planet.

Katey nodded. "I know, but I feel like we're going behind Darren's back when we do that."

"We're not making love. We're simply sleeping in the same bed." How Logan's tune had changed since the first night they slept together in the same bed. She remembered how wary he was at first. Now, he was the one to reassure her nothing scandalous was going on, even if they did engage in some heavy petting now and again.

Katey's cheeks reddened at the thought of being completely naked and exposed before Logan. It was a concept she would have to get used to in time, especially once they had mated, but he did have a point. They weren't doing anything lascivious by sharing a bed. Logan had long ago made it perfectly clear that he wanted to save such an act for marriage and Katey respected his views.

"I know, but... I'm just not sure if I want to give up the dreams altogether."

Logan dropped the lock of hair and nodded, showing his slight disappointment in her answer.

"But," she recovered, "I can still stay with you some nights. I'm just saying I don't want to all the time. Not yet."

Logan gave her a smug half-smile and nodded in agreement.

A slow grin curled across Katey's face as she watched the morning light dance in Logan's eyes like tiny crystals scattered across steely blue disks, so full of the deep love he gave to her every single day. Even on the days they quarreled and bickered about trivial things, Katey always knew he loved her.

If anyone knew their story, how he nearly drove them apart with his grief over changing her and jealousy toward any man who dared to look at her the wrong way, they might have thought her crazy for staying by his side.

Katey didn't want to remember those fights or the heartache that stemmed from not knowing where they stood as a couple.

Some might have advised her to leave him and his overbearing tendencies, but Katey could never do such a thing. She had loved him since soon after they met and that had never changed, despite their rocky start.

Their love was not a question, not anymore.

The same could be said for the rest of her pack, though, their love was purely platonic. They cared for her as if she were their sister or daughter, especially Darren. The alpha was already in a fatherly role, there to protect and guard his wards, but Katey felt his tenderness in the way he spoke to her and catered to her wishes. He was wrapped around her finger, whether he realized it or not. Yet, there was always the dominant edge in his commands that let her know she was not in charge of this pack. They were the family she never had growing up; the family she had always wanted.

In a short time, so much had happened to turn Katey's life completely upside down, but in the disheveling, something glorious came forth that seemed to wrap everything up in a neat little package. Meeting Logan and becoming a loup-garou was all part of some master plan, an ancient prophecy, but just like he had once told her that day in the cemetery near Morrisville, they all made choices. If she had not been there that cold December night, none of this would have come to pass. If he hadn't loved her so deeply, so desperately, he would have never changed her into what she was now.

"What are you smiling about?" Logan asked, a similar grin on his face.

Katey scrunched her shoulders and wrinkled her nose like a giddy child. "Because I'm happy."

His face lit up with an entirely new level of joy that Katey had only seen once before when she accepted his proposal. Leaning in for another kiss, he held her head between his strong hands. When he pulled away, each pair of lips gliding against the other, he said, "You don't know how glad I am to hear that."

Katey leaned her forehead against his. "Help me to understand."

"For as long as I've known you, I've wanted to mend the brokenness inside. To know that you are truly happy here with me tells me I've done what I sought to do."

What he said was the truth. Before Logan, before she even knew about loups-garous, Katey had been a walking disaster. Depression hung over her shoulders like a heavy mantel, like some punishment for a crime she wasn't even aware of. When Logan came, so did the sunshine and Katey was released from her burden. To this day, she never understood what it was that lifted her sentence of misery and unfounded despair. It didn't matter now, not while he was still with her.

She pulled back a bit and tilted her head. "Does this mean you're done with me?" It was a question she had asked long ago, the morning after he had turned her. Yet, the playful lilt in her voice was vastly different than the desperation she felt when asking the same thing once before.

Logan peered at her in confusion. "How could I ever be done with you?"

"You accomplished your goal, so now are you ready to move on to the next challenge?" Katey wasn't the least bit fearful of what he said. She didn't truly believe he would ever leave. They were stuck with each other for life, if not eternity. Her words were merely a tease.

Logan wrapped his arms around her waist and pulled her toward the edge of the counter, her belly pressed against his rock-hard diaphragm, and her legs split over his hips. A breath escaped from her lips as he held her so tightly, her body practically perched on the edge of the counter with only his powerful arms to support her.

"I will never be done with you," he whispered, his sweet breath engulfing her face. "If I ever left you, my soul would split in two. One-half would remain with you, and the other would wither away. I'm nothing without you."

Katey gave him a toothy grin and giggled. "So poetic."

"It's the truth."

"I know it," she replied, her voice thick with emotion. "And the same would happen to me if I ever left you."

Logan smirked. "So, we're stuck together, huh?"

Katey nodded. "Happily stuck."

They drowned themselves in one more kiss just before Darren, Dustin, and Ben began filing down the stairs and collecting their briefcases from the living room. Logan was shameless and refused to let go of her.

Darren poked his head around the corner and narrowed his eyes. "Logan, let her eat. You don't have much time before you both need to get on the road."

With his alpha's prodding, Logan reluctantly released Katey and helped her down from the counter.

CHAPTER 2

With Katey's hand firmly gripped in Logan's, they walked through the north entrance of the high school. The halls were already teeming with bustling teenagers and faculty as they made ready for another day. Katey smiled as she watched some hustle to first period while others leaned against the painted brick walls and talked with their friends.

She remembered the first time she walked through the halls as a newly turned loup-garou. The chaotic cacophony of laughter and shouts was overwhelming. Not to mention the myriad of odors and scents that assaulted her newly refined senses. It had been a harrowing ordeal, to say the least. Now, Katey had learned to tune them out and focus only on what she wanted to smell and hear. With Logan's coaching, she was able to integrate back into student life with surprising ease. Even Darren was impressed with how quickly she progressed in her training as a "pup".

As they made their way to first period – Darren's environmental science class – Katey met the gazes of other loup-garou students she had met in the last few weeks. Some of them had been with her pack on the trip to Alaska, and it took a while to get over the image of their dirt-smudged faces behind silver bars. Against the odds, they had made a full recovery after being captured and imprisoned by the vampires, and no human was the wiser to what they had suffered on their winter break.

Just like every other day, these loups-garous bowed their heads as a show of respect and appreciation to Katey. It was unsettling the first day they returned, and one freshman boy came up to her and kissed the back of her hand until it was glistening with saliva. When she looked to Logan for help, he only smiled and told her the fellow loup-garou was only expressing his gratitude.

When the freshman lifted his head, Katey recognized him as one of the younger loups-garous that was on the edge of death when they finally escaped the castle. He had a right to be grateful, and from then on, Katey took it all in stride.

A scent caught Katey's attention, and she turned to see her friend, Lily, practically skipping through the masses toward her. She grinned and let Lily pounce on her with her usual bubbly giddiness. How they had maintained their friendship through their differences, Katey would never know. They were nearly exact opposites.

"It's so good to see you!" Lily cried, tossing her blonde hair over one shoulder as she pulled away from the bear hug.

Katey laughed. "It was just a weekend!"

"I know," Lily groaned dramatically. "But you won't believe how much fun we had at the studio last Saturday! You would have loved it."

Katey's smile faltered for only a fraction of a second. Since they arrived back from Alaska, Darren pressured her into quitting her job at the ballroom dance studio, at least until she had completed her training.

It broke her heart to tell Lily and Forrest. Forrest understood, but Katey could already feel the strain between her and Lily. They only shared one class together and those few minutes in passing each weekday was not enough for either of them.

Katey had one thing in common with Lily that she didn't have with Beth, her other close friend. Lily knew about loups-garous. In fact, she was engaged to one. Lily had known about loups-garous long before Katey did. She was the only human to know her secret and Lily was like a lifeline to Katey in more ways than one.

The few times they were able to talk on the phone, Katey splurged details about her struggle to get a hold of pack dynamics and all the difficulties in learning to shift. Instead of being horrified or disgusted, Lily offered advice based off her own experiences with Forrest and his pack, the Deviants. Katey felt as though she had more freedom to talk to her than Beth or sometimes even Logan. Although, she was sure Logan heard every word of their conversations on the phone. There was little she could hide in a house full of loups-garous.

"I wish I could have been there too," Katey replied. This past weekend had been consumed with training and staying cooped up in the house.

Lily's eyes glanced to Logan, and she lost a little of her excitement. "I understand why you couldn't be there," she said as they began to walk together toward the hallway where Katey's locker was located. "Maybe Darren will let you come out to the next party. It'll be this weekend. Plenty of time to plan."

"I don't know if Darren will agree," Logan intercepted before Katey could reply. "But it's worth asking if you feel up for going, Katey."

She still felt a little jolt of pleasure when he said her name. Some things would never change. "I'll have to remember to ask him when we get home today."

They chatted for a little longer, mostly about the fact that Lily's parents would be out of town for the next two weeks on an extended anniversary trip to Europe. Lily would be spending most of her time with Forrest, of course, but Katey wondered if her short burst of freedom from her parents would mean they could hang out more as well. Darren said the human would always be a welcome guest in their home.

After they had finished talking, Lily broke away to go to her first-period class on the other side of the school.

Katey and Logan were about to round the corner when she caught a whiff of something that didn't seem familiar. It was a wonder she could detect it in this crowd, but Katey was sure she smelled something like dog. This wasn't the faint scent of dog hair on a student's clothes, as she sniffed that many times throughout the day. This was much stronger.

They turned, and Katey froze. Halfway down the hall was a man dressed in an officer's uniform, holding a leash for a German Shepherd who was vigorously sniffing the base of the lockers. It was something she had seen many times before at school. It was practically routine for the police station to check for illegal drugs at the high school. However, this didn't seem right somehow.

Logan stopped too, and Katey felt his grip tighten and tremble. She looked at him and saw an emotion she had seen so often. His blue eyes, usually so calm and loving, turned cold as he glared at the officer and his dog. His body went rigid, every muscle tensing as if ready to fight or run. Buried deep within his fiery stare, Katey could see a twinge of fear leak through.

"What's wrong?" she asked. They had been around dogs and policemen before, and Logan never reacted this way. "I'm sure it's just drug dogs. They make the rounds at public schools every few months."

Logan didn't respond, and she looked back at the dog and its owner. The animal lifted its brown muzzle and sniffed the air. The shepherd's fierce brown eyes locked on them and went into a barking frenzy that startled everyone in the hallway. Students jumped away, and a few girls shrieked as the dog strained against its leash. The shepherd snapped its jaws and growled as it stood on its hind legs, eager to charge Logan and Katey.

She flinched and felt the unmistakable urge to run like a frightened deer.

Logan wasted no time and bolted into a run down the hall in the direction they came from. Katey kept pace with him, too confused and startled to ask Logan any questions just yet as they bobbed and weaved through the throng of students and faculty who shouted at them to slow down.

They arrived at Darren's classroom and thankfully it was empty. They stood at the threshold as Darren was already making his way to meet them. She could tell that even he was a little confused by Logan's intensity.

"They're here!" Logan barked out.

Darren went still at those two simple words. His face held no expression at first, but when he turned away to retrieve his briefcase, Katey felt the same paroxysm that radiated from Logan, come barreling from Darren. The empathic vibes were dizzying.

"We'll meet back at the house," Darren said as he joined them at the door. "I'll tell the others. Keep Katey out of sight."

The three entered the hall, leaving the classroom unattended.

"What's going on?" Katey demanded, wrenching her hand from Logan's grasp.

"I'll explain when we get home," Logan replied. "If there's a home to go back to."

Her eyes went wide. "What do you mean? What's happening? Who was that guy?"

Darren looked up and down the hall. "There's no time to tell you everything right now."

She stamped her foot and dropped her book bag like an obstinate child. "I'm not going anywhere until someone tells me what's going on!"

Logan moved in front of her, consuming her entire field of vision. He held her face in his powerful hands and she could feel the sliver of panic. "Katey, one of the things I love about you is your stubbornness, but you're going to have to give that up for just a few minutes. We have to get out of here."

Darren had already left them and was practically jogging down the hall with his cellphone pressed against his ear. Katey looked behind them as she heard the sharp tips of nails scraping the tile floor, almost lost in the din of shuffling feet.

Logan grabbed her hand and swept up her bag onto his shoulder before pulling her toward the nearest exit.

"Can you talk while you walk?" she asked, still lagging a bit.

"Hunters," was all Logan said.

Katey nearly tripped over her own feet as soon as he spoke. The reality of their fear finally hit.

Hunters. Loup-garou hunters. She remembered when Logan explained to her about the town of Devia and how hunters had nearly completely wiped out the loups-garous there. Forrest was with those who managed to escape over a hundred years ago, but she recalled the gravestones of so many more who had fallen prey to the hunters.

Without the help of her empathic abilities, their resolve became her own and Katey matched Logan step for step as they escaped outside.

They mounted Logan's black motorcycle and peeled out of the parking lot speeding and snaking through traffic as if death itself were chasing them. As far as Katey could tell, no one was following them, but that was no excuse to slow down. Logan constantly looked around and behind them as they flew down the highway, and she could feel the tautness of his body between her arms as she hung on tightly.

They were the first ones back to the house, miles away from civilization and tucked into the backwoods outside of town. Besides a narrow dirt path that served as their driveway off the main road, no one was likely to find them. The pack built this house here for that very purpose. It was secluded enough for when they took their monthly turns shifting into their loup-garou forms, and away from the prying eyes of the human world.

Logan pulled her off the bike and led her inside where he ordered her to stay on the main floor while he inspected every room of the house, sniffing and scrutinizing everything as if he were looking for something out of place.

"Do you think they were here?" she asked, trying to hold onto any bit of composure she could muster. She didn't need to have a personal experience with hunters to know that they were dangerous.

Logan returned from upstairs and stood beside her, a little of the edge chipped away now that they might have been in a safe place. "I don't think so. I'm going outside to search the property." He shot her a stern look. "Stay here and wait. If someone comes in, yell, and I'll come back. I'll hear you."

With that, he darted out the back sliding glass door.

Katey paced the living room floor, biting her thumbnail while she listened to Logan searching the forest, keeping track of his swift pace as he encircled the house.

Her mind raced to a million different worst-case scenarios. What if hunters were watching their home right now? What if they were to capture Logan? What if the others didn't get out of the school in time?

Would hunters openly fire silver bullets on loups-garous in a public setting? Or would they bide their time and stalk them like predators waiting for the right time to kill? Katey knew nothing of hunters or their tactics, even less than she knew of vampires. However, Logan and Darren did. That might have been comfort enough, but as long as her betrothed wasn't within her sight, Katey wouldn't feel at ease for anything.

Logan returned shortly and met her in the living room. Even though all she wanted to do was hold him until this was all over, she restrained herself and silently pleaded for answers.

He ran his fingers through his hair, taming a few long strands that had worked themselves out of the short ponytail at the base of his neck. "That man in the hall was a hunter," he began, his voice audibly shaking and Katey wasn't sure if that was from the exertion of energy during his run outside or the fear that still lingered under his tough exterior.

"How do you know?" Katey asked, trying to force herself to remain calm when that was the last thing she truly felt.

"Some things are just instinctive."

"We just left school and raised a level ten alarm to all the loups-garous in town over a hunch?" she asked dubiously.

"A hunch is not the same thing as instinct," Logan snapped, a new fire blazing in his eyes.

Katey recoiled but kept her feet firmly planted in place. "I didn't feel anything. Don't you think Darren or someone else might have sensed the same?"

"I don't know why they didn't sense it." Logan looked away, and Katey saw a glint of doubt in his eyes as he must have been mentally retracing what had happened in the hallway. "That's a common strategy hunters use. Dogs and other animals can tell when a loup-garou is nearby, so they train them to hunt us down. They must have used the drug dog cover to get into the school. Hunters haven't come this close to Crestucky in over a century. Our presence here isn't significant enough to rouse suspicion."

Katey crossed her arms over her stomach, willing it to stop doing backflips. She took a few seconds to reach inside herself and consult with her wolf. It was just as nervous as she was, but Katey couldn't recall if she felt this same hesitance in the hall when they saw the dog. She should have sensed it too, just the same as Logan did. She recalled feeling like something wasn't quite right about the scene, but the feeling couldn't express itself as anything more than that.

Logan turned toward the back sliding glass door that opened out onto the back porch and gardens beyond. Dustin was there, knocking the mud off his shoes before he came inside.

"Are you two all right?" he asked, sounding a little breathless.

"We're fine. Where's Darren?" Logan asked, guiding Katey to sit on one of the sofas.

"He should be here soon," Dustin replied as he joined them in the living room. From what she could read, he wasn't nearly as concerned as Logan or Darren had been, but there was an undeniable current of apprehension. "He's calling the local alphas to let them know about the hunters. Ben left shortly after I did, but he's taking his car. The fool wouldn't listen to me when I told him he could get his car later. I didn't want to risk taking too long to book it out of there."

As the two men stood side by side, Katey couldn't help but notice the uncanny resemblance between them. Same eyes, same jaw, and same hair, only Dustin's was much shorter and not streaked with blonde like Logan's. It still amazed her that two people, so unlike in their personalities, could be related.

"What are we going to do?" Katey asked softly, looking back and forth between the two older, more experienced pack members. There had to be a procedure or some list of guidelines for this kind of situation, though Logan just admitted they hadn't encountered a hunter this close to Crestucky since the eighteen hundreds.

Dustin took a deep breath and went to the kitchen. "For now, we do nothing. Darren will be here soon with the plan." Katey watched him take down a plate from one of the cabinets and begin to fix himself a snack of raw deer meat from the fridge, even though they had breakfast less than two hours ago. Between all of them, Dustin had the most voracious appetite.

"How can you eat at a time like this?" Logan asked with more than a little impatience.

"Very easily," Dustin replied as he poured himself a glass of water. "I feel hungry, I pull out a plate, and I eat. Hunters will not keep me from feeding myself."

Rage flickered in Logan's face. "Don't you care that hunters could be closing in on us right now? We should be out there!"

Dustin slammed his hands on the countertop. "Thank you for reminding me, Logan," he replied scathingly, his voice shifting into his Irish tongue. The heavy inflection of his native accent came out every so often when Dustin became overly excited or angry. "Yes, I care deeply, but until our alpha comes waltzing in here with a plan, I'm going to eat my snack and wait."

The pack beta tore off a chunk of deer steak from the slab and chewed on it, giving Logan a challenging stare. Logan let out a subdued growl and began to pace the floor like a caged animal, the way he so often did when he was upset but unable to do anything.

Katey leaned on her knees and tried to make sense of it herself without inciting further conflicts between them. Logan's argument made the most sense to her. If the hunters were a true threat, they should have been confronting them head-on. In the same train of thought, Katey couldn't deny the tremor of fear for the safety of her pack and the longing to have their leader close by.

Dustin finished his snack and retreated to the back billiard room, where he spent most of his free time. Ben came through the front door moments later as if he were coming home from a usual day at work. Katey sensed no agitation in him whatsoever. No worry, no panic, nothing. He was simply indifferent to the danger.

"Have you heard from Darren?" Logan asked as soon as the omega sat down his briefcase by the front door.

"Smooth out your hackles," Ben quipped flatly. "I called him as soon as I left and he assured me that he would be back shortly."

"Did he manage to get a hold of the Devian alpha?" Katey asked, thinking of how Forrest's pack would survive another onslaught by a group of hunters.

Ben turned to her with patient eyes. "He contacted several alphas within a fifty-mile radius. That's all he would tell me. He will be here soon to—"

They all turned to the dull roar of an engine plowing up the path to the house. A car door slammed in the driveway, and the front door opened just seconds later. Darren came charging into the living room, passed them all by, and hurried up the stairs to the bedrooms on the second floor. The other three remained silent as she listened to him gather up something and then returned to the living room.

Between his arms, he toted a wooden sea chest that looked to be a couple of hundred years old. Darren slammed it down on the wood flooring just as Dustin came into the living room holding a pool stick in one hand and a cue ball in the other. Along with the rest of the pack, billiards was a favorite pastime of Dustin's. He once remarked how it helped him focus in challenging times. They had played billiards quite often in the few weeks since Katey had been changed.

She watched as Darren threw open the trunk lid and began pulling out pistols, sheathed daggers, and short-barreled rifles. Some were new, and others looked as if they had been sitting in the chest for decades or longer. All, however, were in mint condition. Katey thought she had smelled something like gun oil late at night when everyone else should have been asleep. Darren must have known this day was coming and wanted to be prepared.

No one spoke as he began to stack the weapons on the opposite sofa, enough for all five of them to arm themselves with – and then some. Then, he closed the trunk and stood up straight to regard each of them with a deathly serious stare. His guard was as high up as Katey had ever seen it, projecting a full spread of authority that held everyone's attention.

"From what we can determine, the hunters have been sending out feelers to the surrounding counties. Small scouting parties have been sighted in almost every town, but no kills have been reported. They're making their way east and north from what other packs can gather."

"How do you know that much?" Katey asked, feeling lost in the midst of it all.

"Word has been trying to get around. Jacob, the Devian alpha, has known that hunters were nearby and has been slowly evacuating his pack out. He didn't want to raise any alarms until he knew for certain the hunters would be coming here and what their intentions were, but he's taking no chances. He may be a second generation Devian, but he knows the dangers when hunters are concerned."

"What about the rougarous?" Dustin asked, his grip tightening and loosening over the pool stick.

"When I tried to contact Gregory, he said his pack had left a week ago. It was a mass exodus, and that might have raised suspicion—exactly what Jacob didn't want. They're in another state, but Gregory wasn't interested in chatting to tell me much of anything else."

Katey thought it strange that Erik hadn't shown up at school, but she wasn't going to be overly worried about the loup-garou who had almost killed them all during the Alaskan incident. It was his fault the vampires knew where to find Katey and her pack on the night of the great gathering of the loups-garous. Although she had forgiven him for his foolishness, they hadn't spoken since. His father, the rougarou alpha, must have given him a severe reprimand about his betrayal when they returned home.

"Did they know the hunters were coming?" Katey asked.

Darren shrugged. "He wouldn't tell me much, and I had other alphas to call. They're safe for the time being."

"What do we do now?" Ben asked, his arms folded over his chest.

Darren was silent for a moment, but Katey could see the gears of his mind hard at work. He had been prepared, that was for certain, but he might not have had time to come up with a plan for all the possible scenarios.

"Under different circumstances, I would say we need to evacuate with the Deviants. Jacob has accelerated his plan to get everyone out of Crestucky, but now that they know the hunters are here, they will need extra protection."

"Are you hinting that we go help them escape?" Katey asked, feeling a new, heavy dread settle in her stomach. She could picture convoys of loups-garous and their families leaving Crestucky, trudging through the woods like refugees under the surveillance of an armed escort. Was that too old-fashioned? Or would they leave in caravan style with their belongings piled high on top of their vehicles as they took the interstate out of town?

Darren gave her a stern look. "You aren't stepping foot out of this house until the hunters have passed through. Logan, myself, and Dustin will accompany the Deviants and their families as they make their way out of town. They have a safe house in central Alabama they can go to during times like this."

Katey's chest ached as if Darren had shot her. "Why can't Logan stay with me?"

"Because Logan has been through an evacuation like this once before," Darren replied. "He knows the routine as well as I do and Dustin is our beta. Ben is strong and can protect you if something happens. He has military training. They're beginning the first wave of evacuations in a couple of hours, and we have to get ready."

Katey looked between them all, eyes begging for a reconsideration, but they all had turned their attention to the weapons and Darren as he began to brief them on the progress of the evacuations. Even Logan had turned his back to her to inspect an antique-looking pistol with a revolving chamber.

Their voices became like deadened rumbles in her ears as she let the idea sink in that Logan would not be with her. Even her wolf whined and whimpered for an alternative. She would have sooner gone with them on their mission rather than sit at home like a helpless child. Wasn't this what she was born for? To protect and aid the loups-garous?

Though she wasn't sure what exactly she could do, Katey thought once she was in the situation, it would all come to her as if she were riding a bike for the first time in years. The trouble was, she didn't know how to ride that bike. Apart from the mediation she did in the castle between the loups-garous and vampires, she knew nothing about what it took to protect her kind against a menace as serious as hunters, but she had to try. She needed to accompany the Deviants, not Logan.

"What if I lose you?" she whispered, staring vacantly at the rug in the middle of the living room, a numbness dominating her body in response to the overwhelming fear.

Her words caught Logan's attention and he rushed to Katey's side to wrap his arms around her. "You won't lose me," he whispered back in her ear, his breath feathering her skin.

Katey only gripped his shirt tighter, bunching it in her fists, and refused to let go, her insides roiling with emotions she couldn't begin to name, let alone control. "What if something happens to you?"

"Nothing will happen to me," he assured her.

Katey felt tears gather at the corners of her eyes as she shook her head. "No, I need you here with me," she demanded, calling on her wolf for strength. "I'll go in your place. This is what I'm alive for, isn't it?"

Darren turned, and she felt an upsurge of dominance pulsate in the room. "You will do nothing, Katey. We can't afford to lose you. We will look after Logan."

She lifted her quivering chin and met Darren's glare. "How dangerous are the hunters? Don't lie to me."

The alpha's face softened, and he heaved a sigh. "I won't lie. They have the ability to exterminate our kind. If you thought the vampires were advanced in their technology, the hunters are beyond experts in their field. They've had just as long to perfect their techniques as the vampires with twice the motivation. Some families have been hunters for generations, passing the craft down to their children to ensure that one day, we will no longer exist."

"The sooner we get the Deviants out of here," Logan added, "the sooner we can leave as well."

"Leave?" Katey said, muttering the word as if the idea was unthinkable.

"You don't suggest we stay in Crestucky when it could become the next Devia, do you?" Dustin asked as he leaned the pool stick into the crook of his elbow so his hand would be free to inspect the straight blade of a devilish-looking dagger.

"But, my school... What about Lily and Beth? What about – "

"There's no time to worry about lost friendships at a time like this," Ben cut in. "The longer we stay here, the more likely the hunters will find us."

"We will not discuss this any further, Katey," Darren ended before he turned back to the pile of weapons and holstered a gun in the belt he had donned a few moments earlier.

Katey shot up from her place on the couch and took a defensive stance against her pack. "I'm not leaving Crestucky!" she shouted.

Everyone turned to her in alarm—all but Darren. His face went hard, intolerance written so clearly in his features that Katey couldn't mistake it. She fought the urge to withdraw into submission to her alpha.

For a second, she recalled how strange it was that she should want to defy him on this one thing so earnestly. A few months ago, she would have wanted nothing more than to leave Crestucky, but she had the new life she had wanted so badly. Her pack and her friendships were even more valuable to her in the last few weeks than they ever had been before. Katey couldn't fathom the idea of leaving all of it behind.

"I said we will not discuss this further," Darren growled, baring his teeth in a way Katey had seen before, but she had never been on the receiving end.

"I say we will," she barked, letting her golden wolf eyes glare back at her alpha.

Katey watched as Darren's shoulders tightened and hands curled into fists. His own golden eyes appeared, taking the place of the brown puppy eyes she admired so much. All warmth and gentility were gone from him.

"You dare to challenge me at a time like this?" he snarled.

Logan and Dustin dashed forward to stand between Katey and Darren. Logan took her by the shoulders and forced her back with little effort while Dustin simply stood close by to serve as a shield of flesh and muscle to intercept any blows.

All went rigid as the two glared at one another, their first major confrontation since she moved under his roof. Everyone seemed ready to come out of their skin from the tension. The dominance the alpha exerted should have been enough to send them all cowering, but she would not let go of her resolve.

Darren's nostrils flared, his eyes fixed on Katey. "You will learn your place, Katey."

Katey took a bounding step forward, but Logan's arm pulled her back. "I won't leave Crestucky. I don't want Logan going out there where he could get hurt. I am the chosen one to fulfill the prophecy. I should have a say in this."

Darren's lips dipped into a deep frown. "You think just because you were born special, you have the right to defy my judgments? You've been spoiled for long enough, and you will do as I say. Logan will help in the evacuations, and as soon as we know every Devian is out of Crestucky, we will follow them as the rear guard. If the hunters move on, we will return in a few months, but no sooner." Darren leaned closer. "Do I make myself clear?"

Katey didn't want to give in to him. The air in the room was thick with the ire they had created, and she was still too sensitive to its negative energy. The wolf within her had little fight left after the outpouring of dominance from Darren's wolf.

She let her body relax, and her eyes returned to their normal green hue. Darren would not recover so easily but turned away to continue assessing the weapons. The others did the same after ensuring Katey would not spring upon Darren unexpectedly or try to bring the subject up again.

Logan gave her a tight squeeze, kissed her with a notable lack of passion, and gave her a few more reassurances before joining the others in arming themselves for the task ahead. Even Ben was giving instructions on how to use certain weapons that were unfamiliar to the others.

Katey returned to the sofa and sat down heavily, knowing there was nothing more she could do to change the course of events that would unfold. She eyed the weapons cagily for a few silent moments before asking, "Are you going to kill the hunters?"

Darren glanced over his shoulder and she saw that his deep brown eyes had returned as the wolf in him had settled back down. "We will kill if they try to kill us first. We have never fired the first shot and never will."

From the gentle tones of his voice, Katey could sense the balance between them had returned to something resembling normal. Though, she couldn't help but wonder if Darren's sudden aggression had more to do with the circumstances than with Katey's futile stab at mutiny. He had never been so quick-tempered before.

"Until this is all over," Darren announced, "everyone is going to drop off the map. Logan, you'll be dropping out of school. Katey,

I'm going to have you registered as away on a medical condition. As for us, we will be gone on extended leave pending a notice of resignation to the school. No one is to have any contact with anyone outside of the Deviants and other loups-garous."

No one contested or questioned his decisions this time and Katey kept her lips held tight, even though she wanted to oppose every bit of it. What about Beth? What would happen to Lily? Who would Katey talk to besides those of her own pack? What would she do with all of her spare time stuck in the house?

As she watched them plan and examine weapons, Katey would have given anything to see the smiles return to their faces. This morning, they were oblivious to the presence of the hunters in their part of the state. This morning, everything was all right, and as far as she was concerned, it would stay that way.

Now, as the ground beneath her perfect world began to crumble like parched earth on the edge of a precipice, Katey didn't know what to think anymore. All she knew was that nothing would remain the same after this. There was no way to know if the hunters were out for blood, and no way to know whose blood they would spill first.

CHAPTER 3

Katey scowled at the wooden chess pieces, her upper lip curled in disgust. Ben had her trapped where if she moved one way, he would take her king, but if she moved another way, he would have her in check. This was the tenth round they had played since the day before when the others left for their first evacuation trip with the Deviants. Ben taught her the game in hopes she would be distracted. She wasn't.

The gnawing ache of loneliness and worry for Logan and the others still filled her gut like an acidic poison. Probably the reason she hadn't won a single game yet was that Katey couldn't stop thinking about her fiancé and all the ways their attempt to help the Deviants could go disastrously wrong. Either that, or Ben had been honing his skills for the last century, and he was too good to beat.

With her chin nestled in her stacked fists on the table, she glanced up at Ben through her lashes. He seemed amused – as he always did – whenever she realized there was no way to win.

"Do you know where you made a mistake?" he asked as he folded his arms over his chest and leaned back in his chair with a smug look of victory plastered on his face.

"I agreed to play this stupid game," she mumbled.

Ben chuckled and pointed to the board. "You used your queen far too much and relied on her to protect the king when you should have positioned the other pieces to guard him."

"Is that some heavy-handed metaphor that I should let Dustin and Darren take care of Logan and stop worrying?"

Ben grinned. "I didn't mean to make it into a metaphor, but it certainly fits."

Katey sighed and tipped over her king to end the game. Ben laughed again and rose from the dinette table in the breakfast nook. "It's close to lunchtime anyway. Let's eat."

"I thought loups-garous were supposed to be geniuses," she wisecracked as he walked into the adjoining kitchen.

"We're not geniuses. We just think faster than the average human. You still have to earn the skills."

Katey groaned and tilted her head so her forehead rested on her arms. It had only been a full twenty-four hours into the evacuation and she was bored out of her mind. Bored and scared. Every minute that ticked by felt like hours of agony while Logan was away. The house was cold and hauntingly empty while the men were on their mission. Darren called the evening before to report on their progress, but he only spoke to Ben and passed along no messages.

She wasn't sure whose decision it had been that the guys stay the night away from the house during the evacuations. Perhaps it was necessary or an order from Jacob, but Katey hated it. If the days were long, the nights were even longer. She hadn't been able to sleep that first night, and she dreaded the one to come as long as Logan was away. Each time she managed to drift off, images of loups-garous trapped in silver cages snapped her awake. Knowing Ben was close by did little to ease her troubled mind and heart.

While Ben prepared two sandwiches of roast deer, Katey felt the unbearable dread consume her. Any word, even one spoken in hate, would have been better than this silence from Logan. How could she know he was alive? Was Ben trying to distract her because Darren had reported Logan to be wounded in an ambush by the hunters? Was Logan angry at her for trying to defy Darren yesterday morning? Had he met the daughter of a Devian loup-garou and become sucked into a whirlwind romance and had totally forgotten about Katey?

The air in her lungs seized, and she wondered if she would ever breathe again.

Katey whipped out her phone and punched out another hasty, pleading text to Logan. It was the fifteenth in a long string of unanswered messages since late last night. It was likely Darren had taken his phone away, or it had gotten smashed somehow, but Katey had to try and reach him, to remind him that she was still there waiting. Certainly, he could feel their bond just as deeply as she did, but what if he had blocked out such a nuisance so he could focus on his job or the pretty girl he escorted to safety?

"That's only gonna make things worse," Ben said from the kitchen.

Katey finished the text, sent it, and tossed the phone onto the chess board, sending some of the playing pieces rolling across the glass tabletop or clamoring to the floor. She could feel Ben's disapproving eyes on her, but she didn't care. This ordeal was nothing short of torture.

"I just need to know he's okay," she said, fighting back the impulse to raise her voice in frustration.

"I know. I understand how you feel, but sendin' him messages he won't see for another few days will do no good."

Katey swiveled in her seat to face him, her hands wringing the ironwork back of the chair. "Why do you say that? What do you know about how I feel?" she countered, the bit of contempt plain in her voice.

Ben gave her an apathetic glance and continued pouring their glasses of water. "Darren told me to keep Dustin and Logan's phones in a safe place while they're gone. Logan didn't even know he was missin' his phone until after they left the house."

Indignation boiled in Katey's chest. "What right did Darren have to do that? What if we needed to get a hold of them?"

Ben brought their sandwiches to the table and then went back to fetch the glasses. "He wants Logan to focus on the job, not spend every moment talkin' to you. He knew you two would feel this way about the separation."

He sat down heavily in his chair and began to pick up the scattered chess pieces. "And I know quite a lot about heartache. Much more than you do, anyway."

Katey wondered if this was a ploy to get her mind off Logan and the resentment she felt toward their alpha. It was a lure, tempting her to ask questions about what exactly he meant. Out of all the guys, Ben was the most cryptic. He hardly showed a flair of personality the way the others did. He was closed off from the world in nearly every way. Katey had read that in him from the very beginning when she listened to him lecture on the first day at school.

He was closed off, yet comfortable with not belonging. She knew the least about him. He was always the last person to speak unless it was truly necessary. Katey often thought he was devoid of genuine emotion. All she knew of him was what he had told her that first day when she learned about the existence of loups-garous.

Ben was a soldier in the Civil War, turned by Dustin on some battlefield. The decades between the time he parted ways with Dustin and when he reunited with the pack were a complete mystery. Not even Logan knew what the old soldier had been up to in those years. After he had joined the pack, he enlisted in the army and fought in nearly all the wars of the twentieth century.

Katey hadn't thought about it until just then, but Ben had probably seen some gruesome things in those wars. Perhaps his flat personality and seemingly calm exterior were the results of training himself to cope with the horrors of war and unspeakable violence. What about his early years? Was he a tender person? Was he sensitive? Did he have a family?

Katey wanted to know, and at the risk of taking his bait, she asked, "What do you mean?"

Ben finished chewing what was in his mouth and then he turned to her with an indiscernible look.

They locked eyes for an indeterminable amount of time before Katey raised her brows. "You're not going to tell me, are you?" she said.

One corner of Ben's mouth slowly pulled up into a pleased smile. "I can, but how much should I tell you?"

The sinister glint in his expression gave her pause. Were there things about his past that he kept hidden for a reason? What deep, dark secrets were lurking behind those amber eyes? Katey began to detest her curiosity. "Isn't it your job to take care of me?" she asked. "A long story will help me stay distracted from Logan and the idea that he could be dead in a ditch right now." She took a bite of her sandwich to show Ben she wasn't as nervous as she really was to know the truth.

He snorted and leaned back in his chair. "Logan's not dead. Darren assured me of that last night."

Katey felt the balloon of anxiety begin to deflate in her gut and she knew she would survive for another day. "Well, tell me the whole story, so I don't have to play another game of chess with you."

Ben looked away, staring aimlessly into space. "I don't think even Dustin knows the whole story."

If Dustin, who was as close as a brother to Ben, didn't know everything, Katey knew he wouldn't dare to unfold his entire life story to her. Crestfallen, she continued to eat in silence while he kept his gaze fixed on a random spot on the opposite wall.

Just when she was about to finish off her glass of water, Ben said, "I was born in Franklin, Georgia in 1840."

Katey set down her glass and folded her legs beneath her, eager to hear the rest, but keeping still as if one wrong move would end the moment.

"I had an older brother, and our family worked on a farm owned by a wealthy tradesman. We lived in a little cabin down in a valley by the farm, and our employer's family lived in a mansion on the crest of the hill. They had a daughter named Abigail." His throat worked as he spoke, but when he said the girl's name, there was nothing but gentleness in his voice.

"We grew up together, Abigail and me. Our parents let us play together as children. When we were older, our friendship grew into love. Her parents didn't approve of my low station, but we were married in the fall of 1860." He paused, his jaw slack briefly as if he were remembering fond moments they shared.

"But, then the war came, and Georgia seceded from the Union. I went to fight like all the other men my age. It was expected. You know how I was injured at Antietam and Dustin changed me to save my life."

His eyelids dropped slowly and silence—ringing and suffocating—filled the house before he shattered it with more misery. "I envy you," he said softly.

Katey was caught off guard by such an admittance. "What do you mean by that?"

"When you woke up from your change, you were coherent. You still had your humanity intact. You could speak human words and understand them when they were spoken to you. When I woke up a few days after Dustin changed me, I could do none of those things."

Ben's eyelids cracked open fractionally, but Katey could see the glittering gold of his wolf eyes staring vacantly. "I was a monster. All I wanted to do was kill everythin' in sight, rip it to shreds, and run far away. I had an insatiable hunger for raw flesh right from the beginnin'. You see, when Dustin changed me, my human life was nothin' but a dyin' ember in the dark. I was almost dead.

When I became a loup-garou, the beast within me took over and dominated what was left of my soul. I didn't change outwardly, but on the inside, there was little left of the man I was. The wolf had to keep me alive."

The immense suffering in his eyes was enough to tempt Katey into embracing him, hoping it would make the broken pieces of his past come together again. She knew it was useless. The damage had been done long ago. Yet, he was sitting there with her, civilized and tamed somehow. Something must have happened to help him recover what he'd lost.

"It took days of nothin' but squirrel and deer meat before I was coherent enough to ask Dustin what happened to me. To the best of his ability, he taught me how to control my senses and new abilities. I hated him for what he made me into. I begged him to let me go see Abigail, to tell her that I was alive – for the most part. He refused, sayin' I wasn't ready to face another human. It wasn't until later that I found out my eyes were not what they used to be."

He looked up at her, showing her the yellow eyes of a wolf. "It doesn't take much effort for me to keep my eyes a human color now. But, back then, I couldn't make them any different. The wolf had conquered too much of me, and any human who saw me would have known I was a monster."

Ben blinked long and when he looked at her again, his eyes were an amber color once more. "After trainin' for a year, I was still no better. All I wanted was to see Abigail, and the fact that I couldn't be with her, that she thought I had died, tore me apart... I ventured close to a Confederate camp and found a silver coin. I took it and swallowed it, hopin' it would put an end to my sufferin'."

Katey let out a tiny sound of distress. She knew how silver felt when it touched her skin. The metal burned like a hot iron. She imagined ingesting silver itself, having it travel down the soft tissue of one's esophagus, must have been excruciating.

"I also thought it wasn't fair my comrades were fightin' and dyin' for our right to independence from the Union while I was sittin' on the sidelines. Dustin found out what I had done and managed to dislodge the coin with the help of a couple of Confederate women. One of the women was Logan's grandmother." He paused and gave her a knowing look. "I won't have to tell you what happened there."

Katey pressed her lips together to keep herself from smiling. Yes, she knew what happened. "After that, though?"

Ben shifted in his chair and sighed. "We left there and came to just outside of Knoxville. I found my way to a Confederate camp and met with an old friend of mine from Franklin. I wore tinted glasses to hide my eyes by that point. We talked and it made me think about my own home and Abigail. I told Dustin I needed to leave and find out if they were okay. Some nasty words were exchanged, and we parted ways. He'd had enough of my uncontrollable behavior, and I'd had enough of his dominance." He huffed with laughter. "Lookin' back now, it was a silly thing to do. It might have saved us all some trouble if we had just stayed together.

"Anyway, I found my way home." Ben swallowed hard and dropped his gaze to the tabletop. "I found my mother in the kitchen, half-starved and insane with loneliness. The house on the hill was burned to the ground, and the fields were the same. The war had found its way to Georgia. Because she was so out of it, I was able to gather that my brother had been killed at Gettysburg and my father had enlisted in a war he had no business fightin' as an old man."

Ben's eyebrows furrowed into a deep frown. "When she had a moment of clarity, she realized who she was talkin' to and began to scream. She called me a demon, and I ran from the house."

Katey bit at her thumbnail, wishing this was the end of the story, but she knew there was still much more tragedy to come. Perhaps he had a right to envy her, more than just the favorable conditions of her change. She had the support of a pack, the acceptance of the guys and so many others.

In all reality, Ben had it tough. She didn't want to think about how alone he must have felt; how discouraged and hopeless enough to want to end it all. She had traveled down that road before but for a different reason.

The fact that Ben was still alive to this day amazed her. There was plenty of heartache and sorrow throbbing in his chest, but just as much – if not more – bravery and strength. She had never admired him more.

"I wanted to see Abigail, but I knew I couldn't face her the way I was. It might have been too much of a shock to see me alive at all. I managed to track her down to the house of a friend far away from the fightin' and rampagin' of Sherman's army. I watched her one night through a window. I will never forget the way she looked, dressed in all black and knittin' a pair of tiny socks."

"Ben," she gasped. "You had children?"

He looked at her, his eyes glazed over with pain. "I did. A son. Though, I had no idea. He was conceived durin' Christmas leave and born right around the time she received the letter that I had been killed in action. That night, I saw my son playin' on the floor by the fire, carefree and happy. I've never told anyone about that."

Katey's throat closed up with tears. "Thank you," she managed to say. She understood the great honor it was to be blessed with such privileged information.

Ben looked away again. "Because they thought I was dead, Abigail was bein' courted by another man. A cavalry officer. I couldn't barge into their lives. I knew if I loved them, I would have to leave them. All soldiers write a farewell letter to their folks in case they die in battle. I had mine already written and slipped it to her the morning I left her. I didn't set foot on Georgia soil for over half a century after that."

"What did you do then?" Katey asked, knowing that wasn't the end. "Logan told me Darren and Dustin found you in the Idaho mountains. That was nearly sixty years later. You had to have been doing something all that time."

Ben nodded. "I was doing somethin' all right... Nothin'. I traveled out west and spent my days scavengin' on buffalo carcasses and dodgin' civilization as much as possible. Worked on the railroad for a while, and some odds and ends jobs, but nothin' else. I was doin' just fine until I got involved in some loups-garous outlaw feud."

Katey held out her hand to stop him. "You're going to have to give me more details about that one," she said hurriedly.

Ben cracked a smile for the first time since before he began, but it was fleeting. "In a nutshell, there are some loups-garous out there that have very twisted views of justice. A sheriff was dead determined to exterminate any rogue loups-garous who didn't belong in a pack, thinkin' they were dangerous because they weren't held in check by an alpha. An outlaw believed loups-garous should make humans their slaves and considered them to be inferior creatures." By the contempt in his voice, Katey knew Ben was not interested in either of these men's ideologies.

"I made the mistake of tryin' to help a young woman hunt down her family's murderer. Along the way, I was captured by that sheriff, and he would have killed me if she hadn't released me from the silver mine they were holdin' me in."

Katey winced at the idea of being trapped in a place abounding with the one thing loups-garous were not immune to.

"I escaped and met with the outlaw. He was the one who murdered the girl's family, but he spun a tale about her father threatenin' to rat out the outlaws to the sheriff. They couldn't risk bein' discovered, so they killed him and all of his family except for the girl. The outlaw told me they would be ridin' out to take care of the sheriff and I joined him, thinkin' I could figure out some way to catch him in a trap or somethin'."

Ben sighed, "But, it turned out the outlaws were just about as mad as a box of frogs. They wiped out an entire Indian village to lure the sheriff into the open. I helped some escape and then tried to team up with the sheriff to bring down the outlaws.

"In the end, I found myself in the middle of a big loup-garou brawl. The leader of the gang and the sheriff were killed, so there was some justice in the end, I guess. But, I'd had enough of society—loups-garous or otherwise—and ran north without stoppin'. I built myself a cabin in the mountains as far from people as I could get and stayed that way for years before Dustin and Darren showed up on my doorstep. I had too many bad experiences with other loups-garous and wanted no part in joinin' this pack."

"How did they manage to convince you?" Katey asked.

A gratified look washed over Ben's face. "Darren promised he could teach me how to make my eyes normal again."

She couldn't help but let out a little laugh at his response, but it told volumes about how Ben would have set aside his prejudgments just to feel a little human again.

"He did help me. I was brought into the pack bond and it was like the wolf in me could finally rest. The gold instantly went away and I got my old eyes back. Darren took it a step further and when we left the mountains, we went straight to Georgia. He told me Abigail was still alive. She was an old woman by then, but I wanted to know if she was okay, if she had lived a happy life after I left. We found her in a nursin' home. We snuck past the orderlies, and I got to see my Abigail one last time. Her mind was slippin' away, but she had never been more beautiful. I saw pictures of our son and grandchildren on her vanity. They were beautiful too."

Ben beamed. "I was blessed with a few moments with my wife and spoke to her as if we were teenagers again. I flirted shamelessly, and her cheeks blushed that rosy red I loved." His smile weakened. "Toward the end, she apologized for remarryin'. I could never blame her for that. She confessed that she did live a full and happy life. Her only regret was that I wasn't there to share it with her. Abigail thought I was gonna take her away to heaven, but I couldn't."

Katey crossed her arms over the tabletop and tried not to cry.

"She gave me the weddin' ring I gave her in 1860." Ben shifted and pulled a tiny golden ring from the pocket of his jeans and offered it to her. "I never leave the house without it."

He placed the ring in her palm and Katey could almost feel the weight of more than a century of love and loss. It was beautiful in its simplicity, even with the few scratches in the surface. She smiled and brushed away a tear that managed to escape before giving the ring back to Ben.

"I let Darren and Dustin train me for a couple of decades before I joined the army." He tucked the ring away in his jeans again. "I wanted to make up for lost time while I was on the benches durin' the Civil War. I stormed the beaches on D-Day and waded through the jungles of Vietnam. My loup-garou abilities were put to good use fightin' for the freedom of others, but I still didn't feel free inside."

"What do you mean by that?" she asked and sniffled to clear herself before she embarked on discovering another piece of Ben's puzzle.

He tilted his head thoughtfully. "I'm not sure if I could accurately describe it," he said. "I suppose I still felt like a part of my humanity was missin'. Joinin' the army didn't help. I did terrible things and saw worse." Ben went quiet, a profound expression almost too arcane for Katey to comprehend developing in his eyes.

"My last battle was in Vietnam. A fellow loup-garou in my regiment and I had been captured by the enemy, who also happened to be loup-garou. I remember bein' so surprised there were loups-garous so far east. They led us into one of their underground bunkers. They fed us and took care of us for a few hours. My comrade formed a quick attachment to the community, but I couldn't. I wasn't even sure if I wanted to. I was a soldier, and they were my enemy.

"The bunker was raided by our men, and we escaped. My friend refused to fire on the loups-garous who aided us." Ben gritted his teeth. "But I had a stash of silver bullets in my bag, and I shot down a few. I remember feelin' the last shred of my humanity slip away. I had never killed my own kind, even though I was prepared for it, and I never wanna again. My friend and I went AWOL that night. He used his connections in Europe, and I took advantage of Darren's good reputation to do the same. I vowed never to fight again if I could help it.

"It's been a struggle since then to make sure the beast doesn't take control like that. So, you see, I know a few things about heartache. I also know you and Logan will survive the next few days, or the weeks to come if you don't see each other. I survived over two years without seein' my wife, and you are so much stronger than me."

Katey wasn't sure how to feel about his confession. War was a terrible thing and the scars that the soldiers kept decades after the fighting stopped were enough for her to abhor the whole thing. Perhaps it was her destiny that made her believe so, but she couldn't judge Ben for what he had done under orders. He was not the same man, that was evident.

As for his admission about heartache, it was plain in the defeat in his words and shame written on his face for the deeds and mistakes he had made. Ben had suffered so much, seen so many horrors, and lived through too much agony to even begin to grasp. His faith in her fortitude to carry on without Logan close by gave her a little strength.

Ben passed a hand over his forehead, and he looked down at his sandwich as if he suddenly remembered it was still there. He didn't pick it up right away. Instead, he took a swig of water and turned to Katey. "Was that sufficient for story time?"

Hardly understanding why, Katey stood and wrapped her arms around Ben's neck. She understood how hard it was for him to talk about his life with someone else. All she could hope was that by talking about it, Ben was healing a little more on the inside. It wasn't just a gesture of sympathy, but of compassion and understanding.

He hugged her in return, and a mutual feeling of solidarity passed between them. They had never been this close, not even a little. To finally bond with the one member of the pack who had stayed so distant made Katey's wolf content. "Thank you," she whispered before pulling away.

She could have sworn she saw Ben's eyes go misty for a moment. He smiled and gave her an assuring nod before he began to eat.

CHAPTER 4

Katey stood in front of her bedroom window, staring out toward the driveway. Her eyes flitted across their property line, her senses straining beyond the pane of glass as her stomach churned. Ben made the mistake of letting her listen in on Darren's last phone call earlier that morning. The boys were coming home after being away for three days, and Katey could hardly wait.

The gut-wrenching situation and lack of sleep made her irritable, but not speaking one word to Logan since he left earlier in the week had made her into a raving mad woman. It was a wonder she had the clarity of mind to speak civilly to Ben at all. Exhaustion and anticipation consumed her, and she didn't know whether to pace the floor or collapse in bed with the knowledge that Logan would be home soon.

How soon they would be back was unknown. They had to wrap things up with the evacuation and conference with Jacob before heading back to the house. The few hours since that phone call had seemed like days, but Katey stayed vigilant, watching the only road in or out of their property.

She could almost hear woodland critters scurrying through the bushes outside and counted how long it took for Ben to turn a page in the book he was reading downstairs.

On the second day of their isolation, Katey had devoured every novel in the house and spent nearly twenty dollars on new eBooks to read to pass the time. Not usually one for reading, Katey was down to her last resort to keep herself occupied. There was little else she could do anymore, and movies did nothing to keep the loneliness at bay. Ben tried to distract her with games and conversation, which helped to a certain extent.

Each time she thought she heard a car engine, her heart skipped and her eyes focused on the break in the trees where she expected Dustin's red pickup truck to come barreling through. She stared until her eyes watered, but Katey convinced herself it must have been a car from the highway miles away.

She sighed, and a subtle pang of hunger brought her thoughts to the present. It must have been close to lunchtime. Eating would have killed some time, but with her jittery nerves, it might have been pointless to eat. It would all come back up soon enough. Plus, she might miss seeing them come home if she were too busy eating or puking.

Katey now knew how a dog must have felt while it waited for its owner to come home from work. Dogs could not judge time, and as far as Katey was concerned, she could relate. Seconds were minutes, minutes were hours, days seemed like weeks or lifetimes. Logan's face was still fresh in her mind, branded there by the love they shared, but she wondered how long it would take for her to forget the sound of his voice or how his kisses felt against her lips. Could loups-garous forget things like that?

She leaned her forehead against the chilled window and her hot breath plumed over the surface. When she took her next breath, her ears picked up the sound of a roaring vehicle again. This time, it seemed closer, and she could hear the popping sound of the exhaust pipe.

Katey straightened and braced herself on the windowsill, her nose less than an inch from the glass as she waited. From the shadows of the path through the trees, she saw the grill of the truck, then the hood, and the front windshield. She could see Darren and Dustin sitting in the front seats. Beyond the cab, Katey glimpsed the quick movement of Logan dismounting from the bed of the truck.

She grinned and turned, planning to meet him at the door, but she only managed to take a step before her bedroom door flew open and Logan rushed in. Katey squealed as he enfolded her in his arms and swung her in circles. She held onto his neck, and when her feet met the ground, Logan's lips met hers with demanding force.

Katey let her eyes close as she drank in his scent, mingled with the aroma of earth and pine. He smelled of the world outside, the forest she had been eager to return to for her training since before the evacuation began. It was intoxicating.

What was more powerful was the relief that flooded her body, chasing away the days of loneliness and revitalizing her spirit. The tether between them strengthened again, and Katey took back all the times she thought his constant presence was annoying or suffocating. If this time apart proved anything, it was that she never wanted to leave his side again.

Logan pulled her close, squeezing her supple body against his own and she could feel the rigid muscles of his abs and chest. Her fingers weaved through his matted hair, savoring the slick feel of the fibers in her palm. A groan rumbled in his chest, and he kissed his way down to her neck. Tiny shocks coursed through her limbs and core as his lips worked on her tender skin.

"I missed you," she whispered breathlessly, burying her nose in his shoulder.

"I missed you too. Damn Darren for sneaking my phone away from me," he grumbled.

Katey pulled away, impatient to see his blue eyes again. When their gazes met, his eyes were not blue, but a lustful red. She wondered if hers were the same and placed her hand in the center of his chest to stop him from carrying their reunion any further. As much as she wanted it too, they weren't mated yet.

Logan made a high-pitched whine, and they waited until both of their appetites for each other had subsided. He leaned in for a gentle, harmless kiss and brushed his nose against hers. "Are you well?" he asked.

Katey smiled and wrinkled her nose. "I am now that you're back. Are you okay?" she asked, looking him up and down for injuries. He was decked out in camouflage pants and jacket that was un-buttoned over a plain white shirt, stained with sweat. It was then that she noticed his face was smudged with dirt as well, making his eyes stand out even more brilliantly.

"I'm fine," he replied and kissed her again. "Now that I'm with you, my world is perfect again."

Katey giggled and heard the front door open to admit Dustin and a raging Darren. She went still and listened to his curses. "What's wrong with Darren?" she asked.

Logan let out a breath. "Some of the Deviants are refusing to evacuate. They don't think there's a reason to worry unless the hunters have been killing. Since there's no body count, they're not budging."

Fear streaked through her. "They weren't there when Devia was wiped out the first time?"

"Some were. Some weren't. There's a total of ten families still in Crestucky that haven't left yet, and Jacob's asked us to stay behind and look after them."

Katey wasn't sure how to feel about it. In one instance, she was thankful she wouldn't have to leave Crestucky or her friends. It had been the one thing she would not be so apathetic about when the time came. Now, she wouldn't have to worry about battling Darren's authority again. On the other hand, she knew how dangerous it would be for those families to stay in Crestucky when the threat of a hunter loomed over them.

"Can't Jacob order them to leave?" she asked with suspicion.

"Jacob was going to, but when Darren agreed to watch over them, he decided to leave it alone."

"So that's why Darren's not happy? He could have said no."

Logan shrugged and rubbed down the center of her back. "There are still many things I don't understand about him." He planted an affectionate kiss on her forehead. "I was so worried the hunters had come here and I wasn't here to protect you, but I knew as long as I could feel the bond between us, you were alive."

Katey rested her head against his shoulder and smiled. She hadn't thought of the bond as a lifeline, but it made sense. As long as his heart still beat, it was beating for her, and their bond would remain. "You shouldn't have worried. Ben was here to look after me."

Logan huffed and hugged her tighter. "That's not much of a comfort."

Katey pulled away and gave him a reprimanding look. "Ben is fully capable of taking care of me. We talked a lot while you were away."

Logan's eyes narrowed suspiciously. "About what, exactly?"

She opened her mouth to tell him the truth, but she had a feeling Ben wouldn't have wanted her blabbing about his life to everyone. He kept his history a secret from the others for a personal reason, and after hearing everything he had to say, Katey understood why. What would they think if they knew he had murdered their own kind in cold blood? What would they do when they found out he had great-grandchildren and great-great-grandchildren run-ning around? Though she understood the purpose of openness in the pack, Ben's business was his own.

"He just told me a lot about himself, and I know if it came down to it, he would do what's best to keep me safe." Logan didn't appear convinced. "Why are you giving me that look like I've got five heads?"

Logan shrugged as if caught in a statement he couldn't sup-port. "Ben just hasn't exactly proven his medal around here, that's all. He doesn't have complete control over his wolf with-out an alpha present. If he changed, he might have hurt you."

She gave him a look. "You're not exactly great in that depart-ment either, you know?" As soon as she said it, Katey knew she had done wrong.

Logan's face went cold, and he let out a long breath, his burning eyes still locked on hers.

"I'm just trying to make a point that Ben's not a bad guy," Katey said quickly, her knees bending a little in submission, appealing to Logan's dominant tendencies that showed up every now and again when they were alone.

He seemed to accept her apologetic body language and stroked her hair while his expression softened. "I know, Katey. I'm sorry. You're safe, and that's all that matters." He kissed her again, and she lifted herself onto her toes to kiss back.

"Will you be staying home from now on?" she asked as his hands cupped around her jaw, his thumb stroking her cheeks.

"I think so. Darren told me that Dustin and Ben would be going out as scouts to patrol around the homes of the families. So, I'm assuming that would leave the three of us together at home."

"Did he mention anything about continuing my training?" she eagerly asked.

Since the others had left Monday afternoon, Katey had been itching to try and change again like they had agreed. However, since they were on a strict lockdown, Katey hadn't had the chance. She had hoped with Darren home, they could pick up where they left off. With luck, taking a break in the last few days would not disrupt her progress.

Logan gave her a rueful smile and shook his head. "No. It never came up. You have plenty of time. Changing on command will be easier after your first natural change. Have you been keeping track of that?"

Katey grimaced. "No. I have trouble keeping up with my own menstrual cycle."

He chuckled and kissed her again. "I love you," he muttered warmly.

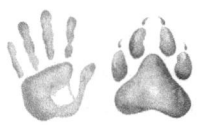

Darren tossed his cap and bag on the couch, still spewing out insults. "Those damn, bloody fools! Do they think the hunters are going to pass them over because they're brave enough to stay? Or are they just ignorant?"

Dustin came trudging in, looking weary. He rolled his eyes and dropped his own bag down next to the one Logan had abandoned before darting upstairs. "I don't know, Darren," he replied tiredly. Ben could tell Dustin had already gotten an earful of Darren's grousing.

"Who's stayin'?" Ben asked, feigning a curious tone. Dustin shot him a displeased look and growled. Ben gave him a cheeky grin, knowing he was prolonging Dustin's suffering.

Darren tore open his camouflage jacket, sending a few popped buttons clattering to the floor. "The Deviants! Some of the families are staying behind!" he roared, waving his arm angrily toward the front door. Ben sneered at the fallen buttons, knowing he would have to refasten them before Darren had to wear that jacket again. Because he had plenty of experience mending his own torn uniforms in the military, the job of pack tailor fell on his shoulders.

Dustin went to the kitchen and began fixing their plates for a late lunch.

"They're stayin'?" Ben asked, snapping closed the book he was halfway through reading for the twentieth time. "I thought Jacob was orderin' an immediate evacuation?"

Darren rubbed at his dirty face with an equally filthy hand. "He did, but these idiots think there's no reason to worry. You'd think that they had never heard of what happened in Devia over a century ago."

"What does that mean for us?" he asked, suddenly interested in this emergency.

Put into a place of true leadership for the first time took him off the sidelines in a way that spurred him out of complacency.

In the army, he only ever had to worry about one person; himself. Even then, he was given orders or was placed under the direction of someone else. In the pack, it was no different. He wasn't dominant enough to serve as an alpha or beta, but he found himself slipping into the role of protector much easier than he anticipated.

Although he would never relinquish his easy life as a subordinate, it made him appreciate the mindset of Darren and Dustin.

The alpha sat down heavily on the sofa beside Ben and rubbed the back of his neck. "Jacob asked us to stay, and I agreed. You and Dustin will look after the families from a distance and make sure they're all right."

Ben watched his alpha for a moment and inwardly cringed at the way he appeared so much older than he had been before the evacuation began, his face haggard and drooping. The stress was getting to him. "When was the last time you slept?" he questioned, his tone rife with concern.

The alpha gave a heavy sigh and looked at him with eyes rimmed in dark circles. "Not since Sunday night."

Alarmed, Ben put his hand on Darren's shoulder. "Go rest. The hard part is over."

Darren's brows snapped together. "What happened?"

Ben blinked. "Nothin' happened. I just don't want you exhaustin' yourself. That's a long time to not sleep, and you're the one usually tellin' us to get a full eight hours."

"I think he means," Dustin interjected, "what happened to make you care at all?"

Ben looked back and forth between the other two men whom he had come to consider as brothers in the last century. He had always cared, but never let it show. He stayed detached from the pack in what ways he could; something else the military taught him.

Soldiers who opened up about their greatest fears and deepest secrets were ridiculed for being weak. Though, oftentimes times he saw the bullies suffer from the same emotional scars as the truthful GI. To stay inconspicuous, Ben knew to shut his mouth and not let the cracks in his armor show. It was better to be calloused in some respects, and he had lived his life that way ever since he roamed through the western territories.

Their puzzled looks and the revelations that Katey inspired over the last couple of days made Ben begin to secondguess everything. It appeared the military had tainted him so thoroughly that there was little left of the farm boy from Georgia and that didn't settle well with Ben. What would Abigail have thought if she faced the cold man he was today?

One thing she loved about him was the way he could carry on a conversation with anyone about nearly everything under the sun. It was his honesty that brought them together because he never pretended to be someone he wasn't. In a society where people were polite and unoffending for the sake of others, Ben was a shining jewel to Abigail. He spoke his mind, but now he kept his problems and comments to himself.

When did that happen? At Antietam? On the beaches of Normandy? In the jungles of Vietnam? Or had becoming a loup-garou stolen his best quality to replace it with some instinct that told him to keep to himself? The days spent apart from the rest of the pack gave him more time to reflect than in all the years he had spent wandering alone.

His hand dropped from Darren's shoulder. How could he possibly answer the alpha's question? Talking with Katey was somehow effortless, but he couldn't fathom how to be candid with his friends.

"How's Katey?" Darren asked, diverting the subject away from Ben for the moment. He must have sensed the confusion in his omega.

"She's fine. Restless, but fine. She was fit to be tied when I told her you took Logan's phone away."

Darren huffed a humorless laugh. "Logan, too," he said before he rose to his feet and walked toward the stairs. "I'm going to take a nap. Don't let hunters burn the house down while I'm asleep."

Ben was not amused by his statement. Did he truly think they would let something like that happen? He stood from the sofa and joined Dustin in the kitchen as their alpha retreated upstairs.

"Don't worry, Mother Goose. I washed my hands," Dustin quipped. Ben let out a short snarl and began helping him assemble the plates loaded with different meats. "So, did you and Katey have a fun time stuck indoors?"

"We played chess on the first day, but she didn't like that."

Dustin laughed. "Did you whip her like you do with us?"

"I let her win one game, but she lost interest quickly."

Dustin elbowed him. "You're turning into a softy all over, aren't ye?" he teased in his Irish accent. Ben went silent and poured their glasses. "I'll bet she didn't like staying cooped up, did she?"

"Frankly," Ben replied, "I didn't either."

"But no trouble?" Dustin asked as he set the plates out on the table.

Ben shook his head, even though he knew Dustin couldn't see him. There was no trouble at all. In fact, it was a pleasant few days. Being separated from the pack wasn't so enjoyable, but he and Katey talked about a variety of things.

He shared with her about the nature of the wolf, explaining in more detail about hierarchy and what he had learned over the decades. He even began teaching her the loup-garou language Darren had promised to teach her weeks ago, but she was too preoccupied with her loneliness to stay interested. He hadn't seen her since earlier that morning after Darren called to let them know the boys would be coming home that afternoon.

"Your shift night was Monday, wasn't it?" Ben asked, remembering the bit of anxiety he felt when checking the calendar on Tuesday morning. Dustin had enough control over his wolf that escorting the Deviants wouldn't be a difficult task for him under the circumstances, but it didn't keep Ben from being concerned.

"I did," he replied. "No trouble at all. I enjoyed getting out of the truck for a little while. I ran alongside the highway until we got to the safe house and it was easier to help offload all the luggage from their vehicles." Dustin came back to the kitchen while Ben set the glasses out. "Do you think we should keep Darren awake for lunch?"

Pondering for a while, Ben joined him and shook his head. "I wouldn't. He can have a double portion at dinner."

The two men leaned against the kitchen countertops, a pause of awkward silence stretching between them.

"You did a good job taking care of Katey," Dustin finally said. "I half expected her to have run away to find us."

Ben snorted. "I'm sure she wanted to. It was hard keepin' her engaged."

"What did you two do besides chess?"

Ben ground his teeth a little, debating whether to tell Dustin the truth or stay obscure. "We talked."

Dustin raised his eyebrows and waited. "Do I have to wrangle the details out of you? I've had to listen to nothing but Logan and Darren arguing for the past few days and little children asking me when they could go back home."

"We mostly talked about me. I told her about everythin' that happened in Georgia and out in the territories. Nothin' you don't already know."

Dustin shifted and crossed his arms, giving Ben a curious look. "That's unlike you."

Ben shrugged. "It kept her attention for a little while, that's what mattered."

"I think there's a little more to it than that."

A deep line creased between Ben's brows as he frowned at his friend's insinuating tone. "She's just a child, Dustin. Why would you even think there would be somethin' more there?"

Dustin's eyes went wide. "I wasn't thinking that at all."

Ben threw up his hands. "Then what do you want me to say?"

Dustin looked heavenward, aggravated as much as Ben was. "I'm not even home for half an hour, and we're fighting like a married couple again. I was just wondering if you had let yourself get wrapped around Katey's finger. That's all I meant."

Ben watched him shed his camouflage jacket, toss it over one of the dinette chairs, and march toward the back billiard room. A tinge of guilt spiked in Ben's gut. Sometimes he wondered if the fights were always his fault.

Dustin read him correctly. Katey had stolen a piece of his shattered heart. She was a sweet girl; a little headstrong perhaps, but a sweet girl. The hug she gave Ben that day during lunch had been so meaningful, so comforting and it filled in the chip on his shoulder that had crippled him for far too long. It melted the ice clean off him, and there was no hiding the change it produced.

After taking a few deep breaths to cool off, Ben followed his friend into the back room with their two plates of food and found Dustin racking the balls on the green felt table.

He set down the plates on a tiny round table in the corner, took up a pool stick, and waited for Dustin to take his first turn before speaking. "Listen, I didn't mean to get defensive," Ben said softly.

Dustin leaned on his stick, assessing where the balls were rolling after he broke their formation. "I suppose we're all a little on edge right now. Darren's not himself either," he said with a sigh. "I can understand why, with his experience with hunters and all, but all that tension is making its way through the pack."

Ben couldn't agree with that statement, even if he knew his own aggression was an internal conflict that was no one's fault but his own. He could agree Darren was not doing well under the stress. "Do you think he's gonna be okay?" he asked as he took his first shot, falling into the game without having to ask. The table was always open to the pack, and formal invitations were never needed for one of them to jump in with a pool stick and take a few turns.

"I think if he gets enough sleep, he'll be all right. We'll have to keep an eye on him, though." Dustin paused with a fascinated look on his face. "It's strange that we're not alphas and we have to look out for him now."

Dustin took his shot and leveled a stare at Ben that somehow made him more alert. He straightened at attention and waited.

"We found out something interesting, though," Dustin began. "Jacob had his scouts search the town and perimeter of Crestucky, and there's no sign of the hunters."

Ben squinted. "Logan said he saw them at the school."

"And many other Devian students did too," Dustin nodded. "None of them thought the police officer was a hunter. That particular officer is an actual member of the Crestucky police force."

"What about the dog barkin' at Logan and Katey?"

Dustin blinked. "Dogs bark at us all the time, Ben."

Ben pinched the bridge of his nose and squeezed his eyes shut, trying to comprehend the whole thing. "So, are you sayin' Logan was the wolf who cried hunter?"

"It's happened before. Not with Logan, but with other packs. Things turn out to be a false alarm sometimes."

"Y'all just evacuated almost a couple hundred loups-garous and their families over this!" Ben exclaimed, looking to Dustin in disbelief. "If there aren't any hunters, what was it all for?"

"We did get confirmation that hunters were in the county, just not Crestucky," Dustin assured. "It might have only been a matter of time before the hunters arrived. If there's an all-clear pronounced, then everyone will come back."

Ben couldn't begin to imagine the kind of upheaval those families went through. Some had to quit their jobs, drop out of school, leave their friends behind, and for what? A hunch? An instinctual assumption? He could never rationalize through senseless commands or executive actions that affected a group of people on such a large scale. The military had failed to eradicate his common sense at least.

"Hey," Dustin said as he walked toward Ben and slapped him on the back. "Don't worry about it. Everything will work out, right? Can't let all that bad juju get to you."

Ben nodded and set his pool stick against the wall. Dustin was completely right. If the families were ushered back, there was a good chance they could continue life as usual. Jacob and Darren had connections in town and jobs could be reinstated. Kids could bounce back and catch up on schoolwork. Ben couldn't think too much about it, or it would drive him nuts.

"Why don't we call the kids down and eat somethin'?" he finally said. "That'll help you too."

Dustin looked up and down the green felt pool table and relented. "All right. As long as we can bring the two love birds in on the game, we can be on a team," he said, jerking his head toward the billiard table.

Ben grinned and nodded. "I reckon we can settle on that condition."

CHAPTER 5

The pack sat at the dinner table that night for the first time since the beginning of the week. The usual talkative group ate silently. No one made eye contact or even showed the least bit interest in starting a conversation, except for Katey.

She and Logan had spent the afternoon together, marinating in one another's company and making up for lost time while he was away. Mostly they napped together in Katey's bedroom, both exhausted beyond what should have been allowed for loups-garous. Logan showered and washed away the dirt and grime from the mission shortly before coming to join the others in the dining room. Katey didn't mind that her sheets were now soiled by his filthy clothes. She was too absorbed in holding him in that way that drove him mad with desire.

The sun was close to setting outside and cast a tawny glow over the room, making it just bright enough that the over-head light wasn't necessary. Logan could see their solemn and thoughtful faces as the minutes ticked by. There was a strange void of emotion about the group as if they were all too numb from the events of the last few days. Logan was too glad to be home to feel such deadness as the others did.

The days spent apart had been pure torture for Logan. With every mile they traveled and each step he took farther north, he felt that unmistakable pull of their bond calling him back home to Katey. If he had his way, he would have stayed in Crestucky, but he knew Darren too well to cross him when it came to matters about hunters. They had lived through a massacre that claimed so many lives and any hint of disobedience within a pack could lead them down a hazardous road.

That was why Logan had tried to indirectly show his disapproval of Katey's outburst that morning before they left. He had hoped it would make her realize her transgression against Darren's authority, but it only served as another thing to feel guilty over as the minutes passed by without Katey in his arms. Logan regretted the level of coldness with which he treated her and was determined to make up for it.

They had all showered, and it seemed things had returned to normal apart from their silent dread. Logan wondered if it had anything to do with their state of emergency with the hunters or if it was simply because there was nothing to talk about. No one had been to work since the evacuation, so they had no stories to share as they normally did during their evening meal.

While he chewed on a mouthful of beef, he glanced to Katey who sat beside him. Her food had barely been touched, and her gaze was vacant, her mind a million miles away. Logan reached under the table and stroked his finger along her thigh.

Katey perked to attention and looked at him as if she had forgotten he was there. He gave her a questioning look, and she returned it with a faint smile. She could feel the void too, and the troubled look in her eyes told him all he needed to know.

Something must have been bothering her. If he weren't scared of upsetting the stagnant balance of the group, he would have asked her what it was. However, Logan knew all too well that Katey hated to have the attention drawn to her like that. After dinner, he would confront her about it, but not now.

Logan returned to eating, but a few more moments of silence passed before Katey finally disrupted it. "So, Darren," she began, starting out confidently. "I was going to ask you about something on Monday, and in all the hysteria, I forgot."

Logan quickly saw where this was going and tapped his foot against her ankle. Katey gave him a quick glance but continued. "There's a weekly dance open to the public at the ballroom studio, and I'd like to go this Sunday."

Darren didn't have to look up from his plate. "Absolutely not," he replied.

He heard Katey suck in a tiny breath. "Why not?" she asked, an obvious warble in her voice.

"I know you're not this dense, Katey," Darren said with a sigh and set his fork down. "There may be hunters hiding out all over

Crestucky, and I won't have you leaving this house until we know they're out of the area."

Katey let out a short laugh of disbelief. "It's just a dance, and Logan will be with me."

Logan winced. He had made no such promises, and he didn't want Darren to think he had anything to do with this scheme. If Katey had consulted with him earlier, he would have advised her to drop the issue. There would be other dances, and the studio wasn't about to close its doors anytime soon.

Darren turned a fiery stare on Katey. "No," he growled, the very walls trembling in the wake of his displeasure.

"Not even if Ben or Dustin went with us?" she asked, the same pleading in her tone as before.

Logan looked up to Ben and Dustin at the other end of the table and saw they were just as distressed as he was. None of them wanted these arguments. As much as Logan butted heads with Darren, he knew where to draw the line . . . sometimes.

"I said no, and that's my final word on it," Darren said before turning back to his meal.

He didn't even manage to bring the next forkful of beef to his mouth before Katey started in again. "How long before I can leave the house?"

Darren went still, and Logan saw the familiar expression of a man struggling to keep his cool while being pushed to his limits. The alpha set down his fork and looked up at Katey. "I'm not sure. If we see more activity from the hunters, it will be a while."

"And what if we see nothing?"

A muscle jumped in Darren's jaw. "Then it'll be a month or so at the earliest."

A deep frown curved Katey's lips. "Earliest? Ben and Dustin are allowed to leave the house, why can't I?" she demanded, her voice raised in agitation, and her body leaned forward over her plate.

"They're going on a scouting mission to protect the Deviants. That's different than a frivolous dance." Darren's words were laced with contempt for the very idea that Katey would want to risk her safety just so she could go socialize with her human friends. For once, Logan agreed with his alpha.

Katey's eyes went wide. "Frivolous?" she exclaimed. "It's not frivolous! I haven't seen my friends all week. I miss going danc-ing."

"I don't care if you miss it or not," Darren replied, his lips curled in a snarl. "You're not going. Not until the threat has passed."

Katey rolled her eyes and threw her fork down onto her plate, the crash of metal on porcelain shattering the still air. "By then, they may stop having these weekly dances altogether."

"That's not my concern," Darren bellowed.

Katey's hands gripped the edge of the table, and Logan wondered if she was going to flip the whole thing over. "All you're concerned about is having your thumb on everyone in this pack!"

Logan couldn't abide by this anymore and reached out to grip Katey's shoulder, hoping his words would somehow ground her in this outburst. "Katey, this isn't the time or the place," he said firmly.

Katey swatted his hand away and turned back to her alpha, eyes blazing gold across the table. "What about my training? Is that going to be put on hold until the hunters are gone?"

Logan was surprised at the amount of control Darren maintained as Katey made her irrational case against him. He was sure the others felt the same as he looked at their fretful faces. No one was eating.

"More than likely, yes."

Katey eased back a bit. "More than likely? So, there's like a twenty percent chance that I can keep training?"

Logan hoped with all that was in him that Darren would give in just this much so Katey would settle down. Her emotional tantrums were grating on everyone, disrupting the pack harmony more than she might have realized.

This side of Katey wasn't completely new to them. They knew she had a temper and headstrong personality, but they thought Alaska had made her realize that such childish ways had to be given up for the sake of her new life and responsibilities. At least, that's what Darren and Dustin had hoped. Logan loved the fire in her that gave her that bit of spice in everything she said and did, but at that moment, he wanted her to bank that fire for another day.

"That's just a formality of speech," Darren replied. Logan covered his eyes and leaned his elbow on the table, feeling exhausted by the whole thing. "I have no intention of continuing your training until the hunters are gone, and we're able to utilize the property and surrounding woods properly."

If nothing else, Logan could admire Darren's calm. The hostility in Katey's voice nearly doubled.

"What happens when we need to go out and shift? We can't do that in the house! You've already made a rule about that."

"We will cross that bridge when we get to it."

"This isn't fair to me or to Logan. The longer it takes to finish my training, the longer we have to wait for our mating ceremony."

Logan felt like groaning at how she managed to pull him into the argument again. Yes, he wanted to be mated to her, more than anything else in this world, but he wasn't willing to test Darren's temper in the process. Not now while they were in the middle of a crisis.

"I'm well aware of that," Darren shouted. "But in our current situation, even if you two were ready, there would be no ceremony. There's no point in preparing for something that won't happen anytime soon."

Katey was silent for a moment, probably out of pure shock at Darren's admittance. "That's not fair!" she whined. "You have no right to keep us from mating!"

From out of left field, Dustin slammed his hands on the dining table and stood to tower over the group, his own eyes blazing gold – which hardly ever happened. "Life isn't fair, Katey!" he roared in his Irish burr, making the very crystals of the chandelier above their heads shiver. "And until you learn your place in the pack and respect Darren as the alpha, you will never understand what it means to be a loup-garou."

Katey's jaw dropped, and her expression morphed from rage, to wounded and terrified. She had never been on the receiving end of one of Dustin's full-blown rebukes. Logan had, and it was often the only thing that would make him fly straight afterward.

Darren looked to his beta, his enforcer, with a mixed look of gratitude and uneasiness. Ben was too stunned to look at anything else except his plate, and Logan was ready to stand up and defend his fiancé.

Katey was too quick. She bolted from the table and dashed out of the dining room. The remaining four listened to her storm upstairs and slam the door to her bedroom. Dustin lowered himself back into his chair, looking less than repentant over his choice of words.

"That was low," Ben muttered before he ate another bite from his plate.

Logan glared at Dustin. "All Katey wants is to belong in our pack, and you throw that in her face?"

"I did what needed to be done to shut her up," Dustin contested. "She was disrespecting Darren, and after that last outburst of hers, I didn't want it coming to blows. I don't want to concoct another bottle of homemade blood stain remover for the carpet." There was no remorse in Dustin's eyes as he resumed his meal.

Darren shook his head. "For once, I think I agree with Logan. I appreciate that you stepped in before she became too upset, but your last comment was unnecessary."

Dustin looked to his other pack members for support but found none. He sighed and stood up a little more gently this time. "I'll go talk to her. I don't know if she will accept my apology, but I'll try."

Logan waited until Dustin was out of the room before looking to his alpha, prepared to make his own plea to follow Katey's. With luck, it would be a balm to the frazzled nerves of the pack rather than an agitator.

"I'm not supporting Katey's argument," he began. "But, you know how much this training means to her. She thinks about it all the time. You know she's behaving like this because you've completely ripped that from her."

Darren picked up his water glass and tilted it to his lips. "I know," he said before taking a long swig. "I also know she will find another diversion. Perhaps you should teach her to draw."

Logan looked away, knowing that would not satisfy Katey. "I'd rather she be granted a little longer leash. Maybe she can practice shifting in the house?"

Darren set down his glass and made his fingers into a steeple on the tabletop. "My first priority is everyone's safety, not their comfort or entertainment." The alpha's deep brown eyes looked up at Logan through dark brows. "I'll take your suggestion into consideration, but if Katey continues to disrespect this pack and me, I'll make sure her training is delayed. I won't reward her behavior."

Silence reigned at the dinner table after Logan nodded and continued eating. Consideration was all Logan could hope for, but as before, he was in agreement with Darren. Before the day was through, he would talk to Katey and see if he could reach her. If Logan could snap her out of this phase, then the pack would be better off for it.

Dustin trudged up the stairs and approached Katey's room. He could hear her soft sniffling from behind the door, and the remorse latched onto his heart like a leech. Before he got too close, she said, "I don't want to talk to you."

From her thick voice, he knew she had been crying, even if he hadn't smelled her salty tears. "Nonsense," he said cheerfully. "Women love to talk to me."

Humor. It was the only thing that saved his hide from countless conflicts and made an effective shield when dealing with reality. It had gotten him out of plenty of messes before and this one should have been no different, but it certainly didn't feel that way.

He could understand her eagerness, her anger, her resentment to authority. Logan had been there once before, and they had to handle him with care over the last century because of it. Disputes abounded, and there had been no shortage of opposition between them for quite a long time. Once Logan began to accept his lot, and he understood that no matter how much training he did it would not change his obvious handicap, he seemed to calm down into a kind of quiet discontent.

Katey had no handicap they knew of yet. She was perfectly well and able to train and excel as a loup-garou, and that must have been the root of her frustrations; to be so close, but shut down at the gate. He understood her need to belong, but not her lashing out to Darren. Perhaps it was her upbringing as an orphan or the lack of discipline in the foster homes she was passed through. Whatever it was, Dustin knew they all had a long way to go, hunters or no hunters, and the only one who didn't know that was Katey.

"Not this woman," she replied.

Dustin guffawed. "I can't imagine why. I'm so likable." He leaned against the doorframe and listened, but Katey wasn't budging. After a pause, he tried the doorknob and found it locked. "You know I've always respected your privacy, but I'd hate for you to have no door after I break this one down."

He waited for that to set in and felt the thrill of victory when Katey unlocked the door and let him in. Dustin stepped inside and hung his thumbs through his pant loops, hoping to seem casual and non-threatening.

Katey stood in the middle of the room with her arms folded and face hardened, but he knew she was putting on a show. The redness in her eyes was testament enough to that. Instead of scrutinizing her too closely, Dustin let his gaze wander around the room.

Since Katey had moved in, she gave the room her own personal touch. It was obvious a teenager lived here and it was evident she did not share in Logan's obsessive tidiness. School books were opened face up on the floor with a smattering of papers all around. One would have wondered if she even used the desk at all. Clothes were slung over her footboard and the back of her desk chair while the bed was unmade.

"I love what you've done with the place," Dustin said. "It's so chic."

He looked at Katey for any response, but she stared at him coldly, obviously replaying what he had said downstairs to keep her anger boiling.

"Do I have to pry the words out of you?" he asked, then put on his best imitation of a female's voice. "'I'm so sorry, Dustin. I shouldn't have been so rude at the dinner table and made everyone nauseous with my angst.'"

"This has nothing to do with angst," she snapped. "This whole thing isn't right."

Dustin blew out his cheeks and realized humor was not going to crack her defenses at all. "He's the alpha, Katey. His word is law."

"But why is he this strict about it? I don't understand why he's keeping us under house arrest when we can handle ourselves as loups-garous. They're just humans."

Dustin shook his head in disbelief. She still had so much to learn. "Do you realize how dangerous hunters are?"

Katey shrugged and lowered her glare. "They can't be more dangerous than a vampire. Vampires are strong like us and have silver bullets, but hunters only have silver bullets. I get they're supposed to be these super soldiers or something, but we didn't go this extreme the last time a vampire was close by."

"Vampires may match us in strength," Dustin replied, "but hunters have the determination. Darren wasn't kidding the other day. They want to see us totally wiped out, more than the vamps do and little is going to change their mind."

"Can't anyone reason with a hunter?" she asked, looking at him with a renewed righteous vigor. "We can make them see that we're not hurting anyone and that they need to go hunt down Erik and Gregory and loups-garous like them that really do some damage."

As much as he disliked the rougarous and those who believed in the same distorted views of how loups-garous and humans shouldn't coexist, Dustin couldn't help but envision the twisted and mangled bodies of the loups-garous who had fallen prey to the hunters centuries ago. Their faces forever etched in his memory.

"I wouldn't wish a hunter upon any of our kind," he whispered. "There's no reasoning with them. They're brutal and don't follow any code of ethics like real soldiers do. They don't see us as humans, or even animals. We're beasts. We're monsters that need to be exterminated. We're alien to them, and they don't see anything wrong with torturing us or giving us a slow and painful death. They'll even justify killing humans who know us to get any bit of information about where we are."

Katey's lips parted, and a cold bucket of water had been dumped over the fire in her eyes. "Has Lily ever been here?"

Dustin peered at her curiously. He had seen Katey and Lily talk in the halls before, but he hadn't realized they were close enough for Katey to care about her. "Forrest's lady? I don't think so."

"Would they kidnap her if they wanted to?" she questioned urgently, taking a step closer and letting her arms drop to her sides. The vulnerable look in her eyes would have broken his heart if he hadn't steeled himself before entering the room.

"As I said, they would justify their actions as long as it benefited their mission to kill us."

"How do you know they'll do that?" she probed. "Killing humans, I mean. Is that just a rumor?"

Dustin could see how badly she wanted all of what he said to be lies, but this was too serious a matter to ever lie about. If she were to ever fully comprehend their situation, he had to tell her the whole truth. "No." He paused, wondering if he should even touch on the sacred ground he was about to trample through. "It happened to Darren. That's another reason why he's so strict."

Without a doubt, he'd get an earful from Darren for sharing his past with Katey without prior permission. Perhaps, given the circumstances, he would understand.

Katey gasped and mutely begged for an explanation.

Dustin began to slowly pace around the room, his eyes fixed on his path so he wouldn't accidentally step on anything. "Imagine a world where superstitions were the religion of the day. Neighbors were suspicious of one another, and the testimony of attention-greedy children was valid in a legal court. Hermits and men of medicine are suspected of being witches. Books on how to kill and identify vampires were printed and sold out of the local bookshops. Public hangings of demon worshipers were the main event of the week, and the stench of burning human flesh hung in the air after a witch was burned. It was the golden age of monster hunters, and everyone was qualified to point out a witch, a vampire, or a werewolf.

"This was the world Darren had to grow up in. When he shifted for the first time, his village in England went nuts. They called him a witch and claimed him to be cursed. His mother got caught in the crossfire and they killed her when she wouldn't tell them where Darren was hiding. Now alone, he fled to France where the persecution was no better. Paranoia doesn't begin to describe what our kind felt. Any given day, our kind were being arrested and put on trial for wild accusations. Sometimes, a loup-garou was executed for the crime of witchcraft, but not for what he might have truly been guilty of.

"Darren found a friend and mentor in John. His training began, and he learned how to integrate into society so he wouldn't be suspected. He didn't hold power, he kept no close friends and made no enemies. Still, it was like walking on eggshells."

Katey's eyebrows rose. "I didn't realize –"

Dustin held up a hand. "Let me finish," he said as he stepped over a pile of dirty shirts. "Before I met up with him, Darren found a woman who accepted who he truly was and they married. She was the daughter of an alpha in Bordeaux. They had a daughter. She was about six years old when Darren and his family took me in. I was fresh from Ireland and not in the best state of mind." He determined that Katey didn't need to know about his suicide attempt, or how Darren found him washed up on the beach, barely alive.

"We went out for my second full shift. When we came back to his cottage, it was burning. His wife's body was inside. He rushed in to try and save her, but she was already too close to death. She had been shot. We found the body of his daughter a short distance away in the woods with a bullet in her chest. It was later that we found out the pack in Bordeaux had been wiped out at the hands of hunters. They must have known where Darren and his wife were and came looking for him."

Katey wrapped her arms around her stomach and her face blanched. "Darren must have been devastated."

"He was. I think he blames himself for what happened. If he had been there... if he hadn't been busy with me, he might have saved his family... He's never married since then. He vowed he would never be so careless with the ones he cared about. Then, he came to America, and he witnessed the destruction of Devia. They killed women and children there, too. He's seen the hunters destroy too many lives to just sit idly by while this threat comes to Crestucky. If he seems a little too harsh or unfeeling, it's because he cares about this pack and the safety of everyone in this town. On some level, he may think it's his responsibility to keep everyone alive. That's why we all need to be in agreement and make sure he doesn't go crazy during the next month or so while we try to get through this. That includes doing as he says without arguing because it will only make him crankier."

Dustin watched Katey, looking for any sign of understanding, but she had turned inward and contemplative. There was not much else he could do or say to tip the scales in his favor. She would just need to let it all sink in. Perhaps then they could breathe a little easier, knowing she wouldn't start a fight every time Darren made a decision.

He turned to leave but froze when she spoke.

"Do you believe there are hunters here?" Katey asked in an almost indistinguishable whisper, so soft he barely even heard her.

When he looked back, Katey had her finger held up to her lips, signaling to him that she didn't want anyone else to hear this conversation. And she was right to want that. He wanted to tell her the hunters were truly here and they were a real threat. However, he had just outpoured so much truth that he couldn't taint it all with a little white lie.

He had already told Ben what he learned from Jacob during the evacuation. There had been no other sign of the presence of a hunter in Crestucky beyond what Logan reported. Darren knew this too, but of course, he was taking no chances. They kept this report from Logan, knowing it would make him doubt himself and his abilities. He didn't deserve the blame for forcing families to abandon their homes without probable cause.

"Beyond what Logan saw," Dustin replied in just as muted a voice as Katey's, "we haven't heard of any other hunters in the area. That doesn't mean they're not there, though."

Katey turned pensive and somehow, Dustin expected her to be surprised or upset. She appeared neither.

"I am sorry for the way I spoke to you downstairs," Dustin said in his normal volume. "I had no right to accuse you of not being a true loup-garou. You've been a fine loup-garou—for a pup. And an even more remarkable woman for what you've had to go through. We will continue your training when this is over, I promise."

Katey's expression softened and her shoulders slumped a little as her defenses fell. Dustin felt a little more confident that he had minutely restored their friendship, but from the way she refused to look at him, he knew he still had a long way to go to regain her trust.

"I'll have Logan bring up the rest of your dinner that you didn't finish," he said. "I'm sure everyone else is done eating by now and you'd rather be alone." Dustin walked to the open bedroom door. "If I don't see you before you go to bed, I hope you sleep well."

"Why don't you sing anymore?" she asked suddenly.

The question puzzled him and he turned to give her a perturbed look. "What are you smoking?"

He saw the corners of Katey's lips twitch with a restrained smile. "Ben told me you used to sing a lot, but I haven't heard you sing at all. Why did you stop?"

Dustin was going to wring Ben's neck when he got back downstairs, but the comment made him think. It was true he hadn't belted out one of his favorite Irish drinking songs in a while. "I'm too busy making sure you and Logan don't put us all into an early grave. I have no time for singing."

"Well, make sure I'm around next time you do."

Dustin rolled his eyes and left the bedroom. She hadn't forgiven him, and he wasn't quite sure if he got through to her, but there was something in that last exchange of words that made him feel lighter in his step as he traveled back downstairs. Maybe a little singing was just the thing this pack needed to lift their spirits and take their minds off the hunters. Dustin remembered with a certain fondness when he and Darren had joined in together on an old ballad or two in their earlier days before they parted ways.

"How'd it go?" Ben asked from the kitchen. He was busily washing dishes while Logan reclined on one of the couches and Darren sat in his recliner with his fingers laced over his lap.

"Not sure," Dustin replied as he retrieved his unfinished dinner and brought it to the living room.

"You told her a great deal, Dustin," Darren remarked, his voice deep with censure. The disadvantage of living in a house of loups-garous was the fact that no conversation was private.

"I thought if she realized why you were going all Adolf Hitler on her, she'd back off." Dustin plopped himself onto the free sofa beside Darren's recliner and inhaled the remains on his plate.

"I'm not being a dictator, I'm – "

"I know, I know," Dustin waved at him. "You just care. I get it."

"Is she going to be all right?" Logan asked, sitting up and gripping his ankles that were stretched out in front of him.

Dustin shrugged. "I'd give her time to cool off," he mumbled through a mouthful of beef.

"What was that she mentioned about singing?" Logan asked as he swung his legs over the edge of the couch and gave Dustin an inquisitive look.

"Singing? She said nothing about singing," Dustin replied nonchalantly.

"Go on, Dustin," Darren egged. "Tell Logan all about your lovely Irish folk songs and how you can play the spoons on your knee."

Logan laughed while Dustin shot his alpha a nasty look. "Logan, go give Katey her dinner so she can finish it," Dustin instructed.

He did as he was told and headed upstairs with the plate of meat and glass of water in his hands.

"At least someone around here is taking orders," Dustin mumbled.

A few silent moments passed, and Dustin knew Darren wanted to say something. The way his fingers squeezed over his knuckles was a dead giveaway. "If you keep your mouth shut, all those words are just going to blow out through your ears," Dustin muttered as he reached for a book on the bottom shelf of the end table between them.

Darren rubbed at his eye and let out a long breath of air, which was usually followed by the announcement of unpleasant news. "I've got to get Katey away from here," he said.

"I beg your pardon?" Ben questioned from the kitchen, his hands covered in soap suds from the dishwater.

"I've been thinking about it and if it were up to me those families left in Crestucky would be forcibly removed from their homes," Darren said with all the gravity in the world as he scratched at his bearded jaw. "I didn't want to say this in front of Logan, but I will not give Katey the option to stay here while there could be hunters in the area. Jacob already did wrong by me when he didn't let me know of the potential threat. Now that it's here, we have no time."

Dustin frowned. "You know I would never oppose you or your decisions, but what made you go from 'staying is fine' to 'we need to evacuate too'?"

"I don't know what's gotten into her. I thought Katey was done being difficult, but I was wrong." Dustin leaned back in his recliner, letting his head rest against the plush back cushion. "I thought Alaska had knocked some sense into her, but she seems just as rebellious as ever."

"Might I remind you she's a teenager?" Ben added as he walked into the living room with his hands folded into a dish towel.

"That's no excuse for disobedience toward an alpha," Darren replied.

"Are you sending her away because you're tired of dealing with her attitude, or because you actually think the hunters – whom we haven't seen for ourselves yet – are a real threat?" Dustin knew he was walking on dangerous ground, but he had been in the same spot with Ben.

Ben was bad-tempered and a handful to take care of at first. They parted on bad terms and Dustin had never forgiven himself for that decision. They should have stuck it out, and perhaps things would have turned out differently. If Darren were on the verge of making the same mistake, just because Katey was being a stubborn brat, Dustin wouldn't be the one to sit by and let him go through with it – alpha or not.

Darren turned a pair of searing eyes on Dustin, but before he could answer, the beta had another comeback. "Everyone in this pack, save for Logan, has accepted your guidance and leadership without question. Even at his worst, Logan disobeyed you and ended up making Katey into what she is. Katey is a whole other ballgame. She's ambitious and determined, more than any of us were. We didn't want this life at first. Katey does, that's why she's demanding more training and pushing you like this."

Darren looked away, his expression seemed unfeeling, untouched by what Dustin had to say. However, he knew his alpha well enough that he was considering everything. He had never been one to ignore an appeal or push aside a kernel of truth just because he didn't agree with it.

Time passed slowly, and Dustin could hear Logan trying to calm Katey down upstairs. Even their relationship was going through rough waters, and it hurt his heart to be in a household full of strife and tension this way.

From what he could tell, Darren was listening to their argument as well, and he tucked his chin against his chest. "Tomorrow evening, Katey will leave on the same route the Deviants took. Logan will go with her and Ben will serve as their protection. You and I will stay to look after the Deviants." He looked to Dustin with surprisingly heartfelt eyes. "I care about Katey. I don't like the way she's behaving, but I want her to be alive in a few more weeks so she can continue her training. As long as I know the hunters are close, I won't be at ease. I'm doing this for her safety, not for my own sake."

Dustin's lips formed a tight line before he replied, "Darren, the hunters are not that close. You heard Jacob say none of his scouts detected any hunters in the area and the cop at the school wasn't a hunter."

"I trust Logan's instincts," Darren said quickly. "Those scouts only look for the obvious signs of a hunter in their scent and appearance. They don't tap into their intuition. Logan had that feeling about Katey and how she would accept the change, so I'm inclined to believe he truly sensed a hunter. The cop could be a hunter for all we know and the dog could have been used by hunters before."

Dustin couldn't argue with that logic. In the past, Logan had demonstrated certain perspicacious tendencies about events or people. It was possible Logan was correct about the cop or his dog. But, there was still the possibility they were wrong and that's what troubled Dustin, Ben, and - as it appeared - Katey as well. It was Darren's confidence that spread to Jacob and the others, convincing them all that they really had detected the hunter and that the evacuation was essential.

"You're my second," Darren continued, "I need you to stand behind me on these things. Otherwise, there will be disorder between all of us." The alpha reached out and placed his hand on Dustin's shoulder. "Are we in agreement?"

Dustin could hardly refuse Darren. If the hunters were here and Logan had been right all along, their precautions were prudent. If the hunters weren't there, then it would have been a waste of time. At least they weren't dead.

He nodded.

CHAPTER 6

K atey stared thoughtfully at the ceiling above her bed, her mind racing with thoughts she could barely put in order. The silvery glow of the moon filled her room, and she could hear the crickets outside, the usual nighttime serenade that would lull her to sleep when all else failed.

After she had cooled off from her argument with Logan and her outburst at the dinner table, Katey was left penitent and with too many conflicting emotions she couldn't keep straight.

When Dustin confirmed that Logan's hunch about the police officer at the school might not have been a hunter, Katey's heart dropped straight into her shoes. It would devastate Logan to know he was wrong and had forced such a burden on the community. It was clear they couldn't tell him and she couldn't use it in a fight against him or Darren to support her need for freedom.

On the other hand, she could finally understand Darren's concerns and the reason for his touchiness in the last few days. It was his job to protect the pack, but she couldn't forget the way he had denied her the very thing she wanted most. She wanted to hate him for refusing to continue her training. She wanted to challenge him for what he said about her and Logan's mating plans.

Most of all, she wanted to hate Dustin for his thoughtless comment that silenced her so efficiently. She thought she knew what it meant to be loup-garou. It meant belonging in a pack, being part of something greater than herself, and being one with the wolf that lived within her. What more was there to learn? What was coming in her training that she didn't know about? What were they keeping from her and why? Hadn't she proven herself enough with everything that happened in Alaska?

Darren hadn't been with them when she stood up against Yaverik and issued the decree about forming the counsel to bring peace between the vampires and loups-garous. Maybe he didn't fully realize she was capable of taking care of herself and continuing her training under the supposed threat of hunters.

Or perhaps it had nothing to do with her pack. There must have been something that happened when a loup-garou shifted at will for the first time. Maybe she would learn some innate truth through the transformation that no one except her inner wolf could teach her, but there was no chance she would learn it at this rate. It'd be weeks, maybe months before everything calmed down and she could resume her training.

Patience was something Katey never had. She pushed back her covers and slipped out of bed, making little more than a whisper of sound. Using everything Logan had taught her about how to creep around, she ducked out of her bedroom and began to make her way down the second-floor hallway.

Katey passed by the other bedrooms, listening to their steady breathing behind the doors. Dustin snorted in his sleep, and she froze, waited for the confirmed pause that he was still unconscious, and then continued.

When she came to Logan's door, she stopped. If anyone had appreciated her desperate need to train, it would have been him. Although he wouldn't have been an excellent teacher, he could have provided protection if she needed it. After the fight they had just a few hours before, Katey wasn't sure she wanted his company. He would just try to stop her, to tell her to go back to bed and probably crawl under the blanket with her to ensure she stayed put.

Logic reminded her that if Logan were to escort her, and if she were discovered, he would have gotten in trouble too. Also, there was nothing for him to protect her from. There were no hunters, and there was nothing she couldn't handle as a loup-garou.

She continued and managed to get to the end of the hall before she heard the soft click of a doorknob turning. Katey wanted to pound at the air or hurry downstairs before anyone saw her, but she knew it was no use.

She turned to face Ben's confused and sleepy face peering back at her in the darkness. He cocked his head to the side, asking without words what she was doing.

Here, she found her ticket out. She made the sign of a drinking glass and tipped it to her lips. Katey had often gone downstairs for a drink of water in the middle of the night. It was a plausible alibi, and he wouldn't have suspected her of anything else.

Ben gave his nod of approval and slunk back into his room, closing the door behind him. Katey waited a few seconds to make sure he was back in his bed and then hurried as quickly downstairs as her quiet feet would take her.

To continue the ruse, Katey went through the motions of getting a drink of water, but she had no intention of finishing it. Instead, she waited a good ten minutes before she was sure Ben was fast asleep along with the others.

She took the back door out through the billiard room and stepped outside where their vehicles were parked safely under the carport. Forgetting the need to be silent, Katey dashed toward the tree line beyond the gazebo and gardens behind the house, using her inhuman speed to carry her far away from her home and her pack.

When she was a safe distance from everything, she skidded to a stop on the fallen oak leaves and pine needles of the forest floor.

Katey breathed in the night air, letting it fill her lungs for the first time in what seemed like forever. How she had missed its cool embrace. Any human would have been shivering in this mid-January weather, but Katey thrived in it.

She curled her toes into the soft soil beneath her and didn't care about the way the dirt would stain the bottom of her pajama pants. The sounds of the earth and forest surrounded her, welcoming her to their domain that she had as much a right to enter as any loup-garou. This was the pull all loups-garous felt to the forest. She felt it rise within her, intoxicating and thrilling like Logan's kisses.

She watched as the branches above her swayed with the gentle wind, making the pale moonlight dance across her skin. Katey stripped away her clothing, standing naked, baring herself to the glory of nature around her.

At any other time, she would have felt silly and vulnerable. The frosty winter wind whipped at her hair, blowing it around her face in a tangled mess. Her skin was riddled with gooseflesh by the time she could focus enough to try the change.

She squeezed her eyes shut and wrapped her arms around her chest, doing exactly what Darren and the others had taught her to do. She tightened her muscles, breathing deeply to get her blood flowing faster. The usual tingle that preceded each of her attempts to change came and coiled through her body. Tiny spasms made her twitch and wince, but there was nothing of the pain and agony that should have come with the shift.

Katey let out a tight breath of frustration and looked to the sky, wondering what she was doing wrong. She turned to the moon above, silently pleading for the answer. For whatever reason, she couldn't capture that same sensation she experienced in Alaska when she almost shifted in front of John and Darren at the gathering. The conditions were nearly the same except she was alone and the ground wasn't frozen with snow.

Somehow, she thought perhaps being alone would help her wolf feel comfortable and come forth more readily. It was just the two of them out there with no one to keep badgering them or telling them what to do.

Don't force me. Welcome me.

The small voice came from seemingly nowhere, but Katey knew it must have been her wolf. Then, the problem was evident. All this time, Katey had been trying to drag the wolf out of her instead of inviting it to emerge. Neither one of them was in complete control and never should be. It was a partnership, she remembered.

After taking several deep, meditative breaths, Katey let her muscles relax, and her body swayed with the winds, becoming in sync with the tranquility of the forest. She closed her eyes and focused on her wolf. With gentle coaxing, the animal awoke and experienced the same sensations of the forest through Katey. The wolf wanted to run free, just like she did. Freedom. It was what she had been denied, what she longed for just as much as a family that accepted her and a man to love her. She and her wolf were in one accord, one mind.

Katey looked up to the moon with her golden eyes, entranced by its majestic shape and simple beauty. Slowly, she let the wolf take dominion, asserting that they were one. A warmth grew in her chest and spread to her belly. It coursed through her veins like a drug and her senses blurred.

The pain came just as slowly, but it wasn't nearly as excruciating as in previous attempts. Her limbs and joints began to ache and pop. Skin pulled, and muscles burned like fire within her. Katey fell to her hands and knees, gasping for air as she could feel her own body begin to morph and her organs expand and contract.

Instead of resisting, she let it happen. She accepted the wolf as it had accepted her, and the shift came easier. Katey kept her lips shut tight against the cries and screams as the pain quickly intensified with the speed of the change. She didn't know which was worse; changing for several minutes with mild pain, or changing rapidly with penetrating pain.

She gave herself no choice. There was no time to hold back as the night was carrying on without her. Even as the wolf was emerging from her subconscious, the wild instinct coming forward in all its splendor, Katey summoned it more urgently. She wanted the wolf to dominate, to take control. To her surprise, the wolf refused.

Instead of demanding her human body as the vessel with which to carry out its primitive desires, the wolf wanted to walk alongside her, to share this body as one. Katey had been told when the shift came, she wouldn't remember anything of her time as a wolf. What luck was it that she should host a spirit willing to coexist so completely?

When the shift was complete, Katey stood on her four wolf limbs. Her paws dug into the earth the same way her toes had. She lifted her head, feeling the weight of her fur coat across her body and around her neck. Her ears rotated at each little sound. She stretched out her stiff muscles, shaking off the last prickling effects of the change.

Then, she heard something behind her. She turned, but it stayed behind her. To her chagrin, she realized it was her bushy tail. Katey's vision was even sharper as a wolf than a human. She could see through the darkness around her, and from what she could tell, her pelt was white. If not white, it was a bright gray.

This, among other things, made her ecstatic because Logan had told her she would be black like all new loups-garous. Witnesses in Alaska had told her that she was a white loup-garou when she shifted at the vampire castle, but she would have never imagined she would be white in her regular wolf form.

Forgetting all propriety, she leaped and yipped like an excited pup, sending leaves and twigs scattering in all directions. Without the aid of her pack, she changed for the first time without complications. She knew there would be trouble in the morning if she were found out, but until then, Katey was determined to make the most of this time.

She sniffed the air, oriented herself to the west and loped forward, weaving between the tree trunks and leaping over bushes with remarkable grace that she could have only dreamed of. Her tongue drooped out of her smiling muzzle, letting the cold air pass in and out through her powerful lungs as her lean legs carried her deeper and deeper into the forest. Where she was going, she didn't know, and she didn't care. As far as Katey and her wolf were concerned, they were where they were always meant to be.

The laptop screen came alive, bathing Darren's room in light. He cracked his eyes open and squinted at the computer until the sleep was cleared from his vision. He saw black and white surveillance video windows checkered across the screen, rotating every few seconds.

When Darren had first gotten the system a few years ago, he was awoken nearly every night by squirrels passing in the underbrush and sparrows flying across the field of view for the cameras hidden away in the branches of the trees around their property. It wasn't until Logan showed him how to change the motion-activated settings that he was able to sleep through the night and the screen only flickered on when anything the size of a deer came into focus.

With the threat of the hunters, he was glad he had made such investments for the safety of his pack. He had asked Ben to keep an eye on the camera feed while they were gone, but he was sure his omega wasn't doing anything of the kind. Ben was the lightest sleeper of them all and would have been driven mad just by the constant whirling of the laptop fan that kept the computer working throughout the night.

Grateful for the break in his fitful sleep, Darren slid out of bed and shuffled to the desk on the far side of the room. He stretched out his tight shoulder muscles and searched through each of the windows, looking for what could have triggered the sensors. The cameras were only positioned around the edges of their property, patrolling a couple of miles worth of woodland forests and a creek that slithered along its northern border. The coverage wasn't perfect, but they watched over the more worn paths through the trees; paths that any large animal or human would be more inclined to take.

Darren thought he had come back around to the beginning of his search when he found the culprit. A doe was peacefully grazing by the creek. He flipped through the feed windows again and was convinced there was nothing else. Still, he felt compelled to watch the deer until it passed on. The screen would not turn off until the deer had moved out of view of the camera anyway, and Darren's tired eyes despised the bright light.

He sighed and sunk into his leather office chair. There was nothing impressive about this doe. It was perhaps a few years old, surprisingly old for an animal of prey around these parts. Apart from the hunting packs of loups-garous that passed through the woods frequently, game hunters were in no short supply this deep in the south.

The mention of hunters stirred unpleasant thoughts for Darren, and he rubbed at his bloodshot eyes. Rest had been an impossible feat this past week. Not only because of the hunters but because of the precarious situation Katey had placed him in.

The alpha side of him wanted to punish Katey harshly for her outbursts and defiant attitude. Such seeds of discontent were likely to spread among his pack, and a mutiny could well be underway. At least, that's what his wolf side wanted to believe. Darren knew his pack too well, trusted them with his life and he with theirs. A mutiny was inconceivable.

He remembered Dustin's words about why Katey balked at his authority so hard lately. It was clear she was different from them. In their early years, they wanted to deny their loup-garou nature and rejected training. Memories of his first few training sessions with John reminded him that even he, an alpha and successful pack leader, had once been hesitant and resentful about what he truly was.

Katey was not that way and probably never would be. He remembered how she had pleaded with him on that long-ago day when she first awoke after Logan bit her, that she wanted this and even asked it of Logan. Even now, Darren still couldn't wrap his head around the idea that she truly wanted to be half human, half beast. Then again, considering it had been a miraculous work of fate that brought her into the world of loups-garous, perhaps it wasn't such a far-fetched idea after all. It was her destiny.

Darren was beginning to consider the possibility of keeping Katey there with them until the threat of the hunters passed. Perhaps he would even continue parts of her training that had nothing to do with shifting.

Getting rid of her or sending her to the safe house in Alabama to wait it out with the Deviants would have been the easier course of action, but what kind of message would that send to Katey? As far as she was concerned, the hunters were no threat, and she might take it as a personal offense against her. Sending her away when she acted out was exactly the kind of treatment she received as a foster child, and this was not one of her foster homes that she would be jettisoned from at the first sign of trouble. This was a pack, a family unit, and Darren refused to let himself pretend it was anything different.

It was the most logical response to keeping her safe and out of danger. Darren stroked his beard, still indecisive as he watched the doe munch away at the winter grasses.

He would need to keep up morale within his pack, now more than ever. No one else seemed as worried about the hunters as him. They didn't understand the danger. He had experienced it firsthand, and that was another reason why sleep evaded him. Images of his family - his deceased family - motivated him to stay strong and vigilant. He had seen Ben's looks of worry and heard Dustin's words of warning, but they didn't understand. They hadn't lost anyone to the hunters, no one they truly knew. He lost friends and loved ones throughout the centuries, and he was going to make damned sure he didn't lose any more.

Suddenly, the doe lifted her slender head, ears working in every direction. Darren watched closer, wondering what had gotten her attention. Then, as quickly as she had become alert, the doe darted out of the camera view, heading further down the creek and away from their property. Whatever had spooked the deer, it did a fine job of it.

Darren was about to drag himself back to bed when he saw another figure blur across the screen. A white streak, much too large to be a dog but too small to be a deer, and much too fast to be a human or small critter.

It darted in and out of the window so quickly that Darren didn't have time to make out what it was. He clicked in a few places and watched the feed of the doe fleeing north. When the white blur came into view, he paused it.

His chest swelled with anger. He stood up so forcefully from his chair, he knocked it clear to the ground. Darren marched out of his bedroom and made his way down the hall, banging on the other bedroom doors as he went.

"Wake up!" he demanded from the three sleeping men. He heard groans and muttered curses from his pack, but he didn't care. He had to know who was on their property – if it were one of his own or a Devian.

When he came to Katey's door, he pounded on the wood, and it gave way, swinging open to reveal that her bed was empty. The covers were thrown back, but her belongings were still there, including her shoes.

"Katey!" he bellowed, charging back down the hall toward the bathroom.

"What's going on?" Dustin asked as he stepped out of his bedroom, rubbing the sleep from his eyes.

Darren pushed the bathroom door open and found it unoccupied. He called out Katey's name again and headed downstairs.

He heard shambling feet move quickly behind him.

"I heard her get up a couple of hours ago to get a drink of water," he heard Ben say as Darren searched the main floor. The full glass of water was set on the kitchen counter, untouched.

When he turned, Logan was practically at his heels while Dustin checked the billiard room.

"Was she sleeping with you tonight?" Darren asked, unmindful of the obvious rage and urgency in his voice.

Logan looked bewildered and shook his head. "No," he said. "We had a fight last night, and she wanted to sleep alone."

Ben joined them, and Darren watched his gaze fall on the unfinished water glass. He balled his hands into fists and the alpha could tell his omega was struggling for composure. "I should have come down here with her," Ben seethed.

Dustin returned from the billiard room. "I know it's nearly impossible to tell since she's been all over the place, but I think I picked up a fresh scent by the back door and in the carport."

The urge to roar like a wild beast pressed Darren, but he swallowed it back, knowing it would do no good to waste his fury before Katey was back. "I shouldn't have left her room unguarded."

"You couldn't have known she would pull a stunt like this," Dustin consoled with a string of his own brand of frustration flavoring his words. "What do you want us to do now?"

"I want you and Ben to go after her. The surveillance feed picked up her trail by the creek on the north side of the property. I don't care if you go as wolves or as men, but get her and bring her back."

He didn't have to ask twice. Ben and Dustin rushed out the back door, following Katey's scent. Logan leaned against the kitchen counter, still somewhat dazed.

"Did she mention anything about running away?" Darren asked Logan, still unable to control the unbridled mix of emotions storming within him.

Logan shook his head with an empty stare. "She mentioned how unfair it was that no one would train her, but other than that, she said nothing." The boy looked up to his alpha for assurance. "Was she injured? Could you tell from the cameras?"

Darren gave him a mirthless laugh and turned his gaze upward, trying to form the words. When he saw that white wolf cross the screen, he had thought it was a Devian at first. At worst, it was a large stray dog that happened to look a lot like a wolf. If Katey was gone, he knew it must have been her.

He wanted to be furious and stricken with grief for her safety. Under it all, suspecting she had managed to shift on her own made him want to puff up with pride. He was unsure why, though. She didn't change with his help. In fact, she changed despite his refusal to help her. What authority did he have left over her? There was still plenty left to teach her, but would she even listen to him anymore?

"Your fiancé may have just successfully shifted."

Darren looked at Logan and saw the same swirling conflict of emotions in his eyes. He didn't know how to feel about it either, and all they could do was wait until the guys returned her to the pack.

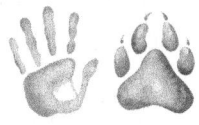

Al stared at the dozens of surveillance monitors, his eyes burning with the effort it took for them to stay open. Luckily, he had a hot cup of coffee steaming between his hands to get him through the last two hours of his shift. Three more grunts were watching their own set of monitors within the same room, but he knew his job was especially important.

They had hacked into the surveillance feeds of countless stores and establishments within Crestucky. Their team had been combing across the south, searching for the boss's intended target. Never had finding a single werewolf been so difficult.

His uncle had welcomed him into this business, and somehow, he pictured his role differently. He wanted to be the one out there with guns and tranquilizers, hunting down the beasts that plagued the earth with their evil, but no. He was stuck in a cramped bunker complex and watching empty storefronts at two o'clock in the morning.

Al's focus wasn't on the stores or streets. They had also managed to tap into the accounts of several townspeople who had bought themselves security cameras for their properties. There were a few citizens who owned farms or small horse ranches bordered by woods. Those were the surveillance footage reels he watched, and they were the best bet at finding a werewolf if it was roaming around outside of town.

He took a sip of his coffee and let the scalding liquid burn his tongue – anything to stay awake until his relief came.

Al's eyes passed over a window a few times, but it wasn't until he marked the time at two-seventeen in the morning that he saw his first sign of movement. A white blur ran across the screen. Thinking he might have truly caught something, he singled out that frame and played it back one more time. It sure looked like a wolf, if not some huge stray dog.

He grabbed the walkie-talkie in front of him. "Hey, I think I found something," Al said into it. He could feel the curious glances of the other surveyors in the room, but they must have brushed it aside because no one asked him a thing.

His superior, Pat, came into the tiny surveillance room and marched up behind his chair, his heavy boots the only sound in the room besides the hum of the computer equipment. Pat looked at the frozen image of the animal and nodded. "Definitely a wolf," he said in his gruff voice, hoarsened by years of chain smoking. "Have you seen anything else?"

"No, sir. I was keeping this window blown up so you would see it."

"You could have missed it again on another feed!" he scolded. Pat snatched the mouse from Al's hand and brought back the rest of the screens. Sure enough, they almost missed something huge.

In one of the video feeds within the same network, they saw a trio of wolves. From the grainy greyscale image, they could determine that two of the wolves were darker in coloration and larger, accompanying the white wolf they spotted earlier.

"Two grown adults and a younger male," Pat speculated. "But I've never seen a werewolf with a pelt that light. Perhaps it's an older male that's shrunken with age – if that's even possible."

Al swiveled in his seat and stared up in awe at his superior. "You've seen a werewolf up close?"

Pat's expression turned hard and calculating. "Son, I've come far too close. You'd soil your pants if you saw what I've seen in the last three decades on the force."

Al looked back and watched the three wolves seem to communicate with one another. The white wolf tucked his tail between his legs, lowering his body in submission to the other two males. One male nipped at the white wolf's neck and then prodded him forward with his shoulder. All three took off out of sight.

"Would an older male cower like that?" Al asked.

Pat straightened and scratched at his chin which was covered in stubble. "Dominance doesn't necessarily come with age, but it sure helps. These beasts are as mysterious as they are vicious." He slapped Al on the back. "Good job, grunt. I'll be telling the boss about this."

"What do we do in the meantime?"

"That's for Andrew to decide. I want the address attached to the owner of those cameras. Use every bit of hacking you can to find it."

Al, a specialist in hacking and computer technology, nodded. "Yes, sir. Shouldn't take me too long. We have it on record here."

A few clicks away and they had the address and name of the owner. "Thomas Hutchinson, sir."

"I want a copy of his driver's license or some other photo ID."

Without breaking a sweat or stumbling his nimble fingers across the keyboard, Al pulled up a copy of Mr. Hutchinson's identification. Pat leaned over, placing a massive hand on the back of Al's chair.

"Now, take that photo and do a facial recognition comparison with every photo ID dating back as far as the records go."

"Sir?" Al questioned, glancing over his shoulder at his supervisor.

"Just do it, grunt."

Al relented, and within moments, they had a match. In fact, they had many matches. "Sir, according to this, Thomas Hutchinson is also Dean Jackson, Kendrick Smith, and there's plenty more. They're all dated differently with different birthdays. Half of these are from school faculty directories. The most recent one is for the same town where he currently lives. He's working under the name Darren Dubose at the local high school. The earliest dated photo has him listed under that same name."

A smile of morbid satisfaction curled across Pat's scar-riddled face as his eyes skimmed over the many faces. The man's cheekbones were the same, and the jaw was square and strong. "He's rotating out names, but the photos are never alike. In this one, he has a full beard. In that one, he's clean-shaven. They're all different in one way or another, but it's the same werewolf."

"You're saying the man who owns these security cameras is a werewolf?"

"Either that, or he's an immortal harboring werewolves on his property. I'm gonna go with the former idea." Pat grinned from ear to ear, showing his yellow tobacco-stained teeth. "Andrew's gonna flip when he sees this."

CHAPTER 7

Katey's body ached from the shift and she found it difficult to sit up straight on the sofa. What she wouldn't have given to pop her stiff joints right then. Clad in her plush robe, she and her wolf had returned to their cage. Although the wolf was satisfied with what they had been able to get away with, it wasn't enough for Katey. The confining walls around her were too close, too suffocating compared to what she had been able to enjoy for the last few hours.

She looked away, her gaze unfocused and distant. Even now, she still thought about the forest and the open arms of nature. Their time in the woods had been short lived when Ben and Dustin came upon them not far from the creek. There was still so much more Katey longed to do, places she wanted to explore beyond the world she had known.

She thought of that deer and how it had narrowly escaped her grasp. Now she understood why wolves hunted in packs. If she had help, perhaps Ben and Dustin would have found her feasting on the carcass of that doe instead.

The cool wash of gold came over her eyes, and she knew that her wolf would have liked that too.

"Katey!" Darren barked and snapped his fingers just inches from her nose.

As if woken from a dream, Katey looked at her alpha. One only had to look at his wide stance, stern and reddened face, and the engorged vein in his neck to know he was far from happy. Ben and Dustin were standing some distance across the room, not as furious but certainly disappointed. She had barely noticed the droning of her alpha's voice and was only vaguely aware that she was not alone in the room.

She observed Logan standing in the kitchen, his back turned to her and arms folded. Every line of his strong back told her he was not pleased in the least. Katey wondered if that was because of their fight earlier or how she had run away the way she did.

His rejection cut more deeply than any of their dissatisfied stares. Somehow, she had thought Logan would be on her side, standing with her as she faced her judges. Instead, he kept his distance and didn't get involved. She hadn't seen his beautiful eyes since she was escorted home.

Katey looked back to Darren and waited for him to speak.

"I don't know what's gotten into you, Katey," he said, a pleading tone echoing in every word he spoke, tainted by his anger. "You knew it was dangerous to go out, especially alone. You could have been killed. What if hunters were out in those woods beyond our property? If you had stayed in the backyard, it might not have been so bad, but you have broken our trust by sneaking around."

Katey bowed her head, her gaze drifting to the rug under Darren's feet. If it had been before this night, she might have bucked at his words and defended her choices, but she lost almost every ounce of courage to stand up to him one more time.

The run in the forest had been spectacular, but it didn't bring her the peace of mind or answers she needed. The secret to being a loup-garou had not been revealed to her in any revelation. If the shift couldn't tell her what she needed to know, then the secret lay with those who had lived longer and had more experience than her. Four such men could teach her and she had successfully pissed them all off.

Her wolf had no desire to fight either, as she began to drift into dormancy in Katey's subconscious.

"What were you thinking?" Darren continued, his voice rising as if that would convince her to answer him. "Was this just an act of rebellion? Were you trying to prove your disrespect for me and this pack?"

"No," she replied. Her voice was little more than the whisper of a quiet church mouse.

"Were you trying to prove yourself to us? You know you've never had to prove your worth around here."

"No."

"Then this was just something to do for the hell of it?" Darren boomed.

Katey cringed, feeling her empathic feelers take hold once more. She had tried to numb that part of herself over the last few days, feeling more chaos and confusion to last her a lifetime. "No," she struggled to say, and the word came out shakily.

"Darren," Ben gently interrupted, taking a step forward with his hands held out in appeal.

"Stay out of this, Ben," Dustin warned, barely shifting his stare away from Katey and the alpha. The omega edged away and rubbed the back of his neck.

Mingling in the fog of anger, Katey could feel Ben's anxiety. He didn't want to see Katey disciplined any more than she wanted to be on the receiving end. She should have thought about that before running away. Perhaps it had been a foolish choice, but at the height of her emotional turmoil, there seemed no other option. What else could she do when it felt as if her insides would burst if she didn't at least try?

"Then why did you do this to us?" Darren demanded. "Why did you put yourself in so much danger?"

Katey paused at his choice of words. What had she done to them? What could she have possibly done? Was he talking about how she had incensed them with her disobedience? Or was this about something else? They didn't have to come and rescue her. There was no danger. They didn't have to let her nightly excursion interrupt their sleep. She never meant to hurt them or make them worry.

She lifted her head and locked eyes with Darren, searching for an answer. What she found was not something she expected. Fear. Had it been there all this time and she was too blind to see it? Or had she been so prejudiced against her own plight, that she hadn't let herself really accept what everyone else had been going through that week?

"I was trying to prove to myself that I could," Katey replied, feeling her own heart crack under the confession.

Darren crossed his arms over his barrel chest. "That you could do what?"

"That I could shift. All I wanted was to keep training."

"And I had told you we would continue training after the hunters were gone."

Katey had plenty of comebacks but pressed her lips together to keep from saying any of them. She could have said there were no hunters, that she was never in any danger, but Logan was within earshot. She could have said she was careful, but that was a total lie.

"I honestly don't understand you, Katey," Darren sighed. "And I don't know what to do with you. It's obvious you have no respect for me or my position of authority as pack alpha." Katey saw his body go rigid as he steeled himself for what he would say next. "Tomorrow, Logan and Ben will take you out of the state to a safe house where Jacob and his pack are staying. Dustin and I will stay behind to look after the remaining Devian families."

Katey's jaw dropped in disbelief. "You can't just—"

She stopped herself. She was about to say that Darren couldn't just get rid of her the minute she started misbehaving. Her wolf even gave her a cautionary growl, telling her to let it go. Darren was completely in the right, not because his decision held merit, but because he was the alpha. At least she would be with Logan. For that, she should have been grateful.

Katey slumped against the couch, letting her tired muscles relax. There was nothing left she could do, nothing left she could say. Perhaps with time, which they had plenty of, Katey would be able to earn back the pack's trust.

Darren let her near-reprisal slide, and he looked over his shoulder to Ben and Dustin. "Go get some sleep. We have a long day tomorrow."

The others obeyed and filed up the stairs. Logan hadn't moved, and that fact wasn't lost on Darren. "You too, Logan."

Katey watched nervously as Logan turned and hurried up the stairs, avoiding eye contact as he went. His slight against her was like a silver knife in her heart. Nothing could have hurt more than his disregard for her at that moment. Would Katey ever earn back her fiancé's favor too? Or would this one act of defiance ruin everything for them?

Everything seemed to shrivel and die before her very eyes. The pack was mad at her and Logan wasn't ready to forgive her. Alone and feeling small, Katey wanted to run away again and leave it all behind, even though that would only make matters worse. She had to find that peace again.

She looked back to Darren with a heartfelt expression of apology and sorrow, hoping beyond all else that he would see it and take pity on her. He did not. Darren turned and stood by the bottom of the stairs, waiting for her. There was no way he would leave her alone again.

Katey stood and tightened the soft belt around her waist before meekly making her way up the steps, her feet heavier than they had ever been.

That night, sleep came easily and swiftly for Katey, despite the emotional and mental disarray storming within her. Her tired body knew nothing of these problems and plunged her into the deepest sleep she had experienced in what seemed like forever.

In result, it didn't take long for her to slip into the world of dreams and visions, the place she had so often seen her parents and been plagued by nightmares of hunters and cages.

Katey opened her eyes and could smell the earthy scent of her father pervading the room. When she pushed herself up from the mattress, her body lighter than mist, she saw him standing at the foot of the bed.

One hand rested on the post of her canopy, the other gripped the footboard panel, his tall frame slightly bent to lean over the foot of the bed. The amber glow of approaching dawn lit the room, casting deep shadows and illuminating her powerful and majestic father.

What struck her most, though, was his expression. "Not you too?" she whined, grimacing at the way his brows pinch together in a look of displeasure. It was the same look Dustin and Ben had given her earlier.

Katey threw herself back under the covers, wishing to blot out this dream somehow. She couldn't take the disapproval of another person, especially her own father. It was too much for her heart to bear and she didn't want to be reminded of how the bitter isolation strangled her chest.

"Katherine, look at me," he asked firmly, his voice like a balm to her raw and tender spirit.

More out of shock than obedience, Katey sat back up and met her father's gaze. Never had he spoken to her in such a direct way. Her other dreams played like broken records, repeating the same words and images. This time was different.

"You did the wrong thing tonight," he said. "Darren is your alpha and should be obeyed. You know your wolf does not want to quarrel with him. Why did you not listen?"

Katey had to take a moment to mentally shake off the awe that came with her father's reprimand. "I... I wanted to learn how to shift, to be like you and all the other loups-garous. I wanted to find out what I was missing. Darren wasn't going to let me train until –
"

"Darren is a wise man and knows what he's doing," her father said. "He's a man of his word, and if he said he would train you later, you should have trusted him. If he tells you to wait, there is a reason for it."

Katey swallowed hard. "You know Darren? Personally?"

Her father gave her the faintest, nostalgic smile. "We met a very long time ago. Even then, he was a wise leader. He is your alpha and deserves to be respected as such."

"You're saying the same stuff he and Dustin were saying. How can I respect him when he won't respect me or what I need?"

Her father straightened and slowly walked around the corner of the bed. "You are not the judge of what you need. He is. He sees what you are capable of and trains accordingly. If you excel in one area, he will move on. If you need more attention, he will give it."

He sat down on the edge of the bed, so close that Katey could reach out and touch him. She lifted her hand with the intention to do just that but thought better and recoiled to let it rest in her lap again. It might have broken the illusion. The sun's rays of the coming dawn sparkled in his green eyes, and for a moment, she thought she saw a touch of wolf gold that was permanently fixed in his irises.

"Then what am I supposed to do? What else am I doing wrong?" she implored, taking advantage of the short time she had with her father.

This time, he reached out to her and ran the back of his fingers against her cheek. His touch was warm and electric. For just a second, she was brought back to the last time they touched when she had died and embraced him and her mother. Then, her chest went tight for another reason completely.

"You are doing fine, Katherine. Despite the difficulties, you shift-ed beautifully, and I couldn't be prouder."

Moisture filmed over her eyes, blurring her vision until she blinked and let the tear roll down onto his fingertips. At least someone had acknowledged the fact that she had successfully shifted. Not once did Darren or the others congratulate her

"You are in such harmony with your wolf. I cannot think of anyone who has ever come this far so quickly."

Katey smiled. "I guess I've got some good genes," she said, her voice cracking under the strain of more suppressed tears.

Her father grinned, his eyes smiling with his lips. It was a beautiful thing to see, and Katey refused to blink again. Even if her eyes burned from fatigue and tears, she wanted to memorize this face forever.

He turned away briefly, looking out the window at the light filtering through the trees on the horizon. "I haven't much time, Katherine."

"Don't go," she pleaded and grabbed at his hand, but it was nothing but an illusion and her hands passed through his arm.

He shook his head. "I'm always with you, Katherine. Respect Darren as your alpha. Respect Darren as if he were me, and know that you are loup-garou. You and your wolf are one, and she will aid you in times of trouble. Never forget that we love you."

Katey watched her father fade into the light, dissolving into the dust particles floating through the air. When she awoke from her sleep, chest aching and heart pounding as it usually did after her vivid visions, Katey looked around her room and saw it was slightly darker than it had been in her dream.

The room was not suffused in an amber glow, but the gray light of the morning before the sun had fully emerged. It had only been a few hours since she had crawled into bed. The day had not begun yet, but it would soon, and this was the day she would leave Crestucky.

Katey hugged her pillow and begged sleep to take her again, but it was no use. Her senses were too alert and her heart racing too fast for her body to rest again. Not only that, but her mind replayed her father's speech, dissecting each phrase, each word, to make sense of it all.

Her father wanted Katey to treat Darren as if he were more than just an alpha. How was she supposed to do that when she never knew her own father while growing up? Living in foster families all her life did not set her up for a functional family unit by any means. Katey was rebellious and strong-willed, and she knew it. She would have to undo years of delinquency in a matter of days, but how?

She knew her wolf would help, just like her father said. Her wolf would know how to be submissive and accept Darren's authority just as it had last night when she was too tired and hopeless to argue. He could tell her to walk through a minefield and she should do it readily, trusting his judgment. She had to do the same that day as they left Crestucky.

Perhaps that was what she lacked. Trust. It was a foreign concept. There was no reason she shouldn't trust her pack. They have never misled her before and wouldn't start now. Katey had been welcomed into this family, but it was evident that she still had a long way to go before she was fully integrated into it as a pack member. That disheartening thought caused even more confusion and doubt to cloud her mind.

If she couldn't learn to trust them, what place would she have in this pack? What use was she to the world that turned to her as the answer to war and hatred? Would her relationships with the others be forever crippled by her inability? Her father's words of wisdom created more problems than they solved.

One thing was for sure. Katey would get no further rest this morning.

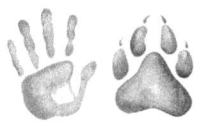

Logan lay in his bed, hands folded behind his head as he listened to the sounds of the house. The pack was sleeping peacefully after the scare Katey had given them, but Logan could not feel the same.

Not only was their previous argument from the evening before still squeezing his heart in regret like barbwire around a tender fruit but now the bitter emotions of betrayal and envy toward Katey kept him from sleeping.

Their argument had been pointless. It only served to make a bad situation worse by trying to instruct her on the way alphas should be treated. He was a poor teacher, and an even worse example and Katey was aware of that. Already raw from Dustin's lecture, she was in no mood for company and rejected what little comfort he wanted to give. Katey had taken her meal from him and ordered Logan out of her room after they were done exchanging some heated words.

It took a great deal of sketching to help numb his spirit enough to sleep. He didn't have that luxury now, with so few hours left of the night to get that much-needed rest.

Shifted, Logan thought to himself. *How could she have shifted and I couldn't?*

It was cruel to believe, but Logan somehow wanted Katey to be just as unable to shift as he was. His loup-garou blood was so diluted by his human parents that he wanted to believe it would be just as hard for Katey to shift voluntarily, knowing her mother was a vampire. Instead, she had done it without help and in record time.

She had been training for only a few weeks. It took Logan decades to get anywhere close to changing at will. After nearly a century of trying, he told the others he had given up the idea. Although he was far from passive about his handicap, Logan had tried to not let it affect his place in the loup-garou community. He tried to convince himself it was an unnecessary luxury and not a useful tool for living his life. Nothing could convince him that he was no less of a man for his disability.

Katey shattered that complacency. Each time she asked to train was like the sharp edge of a knife pressing into his spine. Knowing she had successfully shifted only sliced open the old wounds. She hadn't been a loup-garou for a full month, and she was already excelling faster than any other loup-garou he had ever met. No doubt his astonishment was shared by the others, but it would have been inappropriate to express it under the circumstances.

When they brought Katey back, Logan knew he couldn't face her. He didn't want to say or do something he would come to regret again. Instead, he stayed in the kitchen and tried to not let Darren's fiery rage rub off on him.

His more primal instincts wanted Logan to hate Katey for her natural talent as a loup-garou. No matter what she did or what he couldn't do, Logan knew he would always love her. He just needed time, and so did she, but how much?

The change in her attitude had been plain the moment Darren began to rebuke her for running out on her own. Katey didn't argue, she just let her alpha scold her in front of the others, her voice never raised to return his anger.

Logan wondered if the willful shift, the syncing of wolf and woman, had made her rethink her behavior toward Darren. Was there something about that first shift that fully assimilated the instinctive nature of the wolf with their human counterpart? Did that make them more submissive to alphas? It was just another secret of the shift that he would never know and that caused him great pain.

There was a disturbance down the hall, and Logan sat up, listening carefully. He heard the rustle of fabric and the soft padding of light feet against the wood planks of the floor. Katey's door opened not too quietly, and he listened to her progress down the hall and toward the stairs. It was apparent she wasn't trying to sneak around this time.

Logan took a deep breath to soothe his battered ego. If tonight hadn't happened, Logan knew he would have intercepted Katey in the middle of the hallway and whisked her away to his room. He hadn't moved a muscle. It was this realization that told him they could not continue this way. It didn't matter how he felt or how she had gotten herself into hot water with Darren. They were to be mates, and if they couldn't get past this, it would not bode well for the rest of eternity.

Casting aside his blanket, Logan jumped out of bed and pursued her as quickly as his tired legs would take him. He had no idea what he would say. What was there to say? Repeating Darren's reprimand would do no good at all, and he couldn't behave like nothing was wrong.

There was little time to think of words when he arrived downstairs. He didn't see her right away until he turned the corner into the kitchen. Katey sat on the floor, leaning against the cabinets, a few slices of roast beef pinched between her fingers. Her mouth worked at the bite she had taken already.

Logan hadn't laid eyes on Katey since their fight. It might have been the time they spent apart or some unconscious effect of her first willful shift, but either way, she never looked more beautiful and radiant than she did now. For a moment, Logan couldn't breathe. Katey hadn't even acknowledged him yet, and he was already mesmerized.

He stood there like a dumbstruck fool until Katey heaved a heavy sigh and looked at him. The hopeless expression in her eyes threatened to tear him apart. He hadn't thought about how their treatment of her would have affected her sensitive spirit. She had already told him about how she could feel the emotional energies of the others as if they were her own. The aggression, the disappointment, and the tension must have been eating away at her.

Tenderness was the only way to approach Katey now. Logan found it hard to swallow but managed to gesture toward the fridge. "Is there any more left in there?" he asked, trying to not make this trip downstairs about her at all. He was also careful to keep his tone as neutral as possible, despite his still bruised ego.

Katey blinked, obviously caught off guard by his question and then nodded before she turned back to her own snack.

Logan pushed aside his nerves and put one foot in front of the other, keeping his distance from Katey while he retrieved a couple of slices of meat. He sat down across from her, leaning against the cabinets beneath the sink. Suddenly, it was as if they were strangers again and all the jitters of first love rattled his body. His stomach churned and lungs begged for more air like her beauty had stolen the oxygen out of the room.

Her eyes were cast down, and Logan would have given his world to see her look up at him with love and happiness again. What he wouldn't give to know what she was thinking. How could he have been so selfish to hurt her like that again? He had screwed up their relationship before, but somehow this seemed far worse than any of those other times.

Seconds ticked by and they said nothing to each other. He hadn't even taken a bite of the roast beef in his hand yet. Even if he had tried to eat, he was sure nothing would make it down his swollen throat. If he wasn't going to eat, then he had to speak. The silence could not continue like this.

"Are you okay?" he asked, his voice thick and low.

Katey let out a tight breath and shook her head. "I don't even know," she replied softly.

It felt as if they had been down this road before, back before he had bitten her. He remembered dancing with her in the wrestling gym at school and how she had confessed to feeling so depressed and alone before he came into her life. He remembered knowing right then and there that he would do everything in his power to make sure she never felt that way again. Yet, here he was, breaking his vow.

"I'm sorry for the things I said last night," he said. "Everyone has been giving you a hard time, and you didn't need the same from me."

Katey finally looked up, and Logan felt his heart flutter in his chest. "You were just trying to help. Everyone's been trying to help, and I haven't been listening. I should be the one apologizing for being the problem child of the pack."

Logan wanted to laugh, but the tortured look in her eye stopped him. He used to be the problem child of the pack. Since she had come along, he'd had a reason to set aside his insubordinate attitude – if nothing but to set an example, as Dustin had advised him to do on the night after Logan changed Katey.

"You're not a problem child," he consoled. "It takes time to get used to the way the pack system works."

Katey closed her eyes and sighed, her head listing to the side as if she were tired. "Everyone has been saying these things take time, but I don't want them to. I'm tired of waiting for things to start magically working the way they should."

"It takes work, Katey. It won't just happen overnight." Logan had to keep his tone in check, to show her he wasn't trying to start another argument.

Katey drew up her knees and crossed her arms over them, the meat still clinched in her fingers. "I know, and that's what frustrates me the most." She opened her eyes, but her gaze did not lift from the tile floor. "I had another dream about my dad."

Logan straightened his shoulders against the wood cabinet door behind him. "Was it the same one as before?"

She shook her head. "No. He told me to respect Darren as the alpha like I would respect him as my father. I don't even know where to begin to do any of that." Logan heard the building emotions in her words and her eyes watered. "He said he was proud of me for changing on my own. He's the first one to actually congratulate me for what I did."

Logan could no longer keep his distance when he saw the tear roll down her cheek. He set his meat on the counter and crawled to her side. When he wrapped his arms around her shoulders, Katey's defenses fell, and she began to silently weep into his chest. He couldn't understand why she was crying, but he wasn't about to pry into the corners of her heart that these tears were springing from.

He wasn't sure what to say. Her father had been dead for eighteen years. Logan knew nothing about the afterlife or what spiritual forces could allow anyone to communicate with the dead. When Katey had first told him about the dreams, he wondered if they were just manifestations of what she wanted to see, pulled from her death experience. Now, he wondered if this dream had been a true visitation from her father or if it was just what she needed to hear.

The idea convicted him. He should have been the first to tell her that he was proud of what she had accomplished. Instead, he wouldn't even look at her. Even if he didn't mean it, he should have been supportive. At least he had a chance now to make up for his mistake.

"When Darren told me that you shifted on your own, I was so surprised," he said. "I was surprised, but scared that you were in danger, too."

Katey sniffled and curled against his side like a child seeking protection and comfort. "I shouldn't have run away and tried on my own," she whimpered.

"But you're safe now. That's what matters." Logan braced himself for a white lie. "I am proud of you for changing on your own."

Katey looked up, her eyelashes damp with tears and cheeks glistening in the dim light that came through the kitchen window. "No, you're not," she corrected. "I know you're mad about it just like everyone else is."

He should have known she would be so perceptive. "We're mad that you disobeyed Darren's order to stay inside. We're not mad that you shifted. Being able to shift on your own is a big step in being a loup-garou."

Katey's hand came to rest on his bare chest. Her touch was soft and affectionate, telling him she had forgiven him for all his offenses against her. It felt like an eternity since she had touched him this way.

"I know you're mad that I was able to take that step before you."

Logan went quiet, unsure of what to say.

"I know changing on demand has been the one thing you could never do," she continued.

Logan leaned his head against hers. "You're right. I am mad, but I'm not mad at you. I'm mad at my own inability to do what you've done. I've been trying for a century to do what you did in just a couple of weeks."

Katey slipped her arms around him and squeezed tightly as if that would bring the battered pieces of his ego back together. It just might have. Feeling her embrace chased away some of the demons in his mind and allowed him to love her even more – if that were possible. Logan wondered how it was possible for one mere woman to be in so much pain, yet emit her own kind of peace that others could so easily latch onto.

"I never meant to upstage you," Katey whispered.

"I know you didn't." Logan glided his hand across her slightly tangled dark hair and let the bitterness and decades of self-loathing slip from him. He was like an ox being shed of its harness and able to roam free from his burden. What she said wasn't profound. It didn't erase the past or what he had felt. It was little less than a thin bandage over a severed artery. Somehow, her presence and her warmth in the midst of her own turmoil gave him peace.

"What was it like?" he asked after he gave Katey a few moments to compose herself.

She pulled away from him and searched his face for the anger she must have assumed was still there. After she had found nothing, she smiled. "It was incredible. It still hurt a bit, but I remembered everything."

Logan didn't hold back his unconvinced look. "That's impossible. You shouldn't have been able to remember anything past the change."

Katey took on a new eagerness and gripped his arm. "But I did, and I was white!"

"White? Like you were in Alaska?" Katey nodded. "How is any of that possible? New loups-garous are supposed to be black."

"I know, but..." she said and shrugged.

"Did you do something special with your wolf to make that happen?" Logan asked, also eager to learn what he could from her.

"Darren had been telling me I needed to force the wolf out, but I didn't have to. She came out willingly and I know it sounds crazy, but it was like we were one. One body, one mind, everything."

Logan didn't know what she meant but grinned when he watched the spark of excitement dance in her green eyes. It didn't matter if he understood what she did or how she did it. If she was happy, that was all that mattered.

"Maybe I'll start training again and see if I can do the same," he said, a twinge of woefulness in his voice, knowing that no amount of training or effort would ever make him achieve the level of success she had.

"I can help you if you want," she offered.

Logan kissed her forehead. "I'd want nothing less," he replied with an easy smile.

Footsteps sounded down the stairs, and Logan looked toward the kitchen doorway. Darren appeared, circles under his eyes and face shadowed in weariness. The alpha looked from Logan to Katey to the slices of meat set aside on the counter. Logan wasn't sure if it was weariness that dulled the fury he had seen in the alpha's eyes the night before, or if sleep had taken away the edge, but Darren looked to be in a more amiable mood. Perhaps he had given up on the challenge of disciplining Katey after her show of obvious submission.

"Decided to have breakfast early?" he asked as he shuffled past them toward the fridge.

Katey nestled deeper into Logan, seeking refuge in him, which he was more than happy to give. If Darren so much as raised his voice at Katey this morning, Logan was prepared to defend her this time.

"We were just talking," Logan replied.

"About tonight's plans to leave, I hope."

In all the hysteria of Katey's disappearing act, Logan had completely forgotten about Darren's orders to leave Crestucky. "No, we weren't."

If he were to be truthful, Logan wasn't any happier about leaving the area than Katey was. He was sure they would return once it was safe, but he had never liked living life from a suitcase or running all over the country. This preference had developed during his time with Darren in Europe when they were searching for Dustin. Hopping from hotel to hovel for years made him sick of the idea of fleeing from the most stable home he had ever truly known. If it was Darren's decision to leave, he would honor it with as little grumbling as possible.

Darren pulled out a carton of eggs and a package of bacon from the fridge. "You two will need to pack this evening. Only carry what you'll need."

"We know the drill, Darren," Logan sighed. To his surprise, Darren didn't correct his attitude.

The alpha pulled out a skillet from one of the lower cabinets and turned on the gas range with as much calm as if nothing had happened out of the ordinary in the past week. "I'll also need you to go with Dustin and Ben to check on the Devian families still in town."

Katey straightened up in Logan's arms and leaned in as if she were chomping at the bit. "What about you?" she asked.

Darren sprayed the pan with cooking oil and turned to regard her with a look of indifference. "I will be spending the day with you, Katey."

Logan felt his grip tighten around his fiancé, but her body went slack for a moment, probably from disbelief. She had noticed the lack of hostility in their alpha as well. After all the bickering and fighting, Darren was willing to spend the day with currently his most difficult pack member.

"Why can't I stay with her and you go with the others?" Logan asked, subtly probing for an explanation to his sudden change of heart.

"I have something in mind for Katey and me to do. A little field trip," he replied with a furtive smile.

"Where are we going?" Katey questioned, a sprinkling of hesitance in her words.

"You'll find out," Darren replied before he began to prepare their breakfasts.

CHAPTER 8

They had been driving for over an hour. At first, Katey had been suspicious of Darren's plan to leave the house while they were under a hunter-warning. Once he assured her this field trip was part of the next step in her training, she was more than eager.

From the driver's seat, Darren glanced at Katey beside him. The window was rolled down and her chin rested on her arms that were crossed over the doorframe. The cool breeze whipped at the tendrils of hair that escaped from her ponytail. Sunlight splashed across her face, and a contented smile was spread across her lips.

They had passed nothing but rolling fields of farmland and untouched forest as they drove deeper into the countryside of northern Florida, following the state line that divided them from Alabama. Darren hadn't been out this way for at least six months, but he could remember a time long ago when there wasn't even a paved road to drive on.

Darren looked back to the road ahead as they passed by a few modest homes, the first he had seen in nearly twenty miles. They were drawing closer to civilization, but he would have to make the turn soon that would take them farther away from the town and further into the country.

He judged that it would be safe for them on this route, knowing the hunters were working their way from west to east. It was likely they hadn't scouted around this area yet or they had already passed through after inspecting the small towns, but he remained alert, knowing hunters could be unpredictable.

Hunters had consumed his mind over the last week, infiltrating his dreams and keeping him vigilant at all times. Darren understood his mental and physical health was at risk because of his obsession. The benefits far outweighed what he suffered. Knowing that his pack - his family - was safe, would be the reward for his efforts.

He glanced again to Katey and realized how fond he had become of her, despite everything they had been through in the last twenty-four hours. He had always cared for her. He cared for all his students in the same way and wanted the best that life could offer them. Katey had turned into something special through all of her stubbornness and issues.

Darren had served as a teacher for so many years, educating countless young people. They never stayed in an area long enough for him to gain tenure or raise suspicion of why he never aged. As a result, many of his students moved on with their lives, and he was never able to see the fruits of his labor.

He never knew if a student grew up to be a scientist or an accountant as they had planned. There was the occasional word of gratitude from graduating seniors if he was still around, but he sometimes wondered if any alumni had tried to reach out to him in their adult years to let him know that they finally made it and to thank him for the dedication he gave to their education when they may or may not have deserved it.

They were all, each, shooting stars across his night sky. They stayed for a moment and then passed on in their journey. He stayed in place, watching them brilliantly shine before him and fade out just as quickly.

Katey was different. She was the one shooting star that took her place amongst the fixed constellations in his life. She would be around for centuries to glean from his wisdom, but she had yet to thank him for what little he had done so far. He was tempted to feel embittered by her disregard for the protection and guidance he had given her, but she was still young, and with all they had been through just that week, gratitude was the last thing on her mind.

She wasn't just his student anymore. She had become part of the pack and part of the loup-garou community as something of a Messiah for their race. He hadn't let it fully set in that he was the caretaker of the one person who would mean so much to this world.

Her influence wouldn't be felt by just loups-garous and vampires. Peace between their two races would mean peace for the world as a whole and an end to so many conflicts and internal wars. Looking at her now, no one would truly understand that.

As far as anyone else knew, she was a spirited youth, full of life and an eagerness to please and experience everything. She was too young to have gone through so much. Even Darren wasn't sure if he could have carried her burden at that age. He was still trying to get a grasp on his new life when he was a mere eighteen years old.

"I never meant to take your freedom from you," he said over the roar of the wind blasting through the car.

Katey turned her head toward him but didn't say anything. They locked eyes, but Darren couldn't see any change in her expression. She seemed to be scrutinizing him in the same way.

"You must know I'm only trying to keep you and everyone else safe."

"Maybe that's not your job," she replied softly, her voice almost lost in the noise of the car.

"As your alpha, it is my job," he said sternly before easing his foot on the brake so they could make the next turn.

Katey leaned back inside the car and rolled up the window until there was only a narrow slit at the top for air to blow through. He knew Katey didn't keep the window down for the cold air but for the scent of the pine and earth outside. He couldn't blame her for enjoying the aroma. His wolf responded to the heady smells as well, but he had better control over his bestial instincts.

"I've been doing research about wolf packs, and the alpha isn't always the strongest wolf," Katey said. "It's the beta that keeps the pack safe. So, wouldn't that be Dustin's job?"

Darren wanted to admire her thirst for knowledge, but he didn't appreciate the way she constantly called out the flaws in their system. "A loup-garou pack is still slightly different from a wolf pack."

"And the omega is supposed to be the tension reliever," she continued. "The omega jumps into fights and diverts the attention onto him so no one else gets hurt. They sometimes do that by playing the clown, and that sounds like Dustin. So, Ben shouldn't be the omega. It seems like everyone's position is switched around."

"Dustin wasn't always the clown," Darren replied as they pulled onto another country road, the sun glaring down through the windshield and warming the inside of the car. "Loup-garou packs are structured around dominance. As for roles, we serve where we are needed." He looked to Katey. "Besides, don't you remember last night when Ben tried to intervene, and Dustin had to hold him back? That's a demonstration of their titles, isn't it?"

Katey opened her mouth to reply but then closed it and she turned to stare out the window. He had made his point, but her new submissive attitude made him wonder what had changed. She wasn't as quick to argue anymore.

The way she had behaved in the past few days would have suggested that her wolf was fighting for a higher rank within the pack, despite her greenness. Now, she was resigned and didn't challenge him. Still, that flicker of dominance she had put off made his wolf more nervous than it should have been.

"What was your shift like last night?" he asked, hoping to lure her into further conversation. If they were to repair their pack bonds, Darren had to make her feel comfortable talking to him again.

Katey shifted in her seat and sighed. "Fine."

Darren laughed at her attempt to brush him off. "Are you becoming a one-syllable kid now? I know it couldn't have just been fine. Tell me how it went."

She smoothed back the flyaway hairs from her forehead and appeared to be deep in thought before she replied. "It was hard at first because I was trying to force it, but then I just let the wolf take over, and it was so natural."

Darren let her go on about her night, how she had been so surprised and pleased that she had a white pelt, and the various things she did with her wolf. He was especially intrigued to hear she was able to stay conscious through the experience. He had never known a loup-garou who could do that so soon in their training. No other loup-garou he knew of had white fur either. Even John, who was at least a couple centuries older than Darren, had gray and silver fur, but never the snow-white color Katey prided herself on.

When she was finished, he hardly knew what to say. She had managed to shift on her own without any outside coaching. "Where did you get the idea to just let the wolf take over instead of forcing it?"

As calm as if they were discussing the weather, Katey replied, "My wolf told me."

Darren had never been one for believing that loups-garous were just vessels for the spirit of beasts to inhabit. Even centuries ago, when superstition was the law of the land, Darren knew there had to be some more worldly or philosophical explanation for what he had become. After listening to the way Katey talked so intimately about her wolf partner, he wasn't so sure everything could be explained with science.

"What else has your wolf told you?" he asked.

Katey shook her head and let her gaze fall into her lap. "Nothing else, really."

Darren wasn't so blind. He could see through the deflection and knew there was something more she wasn't telling him. The only solace he could take now was the fact that what he was about to show her was something she would never have learned on her own.

They turned once more down a dirt path off the highway. The unpaved road was clearly marked by a painted sign reading "Florida Wolf Preserve." He watched Katey look over her shoulder at the sign as they passed it.

"I didn't know there was a wolf preserve in Florida," she remarked as she turned back around in her seat.

"It's the only one in the state."

Darren's silver sedan rocked at every little bump and divot in the road. Their few moments of suffering the path paid off when they eased through a break in the trees that opened into a gravel parking area that could accommodate perhaps a little over a dozen vehicles. Two pickup trucks and a minivan were already parked in unmarked stalls.

Darren shouldn't have been surprised by the low visitor count, but it was a Saturday. He wanted to think the vacant parking spaces were due to the winter chill that still hung in the air, despite the warm sun beating down. He also knew the preserve was struggling. It had been since the day it opened. They needed more visitors to keep the wolves fed and the gates open and his monthly donation was not going to make that happen. Tours from the schools were a great way to bring awareness, but what parent in their right mind would allow their child to be within snapping range of a wolf?

He parked close to the welcome center, a wooden building perhaps the size of a single-wide trailer. As they walked up the weed-riddled path, Darren looked at Katey and noticed that she was walking just a few paces behind him, gazing around with a look of amazement and trepidation. Like him, she could probably smell the wolves close by in the enclosures. However, they remained out of sight, hidden in their dens.

Inside, there was a cashier counter manned by a middle-aged woman with short black hair and shiny dark eyes. Her high cheekbones gave away her Native American ancestry. It had been a while since Darren had seen Tessa, but she hadn't changed. Not to him. Despite everything she had been through, she still held her chin up high and kept her gentle deportment. The laugh lines around her mouth and eyes still creased into her dark skin; those lines Chris had blessed her with.

Dressed in a simple sweater and high-waisted jeans, Tessa still retained an element of exotic beauty that had drawn many of their kind to her. Chris was the lucky one to win her heart, but he knew plenty more who were bitter about losing such an appealing prize.

Darren reasoned it must have been the animalistic nature that made sensible men lust after women like her. Many loups-garous craved the strong, independent type of woman, just like Tessa and Katey. Flimsy and shallow females didn't last long within their society. Darren, however, never understood such desires. He never allowed himself to.

When she finally looked up from a spreadsheet gripped between her hands and saw Darren, her lips parted in surprise. Darren swallowed hard and gave her a friendly nod. Katey, oblivious to their greeting, began to roam about the shelves and racks of souvenirs.

Tessa seemed to snap out of her daze and gave Darren the same smile he remembered from years ago. "I haven't seen you in a while, stranger," she said in her husky but feminine voice.

"I'm sorry I haven't visited sooner," he replied, walking heavily toward the counter. "How are things?"

Tessa sighed and held up the spreadsheet in her hand. "The same, but we have fundraiser events planned in the next few months. That should help."

Always optimistic, Darren thought. It was the only way she could have endured the loss and stress.

Tessa glanced toward Katey and the otherwise empty welcome center. "I heard there were hunters in the next county over," she stated in a careful whisper.

Darren nodded. "There are, but I needed to take care of this business before we left the area for a while."

"I thought everyone left already. That's what Jacob said, anyway."

Darren spread his fingers across the polished wood of the countertop. "Most of the families have been evacuated, but a few have stayed behind. Katey, Logan, and Ben will be leaving tonight."

Tessa's eyes went wide. "Katey? Is she..." She motioned to the teenager examining a miniature stone statue of a wolf mother and her pups.

He nodded again. "That's her. She changed on her own for the first time last night." Darren pulled out his billfold from his back pocket. "I was hoping we could get in a private tour to see Chris."

Tessa looked down at the one-hundred-dollar bill Darren offered her with a trembling hand. "I couldn't accept that," she said, shock stealing much of her voice. "You already donate so much to the preserve."

Darren laid it on the counter between them. "We're visitors, just like everyone else."

"Why do you want to see Chris?" she asked, looking up at him with sudden seriousness. He couldn't blame her for being cautious.

"I need to finish up a part of Katey's training, and lately, words haven't been enough to make her listen." Darren cleared his throat. "I want to show her instead."

"Show me what?" Katey questioned as she approached them at the cashier counter with a porcelain figurine of a silver wolf with yellow topaz eyes between her hands.

Tessa was silent, watching Katey with an uncanny interest as if she were a strange species all her own. It was a similar look many strangers had given her that knew enough about loups-garous to know females didn't exist in their race.

"Katey, this is Tessa. She's an old friend of mine. Tessa, this is Katey, the newest member of my pack."

Tessa offered out her hand, but Katey was hesitant. The woman's odd reaction to her must have given her pause.

"Tessa is the wife to another loup-garou I know," Darren added, hoping that would break the ice.

Katey shook Tessa's hand and gave her a weak smile. He would berate Katey about her rudeness later.

"So, can we see Chris today or is he otherwise occupied?" Darren asked, wishing nothing more than to get this unpleasant lesson over with.

Tessa nodded. "Yes, he's here. We have one small group going through the enclosures right now, but Chris is in a different area of the preserve." She slipped Darren's payment into her cash drawer and grabbed a set of keys hanging on the wall. Katey set down the figurine on the counter and fell in beside Darren.

She escorted them out a side door and down a pathway that led toward several different enclosures. Some were for foxes, one for a couple of coyotes, but the majority were for wolves. Signs fastened to their fences read their names and their stories, as well as a few facts about their species. Darren saw Katey reading each one they passed, drinking in the information.

They arrived at the enclosure farthest from the welcome center, and Tessa stopped to open the padlock. Anxiety billowed from her as she struggled to keep her fingers steady with the key. Perhaps it was this building nervousness that Katey had sensed in the welcome center.

Darren could take no more of it and gently took the keys from her hands. "Allow me," he said before easily sliding the key into the lock and twisting it until the bar popped out of place.

They opened the first of two gates. Darren was in the process of opening the second lock when he had to call Katey away from the plaque on the enclosure fence.

"You'll have to forgive me if I don't go in with you," Tessa apologized as she held the gate door open for her visitors.

Darren laid his hand on her broad shoulder. "I understand. I'll lock up when we're done."

Tessa let him take the keys from her and shut the gate for them before retreating up the path. Darren caught a glimpse of her wiping her sweater sleeve against her cheek just before she turned the corner and disappeared behind a cluster of thick bushes.

"Is this Chris guy a volunteer here or something?" Katey asked as she looked about the enclosure.

"I wish he were," Darren replied solemnly. He walked a fair distance into the enclosure, searching for any sign of their host. Katey lingered behind, but he could sense her unease.

"Then what are we doing in here?"

Darren found a shady spot by a boulder and sat down on the ground. "There's something you need to learn about shifting voluntarily," he began as he gestured for her to sit with him. "It's good that you know how, and you can do it so easily, but you have to be careful of how often you shift and for how long each time."

Katey crossed her legs and sat beside her alpha, her eyes still flitting around the enclosure. If she were in her wolf form, her ears would have been pricking toward every little sound. After a few moments of quiet observation, her watchfulness paid off, and a wolf came cautiously loping from the underbrush some distance away.

His pelt was black, tinged with streaks of silver and brown across his back and dense mane. His golden eyes watched them from a distance, and then as if he suspected they might have food for him, the wolf trotted closer and approached Katey first.

Darren watched her grin at the sight of him, but as he came closer and she reached out to weave her hands in his fur, her smile turned sour and brows furrowed in confusion. The wolf knew no difference and sniffed at her face and clothes for the treat he must have been expecting.

"He's loup-garou," she said in disbelief, "but I'm not getting that tingly sensation in my head like I do with everyone else."

"That's right," Darren replied as he scratched at the wolf's shoulders, digging his fingers in deep so the animal would feel his touch.

"When you guys turned into wolves for the first time around me, I wasn't a loup-garou, so I didn't feel anything. I felt something up in Alaska when they turned. So, what's different about this one?"

The wolf turned to Darren and continued his search for a snack, his wet nose skimming around pant pockets and licking fingers.

"This is Chris," Darren sighed. "I've known him for about fifty years. I even worked with him at a university once. He was an educator, like me. He's Tessa's husband and the father of two young boys. They've been married for about ten years now."

Katey pointed back at the plaque on the fence. "But the sign said his name was Kenoa."

"The other wolves here have names like that too. How would it look if visitors came and saw a Shinook, Katara, and Black Paw, but came to this enclosure and read a very human name on the sign?"

Katey bit her lips together and brushed her hand over Chris' chest with such sympathy that Darren had almost forgotten why they were there. For a moment, this seemed as if he were a visitor to an ill friend at the hospital. In a way, it was.

When Chris was convinced the two bipeds did not have a treat for him, he padded away a few paces and began sniffing the air, completely uninterested in his guests.

"About two years ago, Tessa had a miscarriage, and Chris took it hard," Darren continued. "He blamed himself for the complications that came with her pregnancy. I tried to talk him through it. We all did. In the end, he couldn't live with himself anymore and didn't want to bear the pain of the loss.

"When a loup-garou changes too often for too long, the wolf DNA begins to become more active in our bodies. If it happens on accident, the loup-garou may experience difficulty changing back to his human form. After a while, he won't be able to shift back at all and what little control he had over his wolf side disintegrates. Chris changed one night and refused to shift back again.

"After a few days of watching him, we saw that he wouldn't respond to our voices. He began to act just like any other wolf. It was a matter of time before we lost him. There's nothing left of the man now. Just the wolf. Now Tessa must raise her two sons on her own without a husband. When they come of age, their loup-garou gene will activate, and Jacob or some other alpha will have to train them. The job Chris would have taken upon himself has to pass to another because of his choices."

Katey shook her head. "There has to be some way to help him."

"But, Katey, don't you see he didn't want to be helped?" Darren said with a note of urgency. "It was a form of suicide. If a loup-garou is not careful, it could be unintentional, but not for Chris."

They watched the wolf wander away, head low and tail sweeping at the fallen leaves on the ground behind him. "You have to realize," Darren went on, "that everything must be done in moderation."

"Then why shift into a wolf at all if there's the risk?" Katey demanded. "Why not just wait for that time of the month and only shift then?"

"It's not that simple either. We need that release every once and a while. The way it had been explained to me once was that the wolf inside needs a morale boost to stay active and alive." Darren looked at Katey with all seriousness in his eyes, as if this bit of information was even more important than what he had just told her. "If we don't shift enough, the wolf becomes weak and will no longer support our physical bodies. Our joined DNA would disintegrate. For those of us who have been alive for so long, it's vitally important that we make sure the loup-garou gene does not go dormant. If it does, we will stop changing altogether and become human."

Katey's jaw dropped. "So, that's the cure to being loup-garou?"

Darren shook his head. "It's not a cure. It's a death sentence. We're allowed to stay alive for ages, as long as we remain loup-garou. If that gene becomes dormant, if the wolf inside loses vitality and grows weary, then we will too. Without the wolf part of our genetic code, we die. They don't have an exact name for it, but we call it the Disease. I've known many loups-garous who have fallen prey to this Disease. The first signs are when the older loup-garou begins to have trouble changing into his wolf form. Then, they stop changing altogether. Sometimes it takes years after that, sometimes days, but the end result is a painful death by accelerated aging."

"So, if you don't shift enough, your wolf dies and takes you with it. If you shift too much, the wolf takes over, and you die while it lives." Katey looked away. "What about Logan? He doesn't shift at will."

Darren had wondered about that for a long time, and he still didn't have an answer. He could see the fear in her eyes, but there was little he could say to make her any less scared. "Logan is a special case. His loup-garou gene isn't dominant at all. There's no way it could fully take over or die. It's like a recessive gene. We still don't fully understand his biology."

Katey didn't seem convinced as her stare glazed over and her chest rose and fell a little more quickly in her moment of panic. Darren placed his hand on her shoulder. "Logan is going to be just fine, Katey. The Disease never takes a loup-garou as young as Logan. There's still time for him to learn to shift on his own and prevent the Disease."

She swallowed and shook her head. "No, I'm not so much worried about him. It's just... When I changed last night, I wanted my wolf to fully take over. I even begged her to because I wanted to shift so bad, but she wouldn't let me fade like that. She wanted us to be conscious together." Katey lifted her chin. "Maybe she did it because she knew if I just let her take over, that I'd disappear forever too."

"It wouldn't happen after one time," Darren assured her. "It'd have to be dozens of times consistently."

"But what if my wolf was looking out for me like that, you know?"

The way she spoke so passionately about her wolf, the way she was convinced it was truly a merging of two souls within one body, it was almost enough to change Darren's mind again. He had never experienced that kind of bond with his wolf to think it was looking out for him. He'd never known anything from his wolf except the urge to hunt, feed, and run free. Perhaps this child, this savior of the loups-garous, could teach him something for a change.

"I bet she was looking out for you," he replied.

"What's going to happen to Chris?" Katey asked.

Darren let his hand drop as he looked back at the wolf digging into the dirt over by the protruding roots of a tree with his massive, powerful paws. "A pack in Wyoming had been willing to take him under their protection. They have a reserve up there for loups-garous like Chris, but Tessa wanted to keep him close by for a little while. She still hasn't been able to let go of the fact her husband isn't there anymore."

A moment of thoughtful silence had passed before Katey pried a little further. "Was there something going on between you and Tessa?" she asked. "I saw the way you were looking at her in the gift shop."

Darren guffawed. "No, there's nothing between the two of us. We grew close out of necessity, and I was a friend of Chris'. That's all it ever was."

Katey slid a sly glance his way. "I could tell your hearts were beating pretty fast."

He proudly huffed air from his nostrils. "We just hadn't seen each other in a while."

Katey elbowed him. "I promise I won't tell the others," she spurred.

Darren gave her a look. "I've never had feelings for anyone but my wife and I never will."

As if she had unknowingly slipped her hand into a vat of vipers, she withdrew in submission. "I'm sorry. I wasn't thinking."

He rubbed the back of his neck, feeling the tight stress knots beneath his skin. "It's all right, Katey. It's been quite a long time since they... since they passed on and I've done my share of grieving."

Darren could feel her eyes fix upon him, burrowing into him as if to wrench out the story. He would not meet her stare for anything, lest she see that he wasn't telling the whole truth.

"I know Dustin told you about how my wife and daughter died. I don't have to tell you a second time." He wasn't sure why he worded it that way as if to justify his silence.

"I don't want to hear the story again," she said, her voice as light as a caressing feather. "I want to know their names."

Her request was so peculiar that Darren couldn't abstain from looking at her any longer. There was no mocking in her expression, no sign she wanted to use their names against him later. There was no reason to suspect Katey had any malicious intent with the names at all.

"My wife's name was Eleanor. I called her Ellie whenever I was cross with her. Our daughter's name was Lucy, short for Lucianna."

He was sure the only other person in the world who knew that was Dustin, but only because he had personally met Darren's family before they died.

Katey's hand found its way to his and gripped it tightly as a new smile, full of warmth and appreciation, shined his way.

When her skin touched his, the world around him faded and his eyes were clouded by a sudden vision. They came in flashes, as fresh and real as if they were happening in that moment.

Their cottage in the heart of the French countryside, burning. The cinders and flames blazed in the dawn. Darren rushed to the door, shouting out his wife's name. Then she lay in his arms, her delicate flesh bloodied and charred. Her clothes were saturated with smoke and her dark hair singed by the heat. She whispered a word. Centuries ago, he hadn't been able to hear that word or understand her in the midst of the roaring flames. Now her voice was clear as a bell.

"*Dustin,*" she croaked.

Darren blinked, and the image of his wife dying in his arms was gone. In its place was the image of two men traveling through the woods. They held guns and talked of searching for someone. He saw their faces, as vivid and sharp as if they had been inches from his nose. He had never seen them before, but somehow, they still seemed familiar.

When they spoke Dustin's name, Darren blinked and shook the visions away.

When he opened his eyes once more, Katey was in front of him again, a look of befuddlement on her face.

Darren's head throbbed violently, his temples pounding with pain. Inside, he felt the stirring of his wolf. Gnashing teeth and growls filled his mind and the control he had once been able to call on for centuries, was gone. Seeing his wife in his arms, hearing her voice again after so many years, had triggered something within him that he detested.

A violent rage swept through his soul. Darren snatched his hand from Katey's and bolted a few yards away, his teeth bared and eyes golden. Katey's eyes went gold in defense, but she didn't move.

"What did you do?" Darren growled, crouched down like an animal ready to strike or run.

Katey wagged her head and held her hands up in surrender. "I didn't do anything, Darren."

He wanted to roar, wanted to shout and demand an explanation for the strange visions. She had to have done something. Darren had been fine before she touched him.

Katey began to slowly rise to her feet, and Darren bristled in agitation. As if she were approaching a skittish colt, Katey came toward him. The wild wolf that lurked just inches beneath the surface didn't want her to come close. Didn't want her to touch him again.

He snapped at the space between them like a beast, but Katey barely flinched. Behind it all, Darren knew something was wrong and fought for hold of his humanity again, but whatever had consumed him could not be reasoned with.

Darren didn't want Katey any closer, lest he did something he would regret. This had never happened before. Even if it had, then it was a few centuries ago and too far back for him to even care to remember. Nothing had provoked the wolf so suddenly as this before.

Before he realized it, Katey knelt in front of him and touched his cheek with her fingertips.

The effects of her touch spread through his body, subverting his blood like the antidote to the venom she had put there herself. The wolf quieted his growls, and the golden eyes disappeared. Darren felt the peace and balance return to his body, but every tense muscle ached and burned. It took a great deal of strength to keep himself from falling to the ground.

Katey must have seen this and helped to steady him on his feet. "What happened?" she asked.

Darren squeezed his eyes shut as his muscles and joints began to heal themselves and the wolf receded back into the darkness. "I don't know. I..." he paused, wondering if he should tell her about what he had seen and what she had somehow unknowingly caused. He thought better of it. He needed to take this up with the loup-garou his visions had spoken of. "I think tonight is my night for the shift. We should go home now. There's nothing more I can teach you here."

Katey nodded and helped him to his feet. "Should I drive?" she asked.

Testing his legs by shifting his weight from one foot to the other, Darren shook his head. "No, I think I'm all right." With any luck, Katey would believe his lie.

CHAPTER 9

Katey took her time folding her shirts, making each motion as slow and precise as possible. It was the only thing to distract her from the confusion. Ever since they got in the car and made their way back home, Katey found herself replaying what happened between her and Darren at the wolf preserve. Not only was she thinking about Chris and his tragic decision to let his wolf side destroy him, but also about what she had done to Darren.

Although he wouldn't admit what it was, Katey couldn't deny she had unknowingly triggered something in her alpha. She had never seen him so savage. Darren had always been calm, composed, and quietly powerful, but when she asked for his wife's name and touched his hand, all the facades of control broke and Katey wondered if Darren would shift into his wolf form right there in the enclosure.

Yet, when she touched him again, Darren's hackles were soothed, and his human side took over once again. Katey hadn't meant to do it and hardly knew what she had done to be the catalyst. She refrained from even coming close to Darren for the rest of the day and left him alone to deal with whatever it was he personally experienced. He hadn't left the billiard room since they came home and Katey was too terrified to press him any further.

Instead, she stayed in her room and began to pack her things, only taking a break to fix herself a meal. The sun was beginning to set now, and the task of packing was almost complete. She hardly noticed the sounds of a vehicle pulling into the driveway and footsteps through the house. By their scents, she knew it was Ben, Dustin, and Logan, but she wasn't in the mood for company.

That didn't stop Logan from charging into her room. Katey held out her hands to keep him at bay as he rushed forward to embrace her. After their talk that morning in the kitchen, it seemed that all had been pardoned between them. The biting words were in the past, and if they were to cooperate that night on their way to the safe house, they both knew that apologies had to be made.

Now, another problem stood in their way, and Katey didn't know how to fix it.

"Don't touch me," she warned, taking a few steps away from her fiancé.

Logan staggered at her request and gave her a mixed look of hurt and puzzlement. "What's wrong?" he asked.

"Just don't touch me," she repeated, unsure how to even begin to tell him what had happened earlier that day.

"What did Darren do to you?" he insisted, his tone deepening.

"He didn't do anything to me," she said, hoping that she was right. "It's what I did to him." The words sounded so strange and self-condemning, although she didn't know exactly what she could be condemning herself for. No one had been hurt, but somehow, Katey felt as if she had violated Darren's boundaries.

Logan waited for a better explanation, but Katey had nothing to give. After a tense moment, he reached out his hand to touch her trembling fingers. She recoiled, squeezing her arms against her chest, and backed up into her writing desk. The edge of the wood bit into her lower back. She was trapped and vulnerable, and Logan knew it.

Heedless of her warnings, he pursued her and wrapped his fingers around the hand that was tucked under her chin. Katey watched his eyes for any sign of gold or beastly rage but was met with nothing short of devotion.

Katey let herself be pulled into his arms and melted against him, overwhelmed with relief. Perhaps what had happened with Darren wasn't her fault after all, unless it was a one-time freak accident. At least she wouldn't have to deny Logan's warm touch for all eternity.

He smoothed out her hair and kissed the crown of her head as he always did when she was upset. "What happened?" he asked, his voice tender and inviting.

Katey told him about Chris, and all that Darren had shown her at the preserve.

"Did you know Chris?" she asked as she nuzzled against his chest.

"I met him once before he turned wolf, but I know he and Darren were fairly close."

Katey looked up into his icy blue eyes. "You know about the Disease if you don't shift?"

A shadow passed over Logan's face, and he nodded. "Yes, I know, but you don't need to be worried about me. I'm going to start trying again."

"But what if it's too late? What if you can't shift on your own now because you haven't done it in so long?" It was difficult to keep the ribbon of panic out of her words.

Logan shook his head. "We only need to be worried when I stop changing altogether."

Katey hugged him tighter. "And here I thought we were impervious to most things."

A small smile pushed its way forward, and Logan dipped his head down to touch noses. "You still have a lot to learn," he whispered. "I don't see how any of that has to do with us touching."

A grim mantel fell over Katey once again, and she slowly pushed herself back to get a better look at his face. "While Darren and I were in the enclosure, something happened. I touched him and he almost beasted out on me. I don't know what I did, but I touched him again, and he was all right."

Logan turned pensive for a moment, assessing what she had told him and then shrugged. "Perhaps it was your incarnated spirit of peace that did it."

"But if it's supposed to be peaceful, why would it make him so mad that he let his wolf out for a minute?"

"I don't have all the answers, Katey. I'm sure no one does. You're unique, so we're kind of making this up as we go."

Katey didn't want to accept that she would constantly suffer these strange phenomena for the rest of her life. There had to be some ancient manual somewhere, some volume of texts or scriptures to tell her what she had to do and what she was capable of. Anyone who knew was long dead, and any hope of understanding was buried in ruins somewhere if they existed at all.

A sound floated down the hall and into Katey's room. Logan straightened up and turned to face the melody. Katey's lips curled into a wide grin when she realized exactly what it was.

"What in hell fire is that noise?" Logan grumbled.

She tugged at Logan's jacket sleeve and giggled. "Dustin," she whispered before skipping out of her room and down the hall toward the bathroom. The door was closed, with a little steam cloud rolling out from underneath. Through the pattering of water on the shower floor, Katey heard Dustin's baritone voice singing in his lovely Irish brogue.

"O ne'er shall I forget the night, the stars were bright above me, and gently lent their silv'ry light when first she vowed to love me. But now I'm bound to Brighton camp kind heaven then pray guide me, and send me safely back again, to the girl I left behind me."

Logan joined her, his head tilted toward the door as he listened with a screwed-up face of bewilderment. Katey pressed her finger to her lips, enjoying the moment too much for him to ruin it. The rhythm of the ballad was slow, but bouncy, reminding her of rolling green hillsides and everything that personified Ireland.

"Her golden hair in ringlets fair, her eyes like diamonds shining. Her slender waist, her heavenly face, that leaves my heart still pining. Ye gods above oh hear my prayer to my beauteous fair to find me, and send me safely back again, to the girl I left behind me."

Katey watched Logan's expression shift from confusion to something somber like he knew exactly who Dustin was singing about. Katey straightened and felt the joy slip away when she realized that Dustin wasn't singing in joy, but in mourning.

She remembered something about Dustin losing his first wife, but she had never asked about the circumstances. How could such a beautiful song, sung so pleasantly, be about anything but happy times and laughter?

Dustin's voice was in mid-stanza when he suddenly stopped. The void of music in the air left Katey feeling slightly empty and dazed as she snapped out of her thoughts. She opened her mouth to compliment Dustin, but Ben interjected.

"Guys, you better get down here!" he commanded from downstairs, a note of wariness in his voice.

Logan sniffed the air, and his eyes went wide before he rushed toward the stairs. Katey followed, leaving Dustin to cut his shower short.

When they arrived downstairs, Katey tested the air and smelled the faintest whiff of sulfur.

Vampires.

The sun had sunk below the tree line, but there was still enough light to make it difficult for vampires to come out of hiding just yet.

She stopped on the last step and watched as Ben kept his eye on the door, a loaded revolver trained in the same direction. Darren had made an appearance, clad in comfortable sweatpants and a white shirt, and a rifle raised to his shoulder, pointed down the length of the foyer. Katey could see his alert eyes glowing gold.

Without asking any questions, Logan picked up his own gun from the stash near the kitchen - a more modern model - and checked the magazine.

"What are you all doing?" she cried as she made her way to the front door. "We're at peace now, you shouldn't be pulling out your guns at the first sign of a vamp."

Logan darted forward and blocked her path.

"Katey, go upstairs," Darren ordered, not taking his focus off the front door for one moment.

The doorbell rang, and the tension in the room cracked like a mirror put under too much pressure. Everyone looked to the front door and waited in uneasy silence. Katey wondered about the traditional myth that vampires had to be invited in. Not one occurrence during her time at the castle confirmed or denied that myth. From the thread of confusion shared among the others, she knew this must have been odd behavior at the very least.

Katey sidestepped Logan, hoping to catch him off guard, but he blocked her again. This time, Ben went for the door, one hand gripping the ivory handle of his revolver. He clicked the hammer of the gun back as he placed his hand on the doorknob.

The idea of violence breaking out in her own home set her teeth on edge. She was supposed to be the bringer of peace and harmony, and her pack was ready to bring that all out of balance again. She readied herself to dodge past Logan. If she could make it to the door fast enough, she might have been able to intercept their guest and ensure their safety.

He peeked out the narrow window beside the door, and his shoulders rolled back in relief. Ben sighed, and glanced over his shoulder at the others with a look of utter annoyance. He swung open the door and eased the hammer forward on his gun.

An elderly man stood on the front porch, a black cape draped around his body and hood sheltering his face from the fading sunlight. Beneath the cloak, Katey saw a familiar ally, whom she thought she wouldn't see again for a while.

Michael smiled warmly and waited for Ben to invite him in with a casual gesture.

Logan also relaxed and shoved the muzzle of his gun down the back of his pants while Katey slipped past him.

"This is a fine welcome, isn't it?" Michael teased, looking at Darren who had his gun still braced against his shoulder and fixed on the old vampire. Clearly, they didn't get a chance to meet at the resort in Alaska when he and the others delivered her to the clinic to recover from her death experience. If Darren had, he wouldn't have been pointing a gun at him now.

"Darren, this is Michael. He's my grandfather on my mother's side."

The alpha didn't even flinch. "How do you know?"

Michael stepped inside and tucked back the hood to reveal his weathered and wrinkled face. The shock of white hair showed his age, but the sparkle in his wise brown eyes showed a kind and gentle soul. It was no wonder that the spirit of peace would choose him to gather allies for the assembling of the council. He had a charming nature to him that Katey had sensed from the very beginning, even before she knew who he was and her relation to him.

For a moment, she had hoped that perhaps Michael would be the one to explain some things to her. He had known that loup-garou females existed at one time. He had told her so in the library at the castle in Alaska. Michael also knew about the prophecy that she was to fulfill. If anyone knew what she was supposed to do, it was him.

"I was the one who rescued her from those who... dealt with her parents' rebellion against the old ways." His old voice was deep and touched with an accent that sounded foreign, but Katey couldn't place its origins. "While they were executing my daughter, I made sure Katey would be taken care of by one of my maidservants."

Darren didn't lower the gun as Michael moved forward, his heavy boots thudding against the wood flooring. Ben closed the door and followed him, but didn't seem concerned.

Logan, Dustin, and Ben were there when Michael tried to stop Yaverik from continuing the battle in the castle that long ago morning. They also heard the orders concerning him and accepted his help when Katey came back to life after saving Logan. They all knew that Michael could be trusted, but all Darren had were stories and testimonies from the others. He hadn't experienced Michael firsthand.

Michael finally stopped when the barrel of the gun rested against his broad chest. Katey was sure that Darren hadn't blinked in the last few minutes since the alarm was raised. They stared one another down, neither willing to give an inch to the other. They all seemed surprised that Darren hadn't pulled the trigger yet.

"Why are you here?" Darren asked, the hostility palpable in his tone.

"I'm here to see my granddaughter, of course." Michael's jovial voice was quite the opposite of Darren's. Hopefully, the alpha wouldn't take it as mocking.

"Who else is with you?"

"I have my driver outside and a dozen men guarding the house."

"Why?" Darren tightened his finger on the trigger.

"I heard there were hunters in the area and I wanted to make sure that this place would be secure. I've also dispatched men throughout Crestucky to do the same."

"How did you know where we were?"

Michael grinned. "Don't be mad, but your good friend, John, helped me. When I told him that I needed to give my progress report to my granddaughter, he was more than cooperative in letting me know where to find you."

Darren growled and cursed John's name under his breath. "Were you followed?"

"My friend," Michael laughed, "we have our own hunters to watch out for. I have spent centuries mastering how to become invisible. I was not followed."

"I'm not your friend," Darren growled, his teeth bared in aggression.

Michael lifted his hands. "My apologies."

Dustin came trotting down the stairs, wearing a pair of sweats like Darren's and a black shirt, paused at the bottom, and groaned, probably feeling the same annoyance that Ben did. "Darren, what are you doing? Don't be pointing a gun at him!" Dustin chided as he pulled out his own gun that he had hidden behind his back and slammed it down on the kitchen counter.

Katey stood beside Darren and reached out to touch his shoulder, but thought better of it and gripped the rifle instead and gradually lowered it until it was pointed to the floor. Darren put up little resistance, and she wondered if it was because he believed Michael's story, or if it was because Dustin was the one telling him to stand down.

Darren straightened and lifted his chin, his glare still searching Michael for any hint of deception. Michael was no longer concerned about the alpha and turned to Katey.

"I trust you're doing well?" the old vampire asked, oblivious to everyone else in the room and the obvious discomfort amongst them.

Katey smiled weakly and nodded.

In another life, she might have grown up with Michael close by. He might have visited on holidays. He would have been there for every birthday and spoiled her with gifts. He would have been present for every major event in her life like any normal grandparent. Instead, the man that stood before her was her only living blood relative that she knew of and she wasn't sure how to act. Should she hug him? Shake his hand? Or should she continue to stand there like a fool, waiting for a cue or sign to tell her how to behave?

The cue came when Michael held out his arms, offering a hug if she should want it. Katey took the chance and dove into him with the zeal of an innocent child. Despite the stench of sulfur seeping from his skin, she detected the scent of peppermint and the crisp aroma of cologne. This was not how she expected a vampire to smell up close.

Michael's arms encased her for only a few seconds, but it was enough to establish the bonds of their new relationship. Katey stepped back, and Logan came up behind her.

"I don't know if you two have formally met, but this is – "

"Logan," Michael said and offered out his hand to Katey's fiancé. "We exchanged a few unfriendly words last month, but not much else."

Logan was hesitant at first but firmly shook Michael's hand. "I was a bit distracted by the situation. I didn't have time for pleasantries."

"That's completely understandable." Michael looked to Ben and Dustin and gave his respective nods. "It's good to see you all again and in such good health."

Despite his cordial greetings, the energies of the room were savagely different. Katey could sense the prejudicial anger pulsing from Darren. The others were wary but not as hostile as the alpha. Despite the hesitant welcome, Michael was not offended in the least. Katey, feeling that she was the link between them all, wanted to make this meeting easier somehow. Her inner wolf gave her guidance, but not enough to tell her how to handle mediation between these people who meant so much to her.

"How is your apprenticeship coming along?" Michael asked Katey, pulling her from the dizzying anxiety.

"If you mean my training, it's going very good. I just learned to shift on my own last night."

Michael grinned, the wrinkles in the corner of his eyes deepening. "Very good. I imagine that must have taken quite a while to master."

Katey beamed under his praise, the exact thing she had wanted from her mentors all along. "Actually, I've only been trying for the past few weeks since we got back from Alaska."

Michael seemed slightly confused and glanced at the others for an explanation.

"It normally takes us years to nail down that skill," Dustin joined. "So, it is definitely a big deal that Katey was able to shift so quickly."

"Well, then I am doubly proud of you, Katey." Michael's smile widened to reveal the pointed tips of his vampire teeth. "I knew you were special, but if you were able to do something that only seasoned werewolves can accomplish, I'm sure that nothing is impossible for you now."

Katey made no effort to hide her blush.

"Katey did this against my orders," Dubose added, casting a shadow over the conversation. "As you know, hunters may be close by, and I told everyone to stay indoors. She snuck out and changed without our protection."

Michael's face grew dour and he looked to Katey with renewed somberness. "Is this true?"

"Yeah, but nothing happened."

Michael reached out and placed his hand on her shoulder. "You must be more careful, Katey. You are not just a werewolf or a young lady. Many people depend on you. If anything should happen to you, the world would be lost."

Katey felt the heavy weight of responsibility settle back on her shoulders. Michael was right, and once again she felt ashamed for her thoughtless actions.

"I'll never do anything like that again," she said slowly as if to convey her true sincerity with every word. Whether they would accept it, she didn't know. "You mentioned something about a report?"

Michael nodded and moved around Katey, his steps slow and lumbering. "Yes. I have been contacting the various covens in North America, informing them of your arrival and the council."

He positioned himself in front of Darren's recliner as if he were about to sit. The alpha let out a deep and threatening growl that was not only heard but felt by everyone in the room. Katey gulped as the sound vibrated in her chest.

Michael understood the sign of dominance and made a face to show his mild aggravation before moving to the sofa. "Some of the coven leaders are eager for peace, as I am. Others did not take kindly to the news."

"What do you mean by that?" Logan asked.

Michael sighed as he let himself relax in the seat. "There are still some individuals who share Yaverik's warmongering ideology. They crave violence and revenge, regardless of the truth. Most of them also understand how Katey came into existence and despite our seemingly eternal nature, some prejudices remain the same. When the vampire community heard of Adam and Jane's union, they called it an abomination against the natural order of things and they still believe that to this day."

"Adam and Jane?" Katey asked, finding it difficult to breathe under what she suspected.

"They are your parents, Katey. I thought I had mentioned their names before."

Katey closed her eyes and let the names float through her mind. *Adam and Jane.* It felt as if these mere words would complete their identity. The players in her dreams finally had a name, and she could speak them confidently to anyone.

"Wait." Darren stepped forward. "What was Adam's surname?"

Michael pondered for a brief second, then replied, "Swenson, I believe."

Darren reeled and ran his fingers through his hair. The others had similar reactions. Logan went pale. Ben leaned against the far wall and stared vacantly ahead, lost in his own thoughts. Only Dustin and Katey remained clueless.

"What's the matter?" Katey asked of her fiancé, touching his arm as if that would bring him out of his shock.

Logan looked down at her, his eyes searching her face. "I knew your father, Katey."

"As did I," Ben muttered.

"When did you meet Adam?" Darren queried, obviously familiar with the man as well.

Ben blinked and looked at his alpha. "We served in Vietnam together. He was the other loup-garou who got captured with me and served as a radio operator. How do you know him?"

"We spent some time together in Devia before it fell to the hunters," Darren replied.

"He tried to train me during the time I spent there," Logan added, his usually strong voice shaken by ghosts of the past. "I had no idea he had died."

Dustin charged in. "Did you say his last name was Swenson?" Michael nodded. "You've got to be kidding!" he exclaimed. "Was Geoffrey his father?"

Michael's eyebrows shot up. "Yes, he was. Were you acquainted with Geoffrey?"

"We met in passing once in Italy before I came back to the States." He shrugged his brows. "Interesting guy."

Ben started. "Geoffrey Swenson? I think I met him out west. I agree. Interestin' guy. Strange, but interestin'."

Katey felt faint and quickly found her way to the unoccupied sofa before her legs could give out on her. "You all knew my father? And you two knew my grandfather?" she said, disbelief coloring her words. "And none of you told me?"

They helplessly looked at each other with mixed expressions, hoping someone would speak first.

"We had no idea who your father was, Katey." Darren staggered closer, his gaze studying her face, probably looking for any resemblance. "If you're Adam's daughter, then your innate connection with your wolf isn't surprising."

"I don't understand," Katey mumbled.

Logan joined her on the sofa, taking her hands in his. "Adam was an amazing loup-garou. He..." Her fiancé became too choked with the veneration to continue.

Darren picked up for him. "Adam and his father were adamant believers in the spiritual side of being a loup-garou. Adam was half Navajo, so his mother influenced a lot of his spiritual beliefs, and his father encouraged it. They focused on the connection between their human half and their wolf to achieve the kind of balance you have. You must have inherited his unique abilities."

Katey looked to the silently observing Michael and noticed the hint of a pleased smile. "And you have your mother's strong will," he said. "That was clear from the first moment I met you."

"You said her mother's name was Jane?" Darren clarified.

"My daughter's name is Jane Gennari," Michael proudly announced.

Now it was Darren's turn to blanch. "Gennari?"

"Did I stutter?" Michael quipped, raising a giggle from Katey in the intense, emotionally saturated moment.

Darren rubbed the heel of his palm into his eye and groaned. "This is too much for me on my night."

"It's your night?" Dustin questioned, clearly unaware of all that had transpired while they were out patrolling the city.

"Did you know my mom too?" Katey shrieked, hoping to gain more attention this way. Dustin was not about to change the subject on her.

Darren grumbled a curse. "I met your mother once. It was centuries ago in France."

A deep, critical frown formed between Michael's eyes. "When was this?"

For the first time since she had known him, Darren stumbled through his words. "It was an accident really. We were kidnapped by this madman, and I helped her escape."

Michael rose from the sofa and peered at Darren's face. After a moment, his eyebrows shot up. "Yes, I believe I did see you that night. My daughter kissed you before returning to me and our party."

"Kissed?" Katey squealed, unsure whether to be disgusted or amused.

The others chortled and spat out questions in rapid fire, none of which were answered. Darren put a stop to the madness by letting a fresh wave of authority wash over the room, calling for order amongst his pack.

"It was a very long time ago, and I was still a young boy. I never saw Jane after that night, but I am sorry to hear that she is no longer with us." Darren turned to Michael and inclined his head. "I'm even more saddened to learn about Adam."

Michael sighed. "As you say, it was a long time ago. We can't change the past, but we can learn from it, and with Katey with us, the world will be a much better place. Though Adam and Jane are gone, they have given us Katey and created a legacy like no other."

The air of excitement left the room as quickly as it had come, leaving Katey with a heart laden with wonder, worry, and too many questions.

CHAPTER 10

Michael continued to tell the others about the roadblocks he and John had encountered while spreading their message regarding the council. Katey didn't hear a word.

Her mind was still in a whirl. They had known her parents the entire time. They had known Jane and Adam for centuries. Her few dreams and biological and spiritual attachment to them seemed insignificant.

All this time, they had precious memories of her father and all she had were a few fleeting glimpses of who Adam was as a loup-garou. What stories could they tell her? Did he have dreams? Did he have a personality quirk that drove them nuts at times? Or was he as perfect in life as she made him out to be in death?

They all said he was a great loup-garou, but who was he as a man? His spiritual oneness with his wolf set aside, was he a good person? Did he help those in need? Was he a leader? An alpha? Did he ever marry before Jane? What did he do for a living? Darren, Logan, and Ben held the secrets Katey so desperately needed to hear, but when could she learn them?

Looking around at their engrossed faces as they listened to Michael, Katey wanted nothing more than to blurt out her questions and demand answers. She kept her lips tight. There was a time and place for everything. Right now - however much her belly burned with curiosity - was not the time to steal the stage from her grandfather. He was doing so well keeping their attention anyway.

The tension in the room was all but gone and her pack no longer felt as skeptical toward Michael as they did when he arrived. Everyone was seated now as if a council of their own were being held right there in the living room. Logan stayed close to Katey, their thighs touching on the sofa she had lowered herself into earlier. Michael and Dustin shared the other sofa while Darren took the place of honor in his recliner, and Ben perched himself on a barstool near the stairs. All their weapons had been set aside and out of arms reach.

For Michael's sake, Katey was glad they had decided to trust him. Maybe now, they could communicate like the civilized men they all were.

"The alpha in Wyoming seemed particularly pleased, but evidently I was the first vampire he had seen in over a hundred years. They hadn't a chance to develop animosity."

Darren nodded. "Joseph and his pack live in the mountains. That isn't surprising."

Michael smiled. "You seem to know quite a few alphas, Darren."

"I've been around for a while. He and his sons come to the gatherings in Alaska, but not as religiously as some do."

"He assured me that he would be present for the first gathering."

"Where are you planning on having this little shin-dig?" Dustin asked, stretching his legs out in front of him.

"Switzerland," Michael announced. "There is a castle in the Alps that can accommodate the vampire elders and many prominent alphas around the globe. We are only inviting those who wish to come, of course."

"How exactly are you pickin' the alphas?" Ben questioned. "There are probably thousands of them in the world."

"Through John's connections, we are only approaching one alpha from each of the states and countries that have the largest packs. John told me that once they return from the gathering, they will inform the smaller packs of what transpired at the council."

"That's still gonna be over one hundred alphas, plus all of the coven leaders?"

Michael raised an instructional finger against Ben. "A coven leader is not the same as an elder. I, for example, am an elder and hold sway over many coven leaders. There will only be a small group of vampires at the council to serve as representatives."

Katey blinked. "Wouldn't that leave the vampires outnumbered?"

"In a way, it would." Michael chuckled. "I've already had a few companions ask me what I'll do with all the dogs being underfoot."

Darren let out another warning growl, but not one near as threatening as before.

"Pardon my choice of words. They are not my own." Michael let out a breath. "But, it will be crowded. That is for certain. Some alphas may need to share rooms."

"Having that many alphas in one place could be tricky," Logan added.

Michael looked to Katey. "With the spirit of peace close by, I'm sure we will manage."

Katey wasn't too sure about that. She had been able to help avoid major fights among her pack at times, but never an entire castle of dominant loups-garous. With how well she had been able to keep the hostilities down lately, she doubted herself even more. "I hope the fact that they all know each other will keep them from fighting. You shouldn't put all your eggs in one basket with me."

Michael leaned forward, his arms propped on his knees. "Are you saying you don't think you'd be capable of defusing a fight if one should occur?"

"I'm saying that even if I tried, it might not do anyone any good." Katey shrugged. "Who would listen to me anyway? I'm just a kid."

Michael's eyes turned stony. "You're not just a kid, Katey. You're the – "

"I know, I know. I'm the one who's going to bring peace, but see how well I was able to keep everyone from turning a gun on you?"

Michael shook his head. "It's only because you don't know how to channel Tanatia yet."

"What?" Darren, Dustin, Ben, and Logan all asked in unison.

If Katey weren't as mystified, she might have asked the same thing or laughed at them.

Michael looked to them and paused before explaining, probably astonished by their question as if they should have known exactly who he was talking about. "Tanatia. She is the spirit that lives within Katey. Back at the dawn of our civilization, she was a princess, the first one to ever be born from a mixed pair."

"Mixed pair?" Ben asked.

"The king was a werewolf, and his mate a vampire. When Tanatia was born, it was clear that she was different from both races, yet alike in the same ways."

"What do you mean?" Logan questioned, leaning back against the sofa.

Michael straightened. "She could change into a wolf, as any werewolf could, but she could also drink blood without becoming ill. She was also an empath, as all natural-born vampires are."

"Empaths?" Katey whispered. So that explained why she could sense everyone's emotions and be so in tune with her own.

As Michael poured out all of this information, Katey could feel not only her own questions bearing on her mind but the ardent interest of everyone else in the room.

What civilization? Was it the era that Michael had told her about before? A place where vampires and werewolves existed in harmony with one another? Were there no other children who were born to mixed parents between then and now? If Tanatia was a princess, did that mean Katey was too? Above all, how did Michael know so much about these matters?

"Yes. I am empathic, and so was Jane."

Katey tilted her head, wondering how he had managed to keep himself so calm earlier when he arrived. The opposition in the house was enough to make her want to scream, and yet he had been able to smile and carry on as if nothing were wrong.

"So, vampires who are bitten and not born, they aren't empathic?" she asked.

"They are not. Quite the opposite. They are incapable of relating to humans on an emotional level."

Katey thought back to Yaverik and Martel - her old friend who had been turned into a vampire. She recalled sensing a change in him that she despised. Martel used to be caring and sensitive, but the vampire who danced with her at the castle was nothing like that. He had been playing her from the start, she was sure of it.

Perhaps his condition as a vampire was to blame, and not his mentors. A shadow of shame passed over her heart at the hateful things she had thought about him. Instead of disliking him, she pitied him and the terrible change he endured.

If Yaverik were turned into a vampire, it would explain his thirst for violence and war. If only that personality flaw could be reversed. If only there were a cure for those who suffered such a fate to be so careless and inconsiderate of those around them. She wondered how many who were attending the solstice celebration at the castle had been born a vampire and how many were bitten.

Then again, there was a natural design in the way born-vampires were empaths, while bitten-vampires were not. They were the yin and yang, the good and the bad within their race to help balance one another. Just like the loups-garous and rougarous.

"That must come in real handy when you have to kill someone, huh?" Dustin quipped, bringing Katey out of her ponderings.

Michael turned to regard Dustin with a look of impatience, the first he had shown all evening. "I'll have you know that in my eight hundred and fifty years of being on this earth, I have never killed a human being for food."

That staggering age gave everyone pause, but if Michael were telling the truth, that was a massive accomplishment. To live so long and never kill a single human in the throes of hunger must have been difficult. Katey felt a new respect for her grandfather's strong will.

"How did you survive then?" Katey asked.

Michael looked to her. "Animals and willing givers. I have never taken blood from anyone who did not want me to take it."

"So, you just had volunteers line up to give you their necks?"

Katey could sense that Dustin was pushing all the wrong buttons with Michael. She wanted to throw something at him just to get the beta to shut up and let her grandfather continue about Tanatia and Katey's role in this new scheme to save the world from war.

"Not exactly," Michael replied. "In the early years, we kept vassals or serfs. We treated them well in return for the nourishment we needed. After such a practice had become unacceptable, lovers and traveling companions, whom we call blood servants, became necessary."

"Lovers?" Ben dubiously inquired, an eyebrow raised.

"Yes. I suppose I've had as many lovers as any of you have had in your lives."

No one made eye contact except for Katey. She knew all too well that every loup-garou in that room had only one mate in their life; all dead and gone except for Logan's. Michael must have felt the subtle undercurrent of sorrow in the group and sighed at his misspoken words.

"How long will you be staying in town?" Katey asked, feeling the same thread of emotion and looking to shift attention away from disagreeable thoughts. "There's a lot I want to talk to you about."

Michael grinned. "I can imagine that you do. I'll be in town for a few days. If there were no objections, I planned to stay here for most of the evening."

"I'm afraid that won't be possible," the alpha said. Darren looked over his shoulder to the glass doors that led outside. Night had finally come, and Katey could see a speckling of bright stars on the horizon. He then turned back to Katey, looking worn and exhausted. "Are you packed?"

In the height of the excitement, Katey had completely forgotten about their plans to leave Crestucky. The sharp pain of separation from the only home she had ever loved returned to her chest, and she let out a long breath. "Not completely," she replied.

"Packed?" Michael asked, his forehead creased in a frown.

Ben stood to go upstairs, and Dustin was ready to follow.

"Katey, Logan, and Ben are leaving Crestucky tonight because of the hunters," Darren informed the vampire. He slowly rose from his recliner and scowled as if it caused him discomfort. "And tonight is my night to shift. Dustin and I will be leaving for the wood soon."

Dustin stopped at the foot of the stairs and turned to wait for instructions with his arms folded, while Logan gave Katey a squeeze and pushed himself to his feet.

"Leave?" Michael uttered the word as if he hadn't heard it before. "Did I not tell you that my guards were patrolling the house and the city? She is safe here. There's no need for her to evacuate."

Katey watched the two men, waiting with anticipation to see where this conversation led.

Darren and Michael stared at one another, dominance sparking between them. "I am her alpha and the safest place for her to be is away from the hunters, guards or not."

Michael stood. "I am her grandfather. I am concerned for her safety as well, but I can assure you that my guards are well trained."

"I don't know these guards and vampire hunters are much different than loup-garou hunters. I can't be sure they are up to the job."

"Then I will travel with Katey."

Crestfallen, Katey slumped back onto the sofa. For a moment, she wondered if Michael would have been able to convince Darren to let her stay. If he just pushed a little farther, Darren may have conceded.

"I can't be accountable for your life as well," Darren argued.

Michael laughed. "Sir, I am and always will be the only one responsible for my own life."

The alpha's face wrinkled with deep thought, and finally, he nodded. "Very well. If you want to go with her, then I suppose I can let Ben stay behind. We will need all the help we can get to look after the families that are still left."

"Will I still go with Katey?" Logan asked for clarification.

Darren nodded and massaged his temples with his palms for a moment. "Yes. You know the way to the safe house."

"What families do you speak of?" Michael asked, sliding his hands into his cloak pockets.

While Logan left to go upstairs to pack, Katey crossed her arms over her chest, waiting until the last possible moment to continue her own task of packing. Any extra stolen minute in Crestucky was worth being barked at by her alpha. Darren briefly filled Michael in on the Devian families that decided to stay, and Katey's mind went to work on a plan.

With Darren and Dustin out of the house, and Michael more lenient toward the idea of staying, perhaps there was a way Katey could flip the situation so she could stay one more night. The open event at the ballroom dance studio was still niggling in the back of her mind. Despite their argument on the subject the day before, Katey still wanted to go and shake off some of the stress that had been caked on layer by layer throughout the week. Not only that, but she wanted to see Lily. She had to know if her friend was all right and to let Lily know that she was safe as well.

She looked to the two leaders and waited for a pause in the conversation before she said, "Since there's added protection around town, could Logan and I go to the dance tonight?"

Michael and Darren looked at her in unison with questionable eyes, but each pair was inquisitive in a distinct way. Darren must have been wondering why she was still in the living room, while Michael might have wanted to know more about the dance.

"Absolutely not. We discussed this already, Katey," Darren replied with a note of edginess.

"What dance?"

Ignoring her alpha, she responded, "It's an event at this dance studio I used to volunteer at. They're having a party tonight, and I want to go for a few hours so I can see my friends."

Michael shrugged. "I don't see why not."

Darren snarled. "I told her she couldn't go for a reason. Every hour we lose in getting her to safety is just giving the hunters more time to find us."

"I could accompany her to the dance as a chaperone," Michael offered.

"I don't care if she had half the town serve as a chaperone."

"What if I went too?" Dustin piped in from the stairs.

Darren turned on his beta, lips curled up. "Are you more than half the town?"

"I'm just as big of a handful."

Katey saw Darren's hands ball into fists. "Now is not the time to test me, Dustin."

"That sounds like a wonderful plan," Michael remarked, oblivious to Darren's ire. "Katey, Logan, myself, and Dustin will go to the dance, and as soon as we return, we will leave. Ben can accompany you for your shift under we come back. Can you give directions to my driver, Katey?"

She was about to open her mouth when Darren growled again. Dominance pulsated from him, filling the room like a thick gas. She snapped her teeth together and settled back against the couch as if her alpha would strike out against her in his fit of frustration.

"I said Katey is not going and that's final."

The room fell silent, and Michael looked to Darren, an island of calm while Katey and Dustin were drowning in the power their alpha exuded.

Finally, the old vampire spoke. "Darren, I would like you to give me one logical reason why Katey cannot go to that dance for a mere hour. My guards, as unskilled as you believe them to be, are watching this town for any suspicious activity. If they see a hunter, they will call either myself or my driver. Dustin, whom I presume is your enforcer of the pack, will look after her. Logan, her soon-to-be mate who loves her enough to die for her, will be there to make sure no harm comes to her either. You can be sure that her grandfather will keep her safe as well. I've been waiting eighteen years to meet her and centuries to see this prophecy fulfilled. I would never let a mere human take her from me."

Darren was quiet for an indefinable amount of time and Katey could feel the anger regress with the wave of dominance. Slowly, the room regained its equilibrium, and they could breathe again.

The alpha stepped forward, becoming dangerously close to the vamp who was twice his age. "If something happens to her, I won't hold Dustin or Logan responsible. I will blame you, and nothing in this world will stop me from taking my vengeance."

A grin split Michael's face. "I would expect nothing else from her alpha."

Katey didn't have to wait to be told. Before Darren had a chance to change his mind, she bolted upstairs to pack for her trip and to get ready for the dance.

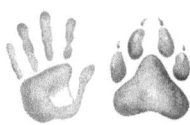

"Ben," Dustin spoke, "could you come down here? There's been a change of plans." He saw no need to shout at the omega, knowing that his ears could pick up every word they were saying in the living room from his bedroom.

Dustin looked to Darren, analyzing the way the alpha wiped his brow and swallowed hard every few seconds. The shift was pressing forward, and it wouldn't be long before he had to leave.

If Michael was the empath he claimed to be, the vampire must have sensed the trouble as soon as he walked into the house. As long as Katey and Logan could pack their bags quickly enough, Ben could usher Darren out into the backyard where he could let the wolf out safely. If what Michael said about having guards around the house was also true, Ben would have a handful in keeping Darren's wolf under control. The stench of vampires was no more appealing in their human forms than in their wolf forms, and their presence would not settle well with their deep-seated instinct to attack or flee from the bloodsuckers.

"Can I get you anything, Darren?" he asked. "Water? Meat? Draw a cold bath?"

Michael let out a short, tickled chuckle, but Darren was not amused by his beta's humor.

"No." Darren looked at him, brown eyes flecked with bits of gold that glittered in the living room light. "I need to speak with you... in private."

A cold streak shot down Dustin's spine. Whenever Darren wanted to speak in private, it never meant anything good. He nodded just as Ben came down the stairs.

"Keep an eye on him," Darren instructed the omega before leading Dustin into the back billiard room. It wasn't complete privacy, that was for sure, but it was out of sight from the others.

Dustin could hear Michael and Ben make casual conversation about Switzerland and the coming gathering, so he was sure that they would not be paying attention to whatever Darren had to say.

"Am I being written up for not unloading the dishwasher? I completely meant to do that before the night was over."

Darren growled, his eyes now fully glazed over by the wolfish gold. Dustin clamped his jaws together to keep from speaking out of turn again. His mouth had been throwing him on the bad side of two powerful men this evening, and it would only get worse unless he curtailed himself.

He had thought a little lightheartedness would help get the pack through this chaotic time. Ben and Logan seemed to appreciate his witty comebacks from earlier that day, and he knew that Katey was thrilled to hear him sing that folk ballad in the shower before Michael showed up. There was a distinct shift in the way Darren behaved. Perhaps the others couldn't see it, but Dustin knew his alpha well enough that something was not right – shift night or not.

"You make one more wisecrack, and I swear on my mother's grave that you will not be able to speak for a week."

Dustin felt himself sink into a submissive stance, knees bent and shoulders hunched ever so slightly. He tilted his chin, proclaiming his obedience, and waited. If Darren were swearing on his mother's grave, he meant business.

Darren sighed and rubbed at his flushed cheeks. "I'm sorry," he grumbled. "It's been a rough day."

Normally, Dustin would have made his agreement known. With Katey and Logan leaving, Michael's sudden appearance, and the sudden prematurity of Darren's shift night – which was not due for another three days – everyone was wound up.

"Today, I took Katey to see Chris." Darren rolled his shoulders to loosen the stiffened muscles. "Something happened. I don't know how to explain it."

Never in their centuries of knowing one another, had Dustin ever known Darren to be speechless. He always had a plan, had an explanation for everything. Whatever happened must have been too fantastic for words or for his logical mind to explain.

"We were beginning to talk about Ellie and Lucy, but I shot it down before it could go anywhere. You know I never talk about what happened, much less think about it." Darren ran his hand through his hair. "She asked for their names. I thought it would be harmless to speak their names after so long. I told her. Then she touched me and..."

Dustin straightened and watched his alpha's mouth hang open, the words just on the tip of his tongue.

With Darren's golden eyes filled with sorrow and pain, he said, "I... I saw her. I saw Ellie."

"What do you mean?" Dustin questioned, his core taut as he listened.

"I had a vision... No, I relived the moment when my wife died in my arms."

Dustin slowly slipped his hands into his jeans pockets, not sure what to say or how to elucidate Darren's experience. His alpha had always been the scientific type, rejecting all spiritual explanations for things that could be reasoned through, seen under a microscope, or touched with their own hands.

These flickers, these visions of the past, were not tangible or able to be studied. Dustin, sometimes tempted to believe in the fairy folk of his homeland, had no trouble in believing that something in Katey's touch had sparked the memory again. The power of names was undeniable, and perhaps that was what conjured Ellie's ghost in his mind again.

"But I remembered something that I couldn't recall at the time," Darren continued, his throat working. "I remembered that she muttered something just before she slipped away. At that moment, I was too distraught to understand what it was. When I relived the memory, the word was as clear as a bell." Darren looked up, locking eyes with his beta. "She spoke your name."

All color drained from Dustin's face. "I can't imagine why she would."

"Did something happen between you two that I don't know about?"

His eyes went wide. "Darren, I was still grieving for my own wife's death. Do you think I would have even wanted someone else's wife? As beautiful as Ellie was, she could never have replaced Cassandra."

Darren seemed to accept that truth. "Then why would she speak your name just as she was about to die? What made your name so significant that she would use her last breath to say it?"

Dustin threw up his hands in a helpless gesture. "I have no idea, Darren."

His eyes narrowed. "I saw something else that I have absolutely no memory of. Two men in the forest, searching for you."

Dustin opened his mouth to refute it, but he found that he had no comeback. "Two men looking for me? Did you know who they were?"

"I didn't, but I knew they were Irish by the way they talked. Were they friends of yours?"

That was even more puzzling, and Dustin shook his head. "I had friends in Ireland, but none of them would have followed me to France. Everyone in Glengarriff likely assumed I was dead too."

Centuries ago, Dustin had married his first wife in his hometown of Glengarriff. On his wedding night, the villagers only knew that Dustin had mysteriously vanished and left what was left of his wife marred and savagely ripped to pieces in their marriage bed. When Dustin awoke the next morning, covered in her blood, and miles away from home, he traveled back to town and saw Cassandra's funeral. Dustin hunted down his sister and she told him they all assumed it was an animal attack and that he was dead as well. It was then that he remembered bits and pieces of that night. It was no animal that killed her. He fled the country and never returned, not even in all his wonderings across Europe after he left Ben.

To hear that someone had pursued his trail all the way across the sea to France was humbling and disturbing. Who could have known the truth and been determined enough to see him hang and follow him all that way?

A face and a name came to mind and with it a flash of fear that was plain on his face.

Darren took a step closer. "You know, don't you?"

Dustin felt like a child, standing before an angry guardian, knowing that he was fully guilty. "My father-in-law, Samuel," Dustin said, his voice soft as the fluttering of dove wings. "He was always superstitious. Believed in the fae, leprechauns, banshees, everything. He even believed in faoladh, the wolf people."

"Would he have suspected you were a faoladh?" Darren probed.

Dustin shrugged. "It's possible."

"Would he have sent hunters after you?"

He felt his heart crumble in his chest. He didn't want to speak it, much less believe it. It was possible that Samuel would have sent a hunter after Dustin if he knew the right men. Between the time that he left Ireland and the time that Ellie and Lucy were murdered, it was possible that a couple of hunters could have found their way to France and tracked him to Darren's home in the country. What if those hunters were part of the massacre in Bordeaux? What if his arrival to France somehow tipped them off?

Dustin lowered his gaze to his shoes and felt the burden of their deaths weigh heavy on his soul. It was pure speculation, of course. If Katey could reproduce what happened millennia ago to cause a feud between the loups-garous and vampires, then she could certainly recreate the events that led to the murder of Darren's family.

But why? Why would she want to bring up old memories to a man who had accepted their tragic deaths so long ago?

Dustin looked up, the light bulb flickering to life in his mind. "So, it wasn't your fault... It was mine." A sadness clouded Darren's features in an indecipherable expression. "Samuel could have sent those hunters, and when they came to your cottage, they must have tried to get information from Ellie. When she refused, they killed her and your daughter and moved on to Bordeaux... The hunters killed your family to get to me. It had nothing to do with you."

"You led the hunters right to us, and you never told me."

Dustin took a step forward. "No, Darren. I never had a clue anyone was after me. You know how I left Ireland. Who would think to look for me at all? I didn't even know my father-in-law suspected me of being a faoladh. You have to believe me. If I knew that I was being followed, I would have distanced myself from you and Ellie the minute I suspected it."

Darren turned his face away, brows knitted together in a glare that Dustin didn't fully deserve.

All the grief, the anger, and the blame resurfaced after being shoved into the recesses of his memory for over two hundred years. Darren had to face the truth once again that hunters had killed his family. They were senseless deaths. The hunters lived on for many years later and probably died of old age in a warm bed somewhere, while justice dictated that they should have choked on their own intestines for murdering two innocent women.

"Don't stay silent, Darren. Yell, scream, anything but the silence. Hit me, kill me, do something. Don't fester in it."

Darren lifted his stare and his face contorted with pain and agony. Night was creeping along outside the walls of their home, and the wolf was itching to run and leave these terrible human emotions behind. "I can't kill you," he snarled. "You couldn't have known that the hunters were after you. Killing you won't bring Ellie back from the dead, and it won't change what those men did to her."

Wisdom won once again, but Dustin could still read the turmoil of grief in his alpha. Like the beta, it was his job to protect both him and their pack. How could he protect Darren from something as metaphysical as a bleeding heart?

"You need to get outside before you rip your clothes."

Darren let his remark slide and nodded as his face began to gleam with sweat. "You're right. Get Ben."

"Comin'." Dustin heard the omega dash from the living room to the billiard room, stripping his shirt off as he went.

"I'll take care of Katey and Logan," he assured Darren. "Don't worry about them."

Darren gave a hard look to his beta and nodded again. "I know you will, but it won't stop me from worrying about their safety."

Ben preceded his alpha out the side door that led to the gardens and grassy lawn beyond. From the gust of frigid air that slipped into the house, he could tell that the vampires had practically invaded the property. Michael had certainly kept his word and Dustin had every intention to keep his. He owed Darren that much after the terrible day he must have had.

CHAPTER II

"Don't think so much about it, Logan. Just relax and focus on the inside. Feel your inner spirit."

Logan curled his fingers into fists, feeling the bitter rage rise in his chest again. "I don't want to feel inside. I don't want to feel anything."

"You must always feel something," Adam said, his deep lilting voice like a pocket of calm air as Logan traversed through the storm. "You and your wolf will always be there, inside. Unless you learn to accept its presence, you will always be at war with yourself."

"But I don't want this!" Logan shouted, his voice echoing through the tree canopy high above them. "I don't want to have anything to do with it."

Adam's sage green eyes narrowed on his pupil. "Logan, this is your life. Your wolf is your life. To reject it is to reject yourself and the air you are breathing right now. It is by your wolf that your heart beats."

Logan felt that familiar wash of coolness fall over his eyes, and he knew the monster was just as irritated as he was. "Maybe I'd rather my heart stop beating altogether. Then I wouldn't have to feel this pain."

Logan blinked and stared out the window from the back seat of Michael's luxury SUV. The windows were tinted nearly black, but he could still see the faint orange orbs of street lamps and neon store signs as they drove toward the dance studio.

Michael's speech about the ancient civilization filled the car, entrancing everyone except for Logan. Yes, it was a fascinating concept, that loups-garous and vampires once coexisted in a perfect world free of war and prejudice. Logan's mind was on far more troublesome things than some fantastical utopia.

He chanced a look at Katey who was perched on the edge of the leather seats, leaning over until she could rest her forearms on the console between the front seats. She changed into a flowing black skirt and equally flattering blouse for the evening, her long brown hair cascaded down her back in that natural beachy wave style that most girls spent hours pruning in front of the mirror to accomplish.

Logan could distinguish the twists and curls of the streaks of blonde in her hair that he had given her after he turned her. It was done unconsciously, but along with giving her the gift of loup-garou, Logan had infused some of his own characteristics with hers. The same phenomenon happened to Ben after Dustin had bitten him. Ben's hair had once been blonde and thin but now was thick and brown like Dustin's. He also wondered how much of their personalities transferred in the process.

The lights from the dashboard illuminated her face and her engrossed expression clearly. The twinkle in her eye and the broad smile across her lips were a dead giveaway that she hung on Michael's every word. She had a right to.

Since Michael walked through the door, he had stolen Katey's interest with his knowledge of her past and future. He was the only one who knew who her parents had been from the start and the expedition to the ancient civilization he spoke of made him an authority on what was expected of the host for the spirit of Tanatia.

Logan watched her and listened to her questions, vaguely aware of Michael's answers. Her beauty hadn't changed, and she was the same woman that he fell in love with, but he could no longer react the same to Katey.

His heart throbbed urgently in his chest, and his palms sweated, but one little fact held him back from wrapping his arms around her waist to serve as the seatbelt she neglected to wear.

Katey was Adam's daughter.

Those words reverberated in his mind like a haunting reminder. In his youth, Logan had been rebellious and insufferable. Still reeling from the knowledge that the beast within him killed his parents, Logan wanted nothing more than to isolate himself from the world and attempt suicide until he couldn't feel that fiery presence of the wolf in his chest.

His new instincts wouldn't let him rest until he found a dominant wolf to latch onto and learn from. He found that wolf in Darren and Adam. Those first few months in Devia had been the most turbulent of his life, filled with tantrums and confusing contradictions in his mind that made no sense.

At the time, he rejected any help that Adam wanted to give. Hindsight shamed him for the way he tuned out sound advice that could have been vital to his training. Over the last century, he had wanted to seek out Adam and apologize for his unruly attitude and perhaps glean more wisdom from the loup-garou.

To know that he was eighteen years too late in reaching out, caused a resurgence of sullenness in Logan that he could scarcely restrain. He hated himself for being so headstrong. He hated the vampires for killing Adam and Katey's mother. He hated the cruel fate that his disobedience had made for him.

Yet, if Katey were anything like Adam, there was hope for him. Whatever wisdom she knew innately might prove useful to him and his efforts to change willfully and correct a mistake made long ago.

Then again, it posed a fresh problem for them as a couple.

Katey now appeared to him as something sacred and untouchable. She was the daughter of his former mentor, an idol within the society of loups-garous all over the world. There was no one who wasn't at least aware of Adam and his father, Geoffrey, and their uncanny ability to tame wolves with old-world methods such as meditation.

All the lustful thoughts and intentions he had toward Katey after they came home from Alaska now seemed even more sinful than at their conception. He no longer felt worthy to mate with the daughter of such a prominent loup-garou. He couldn't even change at will and Katey had already surpassed what other loups-garous had tried for decades to accomplish. Mating with her would have been like an uneducated stable boy marrying a princess. In some ways, she was a princess.

Logan felt humbled just to be sharing the same air with her. He sighed and passed a hand over his eyes, leaning against the car door and distancing himself from the temptation to touch her.

"Katey, sit back," Dustin ordered, giving a slight tug on the back material of her blouse.

She obeyed, and Logan could feel her eyes fall upon him. He refused to even look at her. She must have been aware that something was wrong, but there was no way he could articulate his feelings.

"We took meticulous notes while we were in the temple," Michael explained, "and managed to find some manuscripts written in the ancient language of the society. Yaverik and I later decoded them, but there were only one or two volumes that told us about Tanatia. Interestingly enough, in all of the council minutes, they pause for a moment of prayer to invite the spirit of Tanatia to preside over the meeting to ensure that the most peaceful agreement could be reached."

"Did the assassins who killed her ever stand trial?" Dustin asked, also enthralled by the story. "Or did they even have a justice system back then?"

"Actually, the king and queen did sentence them to death for killing their daughter, but as the legend says, Tanatia appeared in spirit before the assembly and pled for their lives. She was wise beyond her years before she was assassinated, but her appearance at the execution canonized her as the spirit of peace for the society."

"So even after they killed her, she asked her parents to be merciful?" Katey questioned, her attention now back to her grandfather.

"Yes. That's what makes her legend so extraordinary."

"So, if she was supposed to be like the guiding hand in all council decisions," she asked, "how did the feud even get started? Wouldn't she have intervened?"

Dustin huffed. "You talk like she's a god or something, having a divine influence over everything."

"In a way," Michael replied, "Tanatia was like a goddess, but just like all religions, she fell into obscurity. The werewolves and vampires of the civilization forgot about her as the centuries passed and when the war broke out, there was nothing to ground the people in mercy and understanding. The War Beast took the place of Tanatia in their minds and disassembled the society."

"War Beast?" she inquired. "What's that?"

Their driver, who happened to be human, pulled up in front of the ballroom dance studio. Logan could hear the lively music and laughter vibrating the windows of the building outside. Inside, humans mingled in groups and couples sat at tables with votive candles flickering in the middle of an elegant centerpiece.

"The War Beast is the polar opposite of Tanatia. He represented division, confusion, hatred, and every evil thing that plagued their society before Tanatia's time. It was a monster, neither werewolf nor vampire that rampaged through villages, doing unspeakable things to the inhabitants. It took an army of werewolves and vampires to subdue him. He was impervious to sunlight, silver, and death itself. It was only through their cooperation that the War Beast was weakened enough to be killed. Some believe, however, that his spirit still hovers over the earth, waiting for the right host."

Katey shivered. "So, kind of like an Antichrist?"

Michael turned around in his seat to face her. "Much worse, I'm afraid. This is why your appearance means so much to the world. Yaverik, before he came face to face with Tanatia, was ready to offer himself as a host to the War Beast."

"So, if Katey hadn't been there and did what she did –" Dustin began.

"The War Beast would be among us now, and the world would surely be destroyed. With our two feuding races as they are, they would not be able to unite together to capture the War Beast again. It's a lucky thing that not many people know of the War Beast. Besides Yaverik, I know many other vampires who would want nothing more than to herald in the Apocalypse."

"What a lovely thought," Dustin gibed.

The driver snorted a laugh but quieted himself after Michael shot him a look.

Katey blew out her cheeks, and Logan didn't have to touch her to know that she was trembling. Her distant and unfocused gaze told him that she was thinking about all Michael had said. Logan wanted to reproach the vampire for filling her head with far-flung worries that needn't concern her at present. They had enough to worry about with hunters on the loose. None of them needed to think of what would happen if this War Beast emerged.

Forsaking his previous hesitations about drawing close to Katey, Logan squeezed her hand in an attempt to comfort her.

Through it all, even if she were a vampire or a witch, or some other being that loups-garous abhorred, Logan still loved Katey with an abounding passion that transcended beyond sense. Their bond, formed early in their relationship, could never be denied or extinguished. Death was the only thing that could sever their ties, but Logan was sure that even death would not stop him from loving her into the afterlife or whatever awaited when the light was snuffed out in him.

If death couldn't stop his love for her, then a simple matter of her parentage wouldn't stop him either. Logan still felt the kernel of unease in his gut when she locked eyes with him. They were Adam's eyes; he realized that now. Green as the spring forest leaves and just as full of life. When would he be able to distinguish between who Katey was and the inheritance that Adam had left for her?

Certainly, she was her own person with her own ideas and passions. Yet, there were so many similarities that he hadn't noticed before. If he had been looking for them, Logan would have known that she was a child of Adam as soon as he laid eyes on her that night in the cemetery when they met.

Despite her nervousness, he saw the corners of her mouth pull into a smile. The strain between them was abated, but only for a moment.

"Did you two come here to dance or make goo-goo eyes?" Dustin's voice broke through as he opened the car door on his side of the back seat.

Logan opened his door as Michael was sliding out of his seat and with his hand still wrapped around Katey's, he assisted her out of the vehicle.

While they made their way to the front door, Michael advised his driver to come back in exactly one hour and tossed his cloak over the back of his seat. Beneath the cloak, Michael was dressed as if he knew they would be attending a dance. A crisp white button-down shirt was tucked into a pair of black slacks with an equally black vest over top of it. All that was missing was the claw-hammer tuxedo jacket.

Without the cloak, Logan could see what a strong and powerful man Michael was, even in his old age. In a fight, Logan wasn't so sure he could defeat the man, but Dustin or Ben would be more than a match against the vampire.

A breeze made the branches of the guarded trees that dotted along the sidewalk shiver and Logan could detect the faint scent of several vampires nearby. Their presence was nearly cloaked by the city smells of fast food joints and car emissions.

"Do you have vamps all over the city, Michael?" Logan questioned, the first words he had spoken since they left the house.

The elder vampire stepped up onto the curb and fell in next to Katey, opposite Logan and Dustin. "I told you I had my guards patrolling the city. Did you doubt my word?"

Logan hadn't necessarily trusted Michael since they first met in the castle after Katey was shot. In fact, he still struggled with the idea that vampires were their allies now, instead of their enemies. For Katey's sake, he accepted her grandfather's new place in their lives, but he didn't have to like it. With their innate powers of empathy, Logan was sure that they could both sense his intense dislike of the notion that they would have to work closely with the vampires.

"I didn't say that," he replied, turning his attention to the studio.

The last time he was there, Katey had just gotten out of the hospital, and she had twisted his arm into escorting her for the sake of a party just like this one. As they stepped inside, however, he could tell there was a distinct difference between the two events. The one the month before was somewhat organized, and Katey had served in the station of an instructor, alongside Lily and Forest.

Tonight, there were only a small handful of instructors that he didn't recognize from that time before and there was a DJ set up in a corner of the dance floor instead of a laptop and playlist blaring over the speakers.

When they passed over the threshold, Michael and Dustin slipped to the side and found a table away from the activity. Out of the two dozen guests present, only a few turned their heads to acknowledge the newcomers.

"Where's Lily?" Katey asked. "I don't think I even saw her car outside."

Logan scanned the room, but could only confirm her observation. "I don't see her either."

"Did she leave with Forrest?"

Logan met the eyes of a curious woman some distance away. She smiled in a coquettish way that incited disproportionate anger within him. He looked to Katey and bent low to plant a kiss on her lips.

Caught off guard by the act, she still didn't seem to mind and kissed him back, grinning beneath his show of affection.

He pulled away but kept their foreheads just barely touching. "He wasn't in the evacuations. I thought he left earlier."

Katey blinked and gave him a quizzical look as if she didn't understand the point of the kiss if he were only trying to continue the conversation. Logan glanced back to the flirtatious woman and saw she had turned away, just as he intended.

It didn't happen often, but Logan detested the way some women tried to make a pass at him and found the whole incident inappropriate. If the woman were worth it, they would win men's hearts with their personalities and not their unwarranted offers of shallow pleasure that wouldn't extend beyond one evening.

"Why would Forrest leave without her?" Katey asked.

Logan shrugged. "I don't know. I tried to contact him once, but his phone was disconnected."

"I was really hoping to see Lily at least. Do you think she left with him?"

"I'm sure they're both safe and well."

It wasn't a lie, but Logan believed it to be an uncertainty. Jacob said nothing about Forrest during their evacuations, and without being able to get a hold of the man himself, Logan had no idea if Lily even knew about the hunters. If she had known - or if Forrest planned to leave before they became involved in the evacuations - then it would have made little sense for him to leave behind his fiancé. Forrest knew as well as any of them how dangerous hunters could be. He would not have left his future mate behind to suffer.

He did know for a fact that Forrest was not one of the loups-garous that chose to stay behind and there was hope in that.

Katey pulled away and looked across the dance floor. There was a spark of recognition in her eyes and Logan followed her gaze to whom he presumed were the owners of the studio. They waved, and Katey returned the greeting.

"I'll let you socialize," he stated as he let his hand slip from her grasp.

A tiny whimper made its way from Katey's throat, but after a quick peck on the cheek, he strode away to join Michael and Dustin at the table. His heart was heavy to leave her, but mingling was never one of his strong suits, and he would only get in the way while she tried to have fun.

"You own a villa in Florence?" Dustin asked Michael just as Logan was taking a seat across from them.

"I do," Michael replied as he leaned back and made a steeple of his fingers. "The vineyards surrounding it yield some of the best wine you will ever taste."

"And, judging by your last name, you're Italian?" Dustin asked, mouth wide in a grin.

"I am. I was born in Florence, in fact. As far back as we can tell, the Gennari were some of the first inhabitants of Italia, even before the Romans."

"Fascinating. I spent some time in Florence. It's a gorgeous city."

Michael smiled. "It's a gorgeous country, Dustin. Rich with culture and history. It will be a sad day when Italia ceases to be the wonderful place that it is. After the council meeting, I plan to return to my home for a short while before coming back to the States."

"I imagine having to keep up with a house like that can be pretty tough."

Michael gave a dismissive wave. "With the proper passion and knowledge of old architecture, a seven hundred-year-old home is nothing to take care of."

Dustin smiled and propped his chin in his hand as he leaned on the table, thoroughly enthused. "Seven hundred years old."

"Of course. I had it commissioned as a wedding present for my bride. We were married for three hundred years." A whimsical look dawned in Michael's eyes and over the booming salsa music, Logan could hear the old man sigh. "She was a beautiful woman."

"Of your kind, I assume?" Logan asked, folding his arms over his chest as he leaned back in his seat.

"Yes, she was. Our families were close, and she and I grew up together."

Dustin lifted a finger to interject. "I was wondering how Katey's parents met. I never knew Adam personally, but would they not have crossed paths so easily?"

A nostalgic cloud hung over Michael as he spoke. "My daughter and I were not like others of our kind. We kept the company of werewolves, such as yourselves, quite often. I met Katey's grandfather under..." Michael made a face, "not so pleasant circumstances, but we found common ground in our love for the past and hunger for an understanding of the origins of our kind. He also knew of the prophecy and met with the spirit of Tanatia first-hand. I sometimes wonder if his belief in the spirits didn't come from that same experience.

"Anyway, a short time after the Great War began, we all met again – I, Jane, Geoffrey, and Adam." Michael smiled. "And the rest is – as you say – history."

Logan leaned over the table, the votive candle casting a dancing glow on his face. "So, you both knew about the prophecy, and you purposefully came together with your single children so they could meet?"

Michael chuckled. "I know what you're thinking, young man. No, this was not an arranged marriage. We met quite by accident while visiting a mutual friend. Adam and Jane were wary of each other at first, but later my daughter told me that she loved him from the moment she met him. There was no need to coax them."

Logan glanced over his shoulder and saw Katey laughing in a group while the owner told some anecdote about a dance competition a few years ago. So even from the beginning, fate had a hand to play in how Katey came to be with them. Logan did believe in making his own way in life some of the time, but he couldn't deny the obvious forces that were bringing together the masterpiece where Katey starred as the heroine, and he, merely a pawn. He played his part in changing her, but what else was there left for him? What role did he play in the grand scheme of things?

"Now, they were not able to marry for quite a while later, of course. They had to be discrete. I arranged for their secret meetings, but we were not sly enough for the coven Jane had joined at the time."

"They betrayed her," Dustin stated.

Michael nodded. "They did. As I said before, many of our kind believed their relationship to be an abomination. It was unnatural for her to love a wolf, but she did, and he loved her."

Logan let out a long breath and turned back to the others.

"Something bothering you, Logan?" Dustin asked.

With a cautionary glance to Michael, he replied, "I'm fine."

"Will you not dance with Katey?" the old vampire asked, his tone insisting.

Logan rolled his shoulders until he felt the joint pop. "I don't intend to."

He hadn't intended to dance with her the last time they were in the studio, but he did anyway, and both frightening and magical things happened that night between them.

Michael braced his hand against the table and rose just as a waltz melody began to drift from the speakers. "Well, if you won't, then I will."

Dustin let out a laugh as the aristocrat strode across the floor toward the group Katey was standing with. Logan grew hot with embarrassment as the old vamp upstaged him.

When Michael approached, all eyes turned to him in fascination. He offered out his hand to Katey, his body bent forward in a regal and gentleman-like fashion. She smiled and placed her hand in his before they walked onto the dance floor.

With perfect poise, they stepped to the soft ballad as elegantly as any professional dancing couple. Perhaps it was from her vampire genes that Katey inherited her natural grace.

"Why don't you want to dance? I thought you liked dancing with Katey?" Dustin leaned forward as if that would screen off their conversation from the rest of the studio.

Dustin had always been the one for Logan to confide in when he had no one else to turn to. How could he possibly understand Logan's dilemma with Katey? He never had to court or marry a woman so far above his class that it was almost blasphemous.

Logan shrugged. "You know I've never been one for dancing."

"Then why did I waste my time in teaching you if you were never going to?"

Logan looked away, watching Katey and Michael glide across the floor. Their lips were moving, but he could only hear unintelligible whispers. They had their own conversation, but whatever they were saying was intended to be private. His eyes narrowed into slits.

"Well," Dustin continued, "if they start playing 'Rocky Road to Dublin,' I'm tempted to get up and dance a reel myself."

Logan cracked a smile, despite himself and slid an unsavory look to Dustin. "If you get up and start tapping your heels together like some leprechaun, I'll deny any association with you."

"How are you, my dear?" Michael whispered almost too softly for Katey to hear over the music and voices that surrounded them.

They continued to step in perfect time with the symphony and Michael impressed her with his superior talent. It was the first time Katey had danced since that night at the castle when she waltzed with Martel and howled in front of the assembly of vampires. This time, the joy was there, but she knew how to temper herself and her wolf.

Katey made a face. "You don't have to ask that. You know how I'm doing."

Michael's eyes sparkled with amusement. "Katey, I may have a sense of how you are feeling, but only you can explain why."

The entire day had been one strange occurrence after another. First, she made her alpha go ballistic, then she found out that her entire pack knew who her parents were, and now she felt the burden of the entire world on her shoulders. Unlike Atlas, she couldn't shrug it off or pass it to another unwilling victim of fate.

She understood all too well how important, how vital, she was. There was no forgetting what Michael had told her in the vehicle about the War Beast and the legend of Tanatia. The huge shoes she would have to fill made her feel like a child again and not the young woman she had believed herself to be. It was as if she were a little girl trying to slip into her mother's high heels and stumbling around the bedroom, and there was no shortage of stumbling.

Already in her disobedience to Darren and her rebellious attitude, she was going against the tide of destiny. If only her wolf had told her sooner that such behavior was not fitting for the hostess of Tanatia, there might have been less strife within her pack.

"I'm feeling a little lost," she replied, making sure that their conversation was confidential, even to Logan and Dustin who sat on the other side of the room. "I have no idea what I'm doing."

"For the moment, you're dancing with me."

Katey snorted. "I know that. I mean, I don't know what I'm supposed to do when it comes time for the council. How will I make them listen? I'm not a public speaker at all. I still get nervous thinking about having to stand in front of a classroom to give a presentation."

Michael nodded and guided her into a slow walk-about turn that showcased her beauty and grace to those watching. When they came back together, he said, "You don't have to have every detail figured out. There are still a few months before the council will take place."

"But what if I'm not ready by then?"

He gave her a knowing smile and nodded. "You will be. I have every confidence in you."

"Forgive me for bringing this up, but we barely know each other. How can you have faith in me if you barely know my responsibility track record?"

"Because I knew your mother and father."

Katey glanced away and then met his eyes again. "That doesn't exactly help. I didn't realize they were such big players in their own races. I don't know how to live up to being a daughter of Adam Swenson or daughter of Jane Gennari."

Michael grinned. "My dear, you already have. You may not realize it, but when you saved the life of your lover, Logan, you fulfilled every hope your parents would have had for you. You sacrificed yourself for someone you love."

Katey remembered what her mother had said in her afterlife experience. "*Love is what binds us together for eternity.*" At the time, Katey thought her mother was talking about the love they shared as parent and child, but perhaps it was more than that.

Love – or at least its sister forms of peace and tolerance – would bring the world back into harmony. All her parents wanted was for her to be an example, to be like Tanatia.

Still, Katey couldn't help but be a little overawed. How was she supposed to incarnate this princess from millennia ago? It couldn't be as simple as saving the one she loved. If that were true, then she had completed her mission, and there was nothing left to do, yet there was an innate feeling of void and confusion in this matter of her mission.

"Is there like some list of rules? Some guidelines? Was there something in the artifacts you found from the civilization that could give me some clues?"

Michael sighed as the song slowed to the end. "In this matter, unfortunately, there is not. If there was, I would certainly tell you."

He spun her one last time, her skirt billowing out from her legs as she twirled. When Katey came to face her grandfather, he advised, "All I can say is for you to look inside yourself. Tanatia is there. You just have to listen."

Katey opened her mouth to contest that all she felt was her wolf, but they were suddenly not alone.

A young man, a few years older than Katey, stepped up to them. She looked him over from his shiny leather shoes to his navy blue Ralph Lauren polo shirt and curly dark blonde hair. His brown eyes smiled when their gazes met.

"I'm sorry to interrupt, but I was wondering if I could have the next dance?"

Katey stared, her mind trying to understand why he had no scent whatsoever. Everyone had a scent, even a faint one. This man was perfectly blank.

CHAPTER 12

Katey glanced to Michael, and his shoulders squared as if he were ready to give the man a lecture on etiquette, but instead stared at him with as much coldness as a floating glacier in the arctic. Perhaps Michael also picked up on the fact that the man had no scent.

A mellow Latin tune blended into the fading waltz, and though Katey knew a dance for the tempo, she had no desire to accept the stranger's invitation. Yet if she didn't, Michael was liable to tell him off in true noble style, and Katey couldn't bear the thought of a confrontation in the middle of the dancefloor like that.

Without much thought, since her mind was scrambled by the sudden shift in focus, she stepped away from Michael and regarded the man. "Can you keep up?" she asked, issuing it as more of a challenge than a stab at flirting.

The man grinned and took her hand from Michael's. For a second, Katey looked at Logan and saw the crossness written on his face. If only they could reach through their bond and somehow telepathically communicate that this meant nothing to her.

More than anything, Katey was curious why this man had no scent. Not since she had become a loup-garou, had she ever experienced an utter lack of sensation as she did with him. At first, she wondered if his scent was just lost in the crowd, but as he drew closer, Katey confirmed her suspicion that he truly had no signature to his presence besides his heartbeat.

Michael moved away and joined the others at the table without ceremony. Hushed words were traded, and Logan's guttural growl of disapproval rang in her ears just as loudly as the music.

In the flurry of divided attention between her thoughts and what was going on at the table, Katey almost missed her cue to start dancing.

The man stepped forward too soon, and his knee bumped into hers.

"Oh, I'm sorry," he said, quickly withdrawing his leg. It was then she realized there was a vivid drawl in his voice that brought up images of bayous and crawfish. He clearly wasn't from Florida or even Alabama.

Katey hardly noticed the pain in her leg from his misstep. "It's fine. I'm just a little distracted."

"If you don't want to dance – "

"No, no," she said quickly, her hand gripping his to keep him there. "I want to. I just wasn't ready."

Katey watched his inscrutable expression while she counted the beats, her chin bobbing with the rhythm as if she were an instructor working with a student again. Her partner was not unattractive, but he couldn't compare to Logan, that was certain. Her fiancé had nothing to fear, but the room slowly filled with dread like a heavy, suffocating gas and she knew exactly where it was coming from.

"What's your name?" the man asked as they steadily paced their steps with the tango pattern.

After a quick debate with herself, she replied, "Katey. And yours?"

"Drake. It's nice to meet you, Katey."

He was too polite, too tame. Something in the back of Katey's mind screamed that this was not natural. Logan was polite, but only because he was over a hundred years old. Drake, who had no scent and therefore could not be identified as anything other than human, appeared to be of college graduate age. Katey thought it rare to find gentility among her generation.

"I'll admit that I've had my eye on you since you walked in," Drake said.

Katey's eyes darted away, a flush of embarrassment flooding her cheeks, but she refused to smile. "Is that so?"

"Yep. I saw that little kiss your man gave you, but I wonder why he isn't dancing with you."

"Logan doesn't like to dance as much as I do."

Katey wanted to kick herself for giving so much information to a stranger. She bit her lips together.

"That's a shame. You're a wonderful dancer."

"Thank you," she replied, allowing herself one nicety.

"Who are the others with you?"

Her wolf snapped and growled, filling her chest with an ember of defiance. "I'm sorry, but I don't think that's any of your business."

Katey glimpsed toward the table. Logan was halfway out of his chair, and the only thing to hold him back was Dustin's tight grip on his arm. Michael watched with keen suspicion but made no moves to intervene.

"I'm sorry. That was nosy of me."

She squinted at him. Something wasn't right, and perhaps it was her distrust of any man who showed interest in her, but there was a prickly knot in the pit of her stomach. Nothing about this seemed right, and she couldn't put her finger on just what it was. Her wolf would not let her ignore that fact, either. The wolf raged inside of her but had no logical answer for its behavior.

Katey stopped dancing and tried to step away. "Listen, I need to go."

Drake's hand clamped around her wrist. "Wait, I'm sorry if I upset you."

The last thing Katey wanted was to make a scene in front of these people. It shouldn't have been awkward. This seemingly normal guy was dancing with her, but all the adjoining under-current of events and feelings that no one else could see made this into the huge deal that it was.

Logan closed on them within seconds before Katey could give any subdued excuse for her reluctance.

"Back off," Logan growled, a threat behind his words as he glared at Drake.

He let go of Katey, and she reflexively stood just behind Logan, letting him act on his protective instincts, but ready to tug on his arm as soon as he started to draw too much attention.

Drake blinked and smiled in disbelief. "Listen, we were just talking."

"And now you're done," Logan bristled. "Move on."

His eyes darted between Logan and Katey, and then he slowly paced backward. Drake didn't turn away until he was satisfied that Logan wouldn't pounce on him, and then he slipped into the crowd.

"That was unnecessary," Katey mumbled, keeping her poker face so as not to attract more notice than what Logan had already acquired when he bowed up to Drake.

He turned on her, blue eyes flecked with bits of gold, and she wondered if that was why Drake looked so intrigued before he finally walked away. Logan knew better than to let his wolf sideshow in public.

"Calm down," she whispered.

Logan stepped closer. Katey could almost feel his anger hum in her bones. "I don't mind you dancing with your grandfather or even Dustin. They're harmless, but you shouldn't have danced with him."

Katey's eyes wandered to the other guests in the room, feeling their eyes upon them. "Let's take this outside," she advised, straining to keep herself calm under the torrent of emotions and confusion.

"Let's take this home."

A sound of disapproval squeaked in the back of her throat. "Home? We just got here."

"Lily and Forrest aren't here, and that's who you came to see. We have no reason to stay."

He took her arm, none too gently, and pulled her toward the table where Michael and Dustin were pushing back their chairs to stand.

Katey wrenched free, her skin rubbed raw by the force of her efforts. "I'm not leaving," she said, her voice low and asserting. "I didn't just come here to see them."

Logan's nostrils flared, his brows pinching together between his eyes. "So, you wanted to come here and dance with men you don't belong to."

As if the force of the accusation had physically struck her, Katey staggered back a step. Michael was by her side, his thick hands bracing her shoulders so she wouldn't fall over. Dustin attended to Logan, pulling him toward the exit.

Before Katey could recover, they were outside in the cold night air, and Michael was calling his driver on his cell phone. Out of sight from those inside the studio, Katey felt the freedom to turn to Logan, eyes blazing with indignation.

"What did you mean by 'dancing with men I don't belong to'?"

Matching her fury, Logan replied, "You have no right to dance with strange men."

"What? Are we in the sixteenth century all of a sudden?"

Logan stalked closer, every muscle tensed. Dustin stood beside them with his hands held in such a way as to keep them from charging at one another.

"You're my mate. No man has the privilege to touch you without my approval."

Katey rolled her eyes. "Logan, that's not how this works."

"Look what happened when you danced with that vamp last month. I know you were attracted to him."

Blindsided by such an allegation, Katey had to pause. Yes, when she danced with Martel, she had felt a rush of unabridged joy that was completely unexplainable at the time. It might have been his powers of influence over her – the same force that made her stand still while he kissed her on the stairs – or it was purely a platonic joy for the thrill that dancing gave her.

Where was Logan pulling this charge from? Had she smelled of arousal when she fled to the dungeon where they were being held, to escape the wrath of the vampires? She didn't recall such emotions at the time, but it was difficult to sift through the confusion and fear at that moment.

"I was not attracted to him, Logan. How could I be attracted to anyone besides you?"

Katey heard her own voice soften under the realization that Logan wasn't truly angry. He was terrified and insecure. He had been from the moment they left the house and as hard as he tried to hide it, the aura shined through with blaring colors. There was no such thing as a secret between them anymore. There were just unspoken confessions that would work their way out in due time.

At that moment, Logan put up a defensive front against her, and Katey couldn't comprehend why. Despite her words, his hardened expression wouldn't budge.

"Why wouldn't you? You could have any man you want, and they would throw themselves at your feet."

Katey stepped forward, but Dustin pressed his hand against her shoulder to keep her at bay for her own protection. "But I don't want just any man. I've only ever wanted you. Why can't you understand that?"

The low purr of the SUV sounded from down the street and made its way toward them.

"What I can't understand is why you allowed this guy to dance with you. Did he interest you in some way?"

"Of course, not! Logan, please stop acting like this, it makes no sense!"

Katey reached out to touch his cheek, hoping that some tender contact would pull him back from these worthless arguments. Instead, he swatted her hand away and moved to the curb, his back toward a parked sedan.

His eyes glowed a golden hue in the darkness and Katey could hear the rumble of a growl in his chest. Dustin stepped between him and Katey. A current of dominance surged around the group as the van pulled up to an empty parking stall a few yards away. No one moved. Katey didn't even breathe for fear that anything might upset the brittle balance.

Then, she realized that she couldn't be a spectator like this. If she was supposed to learn about conflict resolution and mediation, now was the perfect chance. Loups-garous and vampires alike at the council would be as ready and anxious to fight as Logan was now.

With careful precision, Katey moved around Dustin and stopped within arm's length of Logan. Reaching within herself, she pulled out the words she would need to calm her mate.

"No one will ever take me away from you, Logan. No vamp or human on this earth will have my undying love."

Logan watched her with his feral wolf eyes, fierce and uncontrollable. His breaths came out short and trembling as if she were trying to grasp any bit of logic and reason to bring him back from the brink. Katey had seen him this way before, on the day he changed her in that dark classroom. She hadn't been afraid of him then either.

As they locked gazes, Katey's anxiety ebbed away like a receding tide in the ocean of contradicting emotions all around that threatened to drown her. This calm came from within, and for a split second, Katey wondered if it was the spirit of Tanatia finally making her appearance.

Katey reached out to touch Logan once more, but before she could, Dustin grabbed Logan's arm.

"Come on, kid. We need to get you home."

She opened her mouth to reprimand Dustin for his careless act, but Logan beat him to it in a more direct fashion than she would have liked.

Faster than she could see, Logan had thrown a wide punch to Dustin's jaw and drove him to the pavement. Michael pulled Katey away and ushered her toward the open car door. She wrestled against her grandfather and by the time she looked back to the scene, Logan had vanished.

Dustin groaned and felt his jaw as a dribble of blood leaked from the corner of his mouth.

"Where did he go?" Katey asked frantically, sniffing for any lingering scent of Logan in the wind.

Dustin rose to his feet and staggered to the vehicle. The words that came out were slurred as if his tongue were inoperable.

Michael inspected his slightly swollen face and shook his head. "It looks like he shattered your jaw."

Dustin rolled his eyes heavenward and pointed down Main Street toward the courthouse.

"I'll take care of Logan," Michael said. "You two get back to the house."

Katey stood firm on the sidewalk. "I'll go after him. It's my fault he's acting out."

Dustin cleared his throat and waved his hand as if to say that he didn't like either of their plans.

"We can't all go together," Michael offered. "Katey needs to get to safety, and you need to nurse that jaw until it heals."

"Safety?" Katey asked as Dustin was trying to shove her into the SUV.

"Yes," Michael replied. "I have a hunch about something, though I'm not certain yet. Just get back to the house. We will be along shortly."

Again, Katey found herself where she didn't want to be, and the car door closed on her. She pressed her face against the glass as the driver sped them to the north and away from Logan.

In one sense, she understood why he lashed out at Dustin. Logan had been like a wild animal, and Dustin's rash action set him off. Any loup-garou would have behaved that way, just as Darren might have if she hadn't been able to soothe the beast earlier that day.

What she couldn't understand was the sudden onset of his insecurity. Dancing with Drake hadn't caused it, but it didn't help.

If anything, it pushed Logan over the edge to make him that volatile. What instigated it? Nothing had happened within the last few hours to make Logan question their entire relationship with such skepticism. He had been jealous before, but not so doggedly irrational even after she continually told him the truth about her love and devotion.

What did Michael suspect? Did it have something to do with Logan, or with Drake? Did he also catch that Drake had no scent? If he did, then why didn't he intervene sooner? Michael was older and wiser than any of them, having lived for over eight hundred years, and Katey trusted his instincts completely, but she would have wanted more information than her grandfather seemed willing to give.

Whatever it was, she was determined to find out when both Michael and Logan safely returned home.

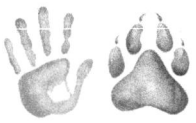

If the chase proved anything to Michael, it was that he was no longer a young man and that he had grown too accustomed to civilized life. Werewolves were always drawn to the woods, while his kind stayed indoors where it was safe and comfortable.

He stood in front of the cemetery gates to catch his breath, taking in the view of the graffitied sign that welcomed mourners and visitors alike. Miles away from Crestucky and well out of sight from human eyes, Logan had certainly picked a strange place to sulk.

"Leave me be, old man," Logan's voice drifted on the whistling wind.

Michael regained his strength and walked through the ajar gate, his footsteps barely making a sound on the crisp, untrodden grass. Even if Logan's scent hadn't led him to this remote graveyard, the trail of heightened emotions would have made his location known like a bright neon sign in the sky.

Since he had come to Crestucky, he knew the werewolves were in a dire situation. Fear and tension loomed like a thundercloud over the city, and especially over the house in which Katey found herself living. Although Michael would have much preferred that she come to live with him, he understood the mind of the were-wolves and their need for camaraderie and familial ties. To take her away from her pack would be like slowly asphyxiating her. To take her from her lover would prove even more disastrous.

From the moment he saw them together in the grand foyer of the castle, Michael knew their relationship was something special and hallowed. Yet, there was a queerness about their bond. Some-thing unseen and probably undetected – even to them – was not quite right and Michael had racked his brain for weeks to figure it out.

Seeing them quarrel made it all too clear. Logan was willing to love, but not willing to lose. He loved too strongly, too passionately, and although Katey loved him with just as much intensity, nothing was holding her back, except for Logan himself.

With care, Michael approached the shaken wolf. Logan was crouched between two graves toward the back of the field. Every line of his body told Michael that he should not venture closer, but he did and stood within striking distance behind Logan.

He took a deep breath and turned to admire the surrounding woods that shaded the edges of the cemetery from the silvery moonlight. After a few moments of waiting, more or less to prove to Logan that he could control himself under the urge to assault the intruder, Michael asked, "Do you come here when you're up-set?"

"I come here to be alone," he replied, a threat-laden in his words.

Michael looked back at the dirt road he had sped down to get to the lonely cemetery. "It's a good place to be alone. I'm sure there aren't more than a dozen people in the world who would know this is here."

Logan looked over his shoulder, eyes still blazing gold and cut-ting through the night. "Many loups-garous know of this place."

Michael avoided looking into the eyes of the beast and continued to observe his surroundings, studying the trees and the way the crickets sang their night chorus. "And now one vampire is privy to its location. Surely, you didn't think we would let you run off while hunters were around?"

The hunters might have been closer than they thought. With his guards stationed around Katey's home and pack, Michael was certain they would be safe for the time being. There was one inkling niggling in the back of his thoughts that refused to be pushed aside. With a few phone calls, he would know if his hunch was correct.

Until then, he had to find some way to get Logan back to the house so he could reconcile with Katey.

Logan turned away and stood, his back muscles stretching under his shirt. They were equally matched in height, but Michael thought himself to be no match for Logan's youth and brawn.

"Was that the first time you ever struck Dustin?" Michael asked, feigning intrigue and admiration.

"No," Logan replied with a sigh. "It wasn't, but it was the first time he didn't deserve it."

Michael bit back a smile. "Then why did you do it? If Dustin wasn't – "

"I don't know," he snapped.

"You don't know who you wanted to harm, or know why you did it at all?"

Logan slowly turned to face him, face seething with self-loathing and a burden that no man could lift. "I don't know why I struck him. I was just so angry."

"At Katey?"

He shook his head. "No, I could never..."

Michael offered his ear to Logan, tilting his head and waiting for him to continue. "Never what? Never hate her? Never be angry with her? Back at the studio, you were furious about what she had done. We could all see that. There's no shame in admitting that you were jealous."

Logan shoved his hands into his pockets and averted his gaze. "I wasn't jealous. How could I be jealous of someone coveting what is not rightfully mine?"

Michael rocked back in his heels and nodded. "Now, we're getting to it. Come, son. There's no one out here to eavesdrop, and you can trust me."

The werewolf shot a glare at him. "How can I? Ever since you showed up, you've been telling Katey how important she is, how her parents were famous and practically royalty. She'll realize she can have something better than me and it's all your fault. If you never came, everything would have been just fine the way it was."

That was not true in the least. If Michael had never come, Katey would have never learned about her heritage and role in this grand design to bring the world back to a stable place. She wanted to know her parents and had wanted it from the very beginning before she even knew that she was the chosen one. Any orphan on this earth yearned for the same truth – to know where they belong and who they were. Michael equipped Katey with that knowledge and probably earned her undying gratitude for it. None of the others even knew she was the daughter of Adam and Jane. None of them could have possibly helped her the way Michael did.

"Has Katey told you this?" Michael asked. "Has she said the words 'I don't want you anymore'? Because, if I recall, she said quite the opposite just a short while ago."

Logan shook his head. "She was saying those things to avoid making a scene."

"No, I assure you that she was sincere. I am empathic, remember? Apart from the fear that you were going to hurt someone, Katey felt nothing but love for you."

"It must have been pity."

Michael's face puckered in bemusement. "Why should she pity you? Why should she think you were not worthy of her love?"

Logan looked away across the field of tombstones, but would not reply.

With a sigh, Michael realized that he would have to learn the hard way. Using another of his vampirical abilities that were usually reserved for hunting or preying upon the weak, he reached into Logan's mind and searched through his many memories.

Without blinking an eye, he sifted through the hate, despair, and utter agony that epitomized Logan's life. One tragedy after another, full of loss and death. The only bright, shining light was Katey herself. Did she know how much he needed her? How much he idolized her and worshipped her as his savior and angel of mercy?

It took only seconds for Michael to know everything; how Logan had unwittingly murdered his parents, how he was unable to change at will, how diluted his werewolf blood truly was. All of it made him wonder more about his origins.

In all of his years, Michael had never heard of a werewolf who obtained their condition from a second generation, such as Logan had inherited from Dustin. He might have been the only one to notice that morning at the castle, but Michael witnessed something extraordinary that left him scratching his head in regard to Logan.

When Katey had died, Logan was inconsolable as he held her in his arms and tears ran in streams down his face. Michael had never heard a man weep in that way for over a century. Perhaps it was a trick of the light or a romantic illusion, but he was sure that he saw one of Logan's tears fall into Katey's gunshot wound. A few seconds later, Katey was gasping for breath.

There was only one thing that could heal a mortal wound like that. Vampire tears had unique medicinal properties. In the Dark Ages, shamans and witches prized vampire tears, and Michael had heard of some vials being sold for a small fortune. They were said to cure the plague and even bring the dead back to life.

Vampires did not often cry, making their tears a precious relic that mystics searched for all their lives.

Michael held his hands behind his back and continued to speculate as he watched Logan struggle for the words. It was lunacy to suggest that the werewolf who stood before him had any vampire blood in him, but the theory of his miracle tears was compelling. Then again, perhaps it was pure coincidence. Katey, after all, did possess the immortal spirit of Tanatia and with that privilege, might have come abilities that they could not begin to fathom.

Unable to wait for Logan to muster the courage, Michael spoke. "You think that because Katey is so special, that you can't possibly match her." He took a few steps forward. "My friend, love is not a competition. If Katey's parentage makes her unattainable, then you don't understand what love is."

Logan looked to Michael, a warning in his glare.

"Love," Michael continued, "does not fabricate excuses. It wants what it will want, and no force on earth can tear it asunder." He held up a cautionary finger. "Unless you allow it to. If you continue to push her away on the grounds that you find yourself inadequate, then you have already lost her."

"Katey deserves better than me."

"No," Michael barked. "She deserves the kind of love that you can give her. If you don't pull up your trousers and realize that she will die inside without your love, then she will never fulfill her mission."

"I'm sure she could do fine without me."

Michael scowled. "So, then you don't love her?"

Logan snarled. "I do love her. She's the only thing I've ever loved in this world."

"All I'm hearing are excuses and lies that you've probably been feeding yourself for your entire life. The pack can do without you. Darren would be relieved that a disobedient pup left him. Dustin would be happier with a more stable grandson. Katey would be better off with a man who wasn't so jealous and insecure. These lies will become the truth if you let them fester in your mind for the rest of your life."

Michael leaned forward. "Or, you can make a choice to believe that your pack cares about you. You can choose to believe that Darren and Dustin love you as if you were their son. You can make a choice to believe every word that Katey tried to pound into your head earlier tonight."

Logan shook his head. "It's not that easy. I don't know how it is for you vamps, but I can't just flip a switch."

"I don't expect you to flip a switch. I expect you to retrace the steps that have led you down this self-destructive path and find where you went wrong in your thinking. It may take years, maybe decades, for you to come back to the place you once were before you decided to make yourself your own worst enemy. When you're there, you'll realize that you've been the mate that Katey has always deserved and the pack member that Darren has always needed."

Logan was silent, and Michael could see the wheels begin to turn in his mind. Yes, it would take a while to reverse the damage, but tonight would be the first night of many where Logan didn't have to hate himself so strongly anymore.

CHAPTER 13

Katey was on the porch before Michael and Logan even breached through the tree line of the front yard. She had changed into a comfortable pair of jeans and a hooded sweater, glad to be free of her skirt and heels. The mating bond buzzed alive just seconds ago, increasing in its draw as Logan came closer to their property.

For the last couple of hours, she and Dustin had been waiting as patiently as anyone might expect a pair of parents waiting for their rebellious child to return home. Dustin's jaw had fully healed on the trip back to the house, but Katey wished it would have taken just a little bit longer because every other word that came out of his mouth was cruel and biting toward Logan and what he had done.

No one could blame Dustin for his anger, but Katey might have been the only one to take her mate's side on the matter. She understood now, more than ever, why Logan behaved so irrationally. If she had her empathic abilities before they left for Alaska the month before, they might have been able to avoid a great deal of heartache and stress. All of Logan's bouts of jealousy could have been dealt with before they blossomed into this new level of insanity.

When she saw their figures dash out onto the field, Katey ran and leaped off the first step of the porch. Logan caught her in his arms before she could hit the ground. Her legs wrapped around his waist and arms around his neck as he held her close. His strong embrace was warm and calming, and Katey couldn't sense the raging emotions that had almost swallowed him up earlier in the evening. Whatever Michael said or did had cured him for the moment.

"I'm so sorry," he whispered against her neck, sending veins of electricity through her nervous body.

"I'm sorry, too. I didn't know." Now she did, and Katey would make wiser choices until Logan finally believed beyond the shadow of a doubt that she was fully and unabashedly committed to him.

Michael stepped onto the porch and entered the house to give them some privacy. Dustin was not as considerate and stood at the threshold, sending an upsurge of negative vibes their way that made Katey shiver. To have been cooped up in the house with Dustin's antipathy had been nearly unbearable and no amount of reasoning got through to him. With Darren and Ben out running as loups-garous in the forested part of their land, there was no one dominant enough to give him a lecture on forgiveness.

"Logan! Inside!" the beta barked.

Instead of insisting on a few more moments of bliss, Logan carried Katey inside as she hung onto him as a baby might cling to its mother. She giggled, despite the coming argument, and dropped to her feet as soon as Logan shut the door behind him.

"I can't believe you just ran off like that!" Dustin raged in his Irish burr. Katey didn't even bother to look over her shoulder but wrapped one arm around Logan's waist in hopes that her presence might soften the hateful words that were about to fly.

Logan surprised her. With his chin lifted, facing his firing squad with dignity, he let out a breath and said, "I'm sorry, Dustin. I'm sorry for striking you, and I'm sorry for running off. I wasn't in my right mind."

There was a spark of confusion at his words, but Dustin continued without a break. "You're damned right you weren't in your right mind."

The heartfelt apology that Logan gave might not have healed Dustin's wounded pride, but it was all he could offer for the time. Though, she did feel a significant difference in her fiancé that she hoped would be explained in time.

Michael's regal stride sounded down the hall, and Katey turned to face them. "Are you packed and ready to go?" he asked, successfully changing the subject.

Dustin noticed the diversion and shot a perturbed look to the old vamp but said nothing in contradiction.

Katey's heart fell at the mention of leaving. Yes, she was packed, but she didn't want to go. "Can't we wait until morning so we can say goodbye to Darren and Ben?"

Dustin's nostrils flared. "Nope. You two are leaving. If Darren gets back and finds you two are still here, I'm going to get my arse chewed out."

"Can I have a moment alone with Katey before we leave?" Logan boldly requested.

Dustin gave him a look as if he had asked for the moon on a silver platter. "You two can talk in the car on the way there."

He shook his head. "No. I want privacy. There are some things we need to talk about."

A sliver of fear pierced Katey's chest, and she looked to Logan for an answer. He gave her a sincere smile in return, silently assuring her that it was nothing serious.

All the time she had waited for him to come home, Katey had wondered if he was beginning to have second thoughts about their mating and future together. Infidelity was never a possibility to her, but it was obviously more than a possibility to Logan. It had become a certainty in his mind, and Katey finally understood that after reading him outside the studio. What she didn't understand was why, after all this time, would he even think that she would want anyone other than him?

Dustin opened his mouth to protest, but Michael's hand on his shoulder stopped him.

"I have to make a few phone calls," he said. "If they go have their talk, it will give me some time to investigate. My guards will escort you two wherever you want to go."

Katey sensed that Logan wasn't completely satisfied with that deal, but he nodded.

Dustin threw up his hands and turned away. "Fine. Fine. I'm going out with Darren and Ben. I need to blow off some steam." He walked to the sliding glass door that led to the back garden. "I'll see you two soon. Don't get into trouble," he said.

"Be safe!" Katey called as he stepped out the door and shut it behind him with little more than a glance over his shoulder.

Logan leaned past Katey and snagged up his motorcycle keys from the dish on the sideboard. In turn, she stooped down to pick up the two helmets sitting on the floor. With Darren not around to police their every move, autonomy seemed within their grasp for the first time all week.

"I'll wait until you return," Michael said as he pulled out his cellphone and began to scroll through his many contacts.

For as old as Michael was, he seemed fairly confident with a modern phone, just as Logan and the others were. It made Katey wonder sometimes how she would be able to keep up with the changing technology over the years.

Logan ushered her out the door before she could say goodbye and whispered, "If we're fast enough, we can outrun the guards."

Katey grinned and hurried to his sleek, black crotch-rocket motorcycle leaning on its kickstand beneath the carport next to Darren's silver sedan. They mounted, both feeling the thrill of escape rise in their chests. The motorcycle wasn't the fastest way to get around for them, but wherever Logan was planning to flee, they must have had to fly past civilians who would spot them running faster than a speeding car.

They zoomed down the driveway and out to the highway that led through Crestucky. Katey remembered how she had once been terrified to straddle behind Logan on his bike. Now, she almost preferred it to riding in a car. Something was liberating about feeling the cool wind whip at her clothes and muss up her hair as it fluttered and twisted behind her. If Logan didn't fuss at her so much, she would have ridden without the helmet on so she could taste the freedom. It was almost like running as a wolf but on blacktop and more rules about where one could and could not go.

After a few moments, Katey looked over her shoulder to see if there were any vamps following along the shoulder of the road or in some tinted-windowed vehicle behind them. She saw no one. Either Michael had not ordered his guards to watch them, or they had successfully evaded their notice.

Just before they reached Crestucky, Logan turned down a county road that was settled by only a few older houses with long driveways leading out to the street. Some of the lights in their windows were on, but others were darkened with only a porch light gleaming to guide visitors to the front door.

They drove until the paved road became packed dirt and the bike wheels kicked up a cloud of dust in their wake. Katey heard the distant rumble of a train and smiled. Although not used for passenger transport, there was one set of railroad tracks that cut through the heart of Crestucky. A bridge allowed traffic to flow over the tracks during the day, but Katey rarely ever saw a cargo train chug down through the town.

The bike slowed, and Logan steered it to the side of the road that was skirted by dense forest and shut off the engine. They were completely and utterly alone out here. The wind didn't carry the signature scent of a vampire, and aside from themselves, no loups-garous were wandering the forests either. They were completely alone except for the crickets and the coming train.

Logan helped her dismount, and when their helmets were off, he tugged on her hand to lead her down a beaten path in the woods.

"Where are we going?" Katey giggled, feeling the responsibilities that had been thrust upon her life to be thousands of miles away. Here, with Logan, nothing else mattered.

"You'll see."

After some trekking through the underbrush, Katey heard the train drawing closer and closer. Ahead, she saw a break in the trees and the unmistakable glare of a bright, round light splitting through the forest.

Beyond the edge of the trees, were the railroad tracks Katey had suspected and the midnight train was making its way slowly toward Crestucky.

They quietly sat together and watched as the train ambled by. Neither of them spoke as they slipped their arms around each other.

"What did Michael say to you?" Katey finally asked, relishing in the night and day difference she felt in Logan.

He squeezed her tight, and she could sense the apprehension in him. "He just made me realize what a fool I've been."

She watched his eyes glisten in the soft moonlight. "What do you mean?"

Logan went still for a moment as if waiting for the words to come of their own free will. When they didn't, he forced them out. "All my life, I've never really had anything good. You know about my parents, and about my struggles to be a true loup-garou, but it's more than that. I've never let myself enjoy life because I know that something or someone always comes along to ruin it."

"And you thought I was just one of those things that would pass away?"

He nodded and swallowed hard. "I thought I knew for a fact that one day you would leave me, or that you would be killed. That's one reason I needed you to become a loup-garou. I couldn't bear the thought of the years passing by without you in my life. When you died, and I held you in my arms..." He paused and looked at her with a measure of sorrow in his beautiful eyes. "I thought that was it for you and me. I had fallen in love, and you were gone, just like that."

Katey nuzzled his shoulder. "But, I'm here now."

"I know you are." He leaned his head against hers. "But I can't help but wonder if there will be something else to take you from me... And when I found out your father was Adam, I began to wonder if you would take yourself from me."

She sat back and frowned. "Why would you think that? What does my dad have to do with anything between us?"

Logan struggled with the words once more. "You see... Adam was more than just a man that tried to teach me how to shift. He was like an idol, a hero. When the Deviants were attacked, he was one of the only loups-garous who didn't belong to the pack but stayed to help them escape. The last time I saw him, he was trying to rescue the women and children from the town. After that time, I heard stories of his heroism, his loyalty, and wisdom. I've never heard a bad thing about Adam in the whole time I've been a loup-garou."

He took a deep breath. "I thought, that if you understood how special your father was and how important you are to loups-garous, you'd start to think that you deserved someone better than me. Someone who can help you do everything that you need to do with the council. You don't need me, a loup-garou who can't even shift at will."

A grin split Katey's face. "If you keep putting me on a pedestal that high, you'll never be able to reach me."

"But you belong on that pedestal," he pleaded. Logan took her hand in his and kissed her palm. "You deserve every good and right thing in this world, and I know I can't give it to you."

Katey flipped her hand and caressed his cheek, letting her immense love shine through her smile. "To me, you are every good and right thing. I don't care if you can't shift at will, or if your loup-garou form had wings or could fit in my lap like a Chihuahua."

Logan chuckled and held her hand against his face, kissing it once more in relief. "You say that now, but what about at the council? When everyone sees that we're together and they know of my failure -"

"Not being able to shift at will is not a failure, Logan. You just haven't been able to do it yet."

He lifted his eyes to her again. "But what if it delays the mating ceremony? What if you change your mind?"

That was certainly something that Katey had feared, but not about changing her mind. Logan had seen how irate she became when Darren denied her training, which would delay their ceremony. Her incensed response did not make him feel any better, she was sure. Even though that was only a day ago, Katey was a different loup-garou now.

"I will never change my mind about you, Logan. If the mating ceremony is delayed a few weeks, a few months, or even a few years, I'll never stop loving you."

Logan leaned forward until their foreheads touched. "I want to believe you so badly."

"Then don't fight it," she whispered before twisting up to kiss his lips.

He didn't fight it. Logan returned the kiss and pulled her close until their bodies pressed together as they once did in a snowy forest in Alaska.

The kiss was cut short as the wind carried the warning of an unwelcome visitor. Logan pulled away and looked off toward the murky forest. "Looks like they caught up with us," he remarked in a grumble.

Katey sighed and leaned her head against his shoulder, sure that she had never disliked the smell of a vampire more than she had at that moment. The train had almost passed them by now, towing along with it countless cargo containers that were vandalized with colorful graffiti art.

"We can't run away from our lives forever, I guess," she said.

Logan hung his arm around her shoulders. "Just know that I'm here for you, Katey."

She squirmed with delight. "I love it when you say my name. You make it sound pretty."

He chuckled and brought his lips to her ears, muttering her name over and over with a lilting, almost musical voice.

His breath tickled her skin, inducing a fit of giggles before she finally pushed away.

Just as she did, Katey heard a strange sound like the sharp crack of a tree trunk being splintered somewhere in the forest behind them. The sound was followed by a shrill ping from the side of one of the boxcars. Logan cried out and grabbed his bicep.

The scent of blood filled her nostrils, and Katey jumped to her feet as her heart began to pound out of her chest. Who else had followed them? Or was the vampire shooting at them?

She heard a scuffle in the bushes. More blood was spilled, tainting the earthy scent of dried leaves, but Katey couldn't make out the wrestling figures in the dense forest. There was a suppressed gurgle, and then utter silence, but who won?

She looked back to Logan, whose shirt and hand were now soaked in the crimson blood that spilled down his arm and dripped from his fingertips.

Logan growled at the pain. "Run!" he ordered as he stood and pushed her with his good elbow. His injured arm dangled limply against his side.

Katey raced down the length of the steadily moving train, making sure that Logan was by her side the whole way.

Logan took the lead and no longer held his arm, but she could still smell the fresh blood gushing from the wound along with a pungent odor of burnt flesh. They turned into the woods after they had almost caught up with the train and found their way back to the bike. There were no other vehicles parked along the road, but Katey could smell the vampire's trail leading into the woods.

Yet, there were no other scents, no tracks, nothing to make her think that someone else had followed. If the vampire had come out to harm them, then who was it that they struggled with? Unlike Logan or other loups-garous, she couldn't yet distinguish blood between the different races.

Without a word, they mounted and sped back down the county road without the headlights on. Katey was careful not to grip his injured arm, but so desperately wanted to ask him why it hadn't healed yet. Upon closer inspection, there were two holes. One was for the entrance, the other for the exiting of the bullet. Around both holes, Logan's skin had been singed as if someone had taken a lit match or hot iron and jabbed it into his skin.

"Silver?" she whispered.

Logan continued down the road, constantly checking behind them. It only took a few moments before a black pickup truck on big tires began to gain speed behind them. She neither recognized the truck, nor could she explain why it pursued them so quickly.

She tapped on Logan's shoulder, but he didn't need to be reminded to speed up. Breaking the limits of road safety, they were traveling at over one hundred miles per hour, and the truck was still roaring up on their tail.

"Hang on," Logan shouted and swerved around two cars which were going half their speed on the two-lane highway. The drivers blared their horns, but Logan refused to slow down.

The truck was not deterred by the maneuvering and made to pass the other cars too. Katey glanced back to see the truck blocked off by an oncoming car. It slammed on its brakes before it could rear-end the cars in front of it. The truck began to fishtail and swerve out of control, buying them a few moments at least.

They passed the Alabama border, and Logan looked to the tree line along the road. A slight break, just big enough for a bike to slip through, was coming up fast. Katey tightened her hold around his waist as he slowed the bike down and skidded through the opening.

The path resembled a hiking trail, not meant for vehicles, but there was no way the truck would be able to follow them. The bike slowed so no displaced roots along the ground would send them flying.

"Hunters?" Katey questioned.

Logan didn't speak but nodded as they crept upon a clearing. She looked ahead and saw the edge of the cemetery near Morrisville where Logan and Katey had once visited.

Once off the bike and alone in the cemetery, Katey allowed herself to feel the fear and panic. The hunters were truly here, and Logan had been right all along. With every chance they took, they were truly putting themselves in danger. Even now, Katey wasn't sure how safe the cemetery was.

"Won't they find us here?" Katey asked.

Logan yanked off his helmet and bolted toward the graves. "I don't know. We have to move fast," he said, a string of firmness emerging in his voice that startled her.

Katey followed, her legs wobbly and weak. "What are we doing here? Shouldn't we go back to the house? The others are still there. We need to warn them!"

She spoke as if they hadn't been expecting this to happen; as if the last week meant nothing but a false alarm. This was real. The bullet wound in Logan's arm was real.

"If the hunters were on our trail, it's likely they followed us from the house," he replied, weaving through the headstones, on a mission. "If they didn't, we'd be leading them right to the pack."

The paralyzing dread slowed Katey's steps. "What if they already got Darren and Ben? What about Dustin?"

Logan was stone cold, his eyes not expressing the terror that gripped his heart as much as Katey's. "We can't think about that right now."

She nodded shakily as if trying to convince herself that everything was all right. "I'm sure they're fine. Michael's guards would have protected them, right?"

Logan stopped at one grave and sat on his heels. "I'm sure they did," he replied with a flat note as if he didn't believe it.

"Did you catch if the vamp took out the hunter back at the railroad tracks?" she asked as she watched him dig his fingers into the earth and pull out the sod and soil beneath.

"I don't know. I was a little preoccupied." Katey crouched down to inspect his arm, but he jerked away. "It will heal. I need you to help me dig," he snapped.

She glanced at the gravestone. "Robert Croxen," she muttered. "Wasn't that the alpha in Devia?"

"Yes. Now, please, dig."

Katey obeyed, clawing at the grass and dirt to keep herself occupied. If she stayed busy, then maybe she wouldn't slip back into the panic that wanted to steal her resolve. After continuous glances toward the dirt road and forest around, they managed to get somewhere and plow through three feet of earth. They hit a solid surface, the lid of a long wooden chest.

"Please tell me there isn't a body in there?"

Logan flipped open the lid to reveal a stash of various items. There was a cardboard box of vehicle tags from nearly all fifty states, a safe deposit box with the key lodged in the lock, boxes of men's hair dye kits, duffel bags of clothing, and nonperishable food items. Another smaller box contained motorcycle plates, and a bundle of fake IDs with identical pictures of Darren, Dustin, Ben, and Logan.

With quick fingers, Logan grabbed one of the empty duffle bags and stuffed supplies inside.

"A bug-out chest?" she questioned.

He nodded as he tucked one of the license plates beneath his arm that was caked with dried blood. "Yes. We compiled all of this together just in case something like this were to happen. We have a similar box at the house, but this is for if we can't make it back there. We didn't have time to add some things in here for you."

He opened the safe deposit box and found wads of cash in the form of twenties and one-hundred-dollar bills. Logan grabbed some and shoved them in the bag just as a familiar scent came barreling toward them.

Katey looked to the forest and saw a vamp approach, his dark clothes spattered in blood. Logan dropped the bag and turned to the vamp, a snarl curling his lips.

The vamp held up his hands, which were visibly trembling. "I mean no harm. Do you require medical attention?" he asked, voice thick with a foreign accent that Katey would have assumed to be Polish or from some other Eastern European country.

"It will heal," Katey replied, repeating Logan's words from earlier. "What's going on?" she questioned, stepping in front of Logan before he attempted to lash out at the vampire with his dirt-stained hands. He was wounded and afraid and wasn't in the mood to play nice with others until they were on their way out of town.

"We've discovered a few hunters hiding around town. We were able to dispose of a few, but more came. That's who shot at you."

"Why didn't you find him in the first place?" Logan spat.

"I couldn't smell him, and by the time I knew where he was, it was too late."

"You couldn't smell him?" Katey asked, recalling the guy from the dance studio who had no scent. Her blood ran cold.

"No," the vamp replied. "None of our operatives have been able to detect the hunters by smell. We've seen them scouting around the homes of the werewolves who stayed behind. We already took care of the threat."

"What about our house?" Katey asked hastily, her voice spiked with distress.

"Michael is still there and hasn't heard anything. I called him just a short while ago, and he said he would go out to check on your pack."

Katey covered her mouth, fighting back the sobs that wanted to rattle out. She hadn't been this terrified since the incident in the castle. Even then, there was time to avoid the threat of death. Now, the threat was upon them, and it was open season on the loups-garous.

"He wanted me to personally escort you out of town," the vamp continued. "He will bring your things once we are sure that your pack is safe."

"How do we know you're not the one who shot at us?" Logan accused as he stepped forward to stand beside Katey.

The vamp pinched his shirt. "See for yourself. This is the blood of the hunter that shot you. He would have fired a second shot if I hadn't killed him first."

Katey staggered backward and felt the back of her thighs collide with the top of the tombstone. Searching for anything to ground her in the present, Katey leaned against it and gripped the edge with her free hand.

Logan sniffed the vamps' shirt and nodded, nearly satisfied.

"We have the convoy waiting outside of town. I'll lead you there."

Katey watched Logan straighten and shake his head. "No. A large group will attract attention. We need to go alone."

"The hunters have already spotted your motorcycle. You need to change vehicles," the vamp advised.

He jerked his thumb toward the grave. "We have plenty of means to disappear. We'll be fine without you guys for a while. There's a safe house compound farther north of here. That's where we're going."

The vamp did not seem pleased. "Michael told me to bring you two to New Orleans. Even if you go alone, you should go there."

After she was sure she had gotten a hold of her sanity, Katey dropped her hand from her lips. "Louisiana?" she asked, voice quaking. "Why there?"

"That's where Michael is going, and he wants you close. He assures that you will be safe there."

Logan balled his dirty hands into fists. "We'll be safer with our own kind, no offense."

The vamp's brows creased together. "I must insist that you come with me. If you won't do it willingly, then I'll have to force you."

"I'd like to see you try," Logan challenged, dominance billowing from him like a smokestack. The vamp couldn't sense any of it. If the vampire - whose intentions were good - pushed any further, then there would be more bloodshed tonight, and Katey was having none of it.

Pushing back her crippling fears, she stepped between them. "Stop it, Logan." She looked to the vamp. "I trust my fiancé's judgment. We're going to the safe house where the other Deviants are. Tell my grandfather that we'll be fine and we'll stay in contact with him. Do you have his number?"

The vampire, disgruntled but accepting of Katey's tenacity, nodded and recited the phone number. They weren't likely to forget it. With a bow of his head, he dashed off into the woods within half an eye blink.

Logan, muttering under his breath, returned to the grave and packed the rest of what they would need. Katey, taking advantage of her lucid moment, pulled out her cellphone and dialed Darren's number. It wasn't likely that he would answer, but at least she could let them know they were all right.

She left identical messages for all three of them, notifying them of their plans to go to the safe house and that they would call when they arrived safely.

When she was finished, Katey tightened her grip on her phone. "I really hope they're safe," she mumbled, more or less to herself.

Logan wiped his brow on his muddy forearm. "I do too, but don't think about it too much or you'll drive yourself crazy."

There was logic in what he said. Katey could already feel her thoughts slip into a dark and destructive place. Images flashed in before her of mangled bodies, blood, and carnage. She could see in her mind's eye, Darren's body pierced with bullet holes and his eyes glazed over with death.

A silent tear dripped down from her lashes as she stood there beside the grave. No, she couldn't think of that now. She knelt beside Logan and wrapped her arms around his shoulders.

He paused in his packing and clutched her arm, offering as much comfort as he could at that moment. Katey glanced down to his injury and found the wound was slowly closing on both sides. They were both scared, both uncertain of what lay ahead, but at least they were together, and they were alive.

CHAPTER 14

T hey had been driving for over three hours now, traveling north toward Birmingham, but slightly east to the Tallade- ga National Forest. Nestled safely along the southern border of the forest was an abandoned military compound, complete with housing for the Deviants and their families.

Adrenaline had kept Logan awake for the first hour as he sped down the interstate with Katey hanging on behind him and the duffle bag laden down with their provisions slung over his shoulder. After that time, he had to keep himself awake with nothing but his own clashing thoughts.

Why didn't he hear the hunter in the woods? Why didn't he smell him or sense his presence somehow? How could he have put Katey in such danger in the first place? He wanted privacy, but what he got was a nightmare. Yet, even if the hunter hadn't shot him, would it have saved anyone the trouble?

Darren and the others must have still been on their property, blissfully unaware that hunters were converging on the homes of those that stayed behind after the evacuations. Logan was not blind to their reservations that he had been wrong all along. Now, he had the last laugh, but it was a bitter victory. Thank- fully, Michael's men were capable of eliminating the threats. Would that be enough to stop the hunters?

Regret, shame, and self-blame fought for prime focus in his mind. If he hadn't been so foolish, perhaps they would have been on their way to Louisiana with Michael long before the hunters decided to strike. If he hadn't been irrational and run off after he struck Dustin, they could have used those precious hours during his absence to flee Crestucky.

Too many *ifs* and Logan couldn't let the rampant emotions cloud his judgment. He had to stay focused. Any time a vehicle looked to be following them, he diverted off an exit ramp to ensure that it was just a coincidence. Once the car or truck passed, he reentered the highway, and they carried on. They didn't stop for a break or for a meal. Both could endure sitting on this bike for several more hours without too much discomfort, but Logan thanked the stars that they wouldn't have to.

The wound in his arm had healed over nicely, though it took its sweet time in doing so. The searing, mind-numbing pain did not keep Logan from acting, but it did humble him. He had experienced silver before, and even been shot with it a few times while in Chicago, but it had been a long time. It was fortunate that the bullet didn't stay lodged in his flesh. Otherwise, he might have had to plead for Katey to take it out before the silver contaminated his bloodstream.

Occasionally, Logan could feel Katey's arms slip down, and he had to buck his shoulder to keep her awake. He hated to force her to stay conscious, but short of tying her hands together around his waist, she needed to stay aware of herself until they could arrive at the compound.

He turned from AL-9 North onto AL-148 South and continued for several more miles until he found the road that led to the compound and turned north once more. The path was well-worn after several caravanning cars had plowed down the deserted service road.

Logan slowed the bike down as they came upon the compound, but he felt no tingling sensation in the back of his skull that signaled the presence of other loups-garous. Instead, he was met with the pungent odors of vampires, black powder, blood, and burnt wood amongst the chaotic scents of old friends spread all around in the woods.

Ahead, he saw the flashing red and blue lights of police vehicles and a few ambulances. Hurried voices of officers and medics echoed through the trees. The bike slowed to a crawl along the dirt road until he had to prop it up with his leg.

Katey came to attention behind him and sat straight in her seat to see what was going on. Dread filled his chest like a painful poison. His mate was the first to dismount, her touch light as she slid her arms away from his torso. Logan hated the feel of the cold against his body where her warmth had once been.

She slipped off her helmet and started off in a brisk jog toward the scene. Logan did the same and led the bike to the edge of the road, out of the way in case any other vehicles needed to make their exit.

When they came closer and stayed within the safe shadows of the concealing trees, what Logan saw made his stomach churn. The compound was in smoldering piles of ash and rubble. All around were the lifeless bodies of men and some women. Police and investigators infested the site, sorting through the corpses and destruction to find an answer to the massacre.

One thing was certain. These were not loup-garou bodies. They were human, but the blood of the loups-garous had stained the ground, as well as vamp blood. Yet, there were no bodies that belonged to a supernatural creature. In that, there was hope, but not much. With the amount of blood that was spilled, there would have been casualties on all sides.

"What happened?" Katey whispered, her voice thick.

Logan watched the scene of bustling officers, trying to piece together what they were saying.

"Someone called in about a fire. By the time the police came, this was all they found."

That couldn't be all to the story. There were guns fired. He could tell that by the distinct scent of black powder discharge. He sniffed the air, following the scent of death. He left Katey to follow it toward the outer edge of the compound where the humans hadn't touched anything yet.

Between the remains of two buildings, Logan found a victim of the battle. He laid face-down in a massive puddle of his own blood that had absorbed into the ground, painting it a dark hue as rain or oil might. Katey, visibly stunned by the sight of so much death, stayed in the cover of the trees while he examined the body, relaying the details to her as he reasoned it out.

"He's not wearing any armor. He has entrance and exit wounds along his back. They were firing from both sides. The entrance wounds are small and made by hollow-point bullets. The exit wounds are large – probably buckshot." Logan turned the corpse over, unblinking eyes staring at him behind a muddy face. His throat was torn open, explaining why he had bled so much before finally dying. "Brutal claw marks on his throat. There aren't any exit wounds for the hollow-point rounds. So, he still has some bullets in him."

He looked around and found a gun in the human's hand, complete with a noise suppressor and a few empty cartridges sprinkled around where he had fallen. Logan picked one up and immediately dropped it after his fingers were burnt. It was as if he had touched a hot iron. "Silver bullets," he remarked.

"They were hunters?" Katey asked.

Logan hung his head and let out a heavy sigh. Hunters had found the Deviants once again. That didn't explain the vampires. By the evidence of blood from all three races, it was clear that they all fought with one enemy in mind.

"The vampires and Deviants were fighting off the hunters," he replied.

The hollow points were older standard ammunition for vampires who wanted to shoot the loups-garous and keep the silver bullets in their bodies. He knew several Deviants who were avid hunters, who loaded their shotguns with buckshot. It clearly wasn't enough. Otherwise, they would still be there, and the compound would not be burned to the ground.

Then again, the various trails of scents that led away from the compound were positive. There must have been enough loups-garous to escape, and they would have taken away the bodies of their dead to avoid the risk of exposure. How many had been killed? Who had been shot down by the hunters? It was expected of the pack to scatter so they wouldn't be found all together again, but did they have a leader to give that order? What became of Jacob? Or Forrest?

And the most pressing question of all: how did the hunters find them? The compound was a secret, even to other loup-garou packs in Alabama. Unless there was a confederate in their midst, the hunters wouldn't have even known about the evacuations or where their final destination would be. How good was their tracking? Or was it some mistake on their part during the evacuations that tipped off the hunter scouts to their activity?

"Hey! What are you doing over there!"

Logan looked up to see two officers at the end of the former alley. He jumped to his feet and darted back into the woods. Katey followed as they made off at full speed back to the bike. They were back on Highway 148 before the cops could even get in their cars to pursue them.

When they arrived back on Highway 9, Logan's questions continued to mount one on top of the other. He made assumptions and guesses, but he was no closer to an answer by the time he brought the bike to a halt at the stop sign, with an old grocery store and a feed store on either side of him.

He looked to his right, which led south and back to Crestucky, where the rest of his pack remained.

He looked to his left, which led farther north and east toward the Georgia state line.

Behind him lay his only plan. They had nowhere else to go that he knew would be absolutely safe. Except for one place.

Logan rubbed the back of his neck, and Katey hugged him from behind, reminding him that they still had one another. He was sure that if it weren't for her, he would have lost his mind back at the compound. All that work to get them to safety and it was for nothing. He was tempted to think that the Deviants might have been better off in Crestucky, but that wasn't true.

"Now what?" she asked gently, though he could feel her arms tense.

Through her calm, Logan saw the deep distress in her eyes. Back at the compound, he knew that she must have been struggling to hold it together, just as she had when the vamp came to tell them that hunters had begun popping up all over town.

Perhaps they were both numbed by the tragedy. Perhaps when the morning came, they would both have their own breakdowns and mourn the possible loss of good friends and allies.

Until then, he had to be strong and make the decisions. He hadn't been on his own without an alpha since the twenties in Chicago, and that didn't turn out as gloriously as everyone had hoped. Yet, Logan was older and wiser now. Another difference was that back then he didn't have anyone depending on him as Katey did now.

He leaned back over the bike and steered to the right to head south. "We're going to Louisiana."

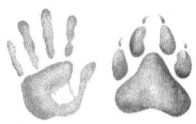

There was little to keep Katey awake and her eyes open. Although falling off the motorcycle at seventy-five miles per hour wouldn't kill her, it wasn't the kind of wake-up she needed.

Her only reward for staying conscious for the entire three hours they drove west, was to see the sunrise behind them as they sped toward – hopefully – safety.

For her own sanity, Katey had to block out all she had seen and felt at the former safe house. She tried not to let the twisted figures of the hunters invade her mind as she held onto Logan tighter. She tried not to think about who could have been killed at the scene. It took at least an hour for the overpowering, residual odor of blood to fade from her senses and even then, she couldn't shake the heaviness of death from her mind.

On top of it all, she could feel the strain in Logan. On the exterior, he was as taciturn and focused as a soldier. Beneath it all, he was grieving and angry. There were no words to comfort him. What could she say to someone who might have lost old friends? What if Forrest and Lily were among the dead who were carted away at the end of the battle? What if Jacob, the alpha, had been murdered by another hunter?

For what seemed like the thousandth time, Katey took a deep breath and let it out slowly. They didn't know for sure who was dead. In time, they would find out what happened and only then would they mourn. It was senseless to do so prematurely when they didn't even know who to mourn for.

They were just across the Mississippi state line when Logan looked over his shoulder. "There's a hotel up ahead," he said. "We're stopping to rest, and we'll move on. I want to be in Louisiana before nightfall."

Katey nodded her consent, eager for a warm bed and a good meal. She hadn't slept in what seemed like ages, and her body ached with fatigue. As far as she could recall, she hadn't been this exhausted since the time she stayed up for two nights straight.

That long-ago sleep-over weekend with Lily and Beth was a piece of cake compared to this torture.

Logan slowed down his bike and turned into a motel parking lot with only a few other vehicles parked in front of the long two-story building. Off to the side was the front office where they were to check in, a smaller building detached from the complex with a lone clerk manning the desk.

When Logan cut off the engine, the comparable silence rang in Katey's ears. For the last few hours, the dull roaring and popping noise was all she had to listen to. With slow movements, Logan nudged down the kickstand for the bike and fished out one of the fake identification cards that matched with an equally fake credit card. Katey fell off her place on the back seat and nearly crumbled to the ground when she discovered that her legs had lost all strength.

Logan caught her around the waist and pulled her back to her feet as he dismounted as well. They made their way inside, both haggard and weary. To their benefit, the clerk was a loup-garou, and perhaps that was why Logan had chosen this hotel amongst others. She didn't have the clarity of mind to ask then, but she would have to inquire later if this was a well-known safe stop for traveling loups-garous.

Katey met the man's questioning eyes. He was young, but that could mean he was anywhere from eighteen to forty in loup-garou years. He leaned forward on the desk as they approached.

"Are you two okay?" he asked, then looked to Katey and froze. "Are you...?"

Logan slapped his card and ID on the counter. "She is. We need a private room for the day."

There would have been a time when Logan beamed with pride over the fact that Katey was a loup-garou, but there was no time for politeness or boasting.

The clerk shook his head. "It's on the house," he replied, then proceeded to pull out a brass key. "I won't even log it. Just don't trash it or anything."

Logan snatched up his cards and the key. "We appreciate it," he said.

"Is there anything I can help you with?" the clerk asked, his face full of pity and Katey knew he was eager to help. He must have been the son of a beta or omega.

Before Logan had a chance to open his mouth, Katey felt his heave of irritation and quieted him with one touch to his shoulder. She looked at the clerk and shook her head. "No, thank you. We just need some rest. We've been traveling almost all night."

The clerk nodded in understanding. "I'll keep an eye on your room, so no one bothers you."

Katey mustered up the energy to smile and thanked him again before they left the front office and moved the bike toward the other end of the complex. Their room was on the first floor and conveniently out of sight from the highway.

They trudged inside, and Katey was surprised by the cleanliness of the room. A single king bed was pushed up against the right wall with two oak nightstands on either side accommodating lamps and an alarm clock. Across from the bed was a dresser, upon which sat a television and TV Guide program. Opposite the front door was a vanity counter with a single sink and tall mirror with soap and other basic bathroom amenities tucked into one corner in a neat pile on top of a stack of towels. The door to the bathroom was to the right of the sink.

Logan walked in and dropped the duffle bag on the floor at the foot of the bed. Katey quietly shut the door and mindlessly stumbled toward the bed until her legs hit the edge and she toppled forward onto the mattress.

She heard her fiancé let out a snort of amusement. As her eyes drifted shut and her legs now curled up comfortably on top of the blankets, Katey vaguely heard the sound of rushing water like a toilet flushing and light footsteps on the carpet.

Through the haze of drifting sleep, she couldn't recall if Logan had ever crawled into bed with her. By the time she opened her eyes again, it was a few hours later according to the clock on the nightstand, and although it was insufficient sleep, her body felt a little more refreshed than it had when they first arrived at the motel.

With stiff muscles, Katey pushed herself up and looked around. The duffle bag was still on the floor, but Logan was nowhere to be found. More awake now than she had been in the last twelve hours, Katey jumped off the bed and rushed to the window. The motorcycle was gone.

Her heart pounded against her chest until it hurt, but she took a small bit of comfort in the fact that their bond was still pulsing strongly in her spirit. Logan was alive. She climbed back on the bed and found a piece of the motel stationary sitting face-up on one of the unruffled pillows. Katey snagged it up and read the familiar, beautiful cursive.

Katey,
If you wake up before I come back, I've gone to the store to get food. I will be back shortly.
Love, Logan

Katey swallowed hard. How far was the store? She tried to search her memory for any sign of a grocery store along the highway they drove down, but couldn't recall any. That wasn't surprising, considering how tired she had been straddling the back of Logan's motorcycle.

She checked the clock again. If Logan wanted to be in Louisiana before nightfall, they would have to leave within the next few hours. When did he leave? Had he been gone the entire time she was asleep, or did he take a nap with her? Perhaps he just left, and his absence woke her up? Or, did he leave hours ago and he should have been back much earlier than this?

Within less than a minute, her head was spinning with all the possible things that could have gone wrong. The loneliness devoured her as it had when Logan was away during the Devian evacuation, but she didn't have Ben's company to rely on.

In one sense, she was terrified for her own safety, but also for Logan. He was just as alone as she was, but perhaps he was not near as vulnerable. She clung to their bond, knowing that if anything changed, she would feel it there. If it ever stopped feeding her its reassuring energy, then she knew that Logan was gone. Her wolf howled for her mate and Katey was tempted to copy the cry for help but held the impulse at bay.

Every possible scenario was explored as Katey held her head in her hands. The panic had nearly consumed her in the silence until her phone rang. Praying that it was Logan, she scrambled to reach her jeans pocket.

Although it wasn't Logan, the caller would be a welcome voice to hear in the chaos that had engulfed the last twenty-four hours.

"Darren?" she hastily answered.

"Katey, where are you and Logan?"

Swallowing back the tears that wanted to leak from her eyes, she replied, "I'm in a motel room. I don't know where Logan is."

"I just spent the last thirty minutes trying to call him, but his phone must be dead."

Katey took a stuttered breath and tried not to break down. What if his phone had been smashed in an accident? "He left a note saying that he went to get groceries, but I don't know when that was, and I was asleep when he left." Without meaning to, her words came out in a gradually building whimper, the threatening tears choking her.

"Hey," Darren said in a peculiarly calm voice. "It's all right. I'm sure Logan is fine."

"Are you and the rest okay?" she quickly asked.

"We are fine. The vamps told us this morning what happened. Michael left sometime in the middle of the night, but he's letting us borrow some of his guards. We're packing up to come to the safe house now."

Katey cleared her throat. "Darren, the safe house... it's not there."

There was a long pause of silence before Darren asked, "What do you mean?"

To the best of her abilities, she began to tell him all about what they saw and what Logan found out. While she spoke, she heard footsteps come toward the phone and knew that Dustin and Ben must have heard her from wherever they were in the house.

She tried to picture them there in the living room or the kitchen and how the morning sun would have been streaming through the windows. Homesickness hit her like a punch in the gut, and she wanted nothing more than for her and Logan to be back in Crestucky with the rest of their pack.

Once she finished her story, she heard a heavy sigh from the other end of the line. "Okay," Darren whispered. Through the phone, over miles of distance, somehow, she could feel the gravity of his emotions. It was the same storm that Logan found himself in, but stronger.

Katey understood his grief. They tried so hard to keep the Deviants safe and in his eyes, it might have been for nothing. Although they didn't know the details, Darren would fill in the blanks and assume the worst, just as she did with Logan.

A thundering noise came from the highway and Katey couldn't dart to the window fast enough. She bumped into a corner of the nightstand in the process and nearly sent a lamp to the floor. It would have been worth the damage.

Logan came cruising in on his motorcycle, making a straight line for their side of the motel complex.

"Logan's back," she nearly screeched.

"Good. Keep me on the phone. I need to talk to him."

The half a minute it took for Logan to park the bike, grab the groceries, and duck inside the room took far too long. As soon as the door was closed, Katey tossed the phone on the bed with Darren still waiting on the line and tackled her mate.

He wasn't the formidable pillar of strength that she was used to. With one arm toting a couple of plastic bags laden with goods, he stumbled backward until he collided with a wall. Katey pinned him there, her arms wrapped around his waist.

She let the heat from his body seep into her bones. It reminded her that he was alive, his heart beating against her ears. His steady breaths told her that he was near and safe with her.

"When did you leave?"

Logan's arm slowly enveloped her, and he made no move to resist her embrace. "I intended to be back before you got up."

"I thought something happened to you." Katey buried her face in his chest, savoring his natural, intoxicating scent mingled with those from the highway and all the places they had been since last night.

"Did you try to call?" His soothing voice pleasingly rumbled in her ears.

"No. I just woke up a little while ago."

"My phone died," he said and held up his armful of bags to show her. "I bought us a charger to share. I imagine your phone is low on battery too."

Then, Katey remembered Darren who probably heard every word they said. She reluctantly pulled away and looked back to the phone on the bed. "Darren's on the phone."

Logan gently pushed her aside, set the bags down by his duffle bag and snatched up the phone. Katey wasn't the least bit offended by Logan's eagerness to talk to his alpha. They hadn't heard from the pack since before they left Crestucky and it was a fair assumption that they could have been harmed by the hunters in the strike on the town.

"Darren?"

"I'm still here," Katey heard from her place by the door.

As she watched Logan set himself down on the bed, she realized that he had not taken a nap earlier. Dark circles hung under his dull eyes, and his lips were turned down in a frown that seemed to mar his face in a way that made her worried.

Another thing she now noticed was that his hair was different. His blonde highlights were gone, and his hair was completely black now. Not only that, but he had cut off his ponytail. Now, his hair was as short as Dustin's but had a sheen as if he had styled it. Covertly sniffing the air, she found this to be true. The traces of hair gel and dye were certainly there. He must have done it while she was sleeping. The empty box of hair coloring that sat on the sink counter was a testament to that.

Logan must have done it to help cover their escape. The hunters would be on the lookout for unique hair like Logan's and the more change to it, the better off they were. Katey was not displeased with the change, but she wondered if she needed to cut her own hair to maintain the disguise. She reached up and touched the tip of a strand that draped over her shoulder and regretted the thought. She loved her hair too much to cut it shorter.

"We're going to Louisiana to find Michael. Do the vamps know where he is?" Logan asked.

"They said New Orleans, but I told them we were going north instead. They didn't give me any details about where in New Orleans he would be... I need to call Jacob."

Their eyes met, and Katey nodded, answering his unspoken question. Yes, Darren knew what happened.

"I wish I could tell you that I could pick up Jacob's scent last night, but I didn't get a chance. We were chased off before I could pick up a definite trail."

"That's fine, Logan." Darren cleared his throat. "If the safe house has been compromised, then we'll go to Louisiana too. Charge your phone and let us know when you get there."

Before Darren had a chance to hang up, Logan asked, "Were any families in town hit?"

Another voice, Dustin's, chimed in. "According to the vamps, no one was killed. A few houses were burned. The reports are saying it was a gas explosion, but the vamps were there and saw the hunters set fire to the place."

Katey crossed her arms over her stomach. "They burned the safe house too. Why would they burn anything?"

Logan grimaced. "Maybe they thought someone was inside at the time."

She shivered and tried hard not to place herself in the shoes of someone about to be burned alive. She couldn't conceive why anyone would want someone to suffer such a traumatic end. Yet, from what she had heard and witnessed, hunters seemed even less human than loups-garous when it came to brutality.

"Those families are leaving town," Darren said. "We'll inform the vamps to not take them north. There's another safe house compound in Georgia. With luck, that's where any survivors might have gone after the attack in Alabama."

Logan nodded but said nothing as his eyes drifted shut.

Katey moved forward and sat on the bed next to Logan. "He's falling asleep, Darren."

"You two get some rest. We'll see you in Louisiana."

Logan's eyes popped open. "Got it. We'll be in touch." With that, he ended the call and rubbed at his face with both palms.

"You should get some sleep."

He grumbled something unintelligible and then stood up. His body swayed for a second as if he were drunk, and then crouched down by the plastic grocery bags on the floor. He pulled out a package containing a charger cord and a handful of packets of jerky.

"I couldn't find a real store anywhere close, but there was a convenience store at a gas station down the road, and it had some things."

The other bag contained water bottles that he stuffed into the duffel bag, but he kept two out for them to drink soon. It wasn't until she saw the jerky that she realized how hungry she truly was. With her stomach growling, she tore open a pack and shoved a few pieces in her mouth with as much grace as a starving animal.

When she looked up, Logan was still crouched on the ground, one palm pressed against his forehead as if it hurt. Forgetting her hunger again, Katey tossed aside the bag and lifted Logan to his feet. "Logan, please. You need to get some sleep before we have to leave again."

He plopped onto the bed and looked at Katey, his blue eyes even more striking against his new hair. If they weren't so bloodshot,

Katey might have thought them more beautiful. She reached up and weaved her fingers through the short locks of hair that were stiffened and chilled by the gel.

"I wanted to get you some hair dye, but they didn't have any at the store."

She shook her head and smiled. "It's fine. We can dye it in Louisiana if you're that concerned."

Logan pulled her hand away from his head and held it between his palms, focusing all his attention on how he held it and rubbed her skin with the utmost care and tenderness. "I didn't want to leave you here alone," he mumbled, his reddened eyes closing again.

"I wish your phone hadn't died," Katey replied, watching how his hands sandwiched hers. "I was worried something had happened to you."

Logan took a deep breath and opened his eyes. He lazily looked around. "I need to get my phone charged."

Katey leaned over and grabbed the package. Using her teeth, she tore open the hard plastic top, something scissors or a pocket knife would have been more equipped to do. The sharp edge cut open her lip, but she barely felt the sting.

"Didn't any of your foster parents teach you not to do that?" Logan remarked as he released her hands and pulled out his phone.

Katey unwound the cord and presented the charger to him. "If they did, I probably wasn't listening anyway."

A faint smile crossed Logan's lips as he took it and leaned over the bed to plug the charger into an outlet behind one of the nightstands. When Logan returned, his gaze fell on her bleeding lip. The cut had already healed, but Katey could still feel the warm blood cooling on her skin just below her lip.

He reached out and in a gesture that would have seemed normal, Logan drew her in for a kiss. What made it unusual was Logan's attention to the spot where her lip had been sliced. His tongue moved along the edge of her mouth, cleaning up the blood, and then slipped into her mouth.

Katey allowed herself to be intimate and grazed her own tongue along his. The metallic taste of blood registered, but she didn't pull away. They were used to blood in their food, just not in other people.

Logan's fingers curled against the nap of her neck, and her skin crawled with pleasure at his touch. Katey scooted forward until their knees and thighs were flush together. Once more, she laced her fingers through his hair, playing with it until the locks were no longer stiff in her hands.

Sparks shot across her body when Logan gripped her waist and pulled her down onto the bed. It then occurred to Katey that they were completely alone. They had never lain in a bed together without one of the pack members close by or in an adjacent room. Here, in the motel, miles away from anyone who might keep them accountable for their actions, Katey and Logan were free to do whatever they wanted, and no one would know about it.

With his body half suspended over hers, trapping her in place, he continued to kiss her. Katey could feel her body reacting to his touch, slow at first and then growing with intensity. Tremors of pleasure flooded through her limbs as she slipped her hand under his shirt, feeling his rippling abs.

Logan let out a muffled groan, and Katey knew she was doing something right. Her fingers ascended higher, gliding over his smooth skin. He tore away for a brief second to tug his shirt over his head and discarded it onto the floor.

When he came back down to connect his lips with hers again, Katey cried out. It was nothing that he did, and it was certainly unwelcome to her. To Katey, it felt as if a pounding force had rammed against her skull from the inside out. It was only a second, a heartbeat of pain, and then it was gone.

She opened her eyes and looked at Logan, his tense body looming over hers. His gaze was a crimson, lustful red, as hers must have been.

"What's wrong?" he whispered.

Katey shook her head and pulled him down to kiss again. Whatever it had been, it only lasted a moment, and she wasn't about to let that stop her from enjoying what might come.

Logan followed her lead, and his hand found the edge of her hooded jacket. She moaned as his fingers slid up her side as they once had a month ago in Alaska. She felt the draft of open air as her shirt and jacket was pushed up over her waist.

Without meaning to, Katey's back arched to the wave of ecstasy. Logan responded by tucking his arm around her waist and pulling her up until their bodies were pressed together. What bit of skin was exposed, touched his and she moaned again. All she knew was she wanted more.

Her muscles tensed with anticipation as Logan's other hand explored further up to her chest.

Before he could even reach her bra, the pulse of pain came again and her body seized under his. Katey winced, and she frowned when Logan pulled away. He removed his hands from her and supported himself, so they were no longer touching.

"What is it?"

Katey whimpered like a heartbroken puppy and raked her nails over his biceps. "Don't stop."

He shook his head, the conflict of desires plain in his gaze. "No. Something's wrong. Tell me."

"It's just a headache. It'll go away."

"Loups-garous don't get headaches." In a gesture of modesty and respect, Logan pulled Katey's shirt down to cover her midsection again, much against her wishes. "I'm sorry. I didn't mean for that to happen."

Through the blinding lust, reason returned to Katey, and she nodded. "It's okay."

Logan stood beside the bed and put his shirt back on before lying beside her. With his arm around her waist and head achingly close to her neck, he simply breathed, and they both came down from the high of fleshly yearning.

After a while, Katey felt she could think straight and looked to Logan, her eyes green once more. He was fast asleep and lightly snoring against her shoulder. She smiled and rolled until they were facing one another.

Although the idea of pre-marital sex was something Logan had opposed, he made it so difficult to refuse. For a moment, she felt more alive than she had in her entire existence. Not even the joy of running as a wolf could compare to the paradise that Logan's caresses brought her to. It was fortunate that Logan was still in control of his senses to pull himself back from almost crossing that boundary they had set for themselves. Once Logan was rested and fed, they would continue onto Louisiana.

What was more disturbing than their near negligence in abstinence, was how the pains had mysteriously vanished. In its place, Katey felt a dull throbbing in her blood that didn't cause her pain, but only a mild discomfort. Nothing she could do in the way of stretches and adjusting her position on the bed would alleviate the sensations.

Her wolf had no answer that she was willing to give. The feeling of expectancy was there, nothing more.

CHAPTER 15

After parking Logan's bike at the Canal Place Garage near the Mississippi River and across from the aquarium, they started their trek down Canal Street, into the swiftly setting sun. To the east, a blue and purple haze lined the horizon and Katey couldn't help but admire how distinct the line was in the sky, dividing their world between night and day.

The air was bursting with scents. The salty river breeze that wafted from behind them collided with the aromas of restaurants and cafes. Katey could smell everything from sugar-powdered pastries baking in ovens to the spiced tinge of true Cajun seafood and authentic gumbo that made her stomach ache. The only thing they had to eat were those few packets of beef jerky at the motel, and that did not satisfy the biting hunger. At the same time, the stench of stale alcohol assaulted her nose and made her lose her appetite.

Music joined the myriad of scents. Jazz, country, and rock melodies wove together, filtering through windows and doors of clubs along the strip. The cacophony of noises roared in her ears as well, but it wasn't more than her senses could handle. After some time spent walking, the modern shopping centers and restaurants gave way to an endless sea of European-inspired architecture with richly ornate facades that shot up three or four stories high in some places.

Lining the streets were all makes and models of cars, towering palm trees, and bright red trolleys that carted tourists down on either side. Somehow, Katey had imagined the French Quarter to be even more touristy and old-world in style.

They had been walking for several blocks before Logan paused, his hand grasping hers, and he sniffed the air. Katey did the same, and she smelled it too. There was a distinct trail of vampire close by. They looked to their right, down Bourbon Street, and she found the French Quarter she had been expecting.

There was hardly any room on the paved street for more than two cars to travel down abreast of each other. The style of the brick buildings was similar, but different as their balconies loomed over the sidewalks where tourists and vendors crowded for space.

With wary feet, they made their way down the street that was dotted with potholes, passing by more shops – some modern and some not – as they searched. Logan had told her they would have to search for any vampire who might know Michael's whereabouts. They had tried to call him as soon as they pulled off the interstate that led into New Orleans, but his phone had been disconnected. Katey was tempted to think the worst – that the hunters had intercepted him before he could leave Florida. Still, they had to try and find him. Unfortunately, the vampires would probably be at some club or bar that catered to their kind and Katey was not looking forward to it.

As the sunlight waned, colorful neon lights sparked to life down the strip, casting a red and yellow glow over the darkening street and shop doors that were more like tall, lime green shutters in some places, opening onto the street under the balconies.

The iron railings and balusters along the balconies were decorated with potted plants whose vines hung low and must have sprouted flowers in the springtime. Some residents – or perhaps tourists – stood upon the balconies and took pictures of the sights below.

In some places, the fronts of buildings were wrapped in scaffolding, cluttered with construction supplies and tools as the edifice was in the process of being renovated. Several blocks away, Katey spotted what looked to be a man mounted on a horse, trotting down the street. When they came closer, she realized the rider was a policeman just before he turned to patrol down a connecting street. She didn't know that there was still a mounted police force on active duty anymore. To Katey, that sort of thing was restricted to old movies and foreign countries.

Somewhere in her baffled thoughts, Katey walked into a wall of odor that she could only distinguish as a horrid mix of urine and vomit that drifted from the north. She had to stop and gag, tugging Logan to a halt just outside a cigar shop that reeked of tobacco and smoke. Her eyes watered and for a moment she thought her own vomit would join in the unpleasant smells of Bourbon Street.

Logan seemed unaffected by the stench and waited until she could get her bearings again. "I know it's bad. It's going to get worse."

"How could it possibly get worse?" she asked while trying to swallow back the beef jerky that wanted to see the light of day again.

Logan didn't answer her, and once she straightened up, they carried on. His hold on her hand tightened as they went and Katey could sense that if they had the time, he would have comforted her more.

Outside of the shops, merchants, and vendors displayed their goods, often shirts and souvenirs for the tourists. In some of the windows were displays of clothing and risqué fashion that Logan paid no attention to. Drunken voices slithered out of the countless bars, and strip clubs they passed and Katey walked a little closer to Logan.

Bands and other street performers came into view. Some of them were single operations with a simple hat out to solicit tips, while others were five or six musician groups playing lively music for a throng of spectators. Katey watched for a moment and admired the raw talent, but had no money and no time to pay them as they continued their search.

The crowds began to thin further north down the block, and the vampire trail grew stronger with each step. Yet, with the potent scent of sulfur came another unwelcome sensation that set Katey's teeth on edge.

It was a nearly imperceptible feeling that started in her bones and snaked its way through her blood. It was unlike anything she had experienced before and with her growing discomfort from what happened in the motel in Mississippi, Katey wanted to scream. It was too much.

Logan looked at her, probably sensing her unease. "It's okay. Just keep walking."

"What is that?" she whispered, looking around as if the answer lay with the shopkeepers or pedestrians that passed them by.

"Magic," Logan replied in a calm voice. "New Orleans is like the mecca of voodoo and witchcraft. Most of them are wannabes or charlatans, but there are a few who truly practice the craft. Some humans can sense the energy, but we can more so. You'll feel better once we pass the source."

Katey cringed as images of shrunken heads and painted witch doctors were conjured in her mind. "Where is the source?"

"It's probably one of these shops. I can smell the herbs they use in their spells and rituals."

Katey was afraid to breathe too deeply, lest the suffocating smells of New Orleans made her dizzy. Instead, she steeled herself against the effects of the magic and whatever else had been plaguing her since they left the motel.

The more they walked and dodged past hustlers, the begging homeless, and drunkards teetering on the sidewalk, the stronger the magic hammered at her spirit. Her wolf, who had been silent up to now, cowered and growled at the bizarre powers.

Up ahead *"Madame Celeste's Voodoo Emporium"* beamed through the darkness in swirly, mystic letters across a sign. Katey gritted her teeth. There were no windows for her to peek through, but she could smell what Logan had been talking about.

The entrance, a set of blue shutter-like doors like the ones scattered along Bourbon Street, released a flow of magic, the essence of incense, spices, herbs, oils, petrified wood, and other aromas that Katey couldn't recognize. Artificial firelight danced from inside, casting a flickering glow onto the pavement.

Just outside the open doors, sitting on a faded stool was a petite woman. She wore a dark, flowing skirt that pooled on the sidewalk around her feet and a white, billowy shirt, embroidered with swirls and flowery designs. Her hands were folded neatly in her lap, her head held high and wrapped in a red turban to contain her hair that was pushed up inside of it. Hoop earrings dangled from her ears as her dark eyes were set across the street.

Katey shrank back and wanted to dart to the other sidewalk to avoid her, but Logan pulled her on. If they acted strangely, they would draw attention to themselves. The only way to cross the river was to go straight through.

They were no more than a couple of yards away when the woman turned and locked eyes with the two of them. The change in her cold expression shifted, and Katey wanted to run. She beamed at the loups-garous and stood from her stool. She didn't seem young, but neither too old. The woman was at a sweet spot in an age where her beauty and womanhood were in full bloom.

Logan guided Katey around his back to stand on the side closest to the street, serving as her shield against the woman and her magic.

Katey averted her eyes but felt the woman's gaze drill into her like a penetrating heat.

"Friends," she greeted in a silvery voice and tinged with a thick accent that seemed neither African nor Creole. "May I have a word?" she asked, seeming eager, but polite.

Logan waved her off. "We don't have the time, sorry."

The woman charged forward and grasped Logan's arm. Despite her fear, Katey stepped up and made her presence known. Something in her wolf flared with territorial rage. The woman saw her and recoiled her hands instantly.

"I'm sorry, princess," she said. "I did not mean to offend."

Katey narrowed her eyes on the woman. "I'm not a princess," she corrected and weaved her arm through Logan's before turning away. Making her claim on Logan was all Katey was interested in.

The voodoo woman blocked their way with her hands held up to stop them. "But, you are. I can see it in you."

Logan scoffed. "And I'm sure for thirty bucks, you'll tell us more, right?"

The woman's smile faded. "Do not insult me, wolf."

They both went rigid. Could this woman tell they were loups-garous or was she simply implying that Logan was like a wolf? He blew air from his nose as a show of dominance and stepped toward her, his blue eyes holding all the excuses she would need to move out of the way.

"Stand aside, woman."

She crossed her arms defiantly. "Please," she crooned. "It's been so long since I stood in the presence of such great creatures as yourselves. Indulge me for a moment only."

Katey felt the muscle in her jaw jump. Yes, the woman knew.

She offered out her hand. "My name is Marie. I am an apprentice here under Madame Celeste. She's away for a moment, but I'm sure she would love to meet you, princess."

Katey didn't accept the hand of friendship just yet. Through the dissonance of voices and feelings that streamed down Bourbon Street, she reached out with her spirit to read this woman. There was no malice in her eyes and no cunning plan of deception about her. It seemed, regardless of what instinct told her, that this woman was kind and willing to help them. Perhaps if she knew what they were, she would know where the vamps were hiding.

In a gesture that might have confirmed everything the woman thought of her, Katey briefly shook her hand and was sure to give it a firm grip to hide her anxiety. "We can't stay long enough to meet your Madame."

The smile returned to Marie's face, showing her pearl-white teeth against dark skin. "Oh, well, I suppose that will be all right. It was my pleasure to meet you, then."

Logan read her words as the cue to break away, but Marie blocked them again.

"No, wait. Please, allow me to grant you with some of my services. I have many spells and talismans that you can benefit from."

He shook his head. "We're not interested in your magic."

A sly, unconvinced glint in her eye made Katey pay closer attention. "What about that problem you've been having? You... can't shift, it seems. That's a very serious thing." She fished out a business card from the folds of her dress. "I have just the thing that can help you if you so choose. Here is my card. I know you're in a hurry, but please know I am here to help you in whatever way I can."

Katey's eyebrows shot up with curiosity. Was there such a potion or herb that could help Logan? More importantly, was it worth the risk to dabble in magic just to settle a one-hundred-year-long battle?

Logan snatched the card from her hand and shoved it into his pocket. "Fine," he mumbled and pressed past her, dragging Katey along.

Marie rushed forward, abandoning her shop front, and grabbed Katey's hand. They all froze, and Katey looked into Marie's dark and haunting eyes.

"My dear, take courage," she whispered. "I sense the trouble in you. It will pass with the morning. And as for the other thing," she smiled, "you will make a fine leader. Even our people have been waiting for you to bring peace. I have been privileged to witness many things in my life, but you are the greatest. I shall tell my grandchildren of the day that I met you."

Marie kissed the back of Katey's hand and then hurried away inside her shop, probably to tell all her friends whom she had just seen on Bourbon Street.

Heedless of the confusion that warred within Katey, Logan pulled her along, and they left the voodoo shop behind them in the chaos of New Orleans nightlife.

"Are you going to go back?" Katey asked once they were a few blocks away and back into the swarm of humanity.

"Are you kidding?" he laughed. "I wouldn't touch magic. My arm is still tingling from when she grabbed me."

Katey felt it too, spreading from her palm to the tip of her fingers. There certainly was something spiritual about Marie, magic or not. Her wolf, however, did not find peace the farther they got from the shop. She still bucked and writhed at the aftereffects of the magic, and it left Katey slightly disoriented.

"Just checking," she replied, hoping to sound more light-hearted than she felt.

The smell of vamps diverted down a narrow alleyway, and the two followed it until they came to a painted door that vibrated with the bass of the music coming from inside. There was no sign, no lights, nothing to indicate that there was anything there at all besides the music.

Logan tested the doorknob and turned it hard until something in the locking mechanism snapped. He released it, and a few flakes of shiny metal finish floated to the ground. The door opened freely, letting the music cascade out into the alley. The stench of vampires and blood plumed with the music, and they ducked inside, no longer afraid of what threat a vamp may pose.

When they closed the door, they were plunged into a complete and total darkness. Any human wouldn't have been able to tell if they were blinking because it was so pitch-black in the corridor. Katey and Logan, on the other hand, could see the edges of the brick that made up the walls of the long hallway that led toward another door at the end.

There were no guards, no sentries posted to keep strangers out of their club. Katey assumed that this must have been a public spot, only known by the locals or those who had been told of its secret location. That must have been a great tourist deterrent. No vamp wanted a human walking in on a feast if that's not what they expected to find.

The music pulsed in Katey's ears, louder than her own heartbeat and thudding in her chest just as hard. Logan led the way down the hall and once more tested the door. It was unlocked.

Inside the inner chamber of the club, Katey's eyes were assailed by flashing strobe lights of reds, golds, and blues. The music was blaring, but nobody was dancing on the designated dance floor in the middle of the club.

To the right was a bar counter that extended for over a dozen seats to the back wall. Behind the counter was a wall of various bottles of liquor and tap stations. A man, undoubtedly a vamp, stood behind the counter and talked casually with a few of his patrons on the side opposite where Katey and Logan stood.

To the left were pedestal tables with rickety wooden chairs pushed up under them and along the wall beyond were plush velvet booths that were occupied by a various assortment of characters.

Many, as Katey was surprised to find out, were human. Some in normal clothes and others in lavish, black, gothic outfits complete with spikes, studs, buckles, corsets, and top hats for their respective genders. Upon their middle fingers were metal, claw-like accessories. All eyes were rimmed in heavy makeup and lips were painted black to match their hair and clothing.

Katey watched with fascination as a couple flirted in a dark corner. The girl was not in a costume as the others were, but her partner was dressed in a dark suit that hugged his thin frame. One moment, they were giggling about something, and then next she offered her neck to him. The man took his claw and tenderly sliced into her skin and sucked on what little blood flowed out.

Katey saw the girl sigh with pleasure, and she couldn't help but flinch at the sight. These were not real vampires as she knew them. If a vamp wanted a meal, he wouldn't take it so compliantly, and his teeth would have served as a better tool than any manufactured claw.

Unsurprisingly, the man pulled away after only a few seconds of drinking.

Logan's attention was not on the cult followers to their left, but on the bar and its occupants. Katey turned and saw their eyes were fixed on them with a fierce intensity. Only the barkeep appeared unruffled by their presence.

They were dressed as civilians in jeans and loose-fitting shirts or jackets, nothing like the humans on the other side of the bar. It occurred to Katey that if those women with the tops of their breasts gushing over their corsets and men downing their red-colored mixed drinks had been vampires, they would have immediately smelled the loups-garous when they stepped into the room.

No, these men at the bar were the real vampires and they were not happy to see Katey and Logan.

Disregarding the filthy looks they shot across the room, Logan strode up to the counter and waited for the barkeep to approach them. Katey observed that he was pale, just like the others at the end of the bar – although it was hard to tell in the dazzling lights – and wore a pair of slacks and a button-down shirt that concealed his broad frame well. He might have doubled as a bouncer if the need arose.

He ran a hand through his slick blonde hair and leaned on the counter in front of Logan. "Listen, I don't want any trouble in my place," he said. Katey could detect the lilt of a Cajun cadence in his warning. "If y'all can't play nice, you're gonna have to leave."

"We have no intention of staying," Logan said, copying the bar-tender's stance by leaning his elbows on the pitted and polished countertop. "We're looking for Michael Gennari. We know he's in New Orleans, but we don't know where exactly."

The vamp's face didn't give him away, but Katey sensed the shard of fear slice the bartender. "What do you want with Michael?"

Katey stepped up beside Logan. "We're friends," she replied. "We're supposed to meet him, but we separated before he could tell us where."

The bartender seemed confused that Katey would call Michael, a vamp, their friend. Despite that, he straightened and shook his head. "I haven't seen Michael in over fifty years. If I knew where he was, I'd tell you."

Logan's hands balled into fists, but one touch from Katey eased him back from getting violent with the bartender. Just like with Marie, she sensed no deception in him. Yet, the twinge of fear made her wonder if he knew more than he was letting on.

"Do you know anyone who might be close to Michael in town that we can ask?" Katey questioned, keeping her voice low and good-mannered. There was no need to make a spectacle.

The bartender thought for a moment, then shook his head again. "I don't agree with my coven's decision to not be involved in this revolution Michael's plannin'. I don't mind servin' werewolves as much as I mind servin' those humans over there." He inclined his head toward the goths in the corner laughing and sipping on their drinks. "As long as I'm paid, I don't care. My coven leader might know where Michael is, but I doubt he will wanna speak to you."

Logan gave a curt nod. "We understand. We don't want a fight either."

From down the counter, Katey heard the muttering words of one of the club patrons, his voice cutting through the blaring music. "You brought the fight in here, ya mangy dog."

There were a few unpleasant words sprinkled in his grumblings, but Logan heard him loud and clear. He looked at the cluster of four vamps at the end of the bar. They were outnumbered and had no weapons on them. Katey squeezed Logan's sleeve, a spell of dizziness smacking her from out of nowhere.

"What did you say, bloodsucker?" he growled.

Katey closed her eyes and sighed. "Logan," she whispered in exasperation.

The vamps stood from their stools and swaggered toward them. "You heard me, dog. You came in here, on our turf, and expect us to just deal with it? You're trespassing, mutt."

He pushed Logan's shoulder, but his muscles were too taut, and he barely moved.

The bartender held out his hand between the two. "Hey, Caz. Back off. He wasn't lookin' for trouble."

"Well," Caz said, "he got it." He puffed out his chest, and Katey felt nauseated by the male egos that clashed in their space around the counter.

"Don't make me call Ezra," the bartender warned. "He won't take kindly to havin' to pay for damages again."

Caz's buddies lost every ounce of fight and backed away, leaving their bold friend to deal with the loup-garou by himself. They didn't want to feel the wrath of whoever Ezra was. Caz, however, was not concerned and through the dominance of both men, she knew Caz had murder on his mind.

"Then we'll take it outside," Caz said. "You wouldn't mind beasting out on Bourbon Street, would ya, mutt?"

Katey couldn't take much more of it and stepped between them, her hands on their chests. "Guys, cool it," she demanded as she tried to send out whatever peaceful auras she could muster to make them change their minds.

A look dawned on Caz's face, and he looked to Katey with eyes wide and unblinking. "You!" he hissed.

She met his shocked gaze, but couldn't place it if they had met once before, perhaps last month at the castle. No, he wasn't familiar in the least. She would have recognized his black eyes and shoulder-length golden hair instantly. The only thing that rang a bell was the look of pure and complete hatred in his eyes. That hatred reminded her of Yaverik as he held a gun pointed at Logan, or how Martel had fought the other loups-garous with such fervor. Perhaps this man had become a vampire by the bite, rather than having been born one.

"You're that bitch they've all been talking about."

Logan shunted Katey aside and grabbed Caz's shirt collar. "Call her that one more time and I promise you won't have a tongue to speak it again."

The two snarled at one another, sharp teeth bared and glinting in the psychedelic lights. Caz's friends stepped up from behind, their eyes darting between their leader and Katey. The bartender pulled out his phone, unwilling to step between them but ready to call his authorities.

Katey stared at the two of them. Had loups-garous and vampires always fought like this? Aside from the wars, the prejudice, and the plots to wipe out one another, how many fights like this would erupt in daily life? How many civilians had been hurt or even killed when they were caught in the crossfire of these two feuding races?

Marie's words came back to her. Even those who were human, but practiced the art of magic, wanted there to be peace between loups-garous and vamps. How many more beings of the supernatural world were glad to have Katey come to restore the balance? How badly would she fail, as she did now to break up a little bar brawl?

A gust of wind came from behind Katey. Logan and Caz were held apart by an intruder, his hands gripping their shoulders tightly. The loup-garou and vampire blinked back their astonishment and looked to their mediator.

Katey leaned around Logan to get a better look. She hadn't heard or seen the vamp come in. Perhaps he had been lingering in a dark corner the whole time. The vamp's frame was slender but powerful under a fitting trench coat that buttoned up around his neck and down his chest. The tails of his coat dusted the ground, concealing most of his legs that were clad in black jeans.

The pale skin of his face and hands stood out against his clothing, nearly iridescent. His deep black hair looked soft and natural. His facial features were sharp with hollow cheeks and a long, angular nose paired with a set of full lips. His deep brown, trenchant eyes looked out from a pair of dark brows and Katey likened him to someone who belonged on the cover of a male modeling magazine.

Instantly, the vamps shrank back, and Katey sensed a reverent fear in them toward this newcomer. He looked at the offending vamp and glared. "Caz, you will leave these people alone. You know the new penalty for inciting trouble."

Katey tilted her head at the vamp's marked Russian accent.

Caz shivered and nodded. "Yes. I'm sorry, Anton."

What kind of authority did Anton possess that the absent Ezra didn't? Anton pushed back Caz, and the vamps darted out an exit door on the other side of the bar. He turned to Logan and reproached, "You will learn to control your temper, young wolf."

Katey looked at Logan and saw the complete and utter terror in his eyes. Did he know Anton as well? Or did he understand why the vampires fled and assumed that he was different and to be rightly feared?

Despite his obvious hesitancy toward Anton, Logan bristled at the innocuous insult and opened his mouth to rebuke, but Katey was too quick and started in.

"Thank you for breaking that up," she said, stepping out from behind Logan to meet the vamp who might have saved them a lot of trouble.

Anton turned to her and the hardness in his face melted into recognition. "Are you Katey?" he asked.

Logan swept her behind as before to protect her, but Katey detected a discrete quiver in his hands. She nodded, sure that a man as powerful as Anton must know all about Michael and the prophecy too. Maybe he was one of the elders that Michael had talked about back in Crestucky and would be attending the gathering.

The vamp smiled and bowed, disregarding Logan's trepidation. "It is an honor to meet you. Michael has been expecting you and Logan. He will be thrilled to know you are safe."

"How did you know who she was?" Logan asked, the aggression simmering down to a manageable level.

Anton looked to Katey with fondness. "She looks just like her mother, Jane."

Katey dropped her gaze. Did everyone know her parents except for her?

"Can you take us to Michael?" Logan asked, his voice tense, but seemingly willing to cooperate as long as Anton seemed to be on their side.

Anton nodded. "Certainly. That's why I'm here."

Katey looked up. "Did you know we were in New Orleans?"

He moved away and led them toward the exit after giving his regards to the bartender. The other club guests weren't paying any attention, despite the near fight that just broke out and the vamps that moved in blurs around the counter.

"I knew you would be coming, but I wasn't sure when or where you would be. It was only when I sensed your essence that I was able to find you here." He opened the door for them.

"You tracked us then?" Katey asked, wondering why he would use the term *essence* instead of scent or trail. Maybe that was the ability that Michael had hinted at in Alaska when they had their long talk in the library.

"Yes," he replied as they made their way back out onto the alleyway. It took a moment for Katey to adjust to the barrage of scents and sounds from Bourbon Street again. Night consumed New Orleans, and the real partiers were flooding the streets. "I found your motorcycle first and worked my way from there."

Logan seemed impressed, but not surprised. "Through all of that, you could pick out our trails?"

"Of course," he replied and walked ahead of them down the sidewalk. Pedestrians and tourists gave him a wide berth. "You will learn that I have many abilities that some of our kind do not."

"That's apparent," Logan muttered.

Katey left Logan's side and fell in next to Anton. "Did Michael send you to find us then?"

"Yes," he answered, glancing down at her for a moment and then chuckled. "I can't believe how much you look like Jane. It's like a photograph."

"Did you know my mother too?" she asked excitedly. Katey felt Logan grab her hand from behind. Looking over her shoulder, she felt the swell of insecurity wash over him again, and she tried to not show her zeal in full force.

"I did. I've known your family for many centuries. I personally serve your grandfather. I suppose you could say I'm something of his personal guard."

Katey let herself drop back to Logan's side and kept her questions to herself. As much as she yearned to learn about her mother and wanted to seize any chance to do so, she realized how this must have looked to Logan.

He just risked his neck to defend her honor against an uncouth vampire, and she hadn't shown her gratitude. Not only that, but she was giving Anton far too much attention, despite her burning inquisitiveness. They didn't need Logan to have a fit about her assumed infidelity again.

In a wolfish display of affection, she rubbed her head against his shoulder and hopped up to kiss the edge of his lips.

Logan looked down at her and smirked, amused by her playful way of thanking him.

They took an alternate path down Toulouse Street toward the river, then turned right onto Decatur Street. They walked under the balconies of the buildings that resembled the others in the French Quarter, while to their left, traffic roared by between them and a massive parking lot for tourists and shoppers.

Some of the scents of Bourbon Street clung to her senses, but the saline breeze of the river began to detox her nostrils with its own wild aroma.

"Michael has taken up residence in an abandoned plantation outside of the city," Anton told them. "It's not far from here. I will escort you back to your bike, and we will go from there."

"My bike won't fit three people," Logan remarked, his words carrying an edge like he didn't want to associate with the vampire more than absolutely necessary.

"No need. I have my own."

"Bike?" Katey clarified.

"Yes. Although, mine is a little more... traditional than yours, Logan."

Logan tilted his head, probably trying to understand what he meant.

At the corner of St. Louis Street, Katey tested the air and looked to her left. The familiar prickling sensation alerted her to the presence of another loup-garou, and Logan turned to look that way as well. Across the street, just outside of an H&M store, Katey saw them standing under a spotlight beneath the awning.

Lily's hands were free while Forrest's were loaded down with shopping bags from various stores. Katey recognized the logos on the bags from stores along Canal Street. When the two friend's eyes locked, they squealed and ran down the crosswalk to collide in the middle of the street, ignorant of the honking cars and weird looks they received from the other shoppers.

CHAPTER 16

"Katey! Get out of the street!" Logan shouted.

"Lily!" Forrest screamed from across the road.

The girls didn't pay any mind to their men. Katey hugged Lily's neck until the human coughed for air. Only then did she let go and look at her friend, whom she thought might have been dead.

Lily's face was clean and grinning and apart from her clothes that smelled of bayou and swamp water, and her oily hair that was pulled back away from her face, she looked unharmed.

Then Katey thought what she must have looked like. She hadn't bathed in over a day, and she'd been riding on a motorcycle for hours all over the south. It was possible Lily thought Katey looked even more ragged than herself.

Forrest came running across the street and ushered the two girls back to the sidewalk where Logan and Anton were patiently waiting. A car blared its horn and swerved to avoid them. Katey heard a few cuss words from the driver, but she didn't care. Her friends were alive, and somehow that gave her hope that many other Deviants might be alive too.

Once their feet were back on the brick walkway, Katey and Lily squeezed each other once more.

"I can't believe you're here!" Lily cried.

"Me neither!" Katey replied. "I'm so glad you two are okay!"

Lily's eyes went dull for a brief second, and her lips pinched together as if she were trying not to say too much. She just nodded and looked to Forrest. What horrors they must have seen if they were at the compound when the attack happened? Forrest had experience with massacres like that, but Lily's constitution must have gotten a good beating after seeing all the blood and carnage.

Forrest gave a wary look to Anton as he set down his bags and then clasped arms with Logan and gave him a brotherly half-hug the way men did.

"We've been to the compound... It's good to see you," Logan muttered, a glossy look in his eyes as well. It was obvious that what had haunted Katey's mind had also troubled him during the long, silent drive.

Forrest nodded after clearing his throat. "Same here."

They pulled away and looked to the girls, their source of sanity in these difficult times. Anton waited good-naturedly off to the side, displaying respect for their emotional reunion.

"Who else is in Louisiana?" Katey finally asked as tourists and shoppers walked around their group.

Forrest took a deep breath and shrugged as he bent down to retrieve the shopping bags. "I'm not sure. We got separated at the compound."

Logan raised a hand to stop Katey's next question from blurting out. "We can talk about this later. Right now, we need to find Michael." He looked to Anton, who in turn nodded and proceeded down Decatur Street toward their parking garage. It was still a good distance to walk.

Anton was head of the pack, followed by Logan and Forrest who walked beside one another and talked in hushed tones about who was all left of the Devian pack and what took place in Crestucky after they left.

Katey and Lily brought up the rear, and Lily wanted to talk about anything but what happened in Alabama. Out of respect for her friend, she listened and tried not to eavesdrop on the men's conversations.

"When we got here, Forrest's great-uncle, Will, put us up on his little shack south of here." Lily groaned and rolled her eyes.

Katey laughed at her friend. "What?"

The words flowed out so quickly that Katey had to pay close attention to follow along. "He lives out in the middle of a swamp with the rest of his pack, and it's like some Cajun community thing. They all live a stone's throw from each other, and they're not quiet neighbors. They're all Forrest's family – by marriage – and they're funny and all, but oh my god, they smell like a sewer. The whole place does. I'm surprised they even have running water. I half expected there to be an outhouse or something. I haven't taken a bath since we got here because the water looks dirty anyway. I don't know how anyone can live out there!"

Katey looped her arm through Lily's and sighed. "The world is made up of all kinds," she said with a smile, simply glad to have her friend back. As soon as they were settled, Katey knew they would be up all night talking, as long as the persistent ache in Katey's body went away soon.

"I know," Lily whined, "but does Forrest have to be related to them?"

"You didn't have anywhere else to go?"

Lily looked to the ground and shook her head. "Not really. The whole pack just scattered and my parents are still on vacation. They have no clue what's going on. Forrest said that Will is his closest living relative, so we came here to New Orleans. We thought about going to the backup safe house in Georgia, but we didn't know if it had been compromised too."

Katey paused to think, and a mischievous grin spread across her lips. "I'm sure Anton wouldn't mind taking you two with us to stay with Michael. Wouldn't you, Anton?"

She didn't have to shout at all, and Anton looked over his shoulder at the two girls with an arresting gaze. He looked between their expectant faces and seemed amused. "I'm sure any guest of Katey would be a welcome guest of Michael as well."

Lily shrieked with delight. "I don't have to sleep on that straw mattress!"

Forrest shot her a reprimanding look. "If that straw mattress was good enough for Will, it's good enough for you."

Lily propped her hand on her hip. "I'm not a four-hundred-year-old sea dog who never knew anything better."

Logan smiled. "You're staying with Will?" he asked, obviously not aware that Katey and Lily had dropped the loup-garou's name a few times already. "I wonder if I can still beat him in a round of poker."

Forrest gave a big laugh. "You wish! The man practically invented all the tricks of the game!"

"Have you met Michael yet?" Katey asked Lily.

"No, I don't think so. Is his pack in New Orleans too?"

She shook her head. "No, he's my grandfather. The one I told you about after we got back from Alaska."

Lily's eyes went wide. "The vampire?"

Katey nodded. "Yeah. He showed up the night we had to leave Crestucky." While they walked, she regaled Lily with the story of their flight from Florida to Alabama, then to Louisiana. She was careful enough not to mention any details about the compound and what they saw. Lily already knew, and there was no reason to bring it up just yet. It was far too soon, and Lily's spirit may have still been raw and sensitive.

If there was one thing Katey knew about Lily, it was that she went shopping whenever she was upset. Judging by the bags of clothing and accessories in Forrest's arms, they had been shopping all day.

They finally came to the parking garage, where Lily and Forrest had parked his gray pickup truck as well, and split off with the promise to caravan wherever Anton led them. Seeing them walk away between the rows upon rows of other parking cars, a slight ache developed in the back of Katey's throat. Her mind tried to remind her heart that she would see them again soon, but with everything that took place, nothing was for certain anymore.

Katey and Logan went to the next floor with Anton still in the lead. The vampire was not a man of many words, but the energy that he gave off was enough to set Katey at ease. If it weren't for Katey's willingness to trust the stranger, she was sure that Logan would have told him off the minute Anton assured them that he could lead them to Michael. The apprehension in Logan didn't abate the longer they spent time with the vampire, but he simply hid it better now that he wasn't blindsided by the whole experience of meeting Anton. That's when Katey finally recognized that Logan somehow knew him, but not completely or personally. Perhaps it was the name that set him off in the bar. Whatever it was, Logan seemed willing to collaborate.

Next to Logan's bike was nothing short of an artifact. It was a motorcycle, but the frame was smaller and appeared lighter than any Harley she had ever seen. Her eyes skimmed from the single round headlight on the front to the flat leather seat and the matching saddlebags behind it. It looked as if someone had taken a modern design and simplified it down to the bare necessities for travel.

Logan let out a boisterous laugh when they came closer. "I haven't seen one of these in decades!" he exclaimed. Stepping up to the side, Katey could see his eyes sparkle with nostalgia.

Anton flipped back his trench coat tails and mounted the bike with a suave and fluid gesture. "It's a 1941 Indian Military Model 841," he announced. "But, I modified it slightly."

The vampire revved up the engine, but hardly a sound came from the bike. A human may not have been able to detect the low whirl, and even Katey could just barely hear it over the din of parking garage noise.

Logan clapped his hands and squatted down to inspect the components. "That's incredible. And you're the one who painted it black, I assume?"

"Yes. This is the ideal stealth motorcycle."

Katey believed it. Black and silent, and if Anton were wearing a helmet and gloves, it would slip through the night, and no one would be the wiser.

"We must hurry," Anton said, knocking Logan out of his daydream.

Katey and Logan climbed onto the more modern bike and sped out of the French Quarter and out of New Orleans. Forrest and Lily followed close behind as they traveled down Highway 18 alongside the Mississippi River. After several miles, they turned south, down an unmarked road concealed by birches, elms, oaks, and pines that closed in around them. The path wasn't paved, but the way was smooth enough for their motorcycles and trucks to pass through without rattling their bones at the same time.

The farther they traveled away from civilization, the more at home Katey began to feel. The rich, earthy scents of the wild consumed her soul. The only thing to make it better would have been the lack of vampire scents that seemed to be all around them. No doubt, Michael had deployed some of his guards to watch over the mansion and ensure that no intruders were permitted in.

At first, it was peaceful, and Katey relished in the droning buzz of nocturnal insects. As the trees and foliage became thicker with every mile, Katey began to feel the strange and painful ramming inside of her skull like she had felt in the motel.

Her wolf sprung to life, exhorting her to dismount from the speeding motorcycle and disappear into the woods. Katey resisted and paid dearly for the refusal. The pain intensified and she gripped Logan's shirt front in her fists.

He looked over his shoulder. "You okay?" he asked.

She lied and nodded. The slamming inside of her skull continued until Anton slowed. Ahead was a break in the trees that opened out onto the front lawn of Michael's mansion.

The home was massive and screamed of antebellum influence. The wrap-around porch extended along every side and was supported by immense columns that stood like sentinels to guard the two-story building. The top story was skirted by wrought iron railings that dripped with wiry moss and vines. Along the front face of the mansion, Katey counted three floor-to-ceiling windows with black shutters on either side of a grand set of doors. Around the doors, she could see skinny windows that were boarded up from the inside to block out light, but through the several glass panes of the larger windows, she could see the glow of firelight.

The stone and wood that made up the mansion must have once been painted a bright, gleaming white, however, after over a century of abandonment, the paint was peeling. The shutters looked to be newly fashioned for the vampires who lived inside, but otherwise, the place seemed as if it hadn't been touched by humanity in decades or longer. Shingles on the roof were bent and missing in many spots. Some of the railing along the second story was rusted out, and cracks in the stone columns snaked along its surface.

Moonlight shined down upon the wild, unkempt lawn that was overgrown with weeds and various native flora of Louisiana. The drive up to the front entry was bordered by weeping myrtle trees, whose tendrils of moss and leaves swayed majestically in the night breeze.

Around the side of the building, she spotted the glint of metal from the numerous cars parked out of the way from the front walk. Among them was Michael's SUV. However, Katey wondered who else Michael was hosting in his elegant but slightly dilapidated plantation home.

Before they even had a chance to touch foot to ground, Michael opened the front door and stepped out on the expansive porch. The light from behind the old vampire made him seem more like a silhouette from their view, but Katey would know that proud stance anywhere.

Anton led them to park around the side of the building with the others. Behind the house, Katey saw something she hadn't expected. In several neat rows, stood shack-like homes with patched-up roofs and crooked porches. The cut-outs for windows and doors were darkened, but she could hear the softly spoken words of the inhabitants. One sniff confirmed that the voices belonged to vampires, and some humans.

Seeing the questions in her eyes, Anton said, "The fields have been overgrown for many years, but the slave quarters remain. Michael refused to tear them down. He said they reminded him of how racial prejudice can ruin a society."

Michael came down the length of the porch and stood beside a white column. "Also, there is limited room inside the mansion for all of my guards and their blood servants to sleep."

She smiled and threw off her helmet with the intent to run up the wooden steps to greet her grandfather.

Another figure stepped out into the night, and Katey froze beside the motorcycle. In the dim light, she couldn't be sure, but she knew that she had seen that face before once in the halls at the convention center in Alaska, and once again in the bowels of a vampire dungeon. Of course, in the dungeon he was clad in only a loincloth to hide his nakedness.

Now, he wore a white button-down shirt that gleamed in the moonlight, tucked into a pair of faded jeans. His thick beard that covered the lower half of his face was tinged with silver, similar to Darren's, but his eyes were more the color of black coffee.

Gregory was a tall man, towering at least a foot over Michael and broad like a linebacker. He was intimidating, as any member of the rougarous would be, and she could see the uncanny resemblance to his son, Erik, in the way he lifted his chin and smirked down at them with arrogant smugness.

He stood beside Michael with his hands clasped behind his back, watching the new arrivals. Logan's posture stiffened with his stance wide as if he were ready to charge up the porch and attack Gregory at the first ill-spoken word.

Lily and Forrest hopped out of their truck. Lily joined Katey, but Forrest stood still with his chest out and brows knitted over his nose. The loups-garous present all knew one another, and the relations were far from amicable.

Through her own riotous feelings and persistent agony, Katey felt suffocated by their shared contempt for the alpha. Gregory had personally done nothing to them. It was Erik who deserved the death sentence in their eyes for the murder of their close friends in Chicago during the Prohibition. His father didn't help matters in any way, but neither did he encourage the butchery.

Gregory only represented a small percentage of loups-garous who were scattered across the country in various packs that held no regard for the life of the humans they had to coexist with. When Darren once explained it to her, she learned that some of the rougarous took the law into their own hands and did away with murderers, rapists, and child molesters. They killed them when the government couldn't find them or didn't dish out the justice they thought was appropriate. Others, simply killed for the joy of it and believed that humans were inferior to their kind.

Although Katey didn't believe in vigilante tactics, she couldn't hate a man for trying to get rid of the scum of the earth. It was his disregard for human life that made him such an enemy to Logan and the Deviants and other loups-garous of the world.

They were the monsters told in storybooks, back before they changed their targets from the innocent to the criminals. It was loups-garous like them that made their kind feared by the masses and the stars of sensational horror films. It was they who inspired the hunt against loups-garous.

"I'm sure you have all met Gregory Jennings," Michael formally introduced, gesturing to the alpha of the rougarous beside him.

The alpha gave a short nod to the group but said nothing.

"You said this was a safe place, Michael," Logan grumbled.

Her grandfather frowned. "And it is. Gregory is aware of the consequences if he misbehaves and I'm sure I don't have to tell you the same."

Logan didn't move.

Gregory took a step forward and sighed. "I've come to speak with Michael about the peace gathering. I have elected to come as a representative of my pack."

Forrest guffawed. "You? Peace? What do you know about that?"

A sneer spread across Gregory's face. "I've lived twice as long as you, boy. I know the difference between peace and war. My pack doesn't like the feud between the vampires and our kind any more than you do. This past December should have proven that enough."

They all knew what the vampires were capable of. They didn't discriminate against the good and bad loups-garous. They were all dogs, just the same, and Gregory had every right to wish for peace too. She couldn't forget how they all fought side-by-side in the castle foyer and that was what made Katey respect him more than anything else.

To lead by example, Katey moved away from her friends and stepped on the porch to stand in front of Gregory.

After a tense moment, he blinked and gave a short bow to Katey, recognizing her as the one who held the spirit of peace. Through the constant pain she felt in every drop of blood in her body, she reached out and offered her hand to him.

A grin curled his mouth, and he shook it in return. For a loup-garou who was supposed to represent the worst of their kind, Katey did not sense any evil in him. Beneath his cold exterior, she could see that he meant well. That was plain to her when he ordered Erik off her that day at the charity luncheon and when he thanked her for her assistance at the castle. It made her wonder if, just like the vampires, they had all misjudged one another.

Logan, Forrest, Lily, and Anton moved onto the porch. Unlike her, the other loups-garous did not show their esteem in the same way. Forrest averted his eyes while Logan let out a short, but hostile growl at the alpha before guiding Katey away.

They all made their way through the front door upon Michael's invitation. Katey almost expected the interior to be as dingy as the outside and in want of serious cleaning.

The foyer was brightly lit but bare in the way of furnishings. A few oil paintings hung upon both walls with candle sconces separating them. Ahead was a stunning staircase, the polished wood gleaming in the candlelight and treads lined with red carpet. At the top of the stairs was a corridor that stretched across the second floor.

The door to the left was closed, and Michael led them into the parlor on thc right.

Katey gasped at the traditional beauty that they had stepped into. The parlor was crowded with ornate, antique furniture styled with complex wood veneer designs on the tabletops and red velvet upholstery on the chairs and sofas around the room. The freshly polished floor was covered in Persian rugs with hand-woven de-signs. An immense fireplace gave the room adequate warmth and heat while a chandelier hanging from the ceiling over twelve feet above them glittered with crystals and candles.

Above the fireplace was a mirror that reached to the ceiling with an intricately detailed golden edge around it. Candelabras were perched upon the mahogany mantle, and dark emerald, velvet curtains trimmed in gold fringe framed the windows along the front of the house.

A few vases and other knick-knacks sat upon the mantle and tabletops. Michael's decorators had kept the spirit of the plantation alive with their attention to detail and admiration for finery that the previous owners of the mansion must have enjoyed.

Logan stood by Katey in the doorway as others made their way into the parlor. Michael finally picked up on the fact that a human was in their midst and turned to Lily.

"I don't believe we have met, signorina. My name is Michael Gennari. Welcome to my home." The old vamp took her hand and kissed the back of it with all the gentlemanly poise that Katey came to expect out of her grandfather.

Lily blushed. "Lily Rangan. I've heard a lot about you," she replied.

Michael grinned. "I hope you will not judge me from the opinions of others, but on what you find me to be."

Forrest moved in and wrapped his arm protectively around Lily. "We're engaged to be married," he stated with a challenging smile. Katey snorted, knowing that Michael would have picked up on Forrest's territorial airs. Apparently, Logan wasn't the only one who didn't appreciate other men flirting with their women.

Michael nodded and grinned. "You have my congratulations. Do send me an invitation."

The couple took a loveseat by the fireplace, and Lily gave Forrest a questioning look as if she didn't understand the one-sided power struggle that just took place.

The vampire looked at Katey and Logan. "You must have had a long journey, but I am thrilled to see you safe at last." He gestured toward one of the unoccupied sofas after giving Katey a tight hug. "Come, you're weary. Take a rest, and I'll have someone fetch you a meal."

At the mention of food, her stomach joined in to torture her body further. She opened her mouth to protest and say that she wanted to go to bed, but Logan gave her a light nudge, and she obeyed.

The sofa was not nearly as hard as she anticipated it to be. Then again, anything would have been comfortable compared to the hard seat on Logan's motorcycle. No number of comfy sofas or plush mattresses would ease the bombarding pain. Every muscle ached, every bone felt as if it were splintered, her flesh raw to the touch and even her senses dulled every now and again, making her believe she was going to faint.

She looked around at the faces in the room, but they blurred in the firelight. When she blinked, they came back into focus for only a few seconds. Their voices were little more than a garbled roar at times. When a servant vamp came into the room and presented the loups-garous with a plate of meaty hors d'oeuvres, she couldn't even smell it.

After a few seconds of stillness, Katey reached out and picked up a slice of meat and nibbled as if she weren't hungry at all. The roiling and seizing of her inner organs made her wonder if she could even keep anything down. All she wanted to do was sleep. Something was terribly wrong, she knew that now.

After a few bites, Katey finally registered that the group had been carrying on some conversation without her and she hadn't a clue what they were talking about. She looked in the direction of her grandfather. Sure, that she was cutting off someone who was speaking, she asked, "Can I be shown to whatever room I'm staying in? I don't feel well."

Logan turned to her, his comforting arm slipping around her hips. "What's wrong, Katey?" he asked.

She shook her head. "I'm just tired," she replied and lowered her eyes, knowing that every gaze in the room was on her.

Michael's voice broke the breathless silence. "Of course," he said. "Anton, please take Katey to her room upstairs."

Katey wanted to cringe at the mention of the stairs, unsure if she would be able to climb them or not. Anton helped her to her feet and escorted her out of the parlor, leaving Logan alone on thc sofa.

When they came to the foot of the stairs, Katey tried to lift her feet high enough to reach the first tread, but her joints protested.

"Anton, I might need you to carry me," she whispered, hoping that Logan wouldn't hear. He didn't need to worry about her any more than he already did. They were all concerned, she could sense that instantly. Whatever this was, Katey was sure that it would pass after a good night's rest.

When Anton lifted her into his arms and carried her upstairs, Katey marveled that she didn't feel jarred or uncomfortable in the vampire's care. It was as if he took no steps at all, just glided upwards like he was mist or fog.

Somewhere between the corridor and her bed, Katey fell unconscious.

"If there are hunters in the bayou, then why did you ask all of us to come here from Crestucky?" Logan hollered at Michael.

It had been an hour since Katey went up to bed and through the haze of fretfulness about what ailed her, Logan was still able to contribute to the conversations.

After Forrest had told Michael all about their staying with Will and the other loups-garous in the swamps, the vampire ordered him to call his great-uncle and have them come up to the mansion. He claimed the bayou was not safe, but wouldn't say why until now.

Up until that point in the discussion, they conversed about the details of what happened in Alabama with the safehouse. Through the vampire grapevine, the coven leader had learned of the dire straits that the Deviants were in and under Michael's direction, set up a sentry around their compound but far enough out of range that the Deviants wouldn't know they were there.

When the hunters came, they tried to fight them off but with the lack of experience regarding loup-garou hunters, the vampires faltered, and a few leaked through their blockade. The Deviants were well armed, however, and with the vampires trapping the hunters in and the loups-garous fighting back from the inside, they didn't stand a chance.

Forrest's life had been saved by a vamp who sacrificed himself for the Deviants. Logan had never seen a more grateful man. Lily, on the other hand, stared blankly at the floor, her heart racing as they talked of the body count. These were things that the loups-garous and vampires were accustomed to. Death and massacres were part of their lives when dealing with one another and the hunters who hated them. For a human, the destruction must have been difficult to grasp.

Another thing that Forrest could confirm was that Jacob, his alpha, was alive and well. He and many of the others went to their alternative safehouse in Georgia, though they hadn't been sure from the beginning if it would prove any safer than the one in Alabama. With the detachment of hunters taken care of, they hadn't heard of any more attacks, so it was assumed they were in the clear. The alpha's phone was destroyed in the raid, hence why he was unable to contact Darren or the others about what happened.

Logan especially watched Gregory's expression during the debriefing. The rougarou alpha stayed perfectly neutral the entire time. Although Katey seemed to be willing to set aside differences and trust Gregory, Logan was not. They had betrayed their pack once before, and he could do it again just as easily.

If Katey were there, he would have asked what she empathetically read off the alpha.

If Gregory had sent the hunters to Alabama or Crestucky, it would explain his pack's sudden departure even before Darren and Jacob had been aware of the threat. Now, with him in Louisiana, there was no telling what he might have been up to.

Anton stood behind Michael's wingback chair, silently observing the group with dark, severe eyes. Logan didn't trust him either. It was too convenient the way he swooped in and interceded in the fight at the bar on Bourbon Street. Not to mention that he had heard too many stories about Anton for Logan to simply give up any entrenched cynicism he carried for the vampire.

They were nothing but ghost stories and legends to many, but now Logan knew there was a flesh-and-blood vampire behind the tales. The fearless, ruthless assassin of the vampire horde was in the same room with them, idly standing by and waiting for orders from Katey's grandfather. It seemed too unbelievable. Logan always pictured Anton to be hulking and monstrous, but besides his silent intensity, no one would have suspected him to be the villain of so many loup-garou horror stories.

Who was to say that he hadn't been waiting for them the whole time? Yes, he worked for Michael, but it was too easy the way he was able to convince everyone to come to the mansion. Michael had an alpha and three other loups-garous in the prime spot for holding as hostages if needed. Although, with Katey here, would that truly be Michael's intention?

Paranoia had ruled every decision since they left Crestucky and especially since they left the compound. With Michael telling him that the reason he had them all come to Louisiana was that hunters were also in New Orleans, none of it made sense. If he needed to, he was ready to barge upstairs, grab Katey, and whisk them far away from hunters and vampires alike.

"Because, Logan, we have been keeping track of the hunters. What better place to be when lions are out on the hunt, than to be in the lions' den? They would never suspect it."

Logan gripped the edge of the sofa, his nails digging into the old wooden frame. "And what if they do? We thought they wouldn't know where the safehouse was, but they found it anyway. Who's to say they won't find us here?"

"My guards are constantly patrolling these woods. If a human stepped one foot on this property, they would know."

Logan sneered. "We were nearly killed back in Crestucky when a hunter snuck up on us on your guard's watch. To me, your guards mean nothing."

Michael neatly folded his hands in his lap and his eyes went flinty. "I received the full report from that guard, and we have learned a valuable thing about the hunters. Somehow, they have invented a scent-masking formula that eliminates all body odor. My guards have been informed of this development and are no longer relying on their noses. Instead, we're focusing on our sense of hearing. No human can mask their heartbeat or breathing from a vampire. It's what draws us to our prey." He gave Logan a slightly sinister smile. "And since we have no heartbeat, out in the empty forest they will be easy to catch."

Logan was nearly satisfied. "Why have you been watching the hunters? If you know where they are, why not just wipe them out?"

One of Michael's fingers shot up. "One has already won the war if you know your enemy well enough. We have been watching their movements and listening to their conversations. Their headquarters are fortified against other werewolves, but not vampires. We have been able to sneak in unnoticed and learn what it is they want."

Lily looked up. "What do they want?" she asked, a ribbon of nervousness rattling her words.

Anton finally spoke in his thick Russian tongue, "From what we can gather, they're after one werewolf. They know approximately where he is, but they haven't said a name. Wherever he was, he was in Crestucky. The headquarters are getting reports every day, and a few days ago, they received a call saying that they might have found him. That's when they attacked the Deviants and those still left in Crestucky."

Every vampire and loup-garou in the room froze when they heard an other-worldly halloo come from across the lawn outside. They all turned to look out the window, but Forrest only smiled. Lily let out a soft groan.

"What in God's name was that?" Gregory asked.

CHAPTER 17

He got his answer a moment later when the front door swung open. Along with the stench of swamp and outdoors, came a small band of loups-garous and the vampires who were escorting them. Tracking mud into the foyer, they came to the parlor and stood in the doorway.

The first three that led the group were dressed in tattered trousers and shirts that looked to belong in another decade. Their hems were sopping with bayou muck and hair disheveled. Darren once called this particular band of loups-garous "swamp wolves" and with good reason.

They were not uneducated or ignorant but favored the lives of hermits in the swamps where the only visitor may be the occasional frog-gigger or biologist studying the unique ecosystem the swamps had to offer. As a result of their lifestyle, certain things never changed.

"Bonjour, Teddy!" Forrest greeted from his place on the loveseat.

The loup-garou in front grinned and gave a sweeping bow. His dark hair had twigs lodged between his locks and bright brown eyes full of laughter and a zeal for life. "Bonjour, mez ami!" he drawled out in traditional Creole French and turned his attention to Michael. "Thank you for the lovely invitation. I haven't been to this side of New Orleans for quite some time. Last time I was, well, that's not a story for lady ears." He slid a furtive look to Lily.

Gregory covered his eyes and let out an exasperated sigh while the others smiled at Teddy's salutation.

Teddy turned and thumbed toward the loup-garou on his right, a slightly younger man with blonde hair and dark brows and equally dark eyes like his brother's. "This here is Uriah, my second and my brother."

Uriah gave a little salute and before he could give his warm hello, Logan heard more footsteps come down the foyer. Will appeared, wearing distinctively more modern clothing than his comrades. In almost a century, he hadn't changed. He cut his black hair the same tousled way, and his mustache and goatee were exactly as he remembered, only with a little more gray than in the twenties. The bold and swashbuckling features were still there and Logan did agree with Lily that he looked to be more at home on a pirate ship than in a southern mansion.

He looked to Logan and grinned wide. "Well, I never thought I'd see you again, runt." Will's voice was devoid of an accent, unlike his friends. He had lived in too many places to ever retain a certain cadence in his voice.

Without a second thought, Logan stood and embraced Will as if he were a blood relative. After the way he took care of Logan while Darren and Dustin were off looking for Ben, he couldn't help but think of him as an uncle just as Forrest did. Will's nephew was Forrest's father and the founder of Devia in the early eighteen-hundreds.

How Will fell into the swamp wolf crowd was a little less easy to track. From what Will had divulged himself, Logan knew he had met a woman in their pack many years ago before the Civil War threatened to split the country apart. Though she was gone and they never had any children, Will still returned to the welcoming community in the bayou every now and then.

"I trust you're staying out of trouble," Logan said.

With Will's firm grasp on Logan's shoulder, he shook his head and made a disgruntled face. "Me? Trouble? Pah! Not a chance."

Forrest folded his arms. "What about that pig you stole from the Jenson's yesterday?" he asked.

Will shrugged. "Okay, in the last few hours, I haven't gotten into trouble."

The swamp wolves let out a hearty laugh with him, and somehow, Logan felt at home again.

"Gentleman," Michael began, standing to address the growing crowd of loups-garous that were standing in his parlor and foyer. Some were sniffing around at the potted plants, others ogling at the fine decorations and patterned wallpaper they must not have been accustomed to. "My associates will show you to your rooms behind the house."

Uriah jerked a thumb toward the front door. "Ya mean them slave huts out back? Nuh-uh. We ain't gonna sleep in no slave's quarters. We ain't slaves."

Teddy backslapped his brother's belly. "Don't be rude, Uriah."

"My own guards and their families are sleeping in the same quarters," Michael assured. "This arrangement is no reflection on you or your race."

Uriah snorted. "Well, if that's the case, come on y'all!" he hollered at his pack and led them out the doors, followed by some bemused vampire guards.

Only Will and Teddy stayed and took seats on the sofa with Logan to join in the discussion.

"As Anton was explaining," Michael continued, "we know the hunters are looking for a particular werewolf, but we don't know who or why." He sat down heavily in his chair. "I honestly think the subordinate hunters are just as clueless as we are. A man named Andrew is making the orders, but not even his top operatives know why they're chasing down this wolf."

Michael looked to Teddy and Will. "With the hunters set up in the bayou, I wanted to make sure the casualty count would not soar through the roof any more than it already has. No matter how well you hide, the hunters may find your pack, and as long as there is that risk, I'd prefer if they stay close by or evacuate the area immediately."

"Evacuate?" Teddy repeated, his lips curling up in disgust. "We've never run from anyone or anythin'. We never had a reason, and we've never had a problem with any hunters. They probably don't even know we're there!" Logan watched the swamp alpha scratch his head, and the twigs and dirt fall onto the sofa cushions.

Anton shook his head. "All the same, it is not safe in the bayou until we can determine how long they will be there or what their intention is with this werewolf."

Will leaned forward, resting his elbows on his knees and lacing his fingers together. "You're asking an entire network of families to just up and move from a place their ancestors came from. Do you understand how big of an undertaking that is?"

"Do you?" Forrest asked, pinning his great-uncle with a stony gaze.

Will turned to regard Forrest with a hard look. There had been animosity between Will and his brother back during the creation of Devia, but Logan was uncertain of the details beyond that. Though they were blood family, he was sure they had their quarrels like any other.

"No, I've never had to worry about it. But, I know you have." He looked to Michael. "Is this a temporary move?"

Michael shrugged. "It all depends on how long this engagement lasts. If we can gather enough information to strike a fatal blow to the hunters' operations, then you can be back before spring comes."

Will was about to speak before Teddy cut him off. "We will cooperate as long as you don't send us to no Yankee state."

Michael smirked. "On the contrary, we were simply going to escort you farther west and north. Our connections there have confirmed there are no hunters in that area."

"Can Lily and I come along?" Forrest asked Teddy.

Teddy slapped his knee and nodded. "Why, sure! We'd be happy to have you along."

Logan saw Lily cringe, but she said nothing. Michael suppressed a chuckle.

"What about Katey and I?" Logan finally asked. "Are we just going to stay here? Darren and the rest of my pack are on their way. They should be here by morning at the latest."

Michael inclined his head. "You and your pack are welcome to stay here. I would have it no other way. What happened in Crestucky will not happen here, I assure you."

Surprising the group, Gregory lifted his chin to address the vampire. "What happens when you get enough information about the hunters? Will you need reinforcements to help attack their headquarters? My son has taken our pack farther north, but one phone call can have them here if they are needed."

With a pinched expression, Michael replied, "If we can help it, we will solve this matter peacefully using any means necessary. Reinforcements will not be required."

Gregory let out a condescending snort. "Hunters will not negotiate. They find their prey, and they eliminate it. There is no reasoning with them."

As much as Logan hated to admit it, for once, he agreed with Gregory. The hunters were ruthless, and they all knew it. A thought came to Logan's mind that made his chest feel as if it would cave in and his stomach twisted with fear. "What if they find us? What if they find Katey?"

Anton stepped forward, the glow of the fire behind him casting light and shadows across his set jaw and furrowed brows. "You have my word that no harm will ever come to Katey McCoy. As long as I am able to protect her, she will be safe."

The grandfather clock in the upper corridor chimed the first stroke, letting everyone in the mansion know it was midnight.

Katey's eyes opened wide as she lay in the plush, rosewood poster bed, but it wasn't the great gong of the clock that awoke her. It felt as if two fists had reached into her chest and squeezed the air from her lungs. She gasped, but it was no use.

On the second stroke, her lungs were released from the vice-like grip. She took the opportunity to inhale, ready to scream for the help she'd needed hours ago before she passed out.

Before the cry could spill from her mouth, it was stolen by the intense pain that constricted her organs. Contents shifted and clenched under the forces that seized her body.

Katey coiled herself into a ball underneath the silky duvet. She brought her arms to her chest and squeezed her eyes shut, but it did nothing to alleviate her discomfort.

The third chime rang out. The flat, resounding tone vibrated in her bones. Katey whimpered as she felt her joints shift, pulling her legs away from her body. The covers slipped from the bed. The fibers of her bones contracted and cracked, then healed themselves and started all over again.

Her whole body battled against her, the pain too intense to bear, but she couldn't cry out.

The fourth chime roared in her ears and pierced through her brain. She pressed the heels of her palms against her temples, willing it to stop. Blood sizzled and burned within her veins.

At the fifth chime, she opened her eyes. Her vision filled with bright and twinkling dots against blackness, like sparkler sticks on a Fourth of July night. Her joints somehow managed to pop back into place, and she rolled out of bed.

Katey fell nearly three feet and crashed to the unforgiving hardwood floor, but that was nothing compared to the hell she endured on the inside.

"Katey?" a sleepy voice called through the darkness. She recognized the frilly pitch of the voice as Lily's.

At the sixth chime, Katey managed to rise to her elbows and knees with her hands still gripped around her throbbing head. She heard movement to her left, but couldn't see or smell them. The noise was enough to make her feel as if her skull would cleave in two.

"Are you okay?" Lily asked.

With the seventh chime, Katey briefly let go of her head to grab the edge of the bed. Her aching hands found purchase on the railing, and she pulled herself up as her fingers popped in and out of position.

"Logan," she whispered, knowing he must have heard her even if they were across the house from one another. Surely, he could sense her pain through their bond somehow. Something this strong couldn't be blocked out of their spiritual union.

The eighth chime split the air, and with halting, unsteady steps, Katey walked aimlessly. Her vision returned, but the edges of figures and furniture were fuzzy and clouded. She stumbled toward a pair of French doors that led onto the second-story balcony that wrapped around the house.

She was driven that way by the blue moonlight and the promise of fresh air. Just as she reached for the door handle, her knees popped backward.

Her cry of agony was drowned out by the clock's ninth chime. As she fell forward, her hand managed to grab the door handle, and she pushed her way onto the balcony. Katey came crumbling onto the wooden planks littered with dirt and leaves.

The cool night air met her skin but provided no comfort for her body now drenched in sweat and trembling from nose to toes.

On the balcony, the heady scent of the forest surrounded her, filling her senses. She craned her head toward the metal railing. Beyond, she could see the tops of the trees, an endless playground waiting for her, and her wolf that began clawing its way to the surface.

The tenth chime sounded like a distant reminder of civilization as Katey crawled. Her body protested every movement, sending volleys of burning fire and sharp needle-like shocks through every cell.

Voices from inside the house and in the slave quarters below came to her, but they were mere nonsense. Nothing mattered except getting to the woods, to freedom. There, Katey knew there would be a release from the torturous pain.

The eleventh chime found her by the railing and Katey pulled herself up, using every ounce of willpower and strength left in her muscles that wanted to tear her body apart from the inside out.

Heavy footsteps came toward her and more shouts of meaning-less words.

The iron in her fingers cracked like dried and brittle flower petals. The metal groaned against her weight and failed.

By the time the stroke of twelve summoned midnight, Katey was falling, air whizzing past her ears and blowing out her tangled hair. She closed her eyes but felt no fear.

Instead of hitting the hard earth, Katey was cradled in a pair of strong arms. Logan's arms. She looked up into his face, the only clear and welcome thing in her moment of terror. His masculine scent seeped into her foggy mind, and through the pain, she managed to give him a shaky smile.

He did not return her smile, though. His eyes told her, louder than any energy or aura, that Logan was terrified, probably more than her. She knew what was happening now.

Her eyes were golden, and her wolf was ready to run.

Katey opened her mouth to tell him, but the pain came fresh and exponentially worse. Her face contorted in anguish and Logan slowly lowered her to the ground. The feel of rich, wild soil beneath her flushed skin made the shift come quicker.

Her legs and fingers raked and beat at the ground until her clothes were filthy and torn. A cry erupted from her lips, and she could sense those around her watching helplessly. Every moment, every sense that was once deadened, now became sharp and vivid.

She could hear everything for miles around, every voice and every heartbeat crowded in her ears. Her eyes opened to a won-drous world of detail she had never seen before. Smells mingled together in a mess that made her retch.

Then came the last push. Her wolf pressed forward, claws digging into Katey's soul. They merged, and Katey let it all go with one last breath.

Michael watched from the top porch step as Katey's body began to morph. He had known from the moment she came onto the property that something was not right. There was a storm inside of her raging to be let loose. If he had known this would happen, he wouldn't have let her spend one moment alone.

If it weren't for Lily's shouts for help, they would have never known that Katey was shifting. With Gregory and Anton beside him, they witnessed the first female werewolf shift for her monthly cycle. They weren't the only ones.

Logan stood a few feet from Katey, the closest of them all, while Michael's guards formed a circle around her, ready to step in if needed. Behind them, Teddy's pack assembled from their designated shacks and ogled at this rare privilege. Their edgy alpha stood just behind Gregory and beside him was an equally fretful Will.

He had never seen a werewolf's first shift. Every time a werewolf permitted him to see their shift, it was nothing like this. Perhaps it was Katey, or perhaps females in general, but there was something majestic in the way her body shifted into the towering beast he had seen once before in the castle. That shift a month ago, however, was not nearly as painful and excruciating as this appeared to be.

Pain radiated from Katey like a beacon, and Michael felt some of her distress in his own body.

After only a few moments of held breaths, they all watched Katey rise onto her limbs, leaving her clothes in a shredded pool around her feet. A beautiful white werewolf was presented to them, her tail drooping to the ground, pointed ears rotating at every sound, and wolfish head swiveling from one side to the other. Her arms and legs resembled that of a human, except her hands were tipped with claws and the undersides were covered in rough pads. Her torso remained the same, her heavy white pelt covering any immodest details of her figure.

Her golden eyes darted between the vampires and werewolves who watched and her lips curled over her muzzle in a vicious growl. Logan stepped back a few paces and Michael sensed a change in him.

He was no longer scared for Katey but scared for himself. Michael looked to Gregory and Teddy, the only alphas present who could explain Logan's fear.

Gregory glanced his way, jaw clenched, but would not speak. Will was frozen in place as if one move would attract Katey's wrath.

"She needs breakin'," Teddy whispered.

Michael looked back to Katey and saw the savagery in her glare, the sheer ferocity in every bristled hair across her body that stood on end.

"Breaking?" Michael questioned, watching her movements as a scientist would study a newly discovered animal in the wild.

"If this is her first shift," Gregory muttered under his breath, "then she needs to be broken, tamed, by an alpha. If she isn't, she'll be uncontrollable."

Michael turned to them. "Her alpha won't arrive until the morning."

Teddy's eyes slid his way. "It doesn't have to be her alpha. Any alpha. Anyone more dominant than she is."

Michael waited patiently for either of the werewolves to volunteer, but once he realized neither of them would step forward, he looked to Anton.

"Don't harm her," he ordered. "But keep her contained."

Anton nodded and charged forward to stand beside Logan.

Katcy spun around and arched her body in challenge. When the vampire didn't respond, she launched herself toward him. The two men dodged in different directions. The beast turned and roared in a blind rage.

That same rage snaked through Michael's core, and he shuddered. Katey leaped into the masses of vampires and werewolves, slashing and rampaging against them. None would strike back, and they were too fast for her as they scattered in every direction.

Some of the younger bayou werewolves made a game of it and taunted her. They let out whoops and hollers, heedless of the dangers that awaited if the beast caught any one of them.

"Y'all stop that!" Teddy shouted from the porch as he bounded down the steps to confront his pack.

When she grew bored of their evasive moves, she turned toward the slave shacks where the human blood servants of the vampires were sleeping or silently watching the scene.

"She's going to look for anything to destroy," Will told Michael. "If someone doesn't stop her, you won't have much of a home left."

Teddy turned to glare at Gregory and stripped off his shirt. "If you won't do it, then I might as well."

Michael looked to Logan who had distanced himself from the scene. In the shadows of the mansion, Logan watched Katey spring toward the wooden shacks. His face was cold and expressionless, but Michael could feel the terrible, heart-wrenching emotions that constricted his chest. Just like the rest of them, Logan was powerless to stop Katey. He was neither a dominant wolf nor could he shift to even try to control Katey's rampage.

At a full run, Teddy changed into a lean, chestnut-colored werewolf larger and bulkier than Katey in all respects. Michael crossed his arms and watched the two werewolves face off just near the slave quarters. The humans who had been watching quickly dodged into the shacks to take shelter. Gregory and Will stepped forward, both of them ready to run to Teddy's aid if needed.

Teddy blocked her way with his body, but that didn't stop her from ramming into him at top speed. They rolled, a flurry of teeth and claws gnashing and slicing through flesh. Yelps and growls echoed through the forest around the plantation.

Michael couldn't tell which was winning as blood splattered on the grass and weeds. Finally, Teddy found himself beneath Katey with her jowls closed around his neck. What Michael came to recognize as a werewolf's dominance came to flow and slam into Teddy with unrelenting power. Such dominance was reserved for alphas of their kind.

A wave of shock and dismay flowed through the spectating werewolves and vampires.

Teddy used his hind legs to kick Katey off but slunk away to nurse his wounds. Hushed murmurs spread through the crowd and no one could point out a single reason why Katey should have won out over Teddy. She was smaller and less experienced, but Michael knew her feral instincts would be a formidable force to be reckoned with. Not only that, but her dominance would make her a contender for any of the alphas or other werewolves present.

With an impatient grumble, Gregory began to unbutton his shirt. "Damn fool didn't know what he was doing," he growled as he leaped off the back porch to change, leaving Michael and Will behind.

Michael looked at Logan again and saw the grief written on the lover's face. He could see, just as well as they all could, the blood staining Katey's pristine white pelt. She was in pain, however much she wouldn't let on.

Katey was still full of determination to stay wild and untamed. When Gregory bolted for her, a blur of dark brown and black fur in the moonlight, she was not the least bit tired after her fight with Teddy.

Gregory was stronger and older, but he wasn't nearly as agile as Teddy had been. Every pair of nervous eyes watched the two size each other up.

The werewolves paced in a wide circle, snapping and growling to one another as golden eyes locked in inhuman fury. Gregory was the first to strike, his heavy frame surprisingly fast.

Katey let out a yelp and Michael winced as he heard bones cracking under the force of Gregory's attack.

Logan stepped out from the shadows, hands balled into tight fists by his sides. Will's attention was momentarily diverted away from the fight to pin Logan with his glare. The younger werewolf obeyed but under silent protest.

The two wolves rolled and took turns conquering one another. Gashes opened up around Katey's throat and sides, spilling her lifeblood into the soil. It was difficult to tell on Gregory, but by the way he retaliated after every swipe of her claws, Michael knew he was dealt equally harsh blows.

Moments passed like hours, and there were several near misses when Katey looked to be tiring out. Each time Gregory had her beneath his massive paws, she would find a way to slither out of his grip and continue the fight.

She was the offspring of two warriors, two stubborn people who would defy gravity itself to get what they wanted. This fight might have gone on forever if Gregory hadn't made a fatal error.

Logan shouted out in rage as Gregory found his way behind Katey and mounted her. Even Michael hissed at the alpha for his insolence.

Katey was too fast. Before Gregory could take liberties that did not belong to him, Katey let out an ear-splitting roar, mingled with earth-shaking dominance, and recoiled. With speed and strength Michael had never seen before in any werewolf – on the battlefield or not – Katey slashed and bit into Gregory's core and neck until somewhere in the barrage, he conceded and slunk away with his tail between his legs.

Although Michael and Logan were both relieved Katey had not let herself be dominated by Gregory, they all knew they were out of alphas.

If the mighty and experienced Gregory could not tame her, what was left?

Michael looked to Will who stood beside him, but he shook his head. By the surety in his eyes, Michael knew the werewolf refused to fight because he knew it would do no good. It had nothing to do with fear. He was simply not dominant enough to do the breaking alone.

Michael heard Teddy give an order to his pack and one by one, the seasoned werewolves began to shift. At this, Will leaped off the porch and joined the others. If he couldn't break her alone, then he would join the fray with the others under Teddy's command to try and contain Katey.

In an attempt to overwhelm her, they rushed in from all sides, werewolves of all colors and sizes uniting against Michael's granddaughter.

Katey broke into a frenzy and crashed through her assailants, sending them flying in all directions. It was as if with each fight, she grew stronger and smarter in her tactics. Even as a raving beast, she was intelligent beyond expectation.

The werewolves made one last sweep in and tackled her, weighing down her body until she lay flat on the ground and her muzzle pressed into the dirt.

A sigh of relief was breathed, almost in unison. Logan stepped closer, now at the foot of the porch steps, and watched, but he was not relieved with the others. He understood Katey better than anyone, and if he wasn't convinced the fight was over, then neither was Michael.

They were right.

Katey let out another beastly roar and plunged upwards through the bodies of werewolves that tumbled to the wayside. Some were knocked out cold, others were disoriented and unable to defend themselves. Others were intimidated by her burst of dominance and slunk away just as her other opponents had once they were defeated.

The white werewolf stood on shaky limbs, her fur saturated in her own blood and the blood of her enemies. Golden eyes rolled wildly around in their sockets, looking for anyone else who would dare cross her. Her back and chest heaved with each breath that came out in a challenging growl between her sharp fangs. She would have her freedom at any cost.

Logan sat down heavily on the bottom step, his eyes fixed on Katey. Anton looked to Michael for direction, his hands steady and jaw set for the assignment.

Michael looked at the scene before him. The exhausted and wounded werewolves shied away from Katey, and the vampires wanted nothing to do with her. Only Anton remained, loyal and ready to carry out the orders he was given, even if it meant sacrificing his own life. When Michael rescued him from the bowels of the Kremlin palace so many centuries ago, he knew he would have a powerful ally and protector.

He nodded, and Anton turned to the lone werewolf. The cuts and gashes on her body had healed, and her stamina was quickly returning. Every vampire who was able reached out with their minds and held Katey in place.

When she tried to lift one paw or turn her head, their amalgamated powers held her still. Only her eyes moved from side to side, and her throat let out a shrill whine of fear.

"What are you doing to her?" Logan asked Michael, his voice shaky with that same fear that gripped his lover.

"Vampires who were born into this life can control the movements of others. It's commonly misunderstood as mesmerizing, and we don't use these abilities unless we have to."

Katey's muscles twitched and bunched under her fur, and the whine turned into a threatening growl, but the guards held their ground against the beast.

"You're hurting her!" Logan exclaimed.

Michael shook his head, but never took his eyes from his granddaughter. "On the contrary, I can feel her mind fighting against me. She's in no pain."

Logan turned away to inspect the grimacing faces of the other vampires. They all could feel Katey's will bashing against the cage they had created for her. Even Michael struggled to keep his hold, feeling his blood sing with the effort.

Suddenly, Katey tossed her head to the side. The few vampires that had surrounded her fell to the ground. Michael gasped in surprise that he seldom felt. The beast had broken their minds, and they now lay unconscious on the ground. When they awoke, they would need to recover from the blow Katey had dealt, but they would live.

One by one, the guards were thrown aside by Katey's sheer drive to be free. Only Michael and Anton's hold was left, but it wasn't enough. He had never seen anyone, vampire, human, or werewolf, break the powerful psychic hold of a vampire's mind.

Her wolfish eyes turned to Michael, and she snarled maliciously. Even in her fear and confusion, she understood where the true authority lay. With jerky precision, Katey marched toward the backside of the mansion.

A drop of blood seeped from Michael's nose as he pulled on reserves of power he never thought he would need. Katey stopped, but she wouldn't keep still for long.

Michael didn't need to tell his most trusted friend and adviser that the situation had become more serious than any of them could have imagined. Two alphas, an entire pack, and a team of vampires now lay by the sidelines, debilitated. All of it had been done by one little girl.

Anton snapped his fingers and ordered what few men were left of his forces to fan out around her with their guns trained on Katey. The guns were loaded with silver bullets, but Anton and all the others understood who Katey was and the enormous role she was to play. They knew better than to shoot in such a way that would cause permanent damage.

To their surprise, she didn't bolt into a run once Michael and Anton released their hold on her. No, she wanted to fight and wanted to feel the thrill of conquering another foe. If Anton were leading the charge, she would find herself disappointed. Anton never failed a mission in his life, nor did he let an enemy slip through his grasp.

Michael wiped the blood from his upper lip and stared down the beast. He tried to understand how she could have done it. With no training and operating on pure instinct, Katey managed to defend herself against all odds.

Katey had not given up on her mission. She was willing to attack Michael, her own grandfather, to gain her freedom.

Before his men could fire a shot, Logan jumped to his feet and sniffed the air as the growl in Katey's throat rose.

Sidetracked from the battle, Michael tested the air as well. Someone had snuck through their defenses. Either snuck through or had been permitted onto the property. They were making their way through the woods at great speed, heading straight for the mansion.

"Anton!" Michael yelled.

The vampire turned toward the intruders, and the vampires pointed their weapons in the direction of the forest.

Three figures were soon loping through the trees. Three werewolves emerged, and Michael knew exactly who they were by their scents.

The silver werewolf, Darren, led his two other pack members into the clearing. Dustin, the brown and beige wolf, and Ben, the black wolf, fell back as their alpha stormed forward. With dark eyes fixed on his target, he was on a collision course headed straight for Katey.

Anton ordered his men aside, and Katey scrambled to gain her footing on the slippery grass coated in fresh blood. Darren collided with Katey without hesitance.

The world sccmcd to stand still as Katey and Darren tore at one another. Upon closer examination of the odds, Darren seemed to be as equal of an alpha as Gregory might have been. Where Gregory used brute force to get his way with Katey, Darren implemented cunning. He dodged instead of attacking and caught her off guard when she could have been more alert.

Not once did Darren use the same tactics to deal a crushing blow on his subordinate. He kept changing his moves, using her own weight against her and if necessary, he retreated to make her think she had won before turning on her again.

Dustin and Ben moved closer, ready to defend their alpha. Their organization was remarkable and more sophisticated than how Teddy's pack functioned. They were truly a well-oiled machine in combat. When Katey was getting too close to conquering her alpha, Ben nipped at her heels to divert her. When Katey tried to run, Dustin drove her back into Darren's range.

The longer the breaking took, the easier everyone became. Katey no longer seemed the confident beast that nearly ripped them apart. Michael sensed her doubt, and there was a feeling of defeat growing in her heart and violent mind.

Katey's movements became slower and the number of times she tried to flee escalated. Darren wouldn't let her off so simply and would almost goad her into defending herself for a little longer.

Finally, when her tail drooped between her hind legs when her hackles were no longer raised in aggression, Katey slunk along the ground with her muzzle between her front paws.

Darren sprang upon her, pinning her entire body down to the ground and his deadly fangs pressing into the mane of fur around her neck. Katey struggled a few times, whimpering as his teeth punctured into her neck with every movement.

Michael watched her shiver, and then go slack under her alpha, his legs straddling either side of her. Her head stretched, giving more of her neck to Darren in a sign of true submission.

Logan passed a hand over his face, and Michael knew everyone shared the overwhelming feeling of relief as Katey was finally broken. One stage of her training had been completed.

A look into Katey's eyes, however, told Michael the battle wasn't over. Yes, she was broken, but it had been over a few thousand years since a female werewolf had been broken. In her eyes, Michael could see more damage had been done this night than a few cuts and bruises. They had broken her, but at what cost?

CHAPTER 18

The mansion and the surrounding property fell into an eerie silence as the morning progressed. The sun had risen above the tree line, chasing the vampires into the dark rooms they had made for themselves in the big house and slave quarters. Loups-garous were still sleeping, exhausted from the late-night entertainment that Katey had provided.

From the plush wingback chair in the parlor, Logan could hear the stirring of a few loups-garous on the second floor. Darren, Katey, Dustin, and Ben came in from the forest about an hour ago, and they were still trying to get themselves settled.

Logan could not sleep. He had tried for hours, but the comfortable poster bed wasn't enough to block out the subtle sounds of Katey's movements outside the mansion. Her grunts, whimpers, yips of glee, and the soft rustling of paws beating against grass lingered in his ears almost as much as what finally snapped him awake at dawn.

Katey's wailing and weeping as she shifted back into her human form wrapped around his mind and refused to let him rest while she was in such pain. Even after she was done changing, Logan heard the echoes of her agony.

To find some relief, he came to the parlor, but there was no rest for him in Michael's chair. Louder than Katey's screams were another repeating nuisance that he simply could not shake.

You failed. You failed. You failed.

Logan rubbed his knuckles against his brow and squeezed his eyes shut. The coaching Michael had given him seemed eons away, and there was no pushing off the heavy weight on his chest.

If he had been able to shift, Katey might not have gotten so out of control. Perhaps he couldn't break her but possibly deflect her attention. They wouldn't have known one another in their wolf forms, but it would have softened the contact. As she was, Katey's wolf would have balked at the approach of a human. There was no way he could have gotten close unless he appeared as she did.

She had no bond, no connections with Teddy, Gregory, or the other loups-garous. She would never have let them close, but the mating bond between her and Logan might have been enough to calm her if only he could have shifted with her.

Darren's entrance was a blessing. Obviously, he was the only one who could handle Katey and her tenacious temper, even as a wolf. Logan had never personally witnessed a breaking, but he knew from experience that Teddy's approach was too carefree, too unorganized. It was a wonder any of his subordinates obeyed him at all.

Gregory's tactic was much too cruel, and his brute strength got him nowhere with Katey, especially when he tried to mount her. Logan's blood boiled at the thought and his fists tightened until his nails bit into his palm.

Darren's style was calculated and subtle. When he broke Logan, it had taken hours before he finally wore himself out trying to chase and attack the alpha. Katey's breaking didn't take nearly as long, but Logan wondered if the key lay in the collaboration with Dustin and Ben. If they hadn't been there, Katey might not have given in so easily. It wasn't that she was outnumbered, but that she wasn't sure who to fight and where.

A corner of Logan's lip curled up in a smirk. Katey was a force to be reckoned with, a reckless hurricane of wrath and stamina that none of them would have ever guessed. She was smaller than the normal loup-garou, but ten times as feisty and vicious. The way she fought off the mental manipulation of the vampires astounded the whole assembly.

Katey amazed him nearly every day since they met and Logan knew that even in a thousand years, she would still be blowing him away with her courage and spirit.

Now, sitting in the darkness with only the dying embers of the fire to keep him company, Logan didn't feel amazed. The guilt for not being there for her on one of the most important days of her life, was like a rope around his neck, tightening with every breath he took.

No matter how good his reasons, instead of trying to calm her down, he stood by the porch like a dumb animal while she suffered in her fear and anger.

Logan pulled out Marie's business card from his jeans pocket. If this had been another time, another place, he would have shredded it to pieces as soon as they left the voodoo shop. He was thankful he hadn't.

All these years, he had stopped trying to shift at will. He stopped trying to control the beast within him or even think it was possible. Logan felt himself to be destined for this cursed uniqueness, and there was no point in trying to change anything. Now that he wanted desperately to learn what Katey had picked up so quickly, Logan felt the expectations loom over him like a dark cloud.

He didn't even know where to start anymore or how to try. Even now, his wolf sulked in the shadows. Logan's commands fell on deaf ears, and nothing would get his wolf's attention for a moment.

The phone number written in the plain font on the card glared back at him, taunting him. His phone had just enough juice to make the call.

Footsteps sounded down the foyer, drawing closer to the parlor door. Logan stuffed the card away and turned toward the ashes and cinders in the fireplace. One sniff told him who was coming to pay him a visit, but Logan wasn't sure if he was a welcome guest or not.

Darren stood in the doorway, his clothes dusty and hair disheveled. Brown eyes regarded Logan with a look of fatigue that told him his alpha was on the rebound from a difficult night and an even more difficult week. If Michael was correct, and this place was the safest, so close to the hunter's den, then the hardest part of their trial was over.

The alpha leaned against the doorframe and Logan looked away. "You smell like a swamp."

Darren let out a deep breath. "I took Katey around the property to stretch her legs. She wanted to take a swim in the river."

Logan would have laughed if it didn't pain him so much that he wasn't there to swim with her.

"I hope she didn't cause too much trouble before we got here," Darren continued.

Logan didn't reply, feeling somehow distant from his alpha. The last couple of days spent away from the pack had put him in a strange situation. He was the dominant one between him and Katey and was forced to make the decisions.

Although he knew it was an entirely different ballgame to over-see one person as opposed to a whole pack, Logan felt somewhat confident in his ability to lead. The thought of being an alpha one day intrigued him, but he always knew it was out of his reach until now.

As if sensing his thoughts, Darren said, "You did a good job taking care of Katey."

"Not as good as you would have," Logan mumbled, keeping his eyes fixed on the undulating glow of the dying embers.

He didn't have to look at Darren's face to know his eyes were rolling. "You know I never like flattering. Not from my students and not from my pack."

Logan could have cared less if Darren disapproved. The alpha shuffled across the floor, tracking in a light trail of soil from the bottoms of his shoes as he pulled up a chair beside Logan. With a great sigh, he sat down and leaned back.

He slid a glance toward Darren and would have guessed him to be asleep already.

"Is she going to be okay?" Logan suddenly asked, heedless if his alpha was dozing or not.

Darren cracked open his eyes and stared ahead of him, ponder-ing the question. "She's resilient. You know that."

"She was crying when you brought her inside," Logan remarked.

Darren shut his eyes again. "She was just scared and confused. It probably hurt like hell, but she'll be fine after she rests for a while."

Logan went silent and looked away, his fingertips unconsciously raking across the stubble on his jaw. He remembered the way Katey looked at him with such trust while he held her close just before she started to shift.

She wouldn't have died from the fall, but she had given them all a scare, nonetheless. He still wondered if she had fallen on purpose or if it was a simple accident. If she understood what was about to happen to her, Logan didn't put the notion of suicide past her. If he had known what kind of monster he would become that night when he killed his parents, he would have done anything to stop the course of fate.

After a few moments, a door closed upstairs, and another loup-garou made their way into the parlor. Ben smelled distinctly of moss and swamp water as well. His face was not haggard as Darren's was, but strained with worry.

"How is she?" Darren asked in a willowy voice, probably on the cusp of sleep as he spoke.

Ben pulled up a chair on Logan's empty side and eased himself into the seat. "She's... I don't know. At first, she was a little hysterical because of all the blood, but then she passed out from exhaustion. I don't know how she's gonna take it when she wakes up."

Logan felt his spine tingle with eagerness. He should be up there with her, to be there whenever she woke up. Perhaps he could atone for his absence during her shift and comfort her somehow.

He rose from the chair, feeling his legs strengthened by his resolve.

"Don't do it," Darren warned.

Logan turned at the threshold and met his stern gaze. No matter how much Logan tried to admit he could be alpha, he couldn't deny that Darren was still more dominant. A mere look had never stopped him before, but Logan was nailed to the floor where he stood.

"Why not?" he questioned.

"She needs rest, Logan. She doesn't need you crawling into bed with her."

Logan dropped his gaze, trying to form his argument. Before he could even begin, another door upstairs opened.

Gregory's scent came to Logan and abolished all reason and control. Darren's hold over his ward broke, freeing him from his fixed spot so he could meet Gregory at the bottom of the stairs.

The rougarou alpha had vanished shortly after Darren and the pack arrived on the scene, and there was some unresolved business between them.

The slept-in hair explained volumes. Gregory hadn't slunk away out of fear of Darren or the others. His wounds were probably on the mend by that point, but while everyone else was focused on getting Katey comfortable with her new form, he had gone to bed. His well-rested and strong gate was also a testament to that.

Gregory held up his hands to stop Logan, but the gesture was futile.

Logan charged forward and swung his fist at the alpha's face. Much to his surprise, the alpha took the blow and staggered to the side. He grabbed the edge of the railing on the stairs and wiped the blood from his busted lip.

Darren and Ben were at his side less than a second later and took hold of Logan's arms to pull him away before he tried to murder Gregory.

The alpha, without so much as a wince, popped his jaw back into its socket and flexed it to make sure everything still worked properly.

"I suppose I deserved that," he said and stood up straight to face the furious lover. "You have to know it was just business, Logan. There was nothing personal in it."

"You break your new pack members by trying to rape them?" Logan fumed.

Darren and Ben, who were not there to see Gregory try to mount Katey, looked between the two of them with eyebrows raised.

Gregory pulled down his t-shirt in a quick jerk as if offended by Logan's assumption. "No, I don't."

"Then that's how you make your women submit?" Logan snarled.

The alpha's nostrils flared. "Sometimes, that's the only way. I don't have to like it, though."

Logan let out a slew of curses in the loup-garou tongue, not expecting Gregory to understand him. To his surprise, Gregory's throat rumbled in a low, defying growl.

Darren stepped between them. "Greg, the boy's just upset. You would be too in his place."

Taking a deep breath, he nodded. "I will admit that. I wouldn't be so civil, either."

Even though the conflict had cooled between Gregory and Logan, Darren's eyes burned with questions. He stepped up close to Gregory, each one sizing up the other.

"What did you do to Katey?" he asked calmly.

Gregory didn't even break a sweat under Darren's scrutiny. "I was trying to break her, as another alpha tried to do, but... she didn't take well to it." Darren waited for a better explanation, and Gregory sighed. "I tried to mount her, and she turned on me."

Ben snorted, but Darren was not amused.

"You do realize if you had succeeded, we would have a problem."

Gregory finally broke eye contact and glanced up the stairs as a door opened and closed somewhere down the corridor. "I realize that," he said, turning back to Darren. "But, at the time, it was a little difficult to think straight while I was trying to wrestle with your prodigy."

Logan looked to the top of the stairs at a perplexed Dustin. "You four are loud enough to wake the dead," he grumbled as he took lazy and swaying steps down the stairs. He had bathed since they returned from the run that night and no longer reeked.

"If that were true, the vamps would be walking around already," Gregory corrected as he moved away from the rest to wander toward the dining hall. "Michael usually has some food set out."

"How long have you been here?" Ben queried.

Gregory didn't even bother to look over his shoulder. "A few days. I've been waiting for Michael to get back from Florida."

With that, Gregory disappeared through a doorway off the foyer, and Logan heard the light clamoring of dishes and utensils. One thing was for sure, Gregory had not heard the last from Logan on the matter. The alpha was fortunate that Logan didn't tear him apart on sight.

"I trust everything went well getting Katey back inside," Dustin asked, running a hand through his damp hair.

Darren nodded, the movement slow and effortful. "As well as could be expected."

Dustin looked at Logan and ruffled his grandson's hair. "I like what you did there."

Logan rolled his eyes and batted Dustin's hand away. "I'm surprised none of you did the same."

"We thought about it," Ben replied.

Dustin's eyes skimmed over Darren. "You look like trash."

Darren gave a heavy sigh. "I need sleep."

The beta took his alpha's arm and led him halfway up the stairs. "There's a spare bed in my room. Last door on the right."

Darren didn't need to be told twice and made it the rest of the way up the stairs without help. "Don't get into trouble," he cautioned.

"You got it, boss," Dustin assured, then turned to Logan as soon as Darren was out of sight. "So, I want to go to the French Quarter. You in?"

Logan blinked. It couldn't have been a more perfect arrangement. Dustin and the others had no knowledge that hunters were in New Orleans, and Logan had some business to conduct on Bourbon Street. "Absolutely."

Ben stepped in and grabbed them both by the shoulders. "Don't you think you two should be restin'?"

Dustin scoffed. "We're not vamps. We don't need to sleep during the day."

Ben looked between the two, then took his hands off them in a sign of surrender. "All right. Just be back before supper." He turned to trudge up the stairs. "I'm goin' to bed too. Where's an empty room?"

Dustin thought for a moment. "I'm not sure. You can take my bed in Darren's room."

The omega nodded and headed down the same way Darren had gone a moment before. When they were alone, Dustin jerked his head toward the door. "Let's go before someone else tries to stop us. There's a bar on Bourbon Street I want to visit. I know the owner."

Logan shot him a dubious look. "Have you been to New Orleans before?"

"A very long time ago, before I even met Ben. Louisiana was a different place then."

Gregory appeared in the doorway, a container of red meat in one hand and a fork in the other. Somehow, Logan had expected the alpha to eat with his bare hands.

"I don't think the bar will be open this early," he commented, a mouthful of meat tucked into one of his cheeks.

Dustin gave him a dismissive wave. "The bars are always open on Bourbon Street."

They quietly walked out the door into the warm sunshine of the morning, leaving behind the mansion, the vampires, the pack, and the love of his life. When he came back, he'd have the key to everything he had ever wanted out of himself as a loup-garou.

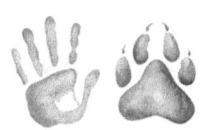

The salty tears had dried on her cheeks. Katey could still feel their long trails along her skin and neck as she lay in bed. Lily had been moved to another room, mostly for her own safety and for Katey's. The ache of isolation hit her harder than ever as she stared at the sliver of light seeping through the bottom crack of the shuttered French doors.

A few hours of sleep had been enough for her to recuperate from her late and terrible night, but it wasn't enough to heal the deep pain within her heart. After changing voluntarily into her wolf form, Katey imagined her first monthly loup-garou shift would be just as seamless. Never in her life had she felt so helpless, so close to death. Even when Logan turned her, even when she died on the floor of the castle foyer the month before, it had not been nearly as painful as shifting for the first time. It was a marvel anyone survived it at all.

Now she understood why no female could be turned into a loup-garou. The frail and fragile feminine body wasn't made for it. If it weren't for her unique parentage, Katey would have died for sure. Laying there in bed, she almost wished she had. To think it would happen again and again for the rest of her life made another tear slip from the corner of her eye and dampen the pillow beneath her head.

It wasn't just the pain of the shift that kept her paralyzed in bed. She could have gotten up and gone downstairs to fill her rumbling stomach. She could have run to see Logan and held him close until the memories of the night before faded into the past, but no. It was the fear that kept her snuggled under the covers.

It was a fear that scarred her mind and weakened her spirit until Katey felt numb and lifeless. No one would have guessed, but Katey was conscious through the whole ordeal. The blood, the carnage, the harried and frightened looks of the loups-garous and vamps that surrounded her, all of it came back in flashes and shadowy images.

She remembered glancing down at her once pristine white fur and seeing nothing but the red blood of her friends and allies. They tried to control her, tried to contain her, and she struck them down one by one. Katey had even tried to attack Michael, who had been nothing but kind and generous to her since the day they met.

Katey buried her face in her pillow when she recalled how Gregory had brutalized her and fought with as much ferocity as she did. When he moved behind and tried to... She shook her head and swallowed back the tightness in her throat. She didn't want to cry anymore, didn't want to remember anymore or even think about it.

Then there was Darren. He accomplished what no other loup-garou present could do. Her legs curled up against her chest and Katey bit into her bottom lip to suppress the whimper of anguish she felt deep in her soul. Never had she felt so violated and betrayed by someone whom she cared so deeply for.

When Darren had beaten her down, Katey could feel the warmth of his body covering her, and she didn't know what was worse: being broken by her alpha or nearly raped by Gregory. She was sure she would never forget his hot breath and saliva on her neck, the feel of his teeth perforating into her skin as she tried to escape.

It had to be done, Katey understood that. If it hadn't, she might have never been able to take the reins away from her wolf. Yet, every ounce of her being wished it didn't have to be so hard to deal with.

Now she understood what Dustin meant. Before last night, she had never understood what it truly meant to be subordinate and part of a pack. Even when her wolf tried to teach her, she couldn't wrap her head around the idea that anyone, Darren or otherwise, could become the master of her body and soul. After the deed had been done, Katey's spirit felt shackled and broken.

No, she couldn't possibly go out and try to pretend like none of it had ever happened. She couldn't face the men she had hurt. She couldn't face the man who nearly raped her. She couldn't face Darren, who seemed to have stolen her free will for all eternity. How could she possibly face any of them? She was sure that not even Logan's company could mend the shattered remains of what was left.

As the rest of the world carried on without her, she could hear voices and movement in the mansion and around the property. Loups-garous awoke and went out to hunt on their own or take the meals left out for them by the vamps.

The smell of cooked and raw meats of all kinds made her mouth water, but Katey's limbs refused to react to her need to eat. All she wanted to do was sleep until the world ended.

But someone wouldn't let her. They had placed her in a room farthest from the others on the eastern corridor of the mansion, so she knew the footsteps down the hall could only belong to someone who intended to visit her.

Katey rolled her head to the side so one eye could watch the door. Her body jumped at the sudden, hard rapping on the wood. Perhaps if she pretended to be asleep, they wouldn't come in.

"I know you're awake, Katey."

Every red flag in her mind flew up, and her eyes went wide. What could Gregory possibly want?

"Go away," she croaked out, her voice tense like her bunching muscles ready to propel her to the window if she needed to run for safety.

"I have food," he replied in a lame attempt to coax her.

Katey gripped the sheets beneath her and felt her heart pound against her aching chest. Over and over in her head, she repeated: *Don't come in. Don't come in.*

A moment passed, and she could hear nothing else but her own heartbeat in her ears, or was it Gregory's? Either way, the alpha hadn't moved from his spot right in front of the door.

He let out a deep breath and jiggled the handle. Katey's body began to tremble, but she couldn't bring herself to flee.

Gregory gave the door a quick tug, and the locking mechanism busted. Katey finally found the courage to spring to her feet and dart to the French doors.

She tugged on the handle, but her burst of adrenaline didn't last long before she crumbled to the floor like a limp fish and wept for fear that Gregory would try to finish what he had started the night before.

Katey leaned her shoulder against the cold pane of the glass panel in the door and with one hand still clutching the handle, she brought her knees to her chest with the other and rocked back and forth, wishing Logan would come to her rescue. Reaching through their bond, she realized he was nowhere close by, and her weeping turned into hysteria.

Loups-garous ran up the stairs to the second-floor hall, but Gregory had already closed the door behind him. Katey fully expected him to rush upon her, but he did nothing. He didn't even step farther into the room beyond the threshold, his body braced against the door to keep everyone else out.

With aching and puffy eyes, she looked up to meet Gregory's steely gaze. There was no malice, no anger, and no lust. He didn't even seem worried or confused by her panic. Gregory just stood there with a plate of food in one hand, watching and waiting until she calmed down.

The loups-garous coming to her rescue banged on the door, but Gregory barricaded it.

"What in hellfire are you doin'?" shouted a familiar voice, one belonging to one of the alphas that first tried to break her the night before.

"Everything is under control," Gregory replied, his eyes fixed on Katey as if his stare was the only thing to keep her from running.

One feeble pull on the handle told Katey the French doors were locked anyway. In her current state, she would never have been able to break the lock as Gregory did. Even if she could, there were the shutters beyond to deal with, and they must have been locked as well. If vamps slept in this room, they would have secured every possible doorway and window against anyone who dared to fry them in their sleep.

"Is Katey okay?"

This time, the voice belonged to Forrest. He hadn't been there last night, and she could only assume the reason was because of Lily. She would have needed consoling after what she had witnessed.

"She's fine," Gregory said. "I'm just giving her some food."

Katey still didn't believe him, but her trembling fingers let go of the door handle and slid down to wrap around her legs.

"Uriah," the first voice said, "stand guard."

"No!" Gregory snapped. "I don't want anyone within fifty feet of this door. You can hear from down the hall."

Katey's lips parted, her chest rising and falling with each quick breath from her lungs.

There were grumbling threats spoken against Gregory, but he didn't even bat his eyes at the insults as the other loups-garous moved away from the door.

Once they were relatively alone again, Gregory let his body lean away from the door. Then, with cautious precision, he moved toward the unoccupied bed on the far wall and slid the platter of assorted meats onto the comforter.

Slowly, he lowered himself onto the bed and made no attempt to approach her. Katey took her eyes off the alpha for one split second to examine the tray from her spot on the floor. Roast beef, turkey, smoked ham, and discs of capicola, salami, and pepperoni. It looked like it belonged in a deli display window and Katey's stomach growled.

"You're hungry," Gregory said. "Eat."

Katey thought for a moment and then shook her head, locks of tangled hair falling around her cheeks. The platter was too far away from the safe spot on the floor and far too close to Gregory. "You're just luring me closer to you," she whispered. "It won't work."

A soft smile spread over his lips, and Gregory nodded. "Smart girl. After their first shift, most of my wolves were still operating on instinct." He tilted his head. "Of course, you're doing the same in a way."

A sickness rose in her gut. "I know what you tried to do to me last night."

The smile faded. "You remember?" he asked, a tone of astonishment in his voice.

"I remember everything."

Gregory lifted his chin in understanding. "No wonder," he breathed. "I promise I'm not going to do anything to you."

"I can't imagine why I don't believe you?" Katey said sarcastically.

A muscle in Gregory's jaw jumped, and she shied away, pressing herself into the door as if that would save her from his agitation. As soon as the flair of emotion showed itself, it was gone, and the sedated look in his stare was back.

True to her words, she didn't trust him. Before last night, she might have felt different. He was interested in peace and contrary to what others believed of him, Katey was inclined to give him a chance. There was still no forgetting the way his arms wrapped around her hips and pulled her against his pelvis.

Katey cringed and looked away.

"I know how you feel," he said, voice softer and gentler than she had ever heard it.

Katey glared back at him. "You have no idea what I'm feeling."

He let out a huff of air and shrugged his brows. "That's what they all say. But you know, you aren't the first to experience the shift after you've been turned."

That wasn't what Katey thought he was talking about, but listened anyway.

Gregory leaned forward, lacing his fingers between his knees. "You see, I was bitten, just like you. Most of the wolves here were born into this life. I was not."

The tightness in Katey's sneer lessened but waited for the rest of his story.

"I was born a human, just like you. I had a family and a stable home. That was a few centuries ago, of course. I had a fiancé and a career." He narrowed his eyes. "Do you want to know what I did?"

Katey blinked, but wouldn't respond otherwise. He would tell her either way.

"I hunted wolves. You see, in Europe at the time, wolves were still a nuisance to shepherds. When they had a wolf problem, I came and took care of it. I was the best wolf hunter in Germany."

Gregory ground his teeth and then continued. "But one day, I killed a werewolf. I shot it with the last of my lead bullets and then had to switch to the silver rounds an old woman in the village had given me a few days before. She suspected it was no ordinary wolf and she was right. When the wolf finally died, it turned into a man. The villagers burned the body, believing it to be some kind of witchcraft. What the old woman couldn't predict was that it was a member of a larger pack.

"You know the alpha, actually. Goes by the name of John Croxen."

Katey's mouth gaped for a moment before she regained her composure and snapped it shut. Gregory seemed amused by her shock.

"He found me and without telling me who he was, he told me to end my career, or he would do it for me." Gregory shrugged. "Being the young man that I was, I refused. I was to be married, and I needed to make enough money to provide for my future wife. Well, he ended my career by turning me into the thing I hunted. It was a form of justice in his mind. Later, he told me I was the first he had ever turned. As far as I know, he's never turned another since.

"I left my fiancé and was forced to join his pack. It became clear after a few days that I was going to be a handful for John. I was stubborn, rebellious, and hungry for power and independence. I never wanted to be ruled over by another man."

Katey dropped her gaze to the space on the floor between them. Perhaps he did know how she felt.

"By the time my first shift came about, I had become somewhat comfortable in what I was. I thought my new abilities would prove useful in a world where power and strength could get you just about anywhere." Gregory took a breath. "When I came to, after the shift and a night of living hell, I realized how powerless I was. John had the power, and I was just a subordinate, someone to control and order around."

Gregory held up a finger. "But, this is what I had thought at the time. Hindsight allowed me to see John was only being the teacher that I never had. He tried to preach peace and coexistence between humans and us, but I never listened. I wanted to rule over the humans. I thought I was superior, just as I once thought I was superior over the beasts I used to hunt."

"Don't you still believe that now?" Katey asked.

"No, not really," Gregory admitted. "One day, I ran away from John to be a lone wolf. In that solitude, I met my wife who taught me love was the most powerful thing, not strength or speed. When she died, and I had to look after our son, my heart felt like it would never mend. I reverted to my old dogmas of superiority and those who thought similar things flocked to me. I became the alpha I always wanted to be, but the wolves under my charge were too... too wild."

Katey looked up. "How?"

A flicker of regret shined in Gregory's eyes, the look of a man who had made bad decisions but had no way to redeem himself. "No doubt you've heard the rumors that we kill humans for food, rather than feeding on wild game... I have never done that. Most of my pack, including my son, have developed a taste for it, but I never could. I'm the only thing holding my pack from erupting into total anarchy. I've never forgotten the principles John taught me, and I've tried to teach them the same, but they're all stubborn and as hardheaded as I had been in my youth.

"Many of my pack members don't make it to see their first fifty years before they find themselves killed by their own ignorance and stupidity. I've had more wolves killed in fights between their own pack members than by hunters. Getting more members is a daily challenge. My wolves aren't the kindest people in the world, so carrying on their gift to another generation isn't always an option. They've resorted to kidnapping women and raping them. The poor woman would kill herself from the grief of what was happening to her before she could carry the child to term. My pack has dwindled down to a mere ten members now, and my son seems destined to be their alpha. Erik is just like me when I was his age."

Katey angled a little more of her body toward the alpha, feeling almost sympathetic to his misfortunes. "So, you're trying to convert them? You're not the reason they kill humans?"

With her whole heart, she wanted to believe he was telling the truth. She wanted to believe he was a saint in disguise, putting on appearances for the world to think he was some evil man instead of a revolutionary reformer, changing loups-garous one at a time.

He ran a hand through his hair. "I don't know why I'm telling you all of this," he mumbled. "I just wanted to let you know that . . . you're not alone. I know how hard it is and so does every wolf here." Gregory leveled his gaze back on Katey, the turmoil of feeling finally under his control. "If you remember everything, then you'll know how hard we tried to keep you from hurting yourself and others."

"I still hurt you. I hurt all of you." Katey shut her gates again and retreated into the darkness of her shame.

"Girl, if you really hurt me, I wouldn't be here trying to give you food. If you hurt any of them, they wouldn't have come running to the door when they heard you cry. The vampires would have shot you with those silver bullets until they couldn't tell you apart from Swiss cheese if they didn't think it was worth keeping you alive after what you had done to them."

Gregory's nostrils flared. "You can wallow in self-pity all you want, stay in this room for the rest of your life, but there will still be those who will guard you even when you've disowned them and tried to shut them out of your life. And do you want to know why?"

Katey slid a glance in his direction and tried to ignore the ache in the back of her throat.

"Because you matter more to us than any amount of pain and irritation you cause us. You're going to do great things for our kind. That's why I'm here because you'll die if you don't eat." He picked up the plate and offered it out to her. "I knew you wouldn't come down willingly."

Katey eyed him and the plate. She took a moment to read him, searching his eyes and the energies he exuded. Like the night before when they met on the porch, there was no dishonesty, no trickery in his tone or body language. Either he was a master at hiding what he really felt, or he meant every word he said.

Each movement was difficult and strenuous, but Katey managed to rise to her feet and took the plate from Gregory.

CHAPTER 19

T he bar was more crowded than Logan had expected. Nearly every table was teetering with vacationers and locals, a tall glass of Guinness or a shot of whiskey in their fists while they laughed and slurred out stories to their friends. The counter toward the back of the hall was just as cramped with humans and loups-garous – to Logan's surprise – sitting upon wooden stools peppered with cracks and impressions from long-term abuse.

The lighting fixtures were tinted red, a color that was supposed to be easy on the eyes in such a dim ambiance. Irish drinking songs and ballads sang through the speakers around the room, matching the décor. Photos of Ireland, Notre Dame football memorabilia, and old farming equipment that must have been straight from Dublin covered the walls.

Logan looked up and saw dollar bills pinned and stapled to the rafters with names and messages scrawled across their faces in thick black letters. Nearly every bar had their customs and the things that they were known for, and O'Malley's Pub and Grill was no different.

Dustin weaved through the tables and headed straight for the bar counter as if he had been there a million times before. A loup-garou was manning the bar, his round face beaming with joviality as he talked with a couple of tourists. Judging by his bright red shock of hair that fell over his ears and equally orange beard, Logan likened him to a leprechaun, though he had the stature of a quarterback.

Squeezing between two drunks, Dustin slapped his hand on the lacquered wood to get his friend's attention. "Carney O'Malley! How's the form?" he shouted down the length of the bar toward the redhead.

Carney turned and let out a boisterous laugh. He excused himself from the tourists and came to face his old friend. "Well, look what the cat dragged in," he said, voice deep and as Irish as a shamrock. "Head like a bag of spuds, as usual."

Dustin chuckled. "And you with a face like a blind cobbler's thumb." Logan heard his grandfather's brogue come out in its full glory.

The men clasped arms in greeting and shook with such force that Logan thought their shoulders would pop out of socket.

"How in the name of Jaysus are ye?" the barkeep asked.

"I'm stickin' it out," Dustin replied. "The boyo and me just thought we'd come out for a little craic. But by the looks of this jammers place, everyone wanted to come out for a lash too."

Carney's bright blue eyes fell on Logan standing just behind Dustin. "All right, boyo?"

Logan blinked and wanted to admit he barely had a clue what they were talking about, but only nodded. "I'm all right."

Dustin glanced over his shoulder, then back to Carney. "The boy's no stook, O'Malley."

Carney held up his hands in defense. "Never thought he was. Just looked a little knackered is all."

Dustin leaned in closer. "We both had a long night." He grabbed Logan by the arm and pulled him up to the counter. "This is my kin, Logan. Logan, this is Carney. We knew each other in the rare auld times back when the Irish ran this city."

Logan and Carney shook hands.

"I thought it was run by the French?" Logan asked.

"Oh, boyo. That may be true, but we Irish have a way of niggling our place into societies all over. Back then, your kin here was just about as mad as a box of frogs and twice as stuttles."

Logan nodded, knowing just how effectively the small green island had brought their culture, slang, and even their music over the ocean. Back when they sailed on the Titanic, there was a party nearly every night in the third-class dining halls, ran and orchestrated by the Irish peasants on board. Two things the Irish were good for: wild parties and even wilder fights.

"Looks like everyone's gonna get locked out of their trees like a monkey who forgot the keys before noontime, Carney," Dustin remarked, looking around at the intoxicated crowd.

"Aye," the bartender said. "Business has been flying for several years now."

"That's good to see," Dustin replied and leaned close. "Ye got any Poitín?"

Carney snorted. "Do I have any Poitín? Of course, I do. But a rawny ponce like ye may get battered by it. At least I won't have to worry about ye getting langered on me."

Dustin looked at Logan. "Want a little traditional Irish moonshine?"

Logan gave him a wary look. "No, thanks. I've got a place I want to go further down the street." His eyes darted between the two crazy Irishmen. "I trust you two won't burn down Bourbon Street if I leave you here."

Carney flipped his wrist at Logan. "Don't be divvy lad. We only tried to do that once."

The two men let out a riotous laugh and slapped the counter, obviously remembering whatever had happened in another century before his time. Logan gave his grandfather a look and turned to walk out, leaving them to their reunion.

"Be back here in half an hour, or I'll send a search party," Dustin shouted out to him over the din of pub clamor.

Logan stepped out into the sun, letting the door close behind him and muffle the bouncy tune of Irish fiddles and flutes coming from the pub. The streets during the bright day were not nearly as congested as at night so he could see for blocks down in one direction without the movement of bodies impeding his line of sight.

After orienting himself, he turned to the northeast and followed the faint trail of magic until it became stronger and pulsed in his core. He was no stranger to the magical energy, but never had he felt it so strongly as he did in front of Madame Celeste's Voodoo Emporium.

Marie was not outside this time, sitting regally on her stool as she had been the evening before. In her place, leaning against the open doorway, was a man in a waistcoat and top hat. His ebony hair trailed down the center of his back as his hands shuffled a deck of tarot cards.

His eyes, blocked out by a pair of round spectacles, seemed to lock onto Logan, but there was no sign of recognition or astonishment in his face. Either he was accustomed to seeing loups-garous, or he didn't have the second sight as Marie was gifted with.

"I'm here to see Marie," he asserted to the man, keeping his eye contact direct and strong, just like his posture. This was no place to show how nervous he was about the exchange. Any sign of weakness and the voodoo apprentice might get the wrong idea to take advantage of his naivety.

The man pushed himself off the doorway and jerked his head inside. "She's here," he replied. "She's been expecting you."

Logan didn't let his confusion show until the man turned away to walk through the open shutter doors. Perhaps Marie had told him to be on the lookout for a wandering loup-garou in the streets. Or perhaps he was a little subtler in his ability to know things merely by looking at a person. Logan could never understand how mystics could read minds or somehow innately know things the way they did. Neither did he understand how Katey could sense the emotions and feelings of others, but he had accepted her skill more readily than Marie's.

The shop was as mutedly lit as the pub, with only a few blue and purple tinted can lights installed in the ceiling. The fire glow effect must have been reserved for the evening when it might have been more alluring to pedestrians who were curious about the world of magic and voodoo. The light shined down upon cluttered shelves and display cases littered with voodoo tourist merchandise that had no magical value or meaning to them.

All around, Logan saw painted skulls, sewn voodoo dolls with needles, idols for other non-Christian religions from all over the world, strings of beads and feathers, shaman masks, and colorful t-shirts with words like "I love voodoo" and other iconic symbols of New Orleans. Somehow, he had imagined the place to be a little more authentic. He pictured rows upon rows of potion bottles and bags of rat bones. This was tame, and it made Logan skeptical whether Marie or even Madame Celeste were the genuine articles.

Marie stepped through an open doorway at the back of the shop and smiled graciously to her visitor. "I knew you would re-turn," she hailed and offered out her hands to him in friendship.

Logan shied from her touch, knowing well what happened the last time their skin came into contact. "I don't mean to be rude, but I don't have much time."

She nodded. "Of course," she replied in her exotic accent. "I'm sure you want to get back with your friend. Come." With long, elegant fingers, she beckoned him toward the back room from which she had come. The aroma of herbs, spices, and incense was coming from the back storeroom where Marie had disappeared.

The man in the top hat left them and returned to his post outside the doors without another word.

Logan gritted his teeth and walked forward with long strides, ready to get it over with.

The backroom was just as dark as the front shop area, but what it contained was the voodoo assortment he was expecting. In the middle of the room was a long table full of knives, mortar and pestles, tiny pots for stirring together ingredients, and leafy herbs scattered over the surface. Along each wall were rows upon rows of bottles containing all manner of liquids and powders. Some spots were dedicated to satchels of unknown contents and dangling talismans of stones and beads.

Logan's nose was assaulted by the odors, but he swallowed back the bile and slowly followed Marie. She hummed a pleas- ant-sounding tune - probably of Creole origin - as she scoured through her stash. Her fingertips dragged along the labels as she went, reading them silently to herself to find just the right thing.

She pulled one powder off the wall, then another, and a satchel of something that smelled like mint and earth, and finally an empty vial with a cork stopper lodged in the top.

Marie brought the ingredients to the table and combined them with the deftness of someone who had made the potion a million times.

"How did she do last night?" Marie asked as casually as if she and Logan were close friends.

He squinted at the voodoo apprentice. "Did you make her shift?"

"Oh, no, dear," she replied with a smile. "But I could sense it in her yesterday. I knew it was coming. I'm surprised she hadn't told you. She had been struggling with the pain almost all day."

Logan looked away. He remembered how Katey had nearly ripped his shirt in her tight grip while they drove toward New Orleans. Was that her cry for help, and he didn't listen? When they almost made love in the hotel room, he knew there was something off, but he was too exhausted and blinded by lust to realize what was going on.

Then there was the way she excused herself from the parlor, complaining that she was only tired. Logan couldn't believe he had been so ignorant the entire day. If he had known, if she had just told him what she felt, then perhaps they could have been more prepared for her shift.

He rammed back the guilt. There was nothing he could do about it now. The deed was done, and now he would redeem himself for a lifetime of carelessness.

Marie poured the contents of her mixing bowl into the vial and wiped clean the opening before resealing it with the cork. "It's a little primitive, but my mistress is very traditional," she said as she presented Logan with the potion. "Drink this when you are ready to call on your wolf. It will give you strength."

Logan snatched it from her hands and felt the essence of magic bleed through the glass for only a few seconds before it died away. He made the dark red liquid swirl within the vial, watching how the tiny sediments of powder and crumbled leaves floated inside.

It was hard to believe that within his hand was the answer to every problem in his life. This little dose of potion would cure him and his wolf, possibly breaking down the wall that had been thickening over the decades. Finally, he would be able to shift at will, and he could be Katey the mate she deserved, one that would be there for every monthly shift. Now, there was nothing stopping them from performing the mating ceremony as soon as this hunter business was taken care of.

"A word of caution," Marie held up her finger. "Some don't take well to what the shift brings out. If you can't get control of your wolf, then there will be little to stop it from consuming you. I advise you to take this in the company of your own kind so they can help you."

Logan looked at the woman's kind face and nodded. "I'll try to remember that."

"And don't worry about your friends smelling the potion. You'll find it has no odor." She grinned with pride. "I've had many wolves come to the shop looking for help in this matter, who are too afraid to ask for help among their own kind."

"I'm not embarrassed," Logan defended.

"No," she said after a half a moment of thought. "But you do hate the situation you're in. There's nothing wrong with wanting to better yourself. Just make sure you're doing it for the right reasons."

"My mate is a good enough reason," Logan replied, a note of firmness in his words. "Thank you for your help."

Marie's pearly teeth gleamed in the light. "It's my pleasure. Peace be with you."

Logan turned and exited the shop as quickly as his legs could carry him. After making sure the stopper was on tight, he slipped the vial into his jeans pocket and entered the pub again to meet up with Dustin.

He had to push aside the strangled nerve that told him what he just committed was wrong. It was for Katey. How could it possibly be wrong?

When he opened the door, he found the place romping with activity. Tourists were huddled against the walls with their beers while loups-garous were brawling in the center. Tables were toppled over, barstools busted into splinters on the floor that was slick with spilled liquor.

In the center of it all was Dustin, fists swinging with a big, stupid grin on his lips. Carney was at the bar counter, laughing himself breathless.

Logan called out Dustin's name to get his attention. After knocking out his current opponent wearing a Steelers jersey, he approached Logan. The brawlers carried on without him.

"I only left you alone for a few minutes," Logan complained.

Dustin spat out a bit of blood onto the floor, probably from the already mending cut on his lip. "Ack, quit yer olagonin'. I was only having a gas with some wanker when he said the Irish were nothin' but a load of feckin' langered gobshites and aren't good for nothin' but brewing Guinness for Americans. I couldn't let that maggot wag his pie hole like that in a place like this."

Logan gave him a perturbed look and watched as another loup-garou grabbed Dustin by the shoulders and threw him back into the fray. Running a hand over his face, Logan groaned and took a seat by the wall to wait for the brawlers to wear themselves out, which might take a while.

Gregory watched Katey devour the plate of meats with intense interest. In the time she ate, they didn't speak. There was no need to.

Erik was completely correct when he said the girl was a prize worth fighting for. Of course, his son had entirely different intentions for Katey that Gregory would never approve of.

Erik had brought home one girl after another, wooing her with the silver tongue he had inherited from his fellow pack mates. Bad influences, all of them. When Erik finally tried to take the girls for himself, when he tried to show them what he really was, they ran from town or would go insane from the shock. Gregory covered up the disappearances the best that he could, but Erik had been completely out of control.

That is until he met Katey. There was a change in his son he couldn't account for otherwise. He was focused, driven, and knew exactly what he wanted. It was only too bad a wolf like Logan got to Katey first. Then again, Katey seemed better off for it, despite the fact she was to be mated with a defective werewolf.

No, Gregory had no interest in Katey as a mate. She was worth far more than a pretty face to him. It was plain as soon as he laid eyes on her the night before that something was different. This wasn't the same girl in Alaska who had stepped in front of a bullet for her mate and ended a millennia-old feud. Katey was a woman now, not a girl to be disregarded.

He had never seen a wolf fight as valiantly and passionately as she did last night. Without hardly breaking a sweat or stopping for a moment to lick her wounds, Katey defeated countless were-wolves and vamps in her rampage. She even threw off two alphas. Although defeating an alpha in such a state didn't proclaim her dominance over them, it certainly made an impression. It was a good thing none of his wolves were there to see his failure.

Besides her fierce tenacity, there was another side to Katey that would serve him for a better purpose.

There was a certain kind of aura that she put out. Before Katey and the others had arrived, Gregory thought he would be driven insane by the stress of being the only werewolf for miles around, surrounded by vampires. He thought the presence of other werewolves would set him at ease, but when he saw Logan and Forrest, mere children in comparison with himself, he felt no relief.

It was only when he and Katey approached one another that he was hit by a violent torrent of peace and tranquility that nearly knocked him off his feet. He was sure no one else felt it, but Gregory did, and that was proof enough for him.

Katey, a female werewolf, would have made a great addition to his pack. Perhaps if she came and spoke to his wolves, they would be convinced to set aside their aggressive, man-eating ways. Up until now, they had ignored his orders, knowing that under the rough exterior, he would never kill them for their disobedience. To kill another of one's own kind, no matter the reason, seemed almost sacrilegious now, though there was a time he didn't think so. It was a sin that Gregory had no intention of committing again.

With Katey, there was hope for his pack, hope for all wolves who had acquired a taste for human flesh. If only she weren't already in a pack. If only she weren't under Darren's watchful eye, then Gregory would be tempted to steal her away. Yet, there would be more than just an angry alpha to deal with if he carried out such a plan. Her mate, her pack, and perhaps Michael's men would come after him. The thought of Anton hot on his trail almost made him shudder.

Gregory was knocked from his thoughts when Katey lifted her head, and wide eyes fixed on the door. He turned his ear and heard a truck rattle down the long, winding path toward the mansion. Katey was on her feet and charged for the door, leaving the meats behind on her bed.

Gregory intercepted Katey just before she could reach for the handle and he looked down at her with stern eyes.

"Where do you think you're going?" he asked.

Katey shied away, the fear of him rolling off her like heavy mist over a hill. It was clear she still hadn't been able to set aside what happened between them the night before. "Logan and Dustin are back," she replied, her voice incongruous with her timidity.

Gregory listened for a moment. Nearly everyone was awake now. Darren, Ben, Will, Teddy and his motley bunch, Forrest, and his mate. Most of them were outside, congregating along the porch like napping coonhounds, or in the dining hall stuffing their faces with the food Michael had set out for them.

A metal truck door slammed, but the two wolves took their time in making their way up the porch steps to the front door. Katey ducked under Gregory's arm and slipped out of the room before he could even realize she had moved. Evidently, she was feeling much better. He marveled at her again. Fresh wolves in his pack normally took days to recover from their first shift.

Gregory walked out the door and into the corridor. Ahead, he could see Katey slowing to a near stop in front of the grand stairs. He came to the second-floor landing where he could look out and see the group that had gathered in the center of the spacious foyer. Teddy, Uriah, and Will were also present to greet Logan and Dustin as they walked through the doors.

None of them had looked up to notice Katey standing at the top of the stairs with a petrified look on her face. Almost everyone below had felt her wrath the night before. For such a strong woman, she shouldn't have been afraid of them now.

"Go on," he whispered, giving her a slight nudge against the small of her back.

Katey took a step, then glanced at Gregory one last time before descending the stairs with precise movements as if she thought she might trip if she wasn't careful enough.

He leaned his elbows against the masterfully carved railing and played the part of a silent observer.

"Why do you smell like beer?" Ben questioned, sounding like an irate wife who had stayed up late waiting for her husband to come home.

"I'm afraid that's my fault," Dustin's said, pinching his sopping shirt. Gregory could see his clothes were torn in a few spots and beer had stained the front of his shirt. "I was sittin' for a spell in my friend's pub and – "

"Pub?" Darren's harsh words cut in. "I told you to stay out of trouble."

"We just went down to the French Quarter for a little while," Logan added softly, his eyes fixed on the approaching Katey as if he were making his excuses to her and not to his alpha. "Nothing happened."

"I can't believe you went to the French Quarter, knowing there were hunters around," Will commented and crossed his arms, regarding Logan with a reprimanding glare. Gregory remembered how Will had been given guardianship over Logan for a while in Chicago. Though he wasn't on friendly terms with the old sailor anymore, it was obvious he and Logan were still close, or at least felt some kind of bond.

"Hunters?" Darren exploded. "Did you know about this?" he asked Dustin, making his beta shrink under his alpha's dominance.

Instead of giving Darren an answer, he turned to Logan. "Did you know?"

All eyes were on Logan and Gregory tried to suppress a grin. The boy had certainly screwed up – again.

Katey was just on the edge of their group now and stood, waiting to be noticed like a shy child. Despite her anxiety, Gregory likened her to a statue of a goddess, standing there apart from everyone and so unlike all of them. In fact, she was far superior, and they didn't deserve her.

Logan wouldn't meet their glares but kept his eyes pinned to Katey, a look of incomprehensible uneasiness written in every line of his face. Gregory thought it right that Logan, of all wolves, should be reverent in her presence.

One by one, the rest turned to see what the boy was staring at. As they realized who was among them, wolves parted like the Red Sea to allow her to approach her lover, forgetting their quarrel for a brief moment.

In one last burst of bravery, Katey ran to Logan, and they embraced without hesitation.

Those who knew of the hunters turned to those who did not.

"There's a group of hunters located just outside of New Orleans," Teddy informed Darren, one alpha speaking to another. "Michael knew it and had Forrest call us up to evacuate the bayou."

Darren's eyes blazed. "He told us it would be safest here."

Will stepped up. "He reasoned that the safest place to be was in the eye of the storm – so to speak. They have operatives keeping an eye on the hunters."

"What operative?" Darren demanded. "There isn't a single person who can stop the invasion of hunters if they had a mind for it."

"Anton Wiatrowski," Gregory announced, the fearsome name echoing off the high ceilings and shaking the dangling crystals of the chandelier.

Some eyes turned to Gregory, while others shuddered at the utterance of one of the most cunning of the vampire race.

Anton was the vamp who single-handedly took out a pack of wolves in the northeast after that same pack had massacred a coven of vamps for stealing one of their women. Anton was the vamp who was rumored to have journeyed across the Pacific Ocean from his homeland of Russia and fed on the passengers and crew of the boat he stowed away on. By the time the ship came into port, he was the only thing left onboard. He was a wolf's first boogeyman and a vamp's first hero. Which stories were true and which ones were exaggerated, might forever remain a mystery to both races.

"Anton?" Darren repeated, all anger lost from his voice.

Will nodded. "We met him last night," he replied. "He's thinner than I thought he would be, but I guess that's why he's as great as he is."

"He doesn't seem like a bad guy," Forrest added. "Logan told me how Anton brought them here from a vamp bar on Bourbon Street and – "

As if being reminded of the serious mischief his wolves had committed, Darren turned to Logan again. "A vamp bar?" he thundered.

Katey pressed herself against Logan's side, her arms wrapped around his waist.

"We were only trying to find Michael. Anton found us first," she answered, her voice meek and slightly trembling. Katey still hadn't found her legs yet when it came to her role in her own pack. That was evident, but Gregory knew it couldn't have been that way before the breaking.

From what Erik told him, Katey was independent. He had known of wolves who were once defiant, then dropped down to the lowest rank in the hierarchy because they couldn't get over the mental anguish of the breaking. Perhaps it was too soon to tell with Katey, but Gregory sincerely hoped she would grow herself another backbone before too much time passed. They all needed her strength for the peace council.

Probably sensing that diffidence in her, Darren softened under her gaze. "I wish you wouldn't have put yourself in that kind of danger. What if there were a vamp in that bar that wanted to harm you?"

"There was," Logan stated. "But Anton stepped in before it could get worse."

Katey looked away and held her lover tighter. Gregory could only guess what kind of trouble would have befallen them if Anton, the fierce and deadly vamp assassin, hadn't jumped in to save the day.

"We wouldn't have had Anton to save either of us if a hunter came waltzing down Bourbon Street," Dustin scolded. "Why didn't you tell me?"

Logan didn't get the chance to explain before a pair of swamp wolves came peeling up the porch and barged through the doors. Teddy came to them, looking up and down at their tattered and torn clothes.

"What in the Sam hell have you boys been doin'?" Teddy inquired.

The two boys, younger than either Logan or Forrest by several decades, stared with unblinking eyes and mouths agape in shock. "We... We just found Bo and Atticus. They're dead."

Teddy opened his mouth to speak, but the words were lost on his tongue. Uriah was the first to ask as he stood beside his alpha, "How? Why didn' ya'll bring 'em back?"

The second boy swallowed. "I dunno. They were just out huntin', and we went to check on 'em. I dunno what killed 'em. It wasn' silver, that's for sure."

The first stepped up. "They were ghost white, and their veins were poppin' out and blue all over. It looked like they were just shriveled up, like a raisin."

"I did see a dart pokin' outta their necks, though," the second one added.

Teddy looked to Darren and the others behind him, entreating for an answer to the strange evidence, but they were too dumbstruck to say anything.

Such a horrific description was enough for Gregory to straighten and grip the railing in his powerful hands. "Wolfsbane," he said.

A ripple of shock seemed to shake the house as wolves turned to one another with frightened and disconcerted looks. The symptoms and nature of the attack could only mean the wolves were shot down with the deadly poison. Silver, even liquid silver as the vamps used, wouldn't make the body dry out like a lizard who had died in the hot sun.

"Wolfsbane?" Katey questioned, looking at her pack.

Ben came forward, his feet dragging with each step. The weight of their flight must have been taking a harsher toll on Darren's pack than any of the rest. They had been on the very brink of danger for over a week, and now, they were in the heat of it again after they had thought they had escaped at last.

"Wolfsbane is one of the oldest ways to kill a loup-garou," Ben explained. "If it's made into a poison, just the touch of it can cripple us. The pollen alone can make us have a severe allergic reaction. It can still hurt a vampire, but it's deadly to us. It's lethal in large amounts to humans if they consume it, but for us, it only takes a little."

"It's the one poison we all fall prey to," Dustin added.

Katey's expression hardened. "If it's deadly to everyone, then who would have used it?"

Will rubbed the back of his neck. "Hunters would be the logical answer, but I've never heard of them using wolfsbane recently. It's too dangerous for them to handle."

"Neither have I," Darren said, a severe look in his eye as if he were ready for battle. "I'm learning not to underestimate the hunters."

"What do we do?" several wolves hollered from the crowd, their pleas sounding like a child's cry for help.

Darren looked over his shoulder to the swamp wolves that had amassed in the foyer, all eyes looking to the alphas for guidance and protection. Gregory stayed at his post, high above the assembly. They weren't his pack, and this wasn't his concern. If hunters were closing in on the mansion or even suspected the former plantation as a hideout for the wolves, Gregory would do what he had always done. He would fight until it was no longer logical to continue.

Darren turned to Teddy and Uriah, whose effort to resist the urge to mourn was prevalent in their stares. "We have to get your pack out of Louisiana," he announced as if he was the only voice of reason left in the room.

Teddy balked. "We can't just leave our homes."

Darren marched forward, the very epitome of leadership in the way his shoulders were back and chest out with confidence. "You can return when the hunters are gone."

"They won't leave until they get what they've been searching for," Will told Darren. "And they've been tracking a wolf from Florida. If they've shown up here after all this time, then the one they're looking for must be here too."

Darren paused in thought, but nothing in his face would betray exactly what he was thinking. Yet, that question was on the minds of Katey, Logan, Ben, Dustin, and Forrest. How did Gregory know? Because they were all from Florida, just as he was, and he wondered it too. Were the hunters after one of them?

"All the more reason for you and your pack to leave this place," Darren answered.

"What about my nephew?" Will asked Teddy. "Can we risk taking him with us?" They understood the connection too. Forrest had also come from Crestucky and was now a suspect in deducing who the hunters were after.

Forrest barged forward, crashing through the other werewolves who were standing idly by and whispering their dissensions about leaving Louisiana.

"If you don't take me, at least take Lily with you," he pleaded. "Then, I know she will be safe."

Teddy nodded. "We can do that much for you, cousin," he agreed, slapping Forrest on the back.

The very mention of her summoned her from the recesses of the mansion, Lily – Forrest's blonde mate – came running down the stairs.

"Katey!" she cried.

Wolves let her by and the two girls hugged one another. They exchanged some whispered words, talking about the night before and the plans hereafter while the other wolves made their arrangements to leave. It was clear the human had recovered from the shock of seeing her best friend shift into a cantankerous beast.

With the help of the two boys, they were able to reason that the hunters must have been coming in from the south, closer to the city and swamps beyond. Teddy's wolves would take the northern route and leave within the hour. Just another pack jettisoned from their homes and comfortable – but oddly detestable – lives living in the backwoods.

While the swamp wolves went north, Darren and his pack, along with Forrest and Gregory, would stay on the plantation to face the hunters as they closed in on the wolf they had been tracking across state lines.

Gregory's gaze jumped between each Floridian present. He knew he couldn't be the one the hunters were after. They had struck too recently for there to be a connection. If they were after him, they would have come onto the property shortly after he arrived a few days ago. They wouldn't have stayed in Crestucky to wreak the kind of havoc that they did with those Deviants and the families still left. They most certainly wouldn't have gone after the fleeing Deviants into Alabama.

Forrest was a likely choice. The destruction had followed his pack all the way to Louisiana, but from what Logan had told them the night before regarding the burning of homes just after they left Crestucky, a day or so after Forrest fled, the timeline didn't make sense. Why would the hunters stay in Crestucky if their target had moved on to Alabama? Then there was the question of, why didn't the hunters attack the swamp wolf colony in the bayou if Forrest was there before moving to the mansion?

Katey and Logan were personally attacked by a sniper in Crestucky and left just as soon as the hunters emerged from their hiding spots to strike against the Devian families, but they weren't present for the Devian massacre in Alabama. They had arrived too late for that.

Then there were the three remaining wolves, brothers in all but blood. They were in Crestucky at the time of the strikes, but not for the attack in Alabama. However, they were the last to arrive at the mansion, and if this new strike by the hunters coincided perfectly, then it might be assumed one of them was to blame. But, it might have been impossible to tell which of them was the target.

If only they knew more, then they could go about this plan of defense better.

Amongst them all, Gregory watched Katey, studying her face and the way her countenance shifted from fear to uncertainty. When she looked to Logan, when she was in his arms, none of it showed. Neither did any of the prior anxiety she felt about being amongst the wolves that she hurt the night before. What emotional resilience she must have had. Or did her strength come from the wolf she esteemed so highly as to claim him as a mate?

There was a new light in her eyes when she gazed up at him, so willing and trusting. No, Logan didn't deserve her love, but neither did Erik in the end. No one deserved to belong to a thing as wild and powerful as Katey. Too bad none of them fully understood that.

CHAPTER 20

Teddy's pack had pried up their stakes and moved north. Carrying their children and women upon their backs, they must have reached the Mississippi state line by now. The sun was making its final descent over Louisiana and within an hour or so Michael and the other vampires would awaken from their sleep.

Until then, Katey and the other loups-garous were assembled and ready to defend the plantation. They didn't have an army to guard their perimeter and the hunters who were on their trail knew that perfectly well.

Katey, presumed to be the most defenseless, was kept inside with Ben and Forrest to protect her. Darren and Dustin stood on the back porch, their senses straining to the north, while Logan and Gregory were teamed up to watch the south side of the property.

Seated quietly on the velvet sofa, Katey's hands fidgeted in her lap. The whole pack was tense, not just because of the hunters but because none of them could predict what would happen. If the hunters came blazing in with wolfsbane darts, there was little they could do to defend themselves. Silver bullets could be ignored for a time while they continued to fight, cuts could always heal, but wolfsbane wasn't something they could get up and run away from.

The loups-garous were hunters themselves, in a sense, with acute senses and faster reflexes than a normal human, but how would they detect the hunters? From what Logan had told her, the vampires were better equipped to hear the hunters coming through the woods than any of them. Now that the hunters had no scent and their dart guns didn't need black powder to propel the ammunition forward, how could they smell them coming?

They were going into this defense strategy nearly blind, but there was nothing they could do until sunrise when Michael and the other vampires could assist them.

Katey had heard talk about taking the fight directly to the hunters, but Darren was still the voice of reason and insisted they stay low and keep their defensive position until they knew more. Anton and his operatives would have to yield more information once they woke up before they made any such offensive moves.

Katey looked to Ben, who stood by the fireplace, his elbow propped against the mantel and facing away from the others. There was a calmness in his façade, but Katey could practically taste the expectation in him.

The soldier would be thrown into another battle, and she knew he wasn't looking forward to it. He might have been the one best equipped to fight, but without the aid of a gun, perhaps he wouldn't fall into autopilot like he might if he had a rifle or pistol in his hand.

Forrest worked at unlocking the shutters of some of the windows that looked out over the front lawn of weeping myrtles.

"Tell me it's going to be okay?" Katey whispered, hoping her intrusion wouldn't throw anyone's concentration off.

Ben glanced in her direction. "I can't do that."

"Why not?" She gulped.

"I can't lie to you," he replied and looked away, the back of his hand rubbing against the underside of his chin.

The strong chord in Ben's voice wasn't fooling her.

"Just say it, even if you're lying."

Ben bowed his head and took a deep breath. "It'll all be fine in the end, Katey."

That's all she wanted. Just to hear the words no one else was willing to speak. It might have been a jinx and too soon to tell, but Katey needed something to hold onto, even if no one else believed it.

Darren's eyes searched the horizon and around the edges of the slave shacks in the distance, waiting for any sign of a hunter. The waning light wouldn't keep them from spotting anything unusual in the woods, but Darren despised the disadvantage of having a useless nose. Sight and sound were the only senses he could rely on. Yet, the sheer population of wildlife in the area threw off his judgment. A squirrel scurrying through the underbrush might have been a hunter moving into position. A bird coming in for a landing on a branch might have been a sniper perched in the treetops.

Dustin stood at the other end of the porch, just as vigilant as his alpha.

The trip from Florida to Louisiana had been longer than expected since Darren, Dustin, and Ben had taken different routes and had to coordinate with one another to arrive at the right place. Since the plantation couldn't be found on any map, Darren had to use geographical coordinates to find the place that Logan had told him about over the phone after they arrived.

No one could imagine his surprise when he felt in his soul that Katey was shifting. The bond they shared as alpha and subordinate was still green, but something in the connection they shared at the wolf preserve had strengthened the ties. Through their pack bond, he felt her pain and fear. To his benefit, it gave him time to formulate a plan and tell the others just what he intended to do.

Sure enough, his tactics worked, and Katey was broken. From what Will and the other loups-garous had told him earlier that afternoon, it was no easy task in the beginning. They told him of the destruction Katey had nearly caused and Darren wasn't sure what to think.

He wasn't going to reprimand her, but neither did he want to coddle her. Her nerves and psyche must have been raw from her breaking. It shocked him most of all when she was so willing to stand in the middle of the assembly in the foyer and speak as an equal with their eyes watching her so attentively.

It only made Darren respect her strength even more.

Dustin stiffened and crouched low, his eyes fixated on something in the tree line.

"I see a gun. The sunlight's shining on the – "

His report was abruptly cut off by the whizzing of a bullet toward the house. The bullet, presumably silver, shattered a boarded window that opened into the kitchen.

Darren spotted the glint Dustin spoke of and took off toward the trees. A few more bullets were fired, but none of them made contact. He found the hunter and launched himself on the human dressed in traditional camouflage and a black mask over his face.

Out of sight, the human must have pulled a dagger. The silver blade lodged high in his left shoulder. Darren's flesh burned against the merciless metal. He felt the pressure of a gun barrel against his chest.

In the midst of blinding pain, Darren's hand wrapped around the gun and wrenched it from his hand to cast it aside. He heard the snap of tiny bones. Darren's left arm was useless as the effects of the silver spread through his nerves and muscles.

The human took advantage of Darren's crippled arm and kicked the alpha off. With the knife handle protruding from his shoulder, Darren rolled away and clenched under the excruciating pain. His free hand grabbed the knife and eased it out of his body as the human stood and retrieved his gun from the leaves of the forest floor.

Another loup-garou, Gregory, crashed through the bushes and tackled the hunter before he could take the time to aim the gun with his only good hand.

The stench of blood met Darren's nose, his first smell of the hunter in the entire engagement.

He stood and regarded his fellow alpha. Much to his surprise, the human's blood was not slathered over his mouth and chin. Instead, his hands and claws were coated in the crimson liquid.

Darren nodded his thanks to Gregory and tossed the knife to the side. Taking one look at the hunter's filleted body, it was clear he wouldn't harm another loup-garou again. The wound in his shoulder began to slowly heal, but Darren's mind was as alert as ever.

"Where's Logan?" he demanded. "You two were supposed to be together."

Gregory wiped his hands on the seat of his pants. "He regrouped with Dustin. They're at the front."

A cry split the air, and the alphas looked to the mansion, nearly a half mile away.

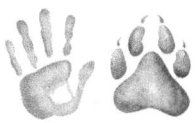

Forrest pulled Katey away from the front window as Dustin came staggering backward on the porch, his hand gripping his side. The bullet had passed through, but she could see the blood begin to seep through his shirt and spread downward to his pants.

Ben took her from Forrest and dragged her to the center of the parlor, just as Dustin backed into the window and slid down, leaving a messy trail of blood on the glass.

A second shot rang out, followed by a grunt from somewhere beyond her line of sight. Katey pushed against Ben's arm, trying to get around him to see how badly Logan was hurt. Tears stung at her eyes, thinking the worst. "No!" she screamed.

Through what she could see out of the window, she saw the two hunters race down the drive between the myrtles. Ben forced Katey to stand behind them as the hunters crashed through the front doors, splintering the timeworn wood.

They came into the parlor, guns blazing, peppering the room with bullets. Glass shattered and antiques like vases and marble statues crumbled into pieces on the floor.

Ben and Forrest charged forward to attack, but the silver bullets brought them to the ground. Katey watched them writhe and growl at the pain in their legs, arms, and chest. Blood oozed from their wounds.

Standing alone, facing the hunters for the first time, Katey found herself paralyzed. These may not have been the exact men that killed so many of her kind in Alabama at the compound. They might not have been the ones that burned the houses in Crestucky or even murdered the loups-garous on the edge of the property earlier that morning.

The anger in her heart toward them was strong and it burned in her belly. She glared, and when they raised their guns to kill her, Katey found the will to move.

Against her better judgment and beliefs that violence was unnecessary, she dashed toward them, ready to disarm by any means necessary.

A flash of black blurred into the parlor. The hunters turned, but it was too late to fire. Logan's eyes were seething gold, and he looked to be on the border of shifting with his claws thick and teeth razor sharp.

He grabbed the nearest hunter and let out another deafening roar. In a movement, nearly too quick for Katey to see, Logan tore into the hunter in a flurry of teeth, claws, and blood.

The other hunter hustled away and fired shot after shot, narrowly missing his target as Logan thrashed his intended kill. Katey dodged behind the sofa whose stuffing and fabric had been shredded away by the shower of gunfire.

She waited, afraid to look at what kind of horrors Logan was committing upon the hunter. When she saw the complete human spine fly across the room and land on the hearth, Katey finally peeked around the corner at the carnage, a cold rush flowing under her skin.

When flesh and bone had been scattered across the room, Logan turned to his next victim and roared with fury.

The hunter pulled the trigger on his gun, but it only responded with a pathetic click. He was out of bullets.

Logan stalked closer, his clothes and skin splattered with the blood of his kill.

The human dropped his gun and fished out a small pellet from his vest pocket. Before he could raise it to his lips, Ben managed to stumble to his feet and tackled the hunter even though the silver bullets still embedded in his body slowed his movements.

Logan came to a halt as Darren and Gregory entered the room. Without question, they helped wrestle the hunter to the ground and pinned him there. Gregory twisted the pellet out of the hunter's hand and sniffed it.

"He was going to kill himself," he announced and tossed it into the fireplace.

Katey stayed crouched behind the sofa until Darren's eyes snagged on her when he turned to attend to Logan. Her alpha was bleeding as well, the evidence caked along his shoulder and torso, but it must have healed already.

The alpha offered out his hand to help her up, and it was then Katey realized how badly she was shaking. Now that the proverbial dust had cleared and the adrenaline high sent her crashing back to the present, Katey could hardly stand at all and merely moved around to sit on the obliterated cushion of the sofa she had been hiding behind.

Logan turned to her with golden eyes still luminous in the dimming light of the parlor. All menace and bloodlust were gone from his expression, but there was a noticeable tremor in his blood-soaked hands. His hands weren't the only thing drenched in blood. The sticky red liquid covered the space around his lips and dripped from his chin.

Darren stooped down to Forrest's side and rolled him onto his back. He was still breathing but had suffered more bullet wounds than Ben, both dripping with blood.

The alpha lifted Forrest onto a lounging bench on the far side of the room, where the battle hadn't touched. Then he set to helping Gregory detain the hunter.

"Go see to Forrest," Darren ordered Ben.

The omega nodded and stumbled to a chair where he proceeded to slide off his own shirt. Katey watched Ben extend his wolfish claws and, with aggressive force, jab them into his open bullet wounds to extract the silver. He couldn't help anyone if he was still injured too, and she marveled at how he could even function through the insufferable pain. It was hard to tell, but Katey guessed he had been shot over a dozen times.

She looked away to the window and saw the streak of blood Dustin had left moments earlier. "Dustin," she mumbled.

Logan, having regained a little of his humanity again, sprang into action and left the parlor to take a look. Through the window, she saw him bend over and then pull Dustin to his feet. He was alive but weak from the loss of blood that wasn't replenishing itself fast enough.

Katey's hands gripped the edge of the sofa, realizing how helpless and useless she was just sitting idly by while the others recovered from the attack. They could have all been killed; some were nearly dead already and what had she done to help? Nothing.

A sickness rose in the back of her throat, and her head swam with nausea.

Gregory and Darren managed to strap the hunter to an arm-chair using shreds of upholstery from one of the destroyed sofas across from Katey. Ben plucked out the last of his bullets and went to Forrest to operate. Logan brought Dustin inside and stretched him out on the sofa the others had stolen fabric from, letting him rest and heal from his gunshot wound. From the smell of it, Katey thought the bullet must have pierced his intestines or stomach.

Logan's eyes locked with Katey's as he straightened, but once again, neither of them made a move. She could sense the unrest in him and the blasting emotions that vied for attention in his soul, but there was no putting order to any of it. Not for either of them.

Katey opened her mouth to speak, but Logan shook his head and left the room, his face twisted with despair for what he had done. If only her legs had the strength, she would have run after him. They needed one another, now more than ever.

"Talk!" Gregory bellowed, making Katey jump.

She turned her attention to the interrogation. Darren slipped the hunter's mask off, and Katey looked up at the face of their enemy. He wasn't a terrible-looking man, but at that moment, Katey regarded him as the filthiest thing on the planet, second only to Yaverik, but equal in their adamant passion to see loups-garous dead at their feet.

The man sneered at the ground, his lips pressed tight together. Waves of anger hit Katey, adding to her own personal grudge against the hunter. Inside, her spirit rebuked her for such feelings, but it didn't lessen her disgust for the man. She was supposed to be a peaceful mediator, but where did justice fall in her destiny? Could she dispense it as she saw fit, no matter the punishment? Or would non-violence and forgiveness be the foundation of her mission, no matter if it meant murderers would go free?

Darren stepped up and grabbed the man by the throat with revenge in his eyes as if this hunter were the one who killed his family centuries ago. "Unless you want to end up like your partner, I suggest you tell us why you're here."

A gurgle slipped out of the hunter's mouth, his words stolen by Darren's tight grip.

Gregory tapped against Darren's arm with the back of his hand to call him off and then stepped in front of the hunter. "You can't threaten death on him if he was ready to kill himself," he said.

Gregory gripped the arms of the chair and leaned in close. "You have to offer him something worse than death."

Katey saw Gregory's head duck down, and jaws latch around the hunter's shoulder. The human screamed, and the anger turned into unrestrained fear as he cried and blubbered for mercy.

For a moment, Katey really thought Gregory was going to change the man. His fangs were latched into the human's flesh for a couple of minutes of intense flailing and pleading.

The malicious alpha pulled back, blood caked on his lips and teeth. He spat the blood out on the floor and looked to the human. "I didn't turn you," he growled. "But if you don't tell us what we need to know, I swear I will, and you can come join my pack. How does that sound?"

Tears streamed down the hunter's face, and he nodded. "I'll tell you whatever you want. Just don't turn me," he implored.

Just then, Logan returned to the room smelling clean and wearing a fresh shirt. Katey found her strength and all but ran to his side, but he held her back at arm's length.

Her eyes were solely secured on Logan, a subdued cry for love and affection ready on her tongue. They couldn't just distance themselves from one another. He could have killed a thousand hunters – whether they deserved it or not – and she would still have loved him the same. The tortured expression on his face rejected her just as harshly as any words could have.

In the background, Katey heard the interrogation.

"How many more are here tonight?" Darren asked.

"Just three. You took care of the others," the hunter sniveled out.

"Why are you here?" Gregory questioned.

"We were after the one who fulfilled the prophecy," the hunter replied. Every pair of eyes in the parlor that were able to open, turned on the human and waited. "We know he appeared last month, and our scouts confirmed he was in Crestucky, Florida. We followed him here."

The hunter looked straight at Logan. "My clan leader told us to bring you back to the headquarters alive."

Katey moved in front of Logan as if to protect him from the intent of the hunter. Her mate's hand gripped her shoulder and moved her out of the way so he would have a clear path to the human. His shoes sloshed through the puddles of blood that pooled on the hardwood floor, some of it seeping through the cracks already.

"If you wanted to take me alive," Logan snarled, "then you should have brought more men. Clearly, you didn't know who you were dealing with."

She slinked back and let him play the ruse out. He did it so they wouldn't suspect the one they had been looking for all along was Katey. If they released the hunter so he could return to his head-quarters, they needed to continue to believe they knew exactly who their target was. Logan had to protect Katey in the end, but she hated the idea. She would no sooner sacrifice Logan than any of her other pack.

The hunter shook in his bonds as Logan treaded closer. Darren brought Logan to a stop, slamming his hand against his chest to hold his charge back from tearing the hunter apart.

"Tell us why you want him," Darren commanded.

Despite the threat of Logan's wrath and Gregory's promise to turn him if he didn't cooperate, the hunter only swallowed hard and shook his head. "I'll never betray my clan. Just like none of you would betray your pack."

Gregory growled, baring his fangs to encourage the hunter one more time. "If you don't betray your pack, you'll become part of ours. Pick your side."

The hunter looked to Logan, the request plain in his eyes. The human would have rather died and the only one willing to do it was the loup-garou staring at him with the angry golden eyes.

"He doesn't know why they need him," a voice from behind them said. Katey turned and watched Michael and Anton step through the doorway.

Michael's sweeping gaze took in the destruction of his parlor, while Anton came forward, unbothered by the carnage he trod on. Katey hardly noticed the sun had gone down, but as she listened, she could hear the vampires rising from their sleep behind the mansion.

Darren stepped away from the hunter, while Gregory and Logan didn't move. Her alpha hadn't the chance to meet the infamous Anton in person yet. He didn't know as Katey and the rest did, that he was on their side.

"I've seen it in his memories," he proclaimed in his thick Russian accent. "There is no need to keep him here."

The hunter looked at the vampire with wide eyes. "We didn't know vamps were here," he exclaimed incredulously.

"You also didn't know we were going to kill you anyway," Gregory said just before slashing his claws through the hunter's throat. The human's dark eyes stared wide as the blood spilled over his chest and into his lap.

Anton's lips turned up into a scowl. "Was that necessary?" he reprimanded Gregory.

The alpha wiped the fresh blood off his hands and onto his already-soiled pant legs. "It was unless we wanted him running back to his superiors to tell them everything."

"They would have come back in greater numbers," Logan offered.

"And now they will know they are missing three operatives," Anton said with a tone of agitation. "They will still return when they realize what might have happened."

Michael made a sound of disgust. "Couldn't you have taken this battle outside?"

Darren turned to the elder vamp and coiled his fingers into fists. "Why did you think this would have been a safe place? The hunters followed us here. They followed Logan here, and you're the one who told us to come," he fumed. "Was this your plan all along? To let the hunters know we were here so they could come during the day when you had an alibi?"

Katey closed her eyes, the room filling with the noxious fumes of hate and prejudice. "Darren, stop."

Michael looked to Darren with indignation. "Do you think I would allow my own granddaughter to be put in danger? We didn't realize what wolf they were tracking. How could we have known when their own men hardly knew? Their leader has been keeping secrets from them."

"Just as you're keeping secrets from us?" Darren asked, his eyes burning gold in the dim light of the parlor.

"I have kept no secrets," Michael corrected, folding his hands behind his back. "If I had known they were tracking your pack, I would have never insisted you come here."

"How can I know you're telling the truth?" Darren challenged, baring his teeth in a low growl.

Katey had enough and stomped her foot, scattering droplets of blood on her pant hem like she had just stepped in a rain puddle. "Stop it! Both of you!"

She looked to Darren. "Michael is telling the truth. I don't read any deception in him. I know you're my alpha and I need to respect you, but I'm the arbitrator between the races, and I'm going to arbitrate now. Michael truly had no idea about the hunters targeting Logan, and he means what he says."

Darren looked at her, his lips closing over his clenched jowls. After a hard moment, he nodded his consent to trust, even though Katey knew it would take more than one reproof to convince him.

"What we need to do now," Gregory addressed Michael, "is make sure Katey and the others are sent away. We will cover their flank and make sure that none follow. We won't repeat the same mistake."

"What?" Katey shrilled. "I'm not going anywhere. I'm tired of running."

"This is for your own safety," Anton told her.

She shook her head, her wolf giving her the confidence she needed to face down such dominant men. "No. I'm not leaving again," she repeated, wrapping her arms around her churning stomach.

Logan came to her side. "Katey, they're right. We can't stay here while we know the hunters will keep coming back. We don't know why they want you."

"Then why don't we find out?" she asked, looking between their faces for any sign of approval. "I'll go to the headquarters . . . alone, so that I don't put anyone in danger, and I'll just straight out ask what they want with Logan. They obviously don't know it's me they really want, and that guy probably didn't have a clue I was loup-garou too."

Darren sliced through the air with his hand. "Out of the question."

"I'm inclined to agree, Katey," said Michael.

Gregory nodded with the others. Looking to Logan, she knew he would not be on her side. When she turned to Anton, he appeared a little more than thoughtful. He was the strategist, from all they said about him earlier that day. He planned operations like this and Anton knew Katey was talking some sense at least. No one else was willing to see it.

"It's what I was born to do? Isn't it?" Katey tried one last time. "I'm trying to make peace. Is the peace between loups-garous and vampires the only thing I'm supposed to do? Or can I make peace between all three races?"

Michael nearly looked convinced, but still shook his head. "You're too valuable to be allowed to go alone, Katey. If something happened to you, if you were taken hostage or they discovered what you are, we wouldn't be able to protect you. It's far too risky, and that's my final word on it."

Katey's brows lowered over her eyes and taking one last furious look at her mentors, she stormed out of the parlor and up to her room, leaving a footprint trail of blood up the stairs.

With great stealth and agility, Anton made his way onto the second-story balcony facing toward the back of the mansion. From his vantage point in the shadows, he looked down on the field of slave shacks dotted across the lawn. The inactive shift of guards ambled about, talking about how inconvenient it was to clean up the mess the wolves had made in the parlor an hour or so before.

They all said if it were them in the heat of the battle, they would have had enough sense to take it outside. Vampire hunters were entirely different than werewolf hunters, Anton understood that much. Their hunters knew only how to kill vampires who were sensitive to light and garlic, two things that could have been cleaned up easily as compared to bullet casings and the kind of slaughter Logan had committed.

Though, he admired Logan's warrior spirit. Primitive as it was, Anton saw the makings of a great combatant. He saw the same in Katey if only those who were too preoccupied with her safety would open their eyes to her potential.

He slunk through the darkness like a formless shadow until he reached Katey's room. She was alone now since her human friend had left with the other wolves earlier in the day.

Darren and Gregory had briefed them on the situation with the hunters, and the two bodies of the wolves that were killed on their perimeter were disposed of since the wolves were unable to get anywhere near the body. The wolfsbane was too potent in the corpses.

The shutters on the French doors had been unlocked, permitting entrance into the bed chamber. Without a sound, he pulled open the door and looked inside to see Katey lying in bed, though she was far from asleep.

She was still preoccupied with the disturbing things she had witnessed that night. Beneath the layers of trauma and fear for the future, Anton could sense a chord of strength in her. In humans, he recognized it as a determination to see things through. In vampires, he knew it as resilience to keep on fighting until there was nothing left of them. In werewolves, it was the tenacity for freedom and a wildness incomparable to any other living thing on earth. Knowing Katey had the genes of both supernatural races and the upbringing of humans, it wasn't surprising to see in such a young person. He admired her all the more for it.

Anton, like all natural-born vampires, could sense the feelings of others. From what she confessed earlier, they now suspected she had empathic abilities as well, just like her mother.

Memories of Jane arrested his thoughts from the present moment.

Anton had only known Katey for a short time, but it was long enough to see everything he loved about Jane manifested in her attitude. No one would have known, save for Michael, all of Jane's little quirks that seemed to pass on to Katey. Her strength was one of those qualities, but the way she walked and spoke was like a woman unafraid of the opinions of others.

Jane was a remarkable vampire. They grew up together, Anton and Jane. Not from childhood, but they served side by side for many centuries. Although she had turned him down to be his blood mate, Jane still held a special place in his spirit.

That's why, when word spread through the coven that she was courting someone, Anton hurt more than any other vampire could have. Sometime later, Jane went missing, and it was rumored she had been kidnapped by a werewolf. No one could have fathomed it was her mate. It wasn't until Michael told him the full truth that Anton understood everything.

Their love was a disgrace. It went against every principle they had been taught and lived by for millennia. Like Michael, he knew of the prophecy that foretold of peace that would manifest itself through the product of both races. He knew this was the beginning of the next era for their kind, but Anton would have never imagined that Jane would be involved in this new revolution. Michael covered for them but told Anton she and Adam, the werewolf, had finally eloped and she was with child.

For months, Anton kept the truth from the others of their coven and diverted their suspicions when possible. When the council decided to send a search party after her, there was nothing Anton or Michael could do. Anton had the right mind to turn down the offer to lead the mission to capture Jane and Adam, but he understood the ramifications. It would jeopardize his life, just as much as Jane's. They might suspect him of being in league with her, and therefore, her crime would become his once they found out the truth.

He accepted, but afforded them more time by leading the troops on wild hunches, tarnishing some of his own reputation as a master tracker. There came a point when he couldn't stall any longer. He sent a private message to Michael and informed him to get the couple out, but there wasn't enough time since Jane had just given birth.

After the child was born, they stormed the cabin and took them. Anton had not been aware of the child's presence beneath the floorboards with Michael and her nursemaid, but by the flatness of Jane's stomach, he knew that the child had to be somewhere.

Anton rubbed at his face, wiping away the image of Jane brazenly facing her executioner, ready to embrace the deadly force of the sun like the bold vampire she had always been. To this day, he wished he had taken the shameful path and defended them. He would have given anything to have Jane by his side in combat again.

He looked up and saw Katey staring at him with probing eyes as she slowly sat up in bed. Anton couldn't save Jane, but he could save Katey and her pack. As long as he had the choice, he would always take her side, and that's why he was here tonight.

Anton held a finger to his lips, beseeching the utmost silence from her, and beckoned her out to the balcony. He would not be able to speak his plan until they were far from the mansion, but Katey was clever enough to know exactly what he intended.

Using the same deftness, Katey joined him on the balcony, and they ran together to the woods, evading the guards and slipping past their ranks. A hunter may not have known their patrol patterns, but Anton knew exactly where the gaps were to allow their escape.

Once they were halfway to New Orleans, Anton turned to Katey and said, "I suppose you know where we're going?"

Katey let out a nervous breath. "Yep," she replied.

"I'll stay close by. If there's any trouble, you know I can't help."

"Why not?" she asked, looking at him with a raised brow.

"I will be severely outnumbered, and with their possession of wolfsbane, they can still harm me. I do not normally conduct missions on so small a team, but Michael would know something was amiss if we left with half of his forces."

She was silent as they ran around New Orleans and through the dense swamps and bogs. "Is what they say about you true?" she finally asked. It had been the question he had been waiting for since the wolves had joined them at the mansion.

Anton smiled. He had heard the rumors and exaggerated stories about his missions through the ages passed down to children as bedtime stories or told around campfires to frighten other wolves. "Some are, but some are not. Do not believe everything you hear, unless you hear it from the source."

Katey, so trusting and eager, nodded and they continued for miles until they arrived.

Easily bypassing the guards that patrolled around the site, they crouched in the bushes outside of a massive clearing. Ahead, was an abandoned sugarcane mill that had been commandeered by the hunters. It had been renovated since it was first left for nature to reclaim decades ago, and now its several buildings accommodated the hunters, their families, and their operations. From the lights shining through many of the windows in each building, Anton knew the compound was humming with activity.

This was not the only headquarters used for hunter operations. There were dozens, one in almost every state, dedicated to the eradication and systematic killing of werewolves. Each compound was run by a leader, a boss, or head of the clan with a hierarchy of soldiers that carried out different tasks. Their field hunters

were the ones who did the dirty work, while the others conducted remote recon or scouted for potential targets.

This compound was different than all the others he had
known of. These hunters had a leader, but he never showed
his face except to his most trusted operatives. Hence, the
reason many of the field assassins knew nothing about their
leader's reason for wanting the fulfiller of the prophecy. Not
even Anton's operatives had seen the face of their leader, the
one they called Andrew.

Once Anton had completely debriefed the compound's assumed floorplan and regular guard rotations, he turned to see
a focused look on her face. She was ready for this and Anton
couldn't help but wonder if she knew exactly what it was she
was getting into. Hunters were not the humans to trifle with,
but she must have known that after all they had been through
already.

"Remember," he warned. "You're only going in as a representative to find out their demands. If you are captured, I'll bring
back reinforcements."

He felt her confused eyes bore into him. "I thought you said
you couldn't do anything?"

"I can't do anything alone, but I can bring back others to help."

"What if you get in trouble for letting me come?"

He slipped her a sly look. "Better to ask forgiveness than beg
for permission."

Katey returned his look with a devious smile of her own.
"Thank you for being on my side," she said.

Anton was sure Jane had said something to that effect once
before, centuries ago. A little bit of Jane shined through in that
wicked grin. If they had more time, he would have told her
everything regarding her mother. He would confess his sin to
Jane's daughter, plead for absolution for allowing her parents
to be carted away like criminals, and then he would tell her of
all their fantastic adventures. But this was not the time. When
this was all resolved, he would tell her everything that weighed
so heavily on his mind.

Without a proper farewell, Katey stood and walked to the
compound where two guards, armed with repeating rifles,
stood at attention. They saw her coming and pointed the barrel
in her direction.

Waving the white flag of surrender and peace, Katey lifted her hands and announced as loudly as she could, "I've come to speak for the loups-garous."

CHAPTER 21

T he chilling scent of gunpowder and steel met Katey as she was escorted into the compound. Pendant lights hung from the high ceilings of the entry corridor where four more guards bearing automatic rifles joined them and surrounded her on all sides. The question was whether they huddled around her to protect her from outside threats, or if she was the threat.

Luckily, none of them had supernatural senses as she did. Otherwise, they would hear her heart pounding away like a jackhammer in her chest. She mimicked their cold, disconnected expressions, but inside she knew how dangerous her situation was.

Katey held onto the security that Anton was right outside and would be there to greet her when she was done talking with the hunters. Appreciation for the vampire spilled over in her heart when she realized exactly why he had brought her here. No one else understood that she needed to do this, not just for her new family, but for herself. Katey so desperately wanted to prove to herself that she could do this, just like when she disobeyed Darren and ran away to change on her own.

If she couldn't convince a band of vengeful humans to give up their mission, then she had no business coordinating peace agreements between the feuding vampires and loups-garous. Everything that happened over the last week told her she wasn't good enough; wasn't capable of the role she had been born into. She needed just one thing to go right, and that would be validation enough.

In the corridor, the guards searched her from head to foot. They even asked her to remove her shoes to show they were empty of anything deadly. It was clear they didn't realize what she was. To them, she was just another human, but she didn't need explosives or guns to cause significant damage.

Once searched and found to be free of any weapons, they led her into a large open area that smelled of moldy brick and fresh oak. Judging from the patched-up and new-looking ceiling, the hunters must have renovated recently. Anton said this used to be an abandoned sugarcane factory and the residual sweet aroma that must have been instilled into the bricks had confirmed it.

Katey thought the room to be bigger than her high school's gym back in Florida, but the hunters didn't play games here. This was their training facility. The floor was covered in padded foam to make it safe for the trainees to tumble and throw one another to the ground in their martial arts exercises. Did they really think martial arts training would help against a loup-garou?

Along the walls were racks of swords and other medieval weaponry that made Katey inwardly squirm. She didn't have to touch the blades to know they were coated in silver.

On the other side of the room from the entrance was an area that had been sectioned off specifically for gun and fire weapons training. Katey could see the plastic handguns lined across a metal table. A doorway just beyond that area led into a room with a viewing window that revealed where the real guns were kept, along with a lengthy firing range for the hunters to practice their aim.

It didn't take her long to realize she and the guards were not the only ones in the room. To the far left of the table loaded with plastic guns, were a group of four humans. Two adults and two children. Katey watched with engrossed fascination.

From what she gathered by their similar features and the whispered endearments, they were a family. The mother was down on her knees, bracing a tall kick bag against her shoulder, and instructed her son - a boy of thirteen perhaps - on the proper technique for a roundhouse kick. His brows and jaw were set in such a way that Katey could almost feel his dogged determination in her soul each time he threw his foot at the bag and tried to get the movement right.

The father's fists were wrapped in athletic tape and threw punch after punch at a mannequin punching dummy, switching up combos and bouncing on his toes like a boxer.

The girl was the only one unoccupied by the art of fighting. Her long dark braid was swept over one shoulder while her eyes slowly scanned through a picture book between her hands. Sitting cross-legged against the wall, Katey wondered if the younger sibling even cared about what her family trained for so diligently. It was the age of princesses and fairy tales for that little girl, and she was surrounded by violence and death.

Katey's heart bled for the innocent as she was led toward the center of the room, the bright lights above glaring down on her.

The mother of the group looked in her direction and stood to her feet. The boy turned, his face dripping with sweat. She called to her husband and he, too, stopped to regard the cluster of guards. As one, the three put up their training equipment, gathered their things together and fled to a pair of double doors that led out of the room.

They were about at the exit when the mother turned and shouted at her daughter. The little girl looked up as if awoken from a dream and scuttled to her mother's side with her book tucked safely under her arm.

As the family left the training hall, another group entered. At first, Katey thought they were more guards, but not all of them carried weapons in their hands.

The guards stopped her and Katey's eyes fell upon the man who led the approaching group.

Drake came forward, a smug look on his face and with a long, proud stride. Katey wasn't surprised. Ever since she found out hunters were using scent-cloaking technology, she made the connection back to Drake from the dance studio. What she didn't expect was that he would be of some importance.

The hunters behind him followed like bodyguards, revering him as some superior officer amongst their own order. At first, she had thought him to be nothing more than a spy or scout, but no. She had the honor of dancing with the leader of the hunters.

More than that, Drake was the instigator of all the chaos that ensued from the past week. He was the reason she had to drop out of school and off the radar. He was the reason families had to evacuate their homes. He was the murderer of the Deviants in Alabama. It was his orders to follow Logan across state lines and try to capture him. Those two loups-garous from Teddy's pack died a horrible death because of Drake's demands. He was the cause of so much misery and panic. For that, she wasn't sure if she could ever forgive him.

Katey's lips pinched together in rage and Drake simply chuckled.

"And I thought you'd be happy to see me again," he laughed.

She refused to respond to his arrogance which contrasted his polite guise so well from a couple of days ago. Katey was in no mood to play his game anymore. With her chin lifted high, she glared as his entourage drew closer.

"I take it our operatives weren't successful in their mission. Otherwise, you wouldn't be here."

Drake waited, but Katey didn't make a peep.

"You said you came here to talk?" Drake asked. "Then let's talk."

Katey took a deep breath through her nose and let it out slowly. She couldn't let her anger get in the way of her job. Somehow, she had to call on the spirit of Tanatia to get her pack through this. "What is it you want from the loups-garous?"

Drake snorted. "Loups-garous? What an archaic name for those animals. I suppose that's the name they told you to use?"

"It's the name they prefer," Katey snapped in defense.

"It's a softer name for them," Drake replied. "That's all. They're still beasts on the inside, no matter what name you call it."

Katey understood. Darren had made that clear the first time she called them werewolves. Although not everyone used the term "loups-garous," she preferred it too, and it had grown on her ever since that day she first found out about this other world of monsters and magic. "You didn't answer my question."

Drake unclasped his hands behind his back, and the smug look vanished. "It's not me that wants your boyfriend. It's my father."

Katey blinked. "Your father?"

A flash of something unrecognizable came to Drake's eyes just before he explained. "My father is still the leader of this clan. I've been acting in his place for a year now. My authority is as good as his, but we've been looking for Logan for over six months now."

"Why do you want him?" Katey questioned, narrowing her eyes on Drake. He might not have been the one who ordered the troops out, but acting as second to his father, it might as well have been his doing to begin with. His father gave the order, and he carried it out.

"That's for my father and me to know. And I'm sorry, but there is no negotiating. We need Logan and only him."

Katey knew it had been a mistake to speak his name that night at the dance studio. It gave Drake and the hunters a level of power they should have never had.

"How did you even find him?"

Drake grinned. "We have our ways. We can tap into any security system on the planet. We just have to know where to look. For months, we didn't know exactly where Logan would be, or if he had even come to full maturity as the fulfiller of the prophecy. After interrogating some of the beasts that witnessed his first appearance, we knew he must have been in a pack somewhere in the southern part of the country. They wouldn't give us a name, so we sent out scouts to find him.

"When we came to Crestucky, we saw a white wolf on a property security footage." Drake shrugged. "Now, we know there are no white werewolves unless they're very old and most of the time, they don't reach that age anyway. Plus, the white wolf on camera was smaller than two other wolves that joined it later in the footage. So, we knew it had to be younger."

Drake began to circle around Katey and her detail of guards, but she wouldn't follow him with her gaze. "After some deep research, we found out who all was living in that house where the white wolf was wandering around. You've been living with four werewolves, and we know all their names and aliases. Logan was the youngest, so we naturally assumed he was the one on camera. And since he has white fur, we knew he must be special. That's how we found him, and that's why we've been following you."

Katey's body went cold and rigid. They didn't know it was her they saw on the cameras. They didn't know there was a female werewolf in existence. She closed her eyes and tried not to let the guilt set in. If she had never gone out that night, the hunters might have passed over Crestucky. It wasn't Drake and his father who killed the Deviants and burned their homes. It had been her fault.

She couldn't slip into despair. Katey opened her eyes and looked to Drake who had almost come full circle in his stalk around her. "If you knew Logan was in Crestucky, why did you murder the Deviants in Alabama? You had your target. Why kill them?"

"Deviants?" he asked, a puzzled look in his eyes. "Oh! You mean the pack that fled town? We didn't know if the chosen one was among them or not. We didn't find out about Logan until after the fact. Our scouts were only supposed to go in and interrogate the beasts, but when the vampires showed up, they had to fight. They were merely civilian casualties. It happens all the time in our business."

Drake gave a flippant gesture as if the lives of the loups-garous, vampires, and humans that died that night meant nothing in the grand scheme of things. Katey couldn't let such an ignorant statement go unanswered.

"Families were torn apart because of you and your father," she spat. "Do you realize the damage you've done? What about those two wolves you killed with the wolfsbane darts? Were those just casualties too?"

Drake chuckled. "Neat trick, huh? We've been developing that for the last few months. We have a lab here in the compound, and a team of botanists working to mass-produce the poison. Hunters all around the globe will have wolfsbane darts as soon as we're done. You see, the silver bullets can be dug out. You can't take a poison out of their blood, though."

Katey clenched her jaw at the horrific reality of every hunter on earth wielding such a weapon. If a hunter found a loup-garou and they had the wolfsbane dart, there was no hope left. It almost didn't matter what she said this evening. If the hunters were successful in producing the poison, her kind was lost already.

"And what about the fires in Crestucky? Is that a usual tactic for you?"

Drake ignored her heated tone and replied, "When you and Logan fled, and we lost your trail, we had to find out where you had gone. They wouldn't give us the answers we wanted. If the vampires hadn't stepped in, we would have taken care of them. The fires were set to cover our presence there."

Katey resisted the urge to growl. "Then I'm so thankful the vampires were there to stop you from killing more innocent wolves."

"Innocent?" Drake laughed. "You think those beasts are innocent? They must have brainwashed you."

"Nobody had to brainwash me to make me understand they aren't the monsters."

"And I suppose you think we're the monsters?" Drake swept his hand toward his following. "Let me tell you, something…" He stepped closer, and the guards hesitantly parted so he and Katey could face one another without a barrier. If she weren't on a mission of peace, she would have attacked him where he stood.

"We've been taking care of these monsters for generations. My family has been in this business for centuries. We can trace our lineage back to the medieval ages when we hunted wolves for the kings. Ever since we've had one mission: to exterminate evil from the world. And we're doing that one werewolf at a time."

Katey balled her hands into fists but didn't reply. Something within her told Katey not to contradict him. There was no point. Drake and all the other hunters like him were too set in their ways, just as the vampires and loups-garous were. It would take a miracle for them to renounce their practices and give up their family heritage. This was not the time or the place.

Instead, she nodded. "I see, and you say there's no way I can convince you to give up your mission to capture Logan?"

Drake must have been expecting an argument, but looked satisfied when she didn't take the bait he had wiggled in front of her nose. "No. My father's demands stand. We need Logan, and we need him alive. If he won't come willingly, then we'll have to take him by force."

Katey tilted her head. "Alive?" she repeated.

"Yes. We need him alive. You can tell him if he comes willingly, we won't have to kill those closest to him. When we're done with him, we'll let him go and give him a day's head start before we begin our hunt again." A sly smile crept across his lips. "You see, I can be merciful."

Katey studied him and found no deceit. If he was telling the truth, there was hope for them. If she could go back and explain the situation to the others, maybe they would let Logan play along. When they had what they thought they needed, Logan would be released, and they could run again. As much as she detested the idea of fleeing, it was a better option than running with the hunters still hot on their tails.

She stepped up closer to Drake, bringing their guards to attention. She could hear them grip their guns a little tighter as skin slipped against the handles. "Do I have your word on that?"

Drake slapped a hand on his chest. "You have my word as a hunter in a long line of hunters."

After a long moment, still watching his eyes for any flicker of doubt, Katey nodded.

As soon as she did, Katey heard a ruffle of cloth and a clank of metal on metal. She turned, but two men seized her arms and twisted them behind her back.

She gave a short cry and then felt the searing silver on her wrists. She had felt silver only once before when she was shot by Yaverik. That was a tiny bullet, and the tight handcuffs burned her skin in such a greater way that Katey hissed and whimpered at the pain.

A wave of shock rippled through the group and nearly every gun in the room was pointed at her in an instant. Drake staggered back and gawked.

Katey trembled and tried to shift her arms so that the silver wouldn't bite into her flesh, but it was no use. She couldn't escape from it.

"It's impossible," he mumbled as a guard turned Katey around so his young leader would see what the cuffs were doing to her. "You're not human, aren't you?"

There was no hiding it now. She shook her head. "No, I'm not. Please, take them off!" she wailed as a tear slipped down her cheek. Blood dripped onto the padded floor and slid down her fingers as the metal cut into her.

"Take her to the detention room," Drake ordered. "We were going to take you as an incentive for Logan to come here, but it looks like we don't even need Logan anymore. We got what we've been looking for."

The guards took Katey and quickly led her toward the set of double doors Drake had marched through earlier. As they exited the training hall, she heard Drake call out to her, "That was a dumb move, Katey. You should have sent someone else."

In truth, there was no one else better for the job. They would take Katey, glean what they needed from her and Anton would go to tell the others what happened. Maybe they would have the sense to leave her and run while they still had a chance.

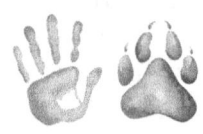

After taking a little over an hour to center himself, Logan left his quiet spot in the shadows on the back porch and went inside the mansion. Voices came from behind the cracked parlor doors, but Logan passed by without poking inside to check on their progress.

Plans were being made for their departure from Louisiana. Darren, Dustin, and Gregory all discussed their proposed escape paths with Michael, while Ben continued to help Forrest convalesce from his wounds. Out of everyone who participated in the battle against the hunters, Forrest was the worst off with his chest riddled with silver bullets.

With Ben's help, they were all physically recovering from the fight as well as could be expected. Their flesh had healed, and the floor was cleaned of the blood that had been shed, but their hearts and minds were not the same as before.

Logan, especially, had a hard time winding down from what happened. He let the beast off its chain for one moment of unrestrained aggression, and he couldn't erase the memory of tearing that man to shreds.

He stopped on the stairway and gripped the railing, and the room began to spin as it had earlier that evening after Katey stormed out of the parlor. He had never committed such a beastly atrocity since his rampage that night in Chicago so long ago.

Things he didn't want to think about came whizzing through his mind. What if that hunter had a family? What of his parents; were they still alive? Did he have a wife or children waiting somewhere? Humans had their packs just like loups-garous had theirs. That hunter, along with the other nameless enemy Gregory killed, would never return to their homes.

Logan mentally grasped for the assurance that those hunters had done the same to his own kind, but somehow that wouldn't pacify the guilt. Yes, hunters had killed their kind, but never so intimately as Logan did.

Though he had washed his mouth out a hundred times, the taste of that man's heart and blood clung to his tongue like a terrible reminder of what he had done. The hunters didn't devour their prey, but Logan had. That human's flesh sat in his stomach and refused to come up, no matter how many times he tried to induce vomiting. What was worse, he found he liked the taste.

The only one who witnessed his crime was Katey. He could not confess to Darren or Michael or even Ben, who was nearly unconscious at the time it happened. The need for forgiveness drove him further up the stairs and down the hall.

More than his need for forgiveness, Logan desperately needed to feel the peace Katey gave so unconsciously. Logan had to feel her hand in his, her heart beating against his chest. Nothing else was going to make this pain go away.

As he neared the door, he listened but heard nothing. No heartbeat, no breathing. He knocked hard on the door, unafraid to wake her from whatever dream or nightmare she may have been having.

While he took a moment to wait, he let his hands slide into his jean pockets. The edge of his finger touched the warm glass of the vial Marie had given him. Logan bit his lip and remembered the moment he was tempted to take the potion before he charged into the parlor to confront the hunters. He had already pulled the bullet out of his thigh by then and was ready to fight them back until he breathed his last.

Not one drop was missing from the bottle. Logan's guts twisted with shame at the thought of having the potion to begin with. It never occurred to him he would have to explain his sudden ability to shift. Darren and the others would ask what helped him and if he told the truth, he knew what a fraud he would become in their eyes; especially to Katey.

He regretted ever going to Marie, and at his next chance, he knew he would have to dispose of the magic somehow.

Logan rapped on the door again and tested the knob. It was then he realized the lock had been brutally broken and he was able to open the door with ease.

The bedroom was empty and the French doors wide open. He took a moment to reach out through their bond, but it only confirmed what he already suspected. Through his grief, he had completely missed that she left the property and had traveled miles away by now.

Logan cursed under his breath and darted down the stairs. He was ready to barge in on the meeting taking place in the parlor when he saw something come up the drive out of the corner of his eye through the open front door.

Logan turned his attention there, thinking it was another hunter coming to claim him. When he stepped onto the porch, he saw Anton slinking through the shadows toward the mansion

Their eyes met, and it didn't take him long to realize the vampire was up to something. Anton paused, a dangling beard of moss grazing against his shoulder. Logan narrowed his eyes when he beckoned him to come closer.

Although he had proven his loyalty, Logan was still leery of the assassin. If the vampire knew why Logan's heartbeat thrashed in his ears, then perhaps he was the one to talk to and not Darren or Michael.

They approached and walked around the side of the mansion into the backfield where the slave quarters and other unoccupied vampire guards were enjoying their break from patrol duty.

"What's going on?" Logan asked, keeping his voice low so no one in the house might accidentally hear them.

"Katey's with the hunters."

It was the rage that made Logan lash out and try to grab Anton by the front of his shirt. It was speed and quick reflexes that stopped him before he could even lay a finger on Anton. The vampire gripped his wrist in a vice and bared his sharp teeth.

"I don't have time for you and your angst. If you're going to help me get her back, I suggest you follow and keep your mouth shut."

Anton released his hand and marched forward like nothing had happened, but Logan stood a little befuddled for a moment. He had been spoken to like that many times before by his alpha and Dustin, but never by a vampire.

However much he wanted to resist such an order, he gathered up his wounded pride and hurried after him to follow like a silent specter in Anton's wake.

He watched as the vamp began to wordlessly recruit other vamps from the shacks. All he needed was a gesture to get their attention, and they trailed behind him like eager pups. Once he had amassed a decent following, he took them to another shack that was free of occupants.

Logan wondered who was really in charge of this coven. Michael was the elder, but these grunts seemed willing to follow Anton just as unquestionably as if he were their leader. With the reputation and prestige that followed Anton, it was no surprise any vampire in the world would jump at the chance to stand by him during battle.

Some of the vampires gave Logan untrusting looks, but they let him glimpse inside their makeshift armory. Hanging on the dilapidated walls of the vacant shack were dozens of guns ranging from simple forty-five caliber pistols to automatic rifles they slung over their shoulders. The guns were the same ones the vampires wielded the other night when they almost open-fired on Katey in her loup-garou form.

Buckets upon buckets of silver bullet rounds were lined up along the walls. Logan took a step back and nearly collided with a vamp who was trying to make his way into the arsenal.

He wanted to turn to Anton, who was loading his own weapons and shoving them into holsters under his coat, and ask how Katey fell into the hunter's hands in the first place. Did she go there alone? If Anton knew about her capture, did he go with them?

Anton looked up, his eyes burning in the darkness. It was as if the vampire read his mind or understood his worry, and said softly, "She went in to talk, just like she proposed earlier. They found out she was the one they were looking for and not you."

Logan turned to the vamps who were busy arming themselves. "If we went with her, she might not have been caught."

"No," Anton replied as he slid the loaded magazine into the bottom side of the handle. "The more that tagged along, the more likely we would have been caught. It was a stealth mission, and it got out of hand. That's all."

Logan snorted and wandered down the creaking, unstable porch, shaking his head. "You say that like it's nothing," he muttered. "She might be dead right now for all we know."

"No," Anton repeated. "She's not dead, and you know it."

As much as he hated to admit it, the vampire was right. The bond still thrummed within his soul, screaming that Katey was still alive, but that didn't give him any assurance or slow his racing pulse.

"Besides," Anton continued, "they don't want to kill her. She was about to make a deal that if you came willingly to them, they would release you once they had what they came for. I doubt they will do any differently with her."

Logan leaned against one of the support posts and heard it groan under his weight. Once again, Katey defied orders to do what she thought was necessary and put herself in front of the gun barrel for him. His chest squeezed, and his hands found their way into his pockets again to touch the vial.

Anton placed a hand on his shoulder. "We're going to get her back, and if it clears your conscience, you're welcome to come along."

Logan owed her that much. He owed her much more than that, but he would take care of it when she was back safe in his arms. With a nod, he turned back to Anton. "What can I do?"

In an imperceptible motion, Anton whipped out one of his guns and handed it to him. "Do you know how to use this?" he asked.

With hesitance, Logan took the gun and marveled at how well it fit in his palm. He curled his hand around the handle but kept his finger off the trigger. Yes, he knew how to use a gun, but after everything he had been through tonight, it seemed like such a tame and humane weapon compared to what he found to be more efficient.

"And don't make too much noise," Anton added and walked away to brief his men on the plan.

Logan listened from a distance, his eyes fastened on the barrel of the gun. He wondered if he had the nerve to kill another human tonight and if he did, would it be his undoing?

CHAPTER 22

Katey sat cross-legged on the floor of the cage in the dark detention center. A single light shined down from the center of the room, but her sharp eyes filled in the rest of the details the light couldn't illuminate. Hers was not the only cage in the room, but it was not the biggest nor the smallest of the dozen or so that were empty.

There were no windows and only one door at least six inches thick with three locks that required passcodes to unlatch. Beyond the room, she could hear almost nothing of the hunters' activities, and the silence rang in her ears so strongly she thought they would eventually bleed.

She remained still, being careful not to move in such a way that would make any part of her body touch the solid silver bars of her prison. The first half hour of her captivity had been spent testing every bar with a single touch, just to make sure there was no way out. Even the padlock was made of silver and some formidable metal she couldn't break or kick open.

With nothing to listen to, nothing to touch, and nothing to watch, Katey sat with her hands folded in her lap and eyes closed. If it weren't for the confined space she found herself in, she would have curled up and slept.

Instead, she dedicated her time to calming her wolf who was frantic and desperate for escape. Now she understood how her pack and the other loups-garous felt while imprisoned in the dungeon below the vampire castle. She didn't have to deal with bodies pressing in from all sides, nor the hungry tempers of other men around her, but what she was left with seemed much worse.

The lonely void made her body shiver with emotions she hadn't experienced before. Like in the hotel room the other day, the disconnect from her pack and her fiancé nearly crushed her spirit. Besides then, she couldn't recall a time when she had been so completely alone. Even in the hotel room, she knew Logan would return eventually. Here, she wasn't sure of anything.

Her pack could be in another state by now, fleeing while they had the chance. Or they could have been wasting precious time coming up with a plan instead of charging into the compound to save her. For all she knew, they could have been trying to get in right then and were shot down by the hunters with their wolfsbane darts. She couldn't hear a thing beyond her prison.

Her inner wolf wailed for company and comfort, but Katey had no means to help her. All she could do was breathe slowly and fight back the waves of panic and hopelessness. She had to hold onto her sanity until all hope was truly lost.

The silence of the detention room was broken as she heard the faint tap of footsteps come closer. She cracked open her eyes to watch as each of the locks snapped back, and the door opened. A team entered, two dressed in lab coats and six more armed with weapons and wearing protective gear.

As they approached the cage, Katey refused to move. These same people had come in some time ago. All they wanted was a blood sample then. Did they need more?

They formed a circle around the cage door, as they had before, and pointed their guns at her head. If she resisted or made any sign of hostility, she would be killed. Although they weren't packing wolfsbane, a silver bullet to her brain wouldn't be something she could bounce back from.

The cage door was unlocked, and a doctor entered with an empty syringe. Katey's eyes watched him take her arm and roll up her sleeve again. She cooperated and refused to listen to her wolf who screamed out demands that Katey take the chance to run away, regardless of the consequences. The process took less than a minute and the tiny hole the syringe made healed as soon as the needle came out.

As the team locked her cage door and prepared to leave for their second time, Katey felt something she hadn't expected. The back of her skull tingled, and she lifted her head to stare at the open door.

Bodies moved in and out, flowing together in such a way that she couldn't pinpoint where the loup-garou was until he was standing in front of her locked cage. A man, tall and built from years of combat training presented himself to her. He wore the same protective body armor that the other guards wore, but he carried no gun.

Their eyes locked and Katey felt her heart seize in her chest. Yes, he was a loup-garou, but something wasn't right. The dark circles under his hazel eyes and scruffy face made him look like he hadn't slept for days. Or perhaps he was ill? His posture was erect, proud. By the way the guards flanked him, Katey knew he must be an important man, like Drake.

He flipped a gesture to the guards, and they left the room, shutting the door behind them, so he and Katey were completely alone. Whatever conversation they had would reach no human ears beyond these walls.

"You're a hunter," she said with such a flat tone that she even surprised herself by how calm she remained under the circumstances.

"I am. My name is Andrew." He squatted down, so their eyes were even with one another. "I'm the leader of this clan."

Katey blinked and squared her shoulders. "You're Drake's dad?"

Andrew nodded, and she could see the weariness in the movement of his head. "I bet you're confused."

"You're a hunter who is also a loup-garou. How confusing is that?" she quipped.

Andrew chuckled and eased himself back, so they were both sitting cross-legged now. At the end of his laugh, he coughed hard into his elbow and took a deep breath to recover.

"How can you be sick if you're loup-garou?" she asked, letting her curiosity inch forward one question at a time.

"Quit calling me something I'm not," he ordered, a snap of impatience in his words.

"But you are," Katey insisted. "I can feel it, just like you can feel that I'm a loup-garou too."

Andrew looked at her with a fierceness that neither frightened her nor would subdue her questions. They were separated by silver, and neither of them could harm the other.

"I was not born a beast," he said. "I was born human, and that's what I am." With a heavy sigh, he continued. "About a year ago, I was bitten while on a solo mission in Alaska. When I got back, I didn't tell anyone. My son is the only one who knows because I needed someone to take my place in the clan. I still give the orders, but I can't go into the field anymore."

Katey laced her fingers together and squeezed. It made sense. How strange would it be if a loup-garou felt the same tingling sensation she felt now with Andrew, and realized that one of their own kind was about to kill them? And if that loup-garou escaped, what kind of mayhem would ensue from the truth? "That still doesn't explain why you look so sick."

Andrew cast his eyes to the ground and pulled out a white pill bottle with no label from his pants pocket. "I've been taking these almost daily since I got back from that mission. A woman in New Orleans made these pills for me and said they would suppress the beast. They've been working."

Slowly, as if he were swimming in a deep sea of pain and mental anguish, he slid his pills back into his pocket. Katey's mouth hung open, and she shook her head. "You can't do that. It'll kill you eventually."

"That's better than being a monster," he whispered.

Keeping the beast locked away without any means of escape would only anger it and bring Andrew to a tormenting end. Even now, she could feel that rage building within him, waiting for the chance to unleash and tear his human host apart.

Katey slipped her legs out from under her and crawled closer to the bars that separated them, being mindful not to get too close. "Listen to me," she begged. "You're not a monster. None of us are. You don't have to take those. You can leave here and join a pack. I know a loup-garou who – "

"Stop!" Andrew exploded.

Katey shrank back and watched his face twist into something terrifying. Hateful eyes glared at her, but they did not turn gold as she had expected. The pills must have been powerful, indeed.

"I will not join your kind," he growled. "I am not one of you, and I will never leave my clan or my son. That's why you're here."

Katey sat back and waited for him to explain while she lowered herself ever so slightly to assume the submissive posture his wolf needed to see in order to feel comfortable again. He might have denied his wolf and kept it locked away, but it still seethed in his soul, and she could sense its dominance. He would have made an excellent alpha.

Andrew's expression slacked back into the haggard look he wore earlier. "I heard a rumor there would be a werewolf who was so special that he would bring peace and harmony to all things on earth. That means he would have the cure for evil. I looked all over the country, sending out operatives in all directions to find the wolf. When we found someone who knew, and we interrogated him, we knew he would be in the South. My son found your pack and through some oversight, we thought it was your mate. We weren't expecting a female werewolf."

Katey heard his words, but the first part made little sense. "The prophecy said I would bring peace between loups-garous and vampires, not the whole world. At least, that's not what I thought in the beginning."

Marie's words came back to her once more and reminded her of how much stock the human race - who were aware of her presence - had put in her. Humans could feel the strain of the imbalance just as much as they did, but to cleanse the world of evil seemed way out of her pay grade.

"What I mean is, since your kind and vampires and all other monsters in the world are evil, you're going to cure them and make them human again."

Katey blinked and shook her head. "No, that doesn't sound right. How can I cure something I already am? Besides, I've been told there is no cure. You're wasting your time."

Andrew glowered. "You're just saying that because you don't want me to be cured. You want me to stay like this forever, but I won't. We already have your blood, and our scientists are working to formulate the cure." He gave her a sinister smile. "Once we have it, you're going to be our first guinea pig. Once we know it works, I'll take the dose and be my old self again. And you're going to stay here until we have the cure."

It sounded like some mad scientist scheme Katey knew would never work. She didn't have to consult with the spirit of Tanatia or her wolf to know that there was no cure. He might as well have been searching for the holy grail, but who could convince Andrew otherwise?

Katey sighed and swung her legs around until she was sitting as she was when he walked in. "So be it," she relented. "I'm telling you that you won't find anything."

"Our doctors have already found some interesting properties in your blood. It's only a matter of time before they can single out that strand of DNA that will cure me."

Katey shrugged. "I'm half loup-garou and half vampire. That's probably what they're seeing. I don't think that will cure you, but knock yourself out." She looked at one of the larger cages tucked away in a corner. "Can I at least get a bigger cage? Or a pillow? The floor is kind of hard."

Andrew stood to his feet with great effort. "You won't be here much longer."

"What if you don't find what you're looking for?" Katey asked as he walked away, each step heavy and shuffling.

Andrew looked over his shoulder, and she saw a glint of remorse in his gaze. "Then we'll let you go, just as Drake promised. We'll drain you dry of all your blood before I'm willing to give up."

The leader of the hunters walked out of the detention room, and the three locks snapped back to trap her again in silence.

Pity enfolded her heart as Katey remembered Andrew's tragic story. If only he could accept what he was, if he could let go of the bitterness that etched itself in every fiber of his being, then perhaps he could have been happier and healthier. A loup-garou who denied their true self might as well have been like an animal who refused to hunt or feed itself. Death was imminent, and Katey was surprised he was still alive at all. She couldn't imagine living one moment without her wolf, let alone nearly a year.

Pity was replaced by disquiet at her next thought. If by some random miracle, Andrew did find the cure for being loup-garou and vampire, what could that spell for the rest of her kind all over the world? She might be the first loup-garou to take their next breath without the aid of their spiritual partner. She was sure there were plenty who would line up at the chance to be human again, but Katey was not eager for it. It made her want to try and escape all the more.

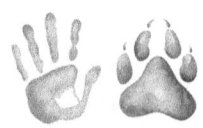

Anton's forces were merciless as they made their way through the guard-infested woods. Bloodless bodies littered the forest floor as the vampires closed in on the old sugarcane mill.

Logan stayed close to Anton but kept his gun holstered. Not a shot had been fired yet, and Anton said he preferred it that way. The vamps were armed only if their stealth attacks were rendered pointless.

Using daggers as long as their forearms, the vamps dispatched their victims with a quick slash to the throat or stab down their spinal cord that killed them instantly. By now, he had been numbed to the blood and carnage, especially now while he only had one thing on his mind.

Not a word had to be spoken between the leader of the mission and his troops. Signals and what Logan could only assume as intuitive telepathy kept them organized as they constricted around the compound.

The two guards at the front were easily dealt with by two vamps who swept in before the humans had a chance to fire their rifles. Two more vamps charged into the mill and scoped out the entry hall before declaring it safe for Anton, Logan, and the rest to move in.

With a tried and proven method, two vamps moved into a room to clean it out and then ushered the others inside with sharp jerks of their heads or guns. Logan and Anton had already discussed the predicted path through the compound since the vamps had studied it well over the last few weeks. Some parts of the building remained unknown to them, but they knew exactly where they would have taken Katey.

Anton informed Logan on the way to the complex, that the night watch would be scarce and many of the lights had been cut off already, so they had plenty of cover in the darkness. The hunters weren't aware of the vampire presence in New Orleans, and if they were, they didn't consider the vampires to be a threat. Therefore, they neglected to build their defenses against them.

The death count rose steadily as they made their way through the complex until they reached the heavily fortified door. Four operatives covered Anton and Logan as they inspected the keypads and dial locks that kept them out of the detention room. They had come so far already, only to be stopped by a few number combinations.

Logan repressed the curses on his tongue and his muscles bunched under his skin, ready to charge at the door himself just to make it open. Anton held out his hand in front of the angry loup-garou to stop him from the foolish impulse and stared at the keypad as if the code would magically reveal itself.

Voices drew closer, but Logan knew more vamps were silently guarding their exit routes. If any hunter so much as wandered too close to the detention room, the vamps would take care of them.

Anton turned away from the locked door and bent down to one of the hunters they killed who had been standing guard over the detention room. Logan watched as the vamp pressed his fingertips against the man's forehead for a solid minute and then came back to the keypad. With nimble fingers, he entered the correct passcodes and spun the dial in just the right combination to open the door.

Logan ogled between the vamp and the corpse he had somehow conversed with, but there was no time to ask questions. He remembered Anton had said something about reading the memories of the hunter they captured at the mansion, but it seemed outlandish to believe he could read the mind of a corpse.

He rushed to Katey's cage as the two sweepers cleared the room. Logan didn't bother waiting for their approval, and he didn't even let Katey speak before he gripped the bars that kept them apart.

The silver burned in his palms, but he hardly noticed as he gave a swift tug on the cage door. The hinges snapped and noisily fell to the concrete floor.

Katey darted out, and they collided, arms enveloping one another.

"I didn't think you'd come so soon," she whispered against his neck as he lifted her to her feet. Anton waited patiently at the door, but Logan knew they didn't have much time.

Logan kissed her hard, but when he pulled away, his eyes conveyed anything but love and admiration for her brashness. "You shouldn't have come alone," he scolded.

Katey hugged him tight around the neck. "I couldn't just stay at the mansion. I had to try."

Yes, he completely understood her reasons. That didn't make it any better. Logan wanted to push aside his crossness with her and be thankful she was alive, but they weren't out of the woods yet.

Katey loosened her grip and met Logan's eyes. "I know why they wanted me," she said. "They think I have the cure."

Logan dipped his chin and squinted at her. "Cure? For what?"

"For us. For loups-garous and vampires."

A sudden coldness hit Logan's stomach. "That's impossible."

"That's what I told Andrew, but he won't listen. He's a loup-garou too and – "

Anton snapped his fingers at the two of them to get their attention before nudging his head toward the door. They didn't have the time for conversation. If any of the hunters stumbled upon their dead comrades, they would come looking for Katey first to make sure no intruders came to claim her.

Logan guided Katey out the door, and the two sweepers followed. They closed the detention room door and retraced their steps back through the compound. Katey's momentum slowed, and after a while, Logan had to practically drag her past the lifeless bodies that marked their path.

Part of him wished she could become accustomed to death. After the battle at the castle, seeing what remained of the safehouse in Alabama, and after the slaughter she witnessed at the mansion, Katey shouldn't have gone weak in the knees at the mess they had made.

Shouts rang through the halls and sirens blared across the compound as overhead lights flickered on and the generators whirled to make the complex come alive. The shadows wouldn't hide them any longer. Anton and the vamps plowed ahead to investigate while a detail of four vamps kept moving with Logan and Katey toward the exit.

Katey's hand gripped tight around Logan's as gunshots sounded through the systems of corridors and rooms that connected several of the buildings. Screams ripped through the once-silent air as their presence was made known throughout the hunter headquarters.

While passing through the last corridor before they could arrive at the training hall, Logan looked down a linked room and saw three hunters in full battle gear.

With little time to react, Logan pulled Katey down to make her crouch. Two of the vamps attending them were shot with wolfs-bane darts. The residual smell of the poison congested Logan's sinuses and both he and Katey were sent into a fit of coughs and wheezes as they hurried on.

The remaining two vamps shot the hunters and evaded the darts, and once they distanced themselves from the corpses now riddled with wolfsbane, their sinuses began to clear, and they could see straight again.

In the training hall, they were met with a detail of hunters guarding their exit. The vamps opened fire, but the hunters out-numbered them.

Thinking fast, Logan whisked Katey toward the sectioned-off gun range attached to the training hall. A silver bullet nicked his side, but he kept going, remembering there was another way out on the floorplans Anton had described to him. The pain seemed like nothing in their rush to freedom.

They ducked down, avoiding the bullets that shattered the observation window and penetrated through the walls of the short gun range. Through another door, they found themselves in an empty corridor where the battle hadn't spilled into yet.

"Where are we going?" Katey whispered.

Logan counted the doors until he found the right one. "There's a kitchen around here somewhere with a door leading to the outside."

He tested the third door on the left. It opened into a debriefing room full of maps, and he let out one of the strings of curses that he had wanted to let loose for a while now. Perhaps he was thinking of another corridor, or he had counted wrong.

He closed the door, but when they stepped back into the corridor, they were met by some of the hunters from the training hall. Shots were fired, and Logan pulled Katey across the hall into another room, hoping somehow it would be the kitchen.

By the time they had barricaded themselves inside, breaking the handle off the door, he had realized this was far from a kitchen. Tables and counters all over the room were covered in computers and other lab equipment with papers, charts, beakers, and burners. Everything in the room was just as the scientists left it when the alarm sounded. They probably evacuated at the first sign of trouble.

Katey grabbed Logan by the sleeve and pulled him away from the door to duck behind a counter and out of sight from the only entrance or exit out of the lab. Hiding wasn't going to save them.

Logan pulled out the pistol from the holster at his hip and Katey yanked on his arm. "Logan, don't!" she cried, her face ashen and hands trembling.

His hands were shaking too. What were the odds those hunters had wolfsbane? It was a long path to clear, and there were at least a dozen hunters coming down that hall. Even if his shots found their targets, he had a limited number of bullets, and he was certain not to find anything to use in the lab.

He tossed the gun aside and reached into his jeans still damp with blood from the gash in his side. His fist clamped around the vial so she wouldn't see it.

Logan looked to Katey, her eyes misting and pleading. As if it were the last time, Logan held her close and kissed her lips. His passion was unrequited. Katey knew he was about to make a suicidal move, but she had done the same for him too many times. He had to repay the favor, even if it meant he wouldn't come back from the change.

"Whatever happens, I love you," he whispered as hunters came to the door.

Katey shook her head, loose strands of hair whipping around her cheeks. "I can't lose you, please!"

"If I don't, we'll all be lost."

Even if he died or disappeared into obscurity, even if he could never become a proper loup-garou or be the perfect mate, he had to keep Katey safe. She was their future and their only hope. If he died here tonight, it would not have been in vain.

He moved away from her, tugged the stopper off the vial and consumed the potion. Before he could drop the glass bottle to the floor, he felt the shift take hold in a violent storm of agony he couldn't force back.

The wolf roared and surged forward to claim the body he had been keeping alive for over a century without remuneration and Logan was thrown back into a dark unconsciousness with no hint that he would ever return.

CHAPTER 23

At first, Katey thought it was nothing short of a miracle, but when she saw the tiny glass bottle shattered on the tile, she knew there was nothing miraculous about what was happening to Logan.

Logan gripped his head between his hands, his body bent over with the pain. He didn't scream as she expected but expelled sharp breaths through his clenched teeth. A guttural growl rumbled from his chest, and he staggered sideways until he collided with the edge of a table.

Katey went to him and stripped off his jacket and shirt, knowing he would need it later. Against the fear that ached in her chest, Katey looked into her fiancé's face. Pinched by the overflowing anguish, he didn't look like himself at all.

Golden eyes glared at her, lips curled back to expose the teeth that grew sharp and deadly.

Love drove her to cup her hands around his jaws and whisper, "Logan, everything's going to be okay."

There was no way of truly knowing if what she told Logan was the truth. Even if he did shift, that wouldn't guarantee an escape. The door to the lab shuddered, and Katey heard the voices of the hunters just outside. She jumped when they pounded on the door.

Logan roared and doubled over as his body began to morph. His skin was blackened with dense fur and bones popped out of place. Katey's quivering fingers found their way to his pants and unfastened them before he could rip the material.

That was as far as she had gotten before Logan lashed out at Katey and sent her flying across two rows of computer desks. She crashed through the monitors and chemistry equipment, bits of glass slicing into her skin and cutting her clothes.

By the time she rolled to the floor, the cuts had healed, but the sharp pain in her ribs told her Logan had broken something. She laid still for a moment, watching Logan from the other side of the room as her heart pounded against her splintered ribs.

Logan fell to his knees. The barrage of hunters ramming against the door was nothing more than background noise. Katey had never seen Logan shift before, but she knew this wasn't the same. When the others shifted, there was pain, but also an element of coordination between the human and the wolf that emerged.

With Logan, it was the complete opposite. They warred with one another, wrestling between the forms like neither could make up their minds about what they wanted to be. There was no harmony, no accord between them.

Katey wondered if this was how it always had been since he first shifted over a century ago, or if this was an effect of the poison he took that stunk of magic.

The shift was complete, and Logan arose onto his limbs as the enormous black loup-garou she remembered from Alaska. This wolf was different and void of any semblance of human under-standing. The beast moved and grunted like an animal, but the loup-garou Katey had met at least had the grace of motion that told her there was an intelligent mind behind the wolfish exterior.

She flattened herself against the ground, feeling the coolness of the floor on her cheek and palms. Steadying her breath was too much to ask, but if she could just lay quiet, Logan wouldn't find her. This beast, unlike the one she knew so well, was dangerous.

The memory of Logan nearly ripping out her throat in Alaska was enough to make her hesitant to approach him. That wolf, the one she met, knew her and accepted her. This new beast, born from powers and manipulation past her understanding, didn't know her and Katey didn't have an alpha to save her.

Neither did the hunters.

The hunters crashed through the door and swarmed into the room. All Katey could see were boots and fur when Logan let out an earth-shattering roar and barreled into the troops.

She closed her eyes against the carnage that ensued, but she couldn't block out the stench of blood, serrated flesh, and loose bowels that spilled onto the floor of the lab. Guns fired, and bul-let casings clinked as they fell to the floor. Grown men let out screeches, and the beast silenced them, slicing their throats open with one swipe of his lethal claws and fangs. Their weapons had no effect on the uncontrollable wrath of the creature.

Just half a moment of horror and the hunters were dead. Logan plunged out the door and down the hall, where she heard more gunshots and bestial sounds of rage and vengeance.

With weak limbs, she hoisted herself up with the help of the nearest chair and table. She kept her eyes aloft, avoiding the sight of the corpses and swallowing back the acidic bile that rose in her throat.

What her eyes did fall on made her skin crawl. She hadn't noticed it before, but the lab was not just made up of computers and chemistry stations. Through a glass door on the other side of the room, she saw the edge of a metal table with leaves and flowers blooming from a long box sitting on top. The bell-shaped petals were a mix of blue and purple, and if Katey hadn't suspected what they were, she would have thought them beautiful. There was only one reason a hunter compound would be cultivating plants.

Slowly, she made her way toward the greenhouse door, stepping over severed limbs and piles of human organs that had gushed out of their bodies during the fight.

Katey pressed herself against the glass and found the indoor greenhouse filled with rows upon rows of the poisonous plants growing in their flower boxes. A dripping sprinkler system kept them hydrated while lights above were supposed to replicate sunlight for future weapons against the loups-garous.

If Andrew had a chance to find a cure, they wouldn't need the wolfsbane, but if Logan had his way, the whole compound would be a mound of rubble by morning and Andrew would never have his cure. If these plants and this lab remained, every hunter on earth would have the means to kill their prey more easily than ever before.

Katey turned away from the glass and tried to think through the din of chaos raging outside the lab. She had to destroy all of this somehow.

Letting adrenaline carry her legs out of the room, she ran down the corridor. Though she slipped several times on the blood that coated the floor, she found her way to the other side of the compound, following Logan's trail of death left behind him.

There was no method to his killing, no order or reason. Katey caught glimpses of pale skin amongst the dead and knew Logan was not prejudiced in who he slaughtered. She remembered the two children from the training facility and hoped they were far away from this skirmish.

Through the rancid odor of blood and butchery, Katey found the garage. When the hunters had dragged her to the detention room, she remembered the potent smell of gasoline and car oil when they passed by one specific door.

She was glad to see the garage empty of corpses, but still full of jeeps and trucks. No one had escaped by that means yet, but if any of the families were to evacuate, they would have taken this route for sure. Logan may be able to outrun a speeding vehicle, but the hunters had a better shot at escaping by car than by running in the woods, where Logan would be in his element and unstoppable.

Katey followed her nose and found several red gas tanks with the long spout at the top.

Without much thought, Katey grabbed two of the tanks and tucked one more under each arm. It might have been too much, but she needed to make sure the wolfsbane would never have a chance to be used against her kind again.

Katey ran back to the lab, and the sound of mindless destruction started to ebb away. Either Logan was running out of steam, or he was running out of targets.

She held her breath before she kicked open the glass door and began pouring the flammable gasoline into the flower beds and across the counters that lined the walls. She would burn everything; the flowers, the seeds, even the fertilizer and hazard suits tucked under the counters. By the time she had emptied half of the tanks, she couldn't even smell the pollen of the wolfsbane and went into the other room to dispose of the rest.

After dumping the last of the gasoline over the computers and scientists' workstations in the lab, she searched for a way to light it all up.

Katey scoured over the countertops where she found a metal striker lying beside a Bunsen Burner. In her sophomore year, she was a whiz at using these contraptions to light burners for her classmates in chemistry.

She grabbed a bundle of papers saturated in gas, ran to the greenhouse room, and quickly pinched the rods of the striker together, making a bright spark at the head.

The papers burst into flames, and the gasoline on the floor ignited from the lit bits that fell from her hands. The greenhouse and lab went up in flames, and Katey ducked out of the room just before she was engulfed as well. Only her ankles and hands were singed in the process, but it was worth it to see the blue flowers turn to ash.

The heat of the flames poured out into the hallways and traveled along the walls and doors of the corridor. Katey bolted down the hall, through the gun range, and back into the training facility where a bloodbath awaited her.

The bodies of men and women were scattered and bleeding, some still groaning from the pain as death took its time to claim them. She sprinted across the training room floor toward the exit where Anton emerged.

His hands and clothes were splattered with blood, and she saw where his shoulder had been shot through, but apart from his harried expression, the vampire looked to be in fine shape. Katey ran into him and hugged his waist, desperate for any comfort in the midst of the massacre and mayhem.

There was no time for a joyous reunion. Anton guided her into the entry corridor and out of the compound. The smell of fresh air was welcome after her nose had been thoroughly hazed by the scent of death.

They bolted to the tree line just as a series of explosions erupted behind them. Katey looked over her shoulder and stopped dead in her tracks as she saw the roof of the hunter headquarters cave-in. Bright flames reached for the night sky and devoured the compound.

Katey looked to Anton. "Where's Logan?"

He shook his head with a dazed, unblinking stare. "I don't know. The last I saw of him was near the housing units."

"Housing units?" Katey cried. The faces of the boy and little girl flashed in her mind.

"Where the hunters and their families sleep," Anton told her. "Come, we can't stay here."

Katey fought against his grip on her arm. "No! I'm not leaving without Logan."

In a frenzy, she struggled harder against Anton until her shoulder dislocated and she screeched like a child in the middle of a temper tantrum. The vampire yanked her back and grabbed her by the shoulders to give her a good shake.

"Katey!" he yelled. "There's nothing you can do for him. I saw his eyes. Logan wasn't there. I don't know what happened, but if you try to find him, he will kill you."

Tears streaked down her cheeks. "I know he's in there!" Katey lied. "What if he's in the middle of all that? I have to get him out!"

A few of the surviving vampires came up behind Anton and watched the compound burn. Their faces were cold and impassive, but she could tell by their clothes and blood-streaked skin that they had a battle of their own to deal with.

Anton's stare lifted for just a moment and then he turned Katey around to face the flames. From the side, she saw him. Logan, still in his loup-garou form, loped toward the trees and disappeared into the night.

She knew Anton was right. There was nothing of Logan in that creature, but Katey still couldn't stand the sight of him running away. Her mind still couldn't make sense of why Logan had the potion in the first place. Why did he take it if he knew the shift would make him so uncontrollable? More importantly, how could they get him back?

On the other side of the burning wreckage, she saw another group emerging. There were some hunters left, and she saw Drake among them as they ran into the forest to escape the calamity.

Anton pulled Katey away and led her deeper into the woods. "We need to get back to the mansion before the survivors know we're still here."

Katey didn't fight him as he hoisted her on his back and the remainder of the party sped to the north. With her head bent low, Katey squeezed her eyes shut and let the tears cool her flushed skin. The only thing she had to hold onto was the tether she and Logan still shared. As long as she could still feel it in her soul, he was alive, and there was some hope of finding him.

With the hunters severely crippled and their wolfsbane technology destroyed, the worst of their troubles seemed to be over. All that was left was the verbal lashing from Darren and Michael, and the hunt for her renegade fiancé. That was nothing compared to the hell she had just been through, but why did she still feel dread sitting in her stomach like a smoldering silver stone?

Drake frowned at the wreckage of his home. His father's remains were in there, along with nearly a hundred fallen comrades and their families. Only a handful stood behind him, their soot-smudged faces turned to the same disaster, and watched the roof and walls cave in with resentful gazes.

The beasts had knocked them down, but he was far from beaten. He was there with his father when they sounded the alarm. Though the pills kept Andrew's sinful nature from consuming him, the keen senses were there, and Drake's body went cold when he heard his dad cuss under his breath about vampires in the compound.

They hadn't been expecting vampires. Never in a million years would a werewolf hunter have prepared for vampires to rescue a beast. When Andrew explained how Katey was half-vampire, it all made sense. The monsters rallied around her and defended her. Because of that, they might have damned themselves from the beginning. If they had known she had such powerful allies, they wouldn't have rushed to capture her like they did. They had known vampires were aiding the beasts in Crestucky and Alabama, but they would never have guessed they had followed her to Louisiana too.

Drake was glad he had refused to join the others in the fight to win back the compound. He might have been killed with the others, and then he wouldn't have had the chance to meet the wolfish eyes of his enemy in the flesh.

The black werewolf must have sensed the presence of another beast in the compound, but when it only found Andrew, its rage was unquenchable.

Drake managed to shoot it with a wolfsbane dart, but the beast didn't falter. The darts couldn't penetrate his thick hide and pelt, which was unusual after the countless tests they conducted to make sure their new weapon would work on the werewolves in both of their forms. Silver bullets wouldn't even slow it down. It was unlike any beast he had ever faced before, and Andrew didn't have a chance.

He watched as his father was torn to pieces by the beast, defenseless and too sick to fight back. Drake ran from the room to start evacuations, but there was hardly anyone left to evacuate.

By the time half of the compound was consumed in flames, he could only round up those who stood with him now. Five hunters, three women, and one gangly teenager who had maybe two weeks' worth of combat training under his belt. It was hardly a force worthy to go after the beasts, but Drake would make due.

A child's scream sliced through his thoughts of revenge. He looked to the housing quarters adjoining the north side of the compound. The flames had already eaten through the top floors, rubble, and burning debris weighing down exponentially as it collapsed in on itself.

Tired and fatigued as he was, Drake bolted into a sprint toward the housing units. One of the older hunters yelled at him to come back where it was safe, but he ignored the order.

He listened for another scream as he neared the scorching flames, but could only hear the shrill wailings of the child somewhere in the age. Throwing aside his instinct for self-preservation, just as his father had taught him to do so long ago, he followed the sound and kicked down a door that was already rimmed in a thin ribbon of fire.

Inside, huddled in a corner, were two children. He recognized them as the Brigham children, Jessie and Mason. Furniture and belongings were encased in flames as black smoke filled the room and billowed out the door.

Drake dodged falling embers across the common room floor and gathered them to his side. Jessie's braid was a frayed mess, and her arm looked to be badly burned. Her older brother was worse off, but he wasn't the one crying. His face was blackened as if he had been wading through the smoke to find safety for himself and his little sister, and his clothes were torn.

The ceiling beams above him creaked, and Drake hurried them outside. Jessie tripped on one of her shoelaces, and he had to gather her up into his arms to get her out the door.

The rest of the housing unit structure failed as they hurried back to the trees. When the three of them returned and had time to catch their breath, they coughed out the smoke that had infiltrated their lungs in the escape.

One of the women took Jessie from his arms and carried her farther away from the sight of their home in ruins. Mason stayed by Drake's side and silently stared at the burning compound. Then, he turned to Drake and asked, "Where are my parents?"

Drake looked to the group around him, but he couldn't see the Brigham couple. One of the hunters, a man Drake trusted from countless missions, heard the question and took the boy aside before Drake had a chance to answer in his usual cold and realistic manner.

He never sugarcoated the truth. If someone was dead, he said it without so much as a crack in his voice. When his mother died years ago, his father taught him to be strong in the face of death. In their line of work, it was the norm. If a hunter couldn't deal with death, then they had no business being a hunter at all.

Mason and Jessie would soon learn that, though he wished with every fiber of his being that they didn't have to learn it so soon.

The eldest of the hunters and a close adviser to Andrew, a man named Cale, approached Drake. "Your father?" he asked, probably knowing the answer already.

Drake simply shook his head and listened to another series of explosions that rocked the earth beneath his feet. The fire had made it to the garage by now, destroying millions of dollars worth of machines and equipment.

"What now?" Cale asked, his deep voice low and rumbling like the inferno they watched from a distance.

Drake had been in command of the clan for over eight months now, but he despised it. They looked to him for guidance and explanations only his father could give. They had put their trust in Drake only because Andrew declared it. To be his father's right hand was a difficult job and it made Drake thirsty for the old days when he didn't have to think on his feet or look after anyone else but himself.

He didn't want to take over as head of the clan, although that was what his father had intended for him all along. Just like the Brigham children, he was about to be thrown into a new life full of unexpected challenges.

This decision was easy. He only had to look into the eyes of his comrades and know what they should do now.

"We're going after the beast," he declared loud enough for all of them to hear.

Jerek, the scrawny teenager who was still hesitant on using a firearm, laughed in contempt. "With what? We don't have a truck, and we can't track it."

Cale nodded. "And we only have the weapons we're carrying. I already wasted all my bullets trying to take down a vamp."

"We'll have all of those things. My father set up a bunker just two miles from here. If we hurry, we can get there and be on the wolf's trail before daybreak."

One of the women, Ginger, stepped forward. "What about the children? We can't take them along."

"My father's bunker has two vehicles. We can split up. Take the kids to the compound in Baton Rouge and stay there until we bring back that wolf's head."

Cale grabbed Drake's arm and whispered, "Drake, we don't have to strike right now. We're all tired, and a few of us have injuries. We have to regroup. Let's all go to Baton Rouge and wait this out. We can pick up the trail in the – "

Drake twisted his arm out of Cale's grip and sneered. "You're just going to let that monster get off free for doing this?" He gave a sweeping wave toward the burning compound, the red glow of the flames flickering against their faces in the darkness.

"I'm not saying that," Cale snapped. "But it'll be wiser to regroup and get more hunters to go after it than fly in half-cocked like you're suggesting."

Drake sized each of them up, their stares fixated on him and waiting for his verdict. Despite everything, they still looked to him for the final word.

"Those who are injured and want to rest, go with Cale to Baton Rouge." He lifted his chin high as his father did when giving a serious order. "Those who want to go after the werewolf who did this, who killed our families and friends, who destroyed our home and livelihood, you all can come with me!"

A pause of silence descended over the group, except little Jessie who was crying some distance off in the woods with her brother.

One by one, the hunters stepped forward to affirm their choices. All but Cale was ready to unite behind him. Then, like the slow turning of the tide, Cale nodded his assent. "Someone has to keep you alive."

Drake took a steeling breath and turned to the east where he knew the safe house and bunker lay hidden in the forest, just waiting for them to pick up where they had left off and track down the beast.

CHAPTER 24

W hen the straggling band came home, the reception was not what Katey had expected. She imagined there would be yelling, blaming, angry fingers jabbed in her face, and lots of groveling to Darren and Michael for her inexcusable disobedience.

Instead, each pair of eyes was marked by a solemnness that pierced Katey's heart more viciously than any silver bullet or wolfsbane dart. They all knew what had happened. The blood-stained clothes and battle-worn faces were testaments to what they had been doing.

Darren didn't say a word to her, though she could feel the rage festering beneath his cool and sober exterior. Perhaps it was too soon for the reprimand she deserved.

Michael was the first one to speak, intruding on the long silence that hung in the parlor when they entered. "Go change clothes, Katey," he said in a gruff and not-so-tender tone. "Ben, keep watch over her."

Ben nodded and followed Katey as she slowly made her way up the stairs, the slick bottoms of her shoes squeaking on the treads. She couldn't blame them for wanting Ben to accompany her upstairs. She had proven herself a flight risk too many times to expect anything less.

Thankfully, he did avert his eyes when she stripped off the grimy clothes and slipped into one of Logan's shirts and jeans. The material hung from her thin frame, but after cinching the jeans tight with a belt and tucking the shirt in, Katey found the big clothes surprisingly comfortable. It made her wonder why she hadn't worn Logan's clothes before.

As his scent invaded her senses, chasing away every rational thought, the grief began to take hold with the force of a riptide.

Katey stared blankly at the floor, the collar of the shirt clutched between her fists. Like all the air had been let out of her, she slowly crumbled to the floor and sat there.

They had no idea where Logan was, and although they had an arsenal of noses to track him, Katey couldn't help but feel a sense of loss somehow. Logan was gone, far out of her reach and anyone else's, and there seemed to be a finality about it, though she had every reason to believe they would get him back one way or another.

More than that, Katey relived the slaughter she had witnessed in the compound. Logan had killed so indiscriminately. The images of the human and vampire corpses came back to her, and the gasping tears convulsed her body. It was simply too much, and Katey's empathic spirit became overloaded by the lavish details of the massacre.

Ben turned and rushed to her side. He only needed to take one look at her to know what was going on before wrapping his arms around her shoulders.

Katey shuddered with each breath and squeezed her eyes shut against the memory, but the darkness only made the visions come back in sharp relief. She was there in the compound again, stepping over the mutilated bodies and the stench of death was everywhere until she questioned whether her own heart was beating.

"Hey, it's over now," Ben whispered, gently rocking her.

Katey wheezed in a breath and said, "It's my fault. If I hadn't run away, they would all still be here."

Ben held her more tightly, and a bit of his calm trickled into her. "Don't go there," he ordered, his voice firm but soothing. "Put it behind you. There's nothin' you can do about it now. All we can do is keep livin', keep fightin'."

She looked at him, meeting his golden eyes with her own. The wolves had always been their strength, their rock to lean on. What could she do when the wolf was so accustomed to death, and she was trying to run from it? The prospect of her own death hadn't shaken her, but this week had shined a spotlight on the reaper as it claimed countless of their kind and their enemies alike.

All Katey knew was that it had to stop. First, it was the hunters who were responsible for the bloodbaths. Now, it was Logan. If allowed loose and without an alpha to control him, the innocent lives of the humans would be in danger. Just like at the compound, Logan would destroy everything in his path without mercy.

Katey sniffled and nodded, knowing she had to be strong. There would be a time to mourn and grieve, but it wasn't now. After a while, the morbid visions would cease, and her mind might repair itself in time, but it wouldn't stop the waking nightmares that were sure to come.

Ben eased away and rubbed her back until she had wiped away the last of the tears.

"I'm sorry. I just lost it there for a minute," she said with an unconvincing laugh.

There was a shift in Ben's spirit that made her look away. "I know what it's like," he said.

He had survived enough wars to know how she felt. Maybe he had a similar breakdown during the Civil War after his first battle. She wanted to ask who was there to comfort him when he experienced more emotion than any soul could handle, but she knew the answer to that.

No one was there. The captains and generals would have had no time to baby their soldiers and back then, men would not have been comfortable with consoling one another.

It was more likely that Ben had to deal with the stress on his own. How many battles did it take before he learned how to cope with what he had seen? How many decades did it take for him to become so wise?

Ben helped her to her feet, and she gave his hand a quick, affirming squeeze before they left the bedroom. Katey took slow and deep breaths as they joined the rest by the front door in the foyer.

Anton was surrounded by Darren, Dustin, Gregory, Forrest, and Michael, telling them all in military-exact detail what took place at the compound. They now knew everything from the moment Katey left the mansion to when they turned their backs on the burning hunter headquarters. Of course, there were some things Anton would never have known about.

"Shift?" Dustin questioned, a perfect blend of shock and disbelief on his face. "That's impossible. Logan's never been able to shift on his own."

"He didn't do it on his own," Katey spoke up, ignoring the concerned looks from everyone. Even though she nearly had a meltdown that everyone could hear on the property, she refused to be pitied. They couldn't afford to waste that kind of energy, just like she couldn't waste time on the guilt-ridden knot in her stomach. "He drank something and then shifted. I was there when he did it."

Dustin's throat worked, knowing that could only mean one thing. Darren knew as well, though he didn't let a single ounce of belligerence bleed through into his visage, though its energy plowed through Katey like a battering ram, along with the unspoken question on everyone's mind.

"I know where he got it," she answered. "And I know just where to find her."

Darren looked to Michael. "I suggest we split up," he said. "You go after Logan, and we'll go take care of his dealer."

To equate Logan's transaction with Marie as something illegal, like a drug deal, placed him in a criminal light that Katey didn't like. Logan wasn't addicted to whatever it was he took, but what else could she call the woman who equipped him with this dreadful poison?

Michael did not readily agree and looked to Anton. The two vampires stared at one another, silently communicating on some level Katey and the others couldn't possibly understand. After working together for centuries, they could probably read each other's thoughts.

After a hard moment, Michael looked back to Darren and let out a sigh. "Very well. But if we find him, we will do everything in our power to not engage him. I won't hold the boy responsible for the deaths of my operatives, but I can't allow the safety of my men to come before his."

Darren nodded. "That will do," he replied and then turned to Katey. "Where did he get the potion?"

Bourbon Street was in full swing, even at three o'clock in the morning. Music carried on the wind and the odor of beer and vomit coaxed out a few gags from Katey as it had the first day they arrived in New Orleans. If she were alone, the partiers and drunkards would have certainly trampled her on the sidewalk. But her pack was with her, gathering around her like a triangular guard detail, buffering the crowds as they made their way toward Madame Celeste's Voodoo Emporium.

Michael and Anton formed their group of searchers and were hot on Logan's trail, but they made it clear if things became too dangerous, they would pull out or use violent force to detain the loup-garou. Gregory and Forrest volunteered to accompany them, and Michael welcomed their assistance, knowing they both had experience with rogue wolves. With luck, the presence of another loup-garou would settle Logan down.

Her affront against the pack seemed to have been forgiven, though no words were spoken about it. The car ride on the way to the French Quarter was quiet, but Katey was unnerved by the wild emotions among Darren, Dustin, and Ben. Hate, rage, and fear dominated the air around them, but no one spoke a word that didn't have to do with the mission at hand. What Katey couldn't tell was which emotion was directed toward her, Logan, or the voodoo apprentice.

Katey knew apologizing would do no good. It wouldn't bring Logan back to them and it wouldn't right the wrongs she had committed against Darren's authority. If this were baseball, this would have been her third strike, but they didn't call her out just yet.

She looked at Darren and Dustin's back, noting their rigid shoulders and tight faces that scanned the masses for trouble or danger. Ben brought up the rear and stayed the closest to her.

Out of all of them, Ben was the one who was the least offended by what she had done. It wasn't his grandson that was missing, and it wasn't his authority she had defied. Once again, she felt a comradery with the old soldier more than any other, and if she were to be ostracized, she knew Ben would be on her side.

They came to the emporium, but the blue shutter doors were shut, and a sign dangled from the knob, saying they were closed and to come back at noon the next day. Darren pounded his fist on the door, but there was no answer.

Just as Katey was about to trespass on the silence between her and her alpha, to suggest they try another way to find Marie, a tired and withered voice came from above.

"Come in, wolves. The door is not locked."

Katey looked up, but the bottom of the balcony blocked her view to see who was speaking.

"We should have just tried the door first," Dustin mumbled and led the way into the cramped shop.

The long room was pitch black and cluttered with merchandise stands and tribal relics hung from the walls. Ben shut the door behind them and turned the few bolts and chains to firmly lock it, trapping them inside.

The pack stood still in the middle of the store and waited, their heads on a swivel and ears open. Katey saw a doorway ahead and slipped between Darren and Dustin to investigate. Her alpha grabbed her arm and pulled her back, keeping her close.

She didn't resist as she had with Anton and bowed her head in submission. "I'm sorry, Darren," she whispered, feeling the need to say something and somehow erase her sins in his eyes. She was sorry for more than one thing.

Darren didn't reply, and it gave some attestation to Katey that his anger truly was reserved for her. Her stomach, already in knots and twists, lurched at the idea that this might really have been her last chance. What greater iniquity was there than to jeopardize the safety of the pack?

Dustin put his hand on her shoulder, a counter to the eddy of emotions that threatened to spin Katey out of control again. He wasn't mad but scared out of his mind. His grandson was out in the world, away from his watchful eye, and hell-bent on a killing spree that might expose their entire way of life. Just one photo shared to a social media site would put them all under the microscope. Katey wasn't sure which was worse: the hunter's wolfsbane or this new threat to their existence.

A pair of light footsteps slowly descended down a flight of stairs out of sight from the main store lobby. Moments later, a frail and elderly woman stepped through the doorway Katey had been eyeing earlier.

In the darkness, she could make out the petite woman and her wiry gray hair that sprouted out in all directions. Her dark face was marked by years upon years of wisdom, the wrinkles carving deep grooves into her skin. The nightgown and coat she wore hung from her thin frame like draping muslin curtains. The hem tickled the floor, concealing feet that might have been clad in a pair of slippers.

A bony hand reached out and flipped the switch on the wall, bathing the store in patches of light from the can lights above. It was only then that Katey noticed something peculiar about the woman. Her eyes were completely clouded over with white cataracts, and her gaze was static. There was a silent, but intense power about her, and Katey shrank back as the magic in the room strengthened with her presence.

"What can I do for you?" she asked, her voice weathered with age just like her body. Her accent nearly matched Marie's perfectly, if not a little thicker.

Darren stepped forward, leaving Dustin to keep Katey at bay. "Are you Marie?" he asked.

The woman smiled. "No. I am Madame Celeste, the proprietor of this shop. Marie is my apprentice, but she has gone home for the night."

The alpha lifted his chin, even though he must have known Celeste wouldn't see his show of dominance. "She gave something to one of my pack, and we need an antidote. He's running wild around Louisiana, and no one can stop him."

Katey couldn't help but appreciate his candor with Celeste and his willingness to admit he was at a disadvantage. An alpha was supposed to be in control of his pack at all times, and he openly stated that one of his wolves had gone rogue. It was not an easy thing, and she could sense the strand of humility in his words.

The thin lips that were once smiling drooped into a frown. "I see. What did Marie give him?"

"Something to make him shift," Katey answered. No one reprimanded her for speaking out of turn.

Celeste folded her hands in front of her and turned contemplative. "I can create an antidote if I believe he drank what I think he did."

Dustin's hand squeezed on Katey's shoulder. "Can't you call Marie and ask?"

Celeste gave a dismissive wave. "That will not be necessary." She turned to hobble into the back room. "Come with me, child."

Darren peered over his shoulder at Katey and jerked his head, telling her to follow as the voodoo priestess suggested. Katey hurried past them and stepped into the room, the aroma of a thousand spices and ingredients like a brick wall that she had run headlong into.

After giving a quick snort to clear her head, she stood by the worktable in the middle of the room. The others followed and did the same, all eyes turned to the old woman who appeared to be searching through the shelves and racks of bottles and satchels.

Katey didn't question Celeste's ability to tell which bottles were which. If she knew they were loups-garous without the benefit of sight, she was sure to pick out the right materials without sight as well.

"What your wolf took was something we've given to many who walk through the shop. They're usually the unconfident, the shy, the doubtful. They don't know their own potential and seek it here when motivational speakers and therapy have failed them." Celeste brought two vials, two sachets, and the black feather of a crow.

"Logan ain't shy," Ben stated.

Celeste gave a soft, bubbly laugh. "No, but he was at war with himself."

"How do you know that?" Katey asked, her fingertips resting on the splintered edge of the table where Celeste began mixing the antidote in a blackened pot set on top of a burner.

"The spirits tell me things, *cher*," she replied. "He and his beast had been at war for a long time. So long that neither of them knows anything different. The tonic only brings out what is hidden within the person. For some, that is the courage to proclaim their unrequited love. For others, it's the confidence to apply for a job promotion. For your wolf, it was the beast within him that would not take orders from anyone, not even his human host. We have had many wolves come through these doors looking for such a quick solution, and it rarely ends well."

Darren stepped up, and Katey edged away from the fuming alpha. "If you know it doesn't end well, then why would Marie give it to him?"

Celeste took a flask and poured a clear liquid into the pot to mix everything well. "Marie is young and might not have known why your wolf needed the tonic to begin with, only that he needed it." The old woman smiled. "She is a sweet girl, but misguided in some ways."

The priestess closed her eyes and stirred the feather into the concoction and mumbled a chant in a foreign tongue. The cadence sent shivers down Katey's back, and her wolf bristled.

Katey looked to her alpha and the way his brows shadowed over his gleaming, golden eyes that had appeared as soon as the woman began her chant. It was clear he didn't trust Celeste. None of them did, and it was a wonder Logan trusted Marie at all.

She understood that Logan longed to shift at will like the other loups-garous, but Katey never suspected he would be so desperate. He even told her that he had sworn off the use of magic and didn't want to return to the shop. What happened between the time they first met Marie and tonight to make him change his mind?

Only one thing came to mind, and the very notion knocked the wind out of her lungs.

Just like the deaths of the hunters, the Deviants, and the vampires, his rash decision to see Marie was her own fault, but it was all unintended. How could she have known her monthly shift would come at such a terrible time? How could she have known that it would spur Logan's envy into the driving force to go to Marie for aid?

Katey wrapped her arms around herself and turned away from the table, finding the air in the room unbearable. Ben blocked her path and held her in place by her quivering elbows. She lowered her gaze, refusing to meet his, lest he saw the guilt in them.

Behind her, Celeste stopped chanting and poured a portion of the mixture into a vial similar to what Logan had been given.

"Make him drink this," she said. "And the beast will be weakened long enough for his human consciousness to regain control."

Darren snatched the vial from the woman and stormed out, followed by Dustin, without so much as a word of thanks. Katey regarded the old, blind Celeste as she gazed vacantly at the wall. There was no hint of offense at Darren's brusque departure, but Katey sensed something of worry in her.

"Is the antidote really going to help?" Katey asked, breaking free from Ben's gentle hold just long enough to address Celeste.

The old woman closed her eyes. "It will give your lover the ability to shift back if he can take control again."

That didn't satisfy Katey. "What if he can't?"

Celeste's lips set in a firm line. "I can't say what will happen then. You must be his strength. I'm sure you know by now that, without you, he is lost."

Yes, Katey understood all too well. It was one of Logan's greatest faults, the way he depended on Katey, to need her love and acceptance every moment of the day. Katey didn't count it that way. She saw a man trying to find his place and keep the only good thing he ever had. Perhaps after this, Logan would realize he was worth far more to all of them than he ever realized.

It never mattered that he couldn't shift, not even for the ceremony. They would find a way to work around his disability. Katey understood that now, but she hated herself for never telling him that enough. If she had, maybe they could have avoided this conflict altogether.

"Thank you," she whispered as Ben guided her out of the voodoo store and into the bustling streets of riotous laughter and jazz music.

By the time Katey and Ben shut the doors to the shop and made sure the closed sign was back in place, Darren was on the phone with Michael. Over the racket of the crowd, Katey couldn't hear the other side of the conversation but waited patiently some distance off with Ben and Dustin.

"He's mad at me," she remarked, knowing it must have been common knowledge to all of them by now.

Dustin sighed and watched a stilted street performer pass them by, tossing candy down on the heads of the passersby. "Of course he is," he replied. "But it will pass."

"Only when he's rid of me," Katey mumbled, looking to the cobblestones of the street covered in glitter and confetti.

Both men looked at her in confusion. "Get rid of you?" Ben questioned. "You can't possibly believe he'd do somethin' like that."

Katey shrugged. "Maybe he'll hand me over to Gregory, so I won't be his problem anymore." The idea of submitting to the rougarou alpha made her innards churn until she wanted to hide in a corner and barf.

Dustin stepped closer to Katey. "You know that's crazy talk, Katey Kat. Darren would never do that to you, and if he did, he'd have us to deal with."

"And Logan," Ben added.

Katey cringed. "Not if Logan doesn't come back from this."

"There's no reason he won't," Dustin replied. "Logan's stubborn. Who knows? Maybe he's shifted back already, and everything is fine."

Katey glanced to Dustin and snorted. "Wishful thinking. You didn't see what he did at the compound."

That's all their talk was; wishful thinking and mindless encouragement. Katey didn't believe words until Darren proved it. After this was all over, she would be kicked out and alone again. Just like in her previous homes, she acted out until the adults had enough and she moved on to the next family. This time, she wanted to stay and be part of something greater than a simple family. At least there was the hope that Michael would take her in.

Before Darren strode up to them, Katey tried to reason through how a loup-garou and a vampire would coexist in the same house with such differing schedules. She set aside her plans and preparations for a rocky future as Darren addressed Dustin.

"They found him about fifty miles west of here near South Vacherie, and he's still in his loup-garou form," he told them. "That's an hour's drive away, but the vamps can't hold him there for that long. He's still moving west, and he'll find a civilization soon. Gregory and Forrest are still with them, but they don't think they can handle Logan either."

"Can we run that distance?" Ben asked as they began making the trek back to Canal Street.

"Once we get out of New Orleans, there's nothing but swamps and forest all the way there along Route 3127."

"Let's do it," Dustin said with a clap as if he were ready to take off right there.

Katey slipped behind her alpha and beta, once more accompanicd by Ben in the back.

"It's still gonna take time to get out of New Orleans, and if the sun comes up before we get there, we won't have the vamp back up," Ben offered. "Can we pull this off without them?"

"Michael said that Logan was running out of steam. Once we get there, as long as the vamps don't antagonize him, we should be able to pull him back. Gregory and Forrest can also help. We just need to strike quickly before he knows what's going on." Darren held up the vial for them to see. The maroon liquid sloshed against the glass walls of its container as he shook it a bit.

Katey steeled herself and reached for it, but Darren was too quick and snatched it back. The group came to an all-stop as Darren turned to face her down with such fervency that Katey couldn't have crouched into submission fast enough.

"You will have no part in this, Katey," he growled.

Dustin stepped between them and took the brunt of Darren's aggression before it could cascade toward Katey in a pulse of dominance that might have reduced her to tears. The beta stood strong against his alpha.

Darren eased back and looked to Katey, a bit of his fire squelched by Dustin's calm composure. "I can't allow you to get hurt. You brought us to the shop, and that's all."

Katey straightened. "What am I supposed to do then?" she asked, a note of diffidence in her voice. "Are you going to leave me at the plantation alone?"

"No," he replied. "You'll come with us, but you're not to go near Logan. If the vamps are still there by the time we get to him, Michael and Anton will take care of you."

Katey gritted her teeth and summoned the last of her defiance, speaking from the convictions she felt so strongly in her soul. "This is my mistake. It's my fault Logan did this. Let me fix it?"

No amount of puppy-dog eyes or pouting would sway Darren. All she could do was speak her mind and hope that somehow he understood her need to clean up the mess she had thrown them all into.

She and Darren locked eyes for an indefinite amount of time, the humans moving around them on the sidewalk as if the four of them were a rock in the middle of a torrent river.

Finally, he offered out the vial to her. "I'm giving you one chance... You may be the only one who can reach Logan. We'll back you up, but if things get bad, we're pulling you out."

Katey took the vial from his palm and clutched it to her chest, nodding a silent thank you. It may have not saved her position in the pack, but it might be the cure to her guilt for the decades or centuries to come. At least she would know she tried, even if Logan was truly lost to the beast.

CHAPTER 25

After centuries of waiting in the darkness, he was finally free and able to quench his lust for blood and destruction. The humans and night-dwellers proved to him that the world was a weak place. They were no match for him, and they were the first to fall. Their flesh sat in his belly, nourishing his body just enough to begin his reign, and how the world would feel the wrath that burned in him.

Padding through this unfamiliar land, he knew it was not suitable. The ground was soft and water-logged, an unstable place to call his own. The beasts that inhabited this land were hardly impressive. The scaly creatures that swam through the swamps may have been vicious, but once he found their soft underbelly, their taste repulsed him. There was nothing here that would benefit him. He had to find a territory, someplace dry and desolate where he could pile the bones of his enemies to make his bed.

All the while he traveled through the marshes, he could smell the noxious stench of the night-dwellers and beasts on his tail. *Let them come after me*, he thought. *They can do nothing.*

Another presence was far more bothersome. The human, the one he had been paired with over a century ago, lurked in the recesses of the dark he had come from. He screamed, he wailed like a child to be given control.

Never again, he proclaimed. *The human will not have this body as long as I can breathe with its lungs and use these fangs to kill.*

The human's pleas for release made little sense to him. After so many years of doubt and feelings of inadequacy, he thought the human would have been thankful. He made them powerful and fearsome. He had the strength that the human had dreamed of and longed for. This should have been the luckiest day of the human's life, but why did he cry out so pitifully? This is what he wanted, after all.

He found himself in forested land, rich with flora and the air was full of spices and song. Humans were some distance away, an entire village perhaps, in the throes of a celebration. They would be more than enough to fuel the rest of his journey to claim a home.

He picked up the pace, weaving through the trees like a black ghost. The night-dwellers did not pursue, but he sensed another group closing in. They were not quiet in their advance, their paws snapping dried leaves and twigs beneath them and their mouths gaped open as they panted in the pursuit.

Not once in his existence had he run from a fight and he could smell that their intent to battle was as deep as his own. He turned to face them.

Three beasts, such as himself. The human knew these beasts, but he did not see friends. He saw enemies in everything, even these beasts who must have come to take back one of their pack.

He roared, proclaiming his challenge. They circled, growling and snapping their jowls to entice him to strike first. Whoever made the first blow would make no difference. They would all die, and he would eat their flesh.

He lunged at the smallest of the three, a black beast with amber eyes. As he did, the beast that was the color of soil and sand leaped upon his back and bit into his throat. He thrashed and rolled to release his enemy's hold, only to be knocked off his feet by the silver elder.

With one swing of his powerful claws, the brown beast was sent rolling. He pounced upon the elder and tore into his shoulder. The victorious taste of blood ran down his throat and gave him strength. The black beast tackled him around the waist and threw him off the alpha.

When he regained his footing to charge, the brown beast attacked again and bit into his leg. Back and forth this went, as he battled against the three, dealing out pain and receiving it in harsh succession.

Another scent, something foreign and yet familiar met his nostrils, and in the heat of the fight, he turned to the trees. A woman stood there, waiting and watching with an anxious look in her green, penetrating eyes. This was no ordinary woman.

The beast recognized the glow around her soul, as white as freshly fallen snow. He thundered in rage at the presence that contradicted his own, opposing him with its mere existence. As long as he was in the world, she could not exist.

A time came when his three enemies did not surround him, and the beast hurdled himself toward the woman. She gasped and dodged behind a tree, but that would not stop him. The silver wolf intercepted, and the battle continued. The others tried to hold him at bay, but the light of peace drove him into a frenzied madness.

All the while, the human in him continued his useless beseeching cries for mercy and leniency for his family, especially for the woman. He should have known she would be their undoing. She was the one who would upset his perfect balance and control over the world.

She had to die.

In the midst of the battle, he felt the pulsating light draw toward him, though his opponents kept him from seeing her approach. With her advance came a weakness that made him fight all the more vehemently. Slowly, he felt the grip on his monstrous body slipping.

The beasts descended on him, taking advantage of his vulnerable state since they could not feel the terrible power of the woman they defended. He struggled and bucked beneath them, but he could not throw them so easily anymore.

He gnashed his teeth as she came close and bent low beside him. With one last surge of willpower, he tossed aside his captors and rammed the woman, her body like fire against his skin.

The sensation of sharp glass sliced into his front paw, breaking something against the ground as he made his escape out of range from the beasts. A coolness like moisture covered his pads, and it wreaked of the same magic that had summoned him into the world.

The more distance he put between himself and the woman, the stronger he became. His enemies pursued him, but the female lagged behind. They fell upon him again, their fervor heightened to nearly match his own as fangs and claws found purchase through thick pelts. Blood tainted the ground and filled his mouth, but he continued to fight. The human wanted to give up, but the beast never would until he drew his last breath.

He sensed the woman drawing close again, her light rushing before her to alert him. The beast scrambled away, but his adversaries would not let him retreat. His body became sluggish, losing momentum as if he were wading through a thick quagmire.

The woman was near, and the beast turned on her like a caged animal and bellowed, his fangs stained red and gleaming in the moonlight. She did not shrink away as she had before. The beast looked upon the woman, the blinding aura around her intensified and her eyes shone white in the darkness that was chased away by her spirit.

In one swift movement, the beasts detained him, and the woman wrapped her arms around his massive neck. Her peace flooded over him, rippling from his black fur that had been caked in blood on this glorious night of conquest.

It was short-lived. He failed, and the woman would have dominion again.

He let out a cry—neither human nor beastly in nature—that shook the leaves on the trees of the forest for miles around. Slowly, the beast within him died away, slinking back into the prison of the soul he had been cursed with. The frail human crawled forward and took control of the body once more.

As they passed one another in their transition, the beast vowed to the man that this was not the end. The day of reckoning was coming, and the world would know him. The woman could not stop him from fulfilling his destiny to rule over the creatures of the world with a mighty paw. Human, beast, and night-dweller would all bow to him in cowering fear. It was only a matter of time.

Logan morphed between her arms. Thick black fur receded into his skin. Bones and muscles shrank and twisted until something more human stood in front of her. Darren and the others backed away, releasing Logan to complete the shift.

Katey helped him to his knees as his legs gave way beneath him. Blood coated every inch of his arms, chest, neck, and lower part of his face and gave him a nightmarish look. Wide, blue eyes stared intently at her as his body began to tremble.

Shaking hands gripped her shoulders. His mouth gaped open and snapped closed as if he were trying to catch his breath or form words that escaped him. Katey tried to smile through her own rattled nerves.

"It's okay. It's all over, Logan," she soothed, her fingers threaded into his short black hair that felt sticky from the blood that had splattered on him.

His face contorted as his eyes were flooded with tears. "So many…" he whispered, punctuated by a shrill whine.

Katey shook her head. "Everything's all right."

Logan shook his head as the tear droplets spilled onto his cheeks, mixing with the blood and dirt. "No. No, it's not."

She pulled him in close and hugged him tighter, pressing their bodies together to feel one another's warmth. Logan broke down and sobbed into her shoulder, wailing and sniffling like a child. He wreaked of death and sweat, but Katey held on even tighter, refusing to meet the eyes of her pack members who closed in around them.

Darren, Dustin, and Ben pressed their muzzles against Logan's back and shoulders, but still, he continued to cry as they gave what comfort they could. Katey rocked him gently as her heart broke in her chest.

In the hunter compound, she didn't get a good look at Logan's loup-garou form, but when they found him in the forest, she knew it was not his usual form. The beast they faced was larger than Logan had ever been with a mad look in its eyes, fangs dripping with drool, and fur nearly standing on end in agitation. It was how she had pictured a werewolf long before she knew the truth about their kind.

It was the monster Logan feared he had become, the monster that the hunters hated and hunted. It was the kind of creature that inhabited nightmares of children when they watched a scary movie before bed, but this was no dream. Logan had become the thing humans feared, but Katey knew well enough that it was not the truth.

That beast was not Logan. Whatever it was, though, it was gone now, and they could rebuild. A single tear slid from the corner of

Katey's eyes. It wasn't a tear of grief or sorrow, but of joy that they could return home and put all of this behind them.

The hunters were taken care of, and although there would be more in the future, there was time to fortify their defenses and next time, they would be ready for another strike. Logan had returned to normal, and although they both had trauma to work through, they could go home. Home to Florida where their friends would be. Nothing sounded more wonderful.

Darren's head lifted for a moment and looked to the east. The sun had not risen yet, but there was a silvery blue halo over the horizon that told them dawn was on the way. It wasn't the sun that caught Darren's attention.

The breeze carried a scent to the group. She could smell the vampires miles away as they kept their distance from the conflict, but there was something else that made her muscles clench. Smoke and human sweat. It was so subtle, but in the hysteria, Katey wasn't surprised they didn't notice it earlier.

Darren growled, and the others moved to surround them. They didn't need to speak the same language to know danger was near.

One dart flew out of the thicket and missed, but that was enough to get their attention.

Katey exploded into action and lifted her naked fiancé to his feet. Logan curtailed his sobs and with weak effort, rose to his feet, while Darren's silver loup-garou body moved in front of them to provide cover.

With one of Logan's arms around her shoulders, Katey helped him limp away as Ben flanked them for protection.

A short whimper prompted Katey to turn, just in time to see Darren crumble to the ground and convulse as the poison entered his system.

"No!" she screamed, but Ben prodded her to continue.

Dustin charged toward the trees where the hunters were lined up, their guns leveled on the loups-garous.

Katey heard the soft firing of the dart gun, then Dustin's whine. She did not turn to watch him die. She held tighter to Logan's waist as her throat closed with restrained tears.

They couldn't escape fast enough.

Ben fell next, and there was nothing to keep them going. Katey and Logan crumbled to the forest floor.

She looked behind her and saw the bodies of her fellow pack members turn ashen, veins standing out purple and bulging against their skin. In the throes of death, they shifted back to their human forms and lay naked amongst the trees. Just as the two loups-garous died outside the mansion, it looked as if their flesh and muscle began to deteriorate under their thin skin.

She saw the dart fired from a nameless point and pin into Logan's spine. He grunted and went rigid in her arms. Katey yanked the dart out, hoping that it would save him somehow. The poison was already in his system and spread through his blood.

With careful movements, Katey laid Logan on his back and covered his body with her own as if that would save him from the reaper who stood amongst them. His eyes and mouth widened, and he gasped for breath. His body jerked and shuddered for three, long, agonizing seconds and then Katey heard his heart stop.

Logan lay lifeless in the dirt, eyes unblinking and lungs empty of air.

Their bond, the constant tether that connected them in life, was severed. For a moment, Katey couldn't breathe. The complete void engulfed her, plunging her into a dark chasm. Her soul plummeted downward until it seemed like nothing was left but her own heartbeat.

"No! Logan! You can't leave me! You promised!" she yelled, beating her fist against his shoulder. "Don't leave me like this! It's not fair!" She wept and tucked her head against his chest, letting the blood that was still wet on his skin to smear across her skin. She could feel his body begin to wither away beneath her.

Now she was alone. There was no pack, no Logan, no family. Most of all, there was no love. The depression that had stolen away the better part of her senior year returned, and it was as if Logan had never existed. Her spirit no longer recognized him. There was no warmth and kindness in the shriveled corpse she had thrown herself upon.

Her wolf howled in mourning and Katey was tempted to do the same, but she was the only one to grieve. The humans who approached knew nothing of her sorrow.

Footsteps came closer, sounding loud in the silence of the forest, only accompanied by the pounding of her pulse in her ears.

She pushed herself up and looked to the path of death that led from the hunters to where Logan lay. They kicked at Dustin's body and then Darren's as they made their way to her, brandishing their guns.

Numbness saturated her body as she turned to face Drake and his posse of murderers.

"Did you really think you could run from us?" he asked, raising his pistol to aim at her head. Even a few yards away, there would be no time for her to dodge and part of her didn't even want to.

Darren, Dustin, Ben, and Logan were all she had, all she ever wanted in this life. They sacrificed themselves to make sure Katey lived, using their bodies as shields against certain death. Now that they were gone, what else was left for her? What held her to this world?

The prophecy no longer mattered. The safety of the world didn't matter. Nothing mattered if there was no love. It had become her strength, and now that it had been extinguished, she would freely give her life to the hunters. What good was the body if the spirit was dead?

Something within her came to life. A new pulse rose from her core and beat in time with her own. She found the courage to stand, her front sullied with blood and eyes softened by woe. The presence built up within her until she felt it overflowing like a bubbling spring from the top of her head. The energy poured from her and a slow smile spread across her face as she realized what was to come. This was not the end.

Drake stopped and pulled the trigger, ready to eradicate this pack and claim the retribution he deserved. The bullet whizzed through the air but stopped short before it found its target in Katey's forehead.

For a moment, he thought he had missed. He fired, and the silver bullet stopped short again, hovering in midair with its partner.

From behind him, one of his associates shot a wolfsbane dart, but it had the same effect. It spun in place with the bullets, as if stopping to admire the delirious smile Katey had plastered on her face.

Frustration consumed him, and he continued to open fire, emptying his last magazine.

When the last bullet was spent, the collection of silver pellets in front of Katey dropped to her feet.

Slowly, a light began to radiate from her, growing, and with it came an intense wall of heat that nearly knocked Drake off his feet.

It surrounded them, illuminating the forest until one could barely tell it was a chilly winter night. Her green eyes were taken over by a white film, but her gaze was locked on Drake. If he were a religious person, he would have thought Katey looked like an angel. That honor belonged to the ethereal entity that began to materialize behind her.

A woman in ancient garb and adorned in golden jewelry appeared in a ghostly form. She towered over all of them in a majestic stance that pronounced her preeminence over them. Drake thought her beautiful, but he could feel her power and authority like the heat of a hot summer day on his skin.

Her dark hair, long and untamed, flowed behind her and her eyes shined a radiant green, just like Katey's. In many respects, Drake could see their similarities and wondered what kind of magic this was that Katey could create some sort of astral projection of herself in the image of a queen.

The other hunters cowered and dropped their weapons in surrender, but Drake kept a firm grip on his pistol as he faced down the spirit.

Katey and the spirit moved as one and looked beside them at the desiccated werewolf drenched in blood. She stooped down and their hands passed in unison over his head and torso. Slowly, the evidence of the wolfsbane in his system disappeared, and his body filled out to its previous living state.

Color returned to the werewolf's skin, and air filled his lungs in a great gasp as his life was restored. Drake looked behind him to the three other bodies, and they recovered in the same fashion. The hunters jumped away from the creatures as they shakily rose to their feet and looked to Katey in awe and wonderment.

"The damage you have done is great," the two women said. Katey's voice was outshined by the saintly voice of the spirit that spoke with a distinct accent that Drake couldn't place.

He looked back to the spirit and its host and felt his palms begin to sweat, knowing that judgment was just a word away. What kind of power did the entity wield? Could it kill as easily as it could gift life? For all he knew, this was nothing but an illusion and had no power whatsoever.

"You're the ones who have done the damage!" he shouted, his voice sounding so plain and mortal after the spirit had spoken. "My father is dead, and we're all that's left of our clan." He jabbed his finger at the one named Logan, who was supporting himself on his elbows and gazing up at the spirit. "He killed them all! He's the one you should be blaming, not me!"

Katey and the spirit looked to Logan, but said nothing and turned their attention back to Drake. "That may be true, but he is repentant of his crimes. You are not." There was a note of definiteness and truth that rang in their last words.

Drake could feel a tendon stand out in his neck as he was ready to defend his guiltlessness. "We kill to keep the world safe and get rid of these – "

"You do not keep the world safe," she interrupted. "You use violence in the name of peace to destroy those who are innocent."

"Innocent? These beasts aren't innocent!"

"They are guilty of only one thing, and it is not a crime worthy of death. They live according to their instincts and have a right to exist as much as you do. There are some who have been guided away from the peaceful way of living, but a day will come when every wolf and vampire will live amongst humans without fear or prejudice. We will all be as one, and you will have no reason to hunt them."

Drake's brows drew together. "Are you talking about a cure?" he asked, remembering his father's last mission.

Katey's expression went hard. "There is no cure for the beast that dwells within every living creature on the planet. There is only a cure for hate, but until humanity is ready to accept its truth, you will know no cure. If you continue to live in violence, it will consume you, and you will become worse than the thing you hunt."

The words echoed in Drake's mind, but they held no meaning. Humans were the rightful stewards of the earth, and it was the job of the select few to eradicate the evil that infected their world. The vampires and werewolves were the true monsters, not Drake. He might as well have been on a mission ordained by God Himself to defeat the minions of Satan, and this spirit was just another agent the devil used to confuse him.

Drake took a bounding step forward, ready to test if Katey's force field was restricted to deflecting bullets. After that, he couldn't move. His body refused to respond to his demands. At first, he thought it was Katey that made him immobile. He looked to his comrades and saw they were just as helpless as he was. Only the beasts were free.

"What are you doing?" he shouted at Katey. Then, figures emerged from the woods wielding their own weapons. He looked to meet the eyes of one of the vampires he had seen at the compound before it burned to the ground. His dark eyes pinned Drake, calm and ready to shoot without hesitance if needed.

It was the mesmerizing powers of the vampires that captured them, and they were following the orders of the spirit. Drake let out a sound of frustration just as he felt his fingers begin to pry open against his will. His useless gun dropped to the ground and his arms raised in reluctant surrender against the unholy creatures that surrounded him and his clan. They were truly defeated.

The other hunters did the same, and without ceremony, the vampires ushered them away from the spirit and the other werewolves who were still recovering from their resurrection.

Drake continued to look over his shoulder at the spirit as his feet moved of their own accord and he memorized the serious but otherworldly look in her eyes. Soon, they were away from the light and heat of the woman who had overpowered them with mere words.

He looked to the familiar vampire who seemed to be in charge and addressed him as one leader to another. "What are you going to do with us?" he asked. Drake imagined a gruesome and bloody end for him and the hunters who had followed him here. If he could request such a thing, he wanted to die first since it was his foolish decision to pursue Logan that brought about their downfall.

The only consoling thought lay in the truth that if they fell tonight, more would rise in their place. There were more of them all over the country and overseas that would continue the fight against evil.

The vampire shook his head. "We will not hurt you if that's what you're thinking."

Drake was caught off guard by the dense Russian lilt to his words. "Where are we going, then?"

Ahead, he saw a break in the trees that led to the country road where their vehicle was parked. He felt a sharp blow to the back of his head, and as his vision narrowed, he heard the vampire say, "You won't know when you wake up."

Logan gazed up at Katey in utter reverence. In the light of her heavenly glow, he felt like a sinner facing the God of judgment. He shouldn't have been so close to her and the spirit that mirrored her every word and action – or was it the other way around? His nakedness and an endless list of wrongs were bared before her without censor.

He should have crawled away or shielded himself from the penetrating light, but he couldn't bring himself to move. He looked to Darren and the others – including Gregory, Forrest, and Michael who stayed behind while Anton escorted the hunters away. They all stared with just as much veneration, but they dared not to approach her.

If the spirit was done with Drake, she would have faded back to the realm she came from, but she remained and looked between the loups-garous as if personally regarding each. Then, her eyes turned to him, and he froze in fear.

She knew what he had done and what beast he harbored. There was no way she couldn't have known. Wearing nothing but the blood of those he had slain was enough to condemn him.

Logan hadn't known the kind of monster he had become. He had never known what he was capable of and what he had been holding back all this time.

He knew now that those walls he had put up should never have been torn down. Taking the potion was a mistake. Katey had seen the darkest part of him that he never wanted anyone to see. Even his pack had witnessed the terrible beast, but they didn't run or try to kill him. They reassured him while he grieved for his sins.

Would the spirit be so forgiving? If he let loose once, who was to say that it wouldn't happen again? If this was the spirit he thought it was – the spirit of Tanatia – then she would know the future and know if Logan would kill again.

It would have been easier if she left him dead where he lay, but she chose to resurrect him. Why? If she could see the monster he gave refuge to, why did she let him live?

Katey knelt in front of him, the spirit looming over them both. Logan didn't know who to look at, or who he should address if he could gather the bravery to speak. What could he possibly say to the spirit that the beast feared?

She reached out, the two hands descending upon him in tandem until the light touched the crown of his head. He closed his eyes as his body was swept up in a piercing force that entered his skull and diffused throughout his limbs and core. A power as sharp as the tip of a silver blade and as filling as a dense ooze penetrated his soul.

For the first time in Logan's life, he felt peace. The threat of the beast was miles away, and all that remained was a wolf he had never known. As if a river had been undammed, a connection finally formed between Logan and this other part of him that was free of rage and hatred.

The wolf he sensed was just as curious about him as he was of it. The toxic sludge of rivalry had been cleansed from his system, all by a simple touch from the spirit.

"You have struggled so long against a burden that was never meant to exist," Katey said, her words sounding like a thousand wind chimes in his ears. "Live now without fear and learn from your wolf, as you should have from the beginning."

When he opened his eyes, the light began to wane from the forest. The darkness of declining night closed in around them, and the spirit grew fainter. The princess's lines blurred until she was gone altogether and all that remained was Katey looking at him with loving eyes.

CHAPTER 26

Katey looked up and down at her reflection in the mirror. It wasn't how she had pictured her wedding day. She had dreamed of a big white dress and a fistful of roses. A plush, white, cashmere robe was not her ideal attire. After thinking about it for the last few days, she realized it didn't matter what she wore as long as she was marrying the man she loved.

And tonight, she was going to do just that.

It had been three months since the incident in Louisiana. Life had returned to something that resembled normal, but the scars remained. Plans had been made for rehabilitation and truths had emerged that brought her pack back together in such a magical way that Katey couldn't help but smile at how far they had come.

Darren had confessed the mysterious experience they had together in the wolf enclosure. Through a heated discussion with Dustin, it was discovered who might have been to blame for the deaths of his wife and young daughter. In his confession, there was an element of healing. Dustin couldn't have known, and Darren was wise enough to realize that now.

She cried when Darren told her that when he stepped in front of Katey and Logan to face the hunters in the woods, he had done so not as an alpha who was obligated to keep his pack safe. He took the wolfsbane dart to somehow absolve his mistake centuries ago when he couldn't save his wife and child from the hunters searching for Dustin.

It had taken Logan some time to warm back up to his family, but they rallied around him to assure him that he was still welcome, no matter what happened at the hunter compound. Of course, they kept a closer eye on him to ensure the magic had been completely worked out of his system.

He made it known that he had eaten human flesh and with the help of Gregory's mentorship, Logan was on the mend. A good thing, too, since there were a few humans in the audience outside around the gazebo. If he got the craving for a human meal again, they might not have been able to go through with this ceremony so soon. The detoxification of his appetite was a slow process, but not as slow as some others who had spent half their lives eating human flesh.

He wasn't the only one who needed time to recover from what happened that night in the forests of Louisiana. Katey still had her own demons to battle after everything the spirit of Tanatia had revealed to her about her intended mate and her own mission to bring balance.

When Tanatia appeared and revived her pack, Katey was shown flashes of the past and future. She saw the moment Logan's mother died, a beautiful woman breathing her last breath in his arms. She saw a man with pale skin and striking blue eyes, just like Logan's. A sketchy and elusive vision of a snowy mountain and warriors decaying in the snow. A lone statue of a ruler in a dimmed and cavernous hall.

She saw their world ruled by both peace and war and the ever-engaging sides of good and evil clashing together in a flurry of power. Nothing was coherent or made sense to Katey now, but she was sure that in time, it would all be clear.

Most of all, she saw the beast that dwelled within Logan. It was like nothing she could have imagined, yet beyond explanation. A formidable darkness lurked in Logan's soul and without the help of Tanatia, it would have consumed him. Katey wasn't able to determine exactly what the darkness was before the spirit placed it within a metaphysical box that could never be opened.

In the darkness, there was nothing but hate and a lust for destruction that seemed so out of place in Logan. How did such an entity become attached to him and for how long? If it was the darkness that kept him from shifting, Katey was grateful to Tanatia for fixing his problem, but the questions weighed even heavier on her mind with each passing day.

Whatever the darkness was, Logan seemed to have moved on. Somedays, she saw a look of sadness in his eyes, but it passed just as quickly as it came and it showed itself less frequently over the weeks and months since the darkness was hidden away for good.

Now that the hunter madness had passed, Ben had started to open up to the pack and play a more active role. He taught them self-defense beyond the use of guns, and shortly after Darren had confessed his revelation about his family, Ben revealed the truth about what happened in Vietnam. None of the pack berated him for the crime of killing a fellow loup-garou. War was war in their eyes, and just as Logan couldn't be held responsible for his actions at the hunter compound, they did not pass judgment on Ben either.

However, there was a strain between all of them after that time. Katey might have been the only one who sensed it because of her empathic abilities, and none of them would admit to it. They were a pack and always would be. One's unsavory past did not change that.

Dustin was his usual carefree self, but the house was never quiet again. Folksongs were hummed, whistled, and belted out in true Irish fashion whenever the fancy struck him. Katey loved the melodies and buoyant lyrics, and some of the others joined in on the songs they knew. After a while, Katey picked up some of the tunes and hummed along from across the house.

Forrest and the remaining Deviants returned to Crestucky. Families were rehired to their jobs and children were reenlisted in school to pick up where they left off. It wasn't hard for Katey to catch up on her schoolwork and she even found the time to help Lily with her own. She returned home, but her parents preceded her and arrived home earlier from their impromptu vacation. Lily was grounded until graduation for being out of state with Forrest, but she was allowed this one evening to attend the wedding.

The rougarous chose to stay away from the town and take up residence elsewhere, but Gregory stuck around to make sure Logan was stable before moving on to catch up with Erik and the rest of his pack.

Michael and John continued their search for elders and alphas to attend the peace conferences. Her grandfather routinely stopped by to deliver good news about their growing attendance number and that plans were in motion for the gathering to take place later in the year.

Three months had passed, which meant Katey had undergone three of her monthly shifts. Each one was just as difficult as the last and the only time her shift experience was a little less agonizing was when she brought the shift on at will. Each shift, she could feel her control over her loup-garou form strengthen and it was only a matter of time before she would have as much control as Darren or Dustin.

Lily stepped up behind her, bringing her back to the present. Her best friend was dressed in a lovely, pink, single-strap gown that draped to the floor. Her bright blonde hair was piled high on her head and dotted with flowers.

It might have been a little too formal for this backyard wedding. Katey had tried to make it clear to Lily that the ceremony was not so traditional, but her friend was hell-bent on looking like a true bridesmaid.

"You look beautiful!" she squealed.

Katey looked from her unpainted nails, to her loose hair that hung over her shoulders, and to her face that was free of any type of makeup. Under the robe, Katey was as naked as a newborn. She would have hardly called the ensemble beautiful, but it was practical.

"You're just saying that," she replied, giving Lily a look of feigned annoyance.

Lily hugged Katey's shoulders. "Every bride needs to hear that they're beautiful on their wedding day. And I hope you'll say the same on mine."

Katey slipped a hand around her friend's waist and squeezed. "When you get married, you'll be in a big white dress and wearing bright red lipstick. You'll actually look like a bride. I look like a girl who stayed the night somewhere and forgot a change of clothes."

The two girls giggled, but their laughter was cut short by a sharp rap on the door.

"Come in," Katey called.

Darren stepped through and took in the sight of the two girls standing in front of her dresser mirror. He smiled, his brown eyes twinkling. It was good to see him happy again, and Katey hoped nothing in the world would steal that joy. The hunter incident had taken a lot out of her alpha and he slept for days after they returned home.

"You both look beautiful," he said as he stepped inside and closed the door. Dressed in a full tuxedo and long tie, he was the picture of handsomeness. A white carnation was pinned to his lapel and stood out against the black material of his jacket.

Lily curtsied. "Thank you," she said so sweetly that Katey thought she might get diabetes just by standing next to her.

Katey rolled her eyes. "Whatever," she grumbled.

Darren chuckled, the deep sound vibrating in her chest to combat the butterflies in her stomach. "Can we have a moment, Lily?"

"Totally, Mr. Dubose," she replied and slipped out of the bedroom after giving Katey one last thumbs-up and a big grin.

Darren walked toward Katey as she turned back to the mirror and took a deep breath. "Nervous?" he asked.

Katey blew out her cheeks and nodded. "Just a little."

Her alpha moved behind her and placed his hands on her slender but strong shoulders, the same shoulders that had to bear so much responsibility.

Her wolf had taught her many things in the last few months as they adjusted back into their routines, but the one thing she could never deny again was her place in the pack.

Katey remembered when she was terrified to face Darren after everything that had happened in Louisiana. She feared she would be exiled from the pack for all the trouble she had caused them. He proved her wrong by accepting her again after she had given him another excuse to give her the boot. Dustin and Ben had been right, and Darren showed Katey she was part of the strongest unit in nature; a wolf pack. Nothing could tear them apart.

"You're going to do just fine," he assured.

Katey looked at him through the mirror. "Are you sure you're okay with this? We can always get Michael to give me away."

Darren shook his head. "No. It'll be my honor to give you away." He gave her shoulders a squeeze. "I know you wish your father were here, though."

Her father and mother were still two mysterious figures to Katey. Each night at the dinner table, they would regale her with stories about Adam from the days they knew him. Whenever Michael visited, she would spend hours listening to him talk about Jane and all the adventures they had together.

For all the stories and anecdotes, Katey didn't feel like she knew them. Their essence, their personalities, fears, and aspirations, they were all merely shadowy shapes in the darkness of her past. Stories could tell a lot about a person, but not about their inner character.

Perhaps she would never fully know her parents, but the dreams still came to her some nights, and she treasured them even more now that she had names to pair with the faces.

Katey felt her throat constrict. "I always knew he wouldn't be. My mom neither." She took another stuttered breath. "But they're here in spirit, right?"

The question might have been a tricky one for a man who always believed in science to explain everything from the reason the sun came up every morning to the reason they shifted into a wolf. After witnessing the miracle of the princess Tanatia appearing in Louisiana, Darren began to concede that some things could never be explained.

He smiled and nodded back at her. "I'm sure they are."

From outside, she could hear the slow beating of the drums and knew the time had come. Darren moved to the side and offered his arm to her.

Fighting back the wave of nervous nausea, Katey looped her elbow in his, and they slowly made their way out of the house. With every step, her excitement doubled. Her unsteady free hand constantly adjusted her robe, even though it covered everything from her chest to her knees and tied together with a sash that cinched her waist.

Darren opened the sliding glass door into the flourishing garden. The cold winter had given way to balmy spring weather and the property around the house teemed with wildflowers and thick, rich grass.

Torches had been set up along the path Katey and Darren would walk to fight back the diminishing light of day. To either side stood loups-garous, vampires, and humans who knew of their kind. The drummers stood to either side of the gazebo, their tempo quickening at the sight of Katey and mimicking the rhythm of her racing heart. Dustin and Lily stood on either side of the gazebo stairs, playing their parts as the best man and maid of honor.

When Katey stepped out, all eyes turned to her, and her stomach rolled in on itself under the pressure of being the center of attention.

Ahead, Katey saw Logan standing at the foot of the gazebo stairs. He wore a matching robe, but instead of white, the soft fabric was as black as his hair and the night sky above. The glow of the fire danced across his face and the skin of his broad chest that the robe did not conceal.

He smiled, the corners of his serene blue eyes crinkling. And just like that, Katey forgot that anyone else was there. They were alone in the crowd, and the quick beating of the drums faded away.

She and Darren walked forward at a slow pace, and by the time she was facing Logan, she forgot why she had been so nervous to begin with. None of the guests mattered though she was glad to see the familiar faces of beloved friends. The fact that she wasn't wearing an expensive dress didn't matter. All that mattered was that moment when Darren handed her to Logan, and they ascended the stairs to stand under the gazebo.

John, who had traveled across the country to officiate the ceremony, waited just inside the gazebo. He smiled to both of them and gave the cue for the drummers to stop.

Logan looked upon her, his eyes soft and abounding with love. It hadn't been so long since they met and she first fell in love with the loup-garou she held hands with, but he still had the power to make her dizzy and ridiculously happy.

John began the opening of the ceremony, but Katey didn't hear a word. Her mind played back every crucial moment that led to this day. There were many chances for them to turn back, to deny their love and carry on with their lives. There were times when they could have given up on one another. All those times that Logan had been insanely jealous, all those times Katey had been difficult and stubborn, all the times they shouted at one another and disagreed. Every single bump in the road and every single celebration had prepared them for this day and Katey wouldn't have changed a thing, even if it meant the road would have been easier for them in the end.

Those struggles and triumphs made their love stronger, and Katey knew she could look forward to the next thousand years together and the eternity that awaited them beyond.

"Now, the husband will speak his vows to his intended mate."

Katey glanced to John and back to Logan and waited with bated breath.

Logan opened his mouth, but the words didn't come right away. After a few seconds of silence, he began, "You know how I've always loved you. You know how I've wanted nothing more than to be with you from the very beginning. Now that we're here, I can only promise that I will protect you, honor you, and run with you wherever you go. As long as you'll have me, I'll never leave you. As long as it's within my power, you'll never be unhappy again. After this night, you'll be my mate for life, and I can't wait to start that life with you."

Katey pressed her lips together to keep the wild giggles of delight from bubbling out.

John nodded. "Well said. And now, the wife will speak her vows to her intended mate."

The words she had intended to say fell straight out of her brain, and she stood speechless, just as he had for a few panicked seconds. "Logan, you have given me the best gift I could ever ask for. When I was lost in darkness, you showed me the light. When I couldn't see the end, you gave me a new beginning. Though the journey here hasn't been easy, it's been worth it, and I can't imagine sharing this life with anyone else. You've given me hope and love that I never dreamed was possible. You've given me a family and a home I can love. You've been more than a friend. You've been my angel, and I hope you don't think that's too cheesy, but it's true." Katey kissed the back of his hand. "I vow to be your mate, your wife, and your companion for the rest of my life, no matter how long that is."

John gave his approving nod again and reached behind him to a table that had been set up. He produced a primitive-looking dagger with a bone handle and presented it to the crowd.

"The couple will now join in the blood covenant that will bind their souls for eternity."

Katey and Logan held out their arms and turned them over to expose their wrists to the officiate. With two quick actions, he sliced into their skin and blood seeped from the cuts. As they had practiced, they twisted their wrists around until the open cuts were pressed together, loose blood flowing from one body to another.

Katey hadn't expected to feel anything, but as the warmth of his blood blended with hers, she felt it infiltrate her body. His essence flowed through her and mingled with her soul, just as John said. The bond they shared before the ceremony intensified and sparked in to a new sensation. Their hearts began to beat in synchronous union, and she couldn't help but grin at the feeling of total oneness with Logan.

He smiled too, and she knew the feeling had to be mutual. They were the first loup-garou couple to undergo this ceremony in thousands of years, but she wondered if other wives felt the bond in the same way. Could a human body possibly feel so attuned to a loup-garou?

The wounds healed quickly, and they separated their wrists. They didn't bother to clean off the blood or wipe it on their robes.

John turned to the table again and unfolded a fur pelt. Katey and Logan stepped closer together as it was swathed over them and held together by John. Katey swallowed hard, knowing what was to come next.

"Disrobe," John instructed.

Logan did so without hesitation, but Katey was a little slower to untie her belt and let the robe drop around her ankles. She had never been naked in front of Logan. All the times she had shifted, Katey had made sure to keep herself covered until the last possible moment so none of her pack would see her nakedness.

Their nudity had become something rather normal and expected. They felt no shame in stripping in front of her every time they were ready to shift, but Katey had never been that willing.

As she stood there, naked before Logan, he understood her modesty and kept his eyes locked on hers. From their angle, John could not see her below the shoulders, which eased her discomfort.

"The couple will now present their true selves to one another and seal the bond of their matehood."

Katey and Logan nodded to one another and held their hands tighter as they brought on the shift. The pain that came with the shift could not outdo the immense bliss that flowed in Katey. From what she could sense in Logan, there was little pain in his shift as well.

It took only a few moments for them to stand together on the deck of the gazebo, golden eyes gazing at one another and the fur pelt of union dropped to their feet. One black and one white loup-garou faced each other for the first time as a mated couple.

Their souls acknowledged one another and Katey licked the bottom side of Logan's muzzle. He returned the gesture and nudged against her head in a show of acceptance and affection.

The audience clapped and cheered, but neither loup-garou paid them any attention.

Katey tucked her head under Logan's as he protectively enveloped her in an embrace that claimed her as his own. With bursting exultation, she nuzzled into Logan's dense fur, savoring the scent of forest and freedom.

SNEAK PEEK - PRECEDENTS

The soft thumping Katey heard was not just in her head. Logan said he heard it, too. She perceived it as slightly more muffled than her own, but still louder than Logan's when he lay in bed next to her.

At first, she thought it was a bug, or perhaps one of the guys tapping their foot in another room. When she sensed that there was no one else upstairs but Logan, and he was fast asleep, she knew something wasn't right.

She just never thought it would be this.

Birth control was a joke to a loup-garou. Katey knew her metabolism would be far too high for any contraceptive pill to be effective. In the heat of passion, they often forgot about condoms, and when they did, it was a hit-or-miss thing for Logan to pull out in time. Such an occurrence happened a week before, but Katey never thought something like this would manifest so soon.

She was too wired to sit, but her legs were too weak to stand or pace as Logan did. So, she crouched in front of the toilet and stared at the plastic pregnancy test sitting on the porcelain lid. Logan's nervousness matched her own as the seconds dragged on, the minutes ticking off sluggishly. So far, there was only one pink line. They were waiting to see if there was a second. The package said they would see a result in three minutes.

They made an agreement not to say a word, knowing that Darren and Dustin were downstairs and would certainly hear them. Logan had been abnormally quick about running to the store to get the test, though Katey had been willing to wait a little longer.

She wanted to enjoy the idea that they would stay an unburdened couple for a few more years, maybe a century, just to enjoy all the wonderful privileges of married life. They could go on dates, sleep in late on the days that neither of them worked, and kiss and hold one another to their hearts' content. Having a child might ruin all of it.

In just a short while, Katey's already complicated life became threatened by new responsibilities that she wasn't sure she could handle. What would having a baby mean for them? How would it integrate into the pack? She had seen plenty of kids with the Devian pack, but they were a larger group. Her pack was small and primarily made up of adults. How could they take care of a child?

What would happen when the child grew up? Would they turn? Katey and Logan were the first loup-garou couple in millennia, since the vampires wiped out all the females of their kind in the war. Would they come out purely human and change later? Would they be loup-garou right out of the womb?

Then Katey thought of the pregnancy. What if they reproduced in the same way wolves did? In litters. She covered her face in her hands, pushing away the nasty thought that she would have to carry four or six babies in her belly for nine months.

This isn't happening. This isn't happening.

She wanted to believe she was still dreaming, that this whole scenario was just the end of some hellish nightmare.

Logan must have sensed her worry through their bond and stooped down to wrap his arms around her shoulders from behind. Feeling his warmth and loving embrace chased away much of the queasiness and tightness in her chest.

"It's going to be okay," he whispered in her ear.

All Katey could do was nod and squeeze her eyes shut against the tears that burned at the corner of her eyes. She wanted to believe him. She wanted to think that as long as she had him and her pack, having a child wouldn't be so difficult. It was the next logical step in their relationship, but they hadn't even been together for a year and she still considered herself to be fresh out of high school.

She had her diploma, but there was plenty more she wanted to do. How would having a child complicate traveling with the pack? How would it affect her budding plans to go to college and get a degree? Would she have to quit her job? Would having a child financially cripple the pack?

She had so many questions, so many fears and doubts. Her wolf was no help. It wasn't scared at all, which was another sign that what she heard earlier was truly the heartbeat of her unborn child. In fact, the wolf was oddly content, perhaps even pleased.

Logan nudged her head to get her attention and she opened her eyes. Blurry with tears, she blinked a few times before leaning closer to the toilet to peek at the little window on the pregnancy test.

Two pink lines.

AFTERWORD

Dear Reader,

I'm so glad you decided to continue in this awesome series with me and I hope you're eager to see where the future is taking Katey and Logan. There's still many more unresolved mysteries and loose ends to tie up and the next installation of this series, Precedents, endeavors to deliver an exciting climax to Katey's growth period as a loup-garou and fulfiller of the ancient prophecy of Tanatia, the spirit of peace. From the beginning of the loup-garou series, I knew I wanted to bring in more characters and highlight the struggle with hunters. Many of the characters, like Anton, Will, Uriah, and Teddy, have backstories of their own and how they came to be so intertwined with the protagonists of the series. Progressively, I'll be releasing a series of novellas that highlight these backstories. As a reader, you'll get to see John's origins, find out all the nitty-gritty details about what happened in Chicago between Logan and Erik, and see Adam and Jane's romance blossom. Keep an eye out for these novellas by tuning into my social media sites for ups on release dates and sneak peeks into my progress. I'm so excited for The Legacies Series and I hope you will be too.

If you enjoyed Beast Within, I encourage you to leave a review on its Goodreads page. It absolutely makes my day to hear that someone loves my characters and wants to read more. I'd also love to see you in person! I'll be making several book signing events across the southern United States. If you'd like me to sign a copy of one of my books, or get your first signed paperback from me, check out my blog site for information on upcoming events.

In the meantime, I invite you to check out my social media sites for more updates and sneak peeks into my progress. You can find me at my blog, www.moonstruckwriting.wordpress.com.

Also, find me on Facebook! I have an author page where you can stay tuned into the latest news, get the chance to earn free stuff, and talk all about your favorite books.

Happy Reading!
Sheritta Bitikofer

ABOUT THE AUTHOR

Sheritta Bitikofer is an author of paranormal and historical fiction. She lives for the deep, engaging stories that enthrall readers from cover to cover. As a wife and mother of eclectic tastes, she can be found roaming Civil War battlefields, haunting her local coffeeshop, or relaxing with a plate of chili cheese fries.

Follow her for upcoming novel releases
www.sherittabitikofer.com

ALSO BY SHERITTA BITIKOFER

Bewitching Darkness
Bewitching Hearts
<u>Wolves in the Open</u>
Highland Howls
Silver Screen
Mourning Moon
<u>The Decimus Trilogy</u>
The Beast of Verona
Amber Ashes
Saving the Beast
<u>Redemption Duet</u>
The Rose
The Lion
<u>Standalones</u>
Escape
Clouds
Passions
By The Book

www.ingramcontent.com/pod-product-compliance
Lightning Source LLC
Chambersburg PA
CBHW072301020726
47501CB00002B/349